Maggie's Boy

Beryl Kingston was born and brought up in Tooting. After taking her degree at London University, she taught English and Drama at various London schools as well as bringing up her three children. She and her husband now live in Sussex.

ALSO BY THIS AUTHOR

Hearts and Farthings
Kisses and Ha'pennies
A Time To Love
Tuppenny Times
Fourpenny Flyer
Sixpenny Stalls
London Pride
War Baby
Two Silver Crosses

MAGGIE'S BOY

Beryl Kingston

First published by Arrow Books in 1995

1 3 5 7 9 10 8 6 4 2

First published in the UK in 1994 by
Century Random House UK Ltd,
20 Vauxhall Bridge Road, London SW1V 2SA

Random House Australia (Pty) Limited
20 Alfred Street, Milsons Point, Sydney,
New South Wales 2061, Australia

Random House New Zealand Limited
18 Poland Road, Glenfield
Auckland 10, New Zealand

Random House South Africa (Pty) Limited
PO Box 337, Bergvlei, South Africa

Random House UK Limited Reg. No. 954009

ISBN 0 09 9 22881 5

Filmset by SX Composing Ltd, Rayleigh, Essex
Printed in Great Britain by
Cox & Wyman Ltd, Reading, Berks.

To Victims Everywhere

Prologue

June 1984

Morgan Griffiths was the first to hear the explosion. He was half way along the tunnel, with his two cousins just ahead of him, trudging back from the coal face, stooping to protect his head and shoulders against the low roof. The sudden, sharp crack stopped him in mid-stride. *Duw!* Quick! The pit props!

Sweating faces gleamed out of the darkness. Then he saw the roof bulge.

'Run!' he yelled. 'Run boys!'

Dai was already on the move, hurtling forward, but Hywell was frozen with fear and shock.

No time for thought. Nothing but terror, instinct, action. Morgan punched his cousin in the small of his back before he knew what he was doing. Hywell was running, his body filling the space between tunnel side and falling earth. The entire roof was caving in. No way forward. *Duwydd mawr!* No way forward! Back! Back! Weight stunned his arm and shoulder, one hand stinging as he struggled to extricate himself. The roar of the fall grew louder and louder. Dust filled his mouth and pushed into his eyes. He had no sense of what he was doing as he stumbled backwards, fell into puddles on the tunnel floor, scrambled up even before he stopped falling, ran and ran, back along the tunnel.

It was over in seconds. The roof was down, the last piece of debris rattled to a halt, the last echo gone. There was only dust and silence and darkness.

Morgan lay where he'd fallen and struggled for breath. He knew he was injured – because he could feel blood running down his arm – and he knew he was trapped and on his own, but there was nothing he could do for the moment. Not until he stopped shaking. This is shock, he thought, recognising the symptoms. I must keep calm or I shall make it worse.

He was surprised at the absence of pain, except for a dull ache in his chest. But the darkness pressed in upon him in a terrifying way. He could feel the weight of it bearing down from all sides, closing him in as if he was in a tomb. A tomb! *Duwydd mawr!*

No, he told himself. Don't think of that. Be practical. Take it step by step. Think of what Granddad would say, '*Go with it, boy. Don't force it. Nothin' ever comes of forcin' things. Go with it and wait for the moment. There's always a right moment. That's the art of livin', boy, findin' the right moment.*'

Wait. That was it. Wait for a bit of strength to come back. There's no rush. I could be here for quite a time. There was no way of knowing how long. It all depended on the state of the roof further along the tunnel. There was no sign of collapse when we made our inspection, but that was a couple of hours ago, and a fall like this could have weakened the pit props further along the tunnel in either direction. The mine had been out of action for nearly twelve weeks because of the strike, and mines deteriorate quickly when they aren't being worked. There was already too much water in this one, and the air was none too good.

Time passed and Morgan stopped shaking. The dust had cleared enough for him to inspect the roof. He got up and walked carefully back to the fall. There were new cracks in the props but nothing was moving. Lots of rubble, no way through the fallen pile, no hope of digging himself out. Still, Dai and Hywell should have got to the surface by now. The rescue teams would be on their way. All he had to do was be patient.

At the pit head, the crowds were gathering, anxious for news. A television crew had arrived, dispatched to pick up a human interest story, glad to leave their vigil at the gate of the steelworks where they'd been filming the picket line for far too long.

Its reporter had already gleaned most of the necessary details. Morgan Griffiths, aged twenty four, born in Port Talbot, six years in the pit at Blaenhydyglyn, working alongside his two cousins, one of a family of seven, mother, three sisters (two married), one brother (still at school), father a steel worker. Grandson of a man who'd been a legend in the pit.

'That's the one you want to talk to,' a woman told him. 'Over there, see. Woman in the green cardigan, next to the three girls with red hair. She's his mam. Grace Griffiths.'

'Who are the redheads?'

'His sisters.'

The reporter, who had learned not to be sensitive about other people's distress, took the crew across at once.

'I believe you're his mother.'

Grace Griffiths' face was strained with worry but she answered him politely. 'Yes. That's right.'

'Would you mind telling me something about him, Mrs Griffiths?'

'What sort a' things?'

'Well. What he's like.'

'He's a good man,' Grace said. 'A very good man. Kind. Quiet. He was always quiet, even as a little boy. Quiet and thoughtful.'

'Strong silent type,' another woman confirmed. 'He don't say much.'

'One of the best,' a young miner said. 'Do anything for you he would. You can depend on him. You only got to look at him to see that.'

'What does he look like?'

How can I answer that? Grace thought, when I've seen him in so many different ways and I don't know whether I'm ever going to see him alive again. That young feller's right. He looks dependable. Solid and dependable, as if he's been carved from a rock, or hacked from the coal seam. Apart from that what else could she say? Walking out of the pit – oh please God let him walk out of the pit – blackened and depersonalised by coal dust, he looks like any other miner. Out in the village, when he's clean and clothed, he's a man to notice. She closed her eyes in the anguish of waiting and being pestered by questions, and saw him clearly: five foot nine tall, broad shoulders, square, scarred hands, big feet, strong craggy face smiling at her under that untidy thatch of thick red-gold hair. Dear Morgan.

Other voices were offering information. 'He's a big

bloke, sort a' chunky.' 'Always helpin' people.' 'Patient.' 'A good worker.'

'Is there anything else you can tell me, Mrs Griffiths?' the reporter prompted.

'Yes,' Grace said, bitterly. 'He don't deserve to be buried alive.'

Down in the pit, there was no sound yet beyond the roof fall. The ache in Morgan's shoulder was deepening into pain. He checked his watch and realised that he had been squatting in the darkness for more than an hour. They're taking a long time, he thought. The fall must be worse on the other side. Or Dai and Hywell didn't get through.

He tried to stand up, conscious that he ought to make his second inspection. But the pain in his back and shoulder was so much worse when he moved that he gave up the effort and remained where he was. He tried to ease his spine into a more comfortable position, but it didn't help and, as he was shifting, his lamp went out.

It was a horrible moment. The darkness was total. Fear clutched at him with rough fingers, making him imagine all the wrong things – that he could be here too long, that all his air could be used up, that there could be fire-damp in the tunnel, that he might never get out.

Think of something else, quick, he told himself. Something pleasant. But what? What? And he thought about Bubbles.

He could see her face evolving against the darkness, heart-shaped and surrounded by blonde curls, watching itself in a mirror. Then the rest of her appeared, sitting at the dressing table in her bra and pants, applying the second layer of mascara to her eyelashes. Bubbles, the girl he'd lived with for the last eighteen months, the girl he loved.

But before the image faded, Morgan knew it was a false one. I don't love her, he thought. I've never loved her really. Not the way Dad loves Mam. Not the way it ought to be. I just wanted to go to bed with her. That's all. It was shaming to have to face such a truth, but it was possible, down here, in the darkness, on his own. Bubbles is gorgeous but we won't be getting married. She's not really interested in me any more than I'm interested in her. Apart from sex, we're not giving anything to one another. We're not involved and I want to be involved.

Dear God, he prayed, let me get out of here. Don't let me die. Not yet. I got too much living to do. I want to be married like Dad, to bring up a family, to see more of the world than just the inside of a pit.

It was growing very hot in the tunnel and Morgan was finding it hard to stay conscious. Mustn't fall asleep, he thought drowsily. Better sit up. What if I . . . ? But the pain pulled him down and down, from one nightmare into another.

He was in a car with Dai and Hywell, driving to the coking plant at Orgreave, and he'd been stopped by a police sergeant.

'Where're you from?' the sergeant said, filling the window with his red face and bulky shoulders.

He answered, giving the Welsh name the full dignity of its lyrical pronunciation. 'Blaenhydyglyn.'

'Where the hell's that?'

'Near Port Talbot.'

'Bloody South Wales.'

'South Wales, yes.'

'Well you can just fuck off out of it,' the sergeant said. 'We don't want any Wogs or Gippoes or South Wales miners on our *patch.'*

He felt assaulted and full of anger, but he knew he couldn't fight back. Because of the road blocks? Or the roof falling? Or was it the horses?

Another wave of pain swept him away from thought, holding him in a vice. When it eased, the police were marching towards him, like a great blue army, standing in line in their bulky riot gear, truncheons in hand, bright blue helmets glinting in the sunshine, long plastic shields held together in a glittering wall. And the wall was parting to let the horses through. There was something practised and deliberate about it, but his mind wouldn't function efficiently enough to tell him what it was. The horses reminded him of something else too – charging into the pickets, chestnut rumps steaming and straining, with their riders brandishing truncheons. Something from the cinema. The seventh cavalry charging the Indians. That was it. Only he was one of the Indians. He was one of the Indians and he was going to get hurt.

The pain returned, wrenching his bones. '*Myn uffern!*' he groaned. I can't stand much more of this. 'Somebody make it stop!'

Voices called his name. 'Morgan! Where are you, man?'

He tried to rouse himself but he was disorientated – by foul air, bad dreams, heat and the blaze of lights bobbing towards him out of the darkness. A familiar face was approaching. Or was that a dream too? 'Granddad?' he called. It couldn't be Granddad, not down the pit. He'd been retired for years. But it *was* him. Thank God. Thank God. 'Granddad! By y'ere.'

'We're here boy,' Granddad Griffiths called back. 'We got you. You're all right. Lie still. We got the doctor to see you.'

They carried him out of the pit on a stretcher. Out to the good clean air, the beautiful colours of the mountainside and the sky.

He was puzzled by the size of the crowd waiting at the pit head. What were they all doing there? Then he saw Mam and his sisters, running towards him and held out his good hand towards them. No sign of Bubbles, but that wasn't a surprise. A reporter was at his elbow, buzzing with questions, but the morphine he'd been given was making him so drowsy he wasn't sure he could answer.

'I been talking to Dai Griffiths,' the reporter said. 'He says you're a hero. Risked your life to save his brother. Is that true?'

Was it true? Was he a hero? He couldn't remember. Everything had happened too quickly and instinctively to be heroic. 'I gave him a shove, like,' he said.

The answer delighted the reporter. And so did the picture Morgan was making, his blackened face silhouetted against the summer green of the mountainside, lying on the stretcher, bloodstained and weary, in his pit boots and filthy overalls, grimed by coal dust. The only things about him that were clean were his eyes and they were clear, sky blue and honest. He was the very image of the struggling miner – noble, invincible, suffering. It was just the sort of picture his producer would love.

But although nobody knew it then, except the doctor, Morgan would never work in the pit again.

Other people were being filmed too on that sunny, summer weekend in 1984.

In Hampton-on-Sea, on the South coast, Alison and Rigby Toan were facing the television camera. They were the two hundred and fiftieth couple to hold their wedding reception at the Royal Maritime Hotel and the local television station thought their wedding would make a nice fill-in for the regional news.

The Maritime was a splendid-looking place, built in Georgian times and always painted a dazzling white. It was set at an angle to the beach and stood well back from the promenade with a wide lawn to protect it from trippers and a long carriage drive to impress visitors and provide parking space for their cars. It was the perfect setting for a television feature on a wedding.

'Give her a kiss!' the camera man called to the groom.

Rigby Toan needed no encouragement. He already had his arm round his bride's waist. He pulled her towards him at once and kissed her passionately for a long time, enjoying the sensations he was rousing – her mouth soft and warm, her nipples hardening. My luscious Ali!

As they kissed the sun flooded through the clouds and shone straight down on to their heads so that they were shimmering with gold. It was the most romantic thing Elsie Wareham had ever seen.

'Don't they look a *picture*!' she breathed.

She was so proud of her daughter, especially today. Dear Alison! She was like a vision from another world in her beautiful fairy-tale dress, all pretty curves and charming blushes, her long dark hair curled over her shoulders and her green eyes clear and loving. Rigby was handsome too, dapper in a cream tuxedo, with a white shirt to set off his tan, a red rose in his button hole to match his bride's red and white bouquet, his moustache neatly trimmed for the occasion and his fair hair bushed like a lion's mane around his face. They were going to look really gorgeous on the local news.

'Can we have you walking into the hotel,' the producer said.

The guests eddied forward, Rigg's mother prominent among them in a mink stole and splendid pearls. She was well over fifty – fifty seven, to be exact, because she'd been thirty when Rigg was born – but she didn't look it. She looked like royalty and she was the first to greet the newly married pair.

I'll bet those are kid gloves, Alison thought, as the cream-encased hands patted Rigg's cheek. The picture hat's from Harrods, she decided, looking at her mother-in-law's silvery fair hair, and so are the pearls. They shriek money. Then she was ashamed of herself for feeling envious. There was no need for that, not now she and Rigg were married, for in a few years' time they would be millionaires too. Rigg was quite sure about it. The trouble was, Margaret Toan's wealthy elegance always made her daughter-in-law feel gauche. Even today, dressed in all her wedding finery, Alison was conscious that she was too tall and too plump, that her teeth were crooked – that she wasn't a patch on either of the good-looking Toans.

But then her brother Mark stepped forward to kiss the bride and balance was restored.

'You look a treat, kid,' he said.

He's such a lovely brother, Alison thought, kissing him back, and so like Dad. Except that Dad had been stocky and stolid and dependable and Mark was tall and rangy and impulsive. But he had the same air about him, the same smile and the same quick, protective temper, and he made her feel loved and cherished exactly as Dad had done. Dear Mark.

'Have you seen your friend Brad?' Mark said, his voice full of laughter. 'She's pulled out all the stops today. What *does* she look like?'

'Your-friend-Brad' was standing by the bar; a Technicolour vision in a black mini skirt, spangled purple jacket and every piece of gold jewellery she possessed. There was a hat like an inverted flower pot wedged into her butter-yellow hair, decorated with an assortment of bright pink and blue flowers and trailing net, and she was smiling hugely, her lips a splendid vermilion and her eyelids sea green. In short, she looked exactly the way Alison expected her to – except that she wasn't smoking. They grinned at one another across the room and Brad mimed a kiss. Good old Brad.

'Say "cheese",' the camera man instructed. 'One last shot.'

It was easy for Alison to smile, for Mum was coming up to kiss her, and after Mum, her older brother Greg and his wife Susan, and her younger brother Andy and his wife Clare.

The foyer was crowded now. Alison and Rigg shook hands and kissed cheeks, as trays full of glasses clinked by and muzak meandered from the plush red walls and the 'last shot' went on and on. There were people everywhere, kissing the air alongside one another's cheeks, slapping backs and booming bonhomie. Now and then, Alison caught snippets of passing conversations; somebody admiring the 'dear little bridesmaids', Brad advising a friend to 'thump him in the kisser', a woman's voice saying, 'not actually the sort of wife I imagined for Maggie's boy', in such a disparaging tone that Alison was momentarily hurt – until the next guest strode towards her, arms outstretched.

At last, the cameras packed up and everyone could relax. The rest of the wedding breakfast went as smoothly as if it had been rehearsed. Mark proposed the toast quite wittily and Rigg was absolutely charming, smiling and handsome. He had a good voice for this sort of thing, rich, deep and expressive.

Waving his hand at the side table where the wedding gifts were displayed, he thanked his guests for 'your presence here and your presents there'. He informed them he was the luckiest man alive to be marrying 'such a beautiful, wonderful girl' and into 'such a lovely, wonderful family'.

'As an only child,' he confided, 'I can tell you it will be wonderful to belong to such a large family, all ready-made so to speak and ready to walk into. Three new brothers, three new sisters-in-law, three beautiful nieces and a very handsome nephew.' He looked across to where the said pageboy nephew was smearing his face with ice-cream, and paused, raising his eyebrows so that the guests laughed. '*Absolutely* wonderful. Which is not to say my own darling mother didn't give me the most marvellous childhood.' He flashed an adoring smile at Margaret Toan, 'Nobody could have been a better mother – nobody in all the world – and I don't care who knows it.'

Then he paused, scanned the tables, smiled at his audience and made them wait for what was coming next. 'It's been a wonderful year for me,' he said, 'what with one thing and another. First a landslide victory for the Tories – and what a difference that's making – and now this wedding. And to put the cherry on the cake – you might be interested to know – yesterday I signed contracts on my second jewellery shop. I don't mind admitting to you that I'm very ambitious. Not over ambitious. I don't think that could be said. But ambitious. We're going to make our mark on the world, aren't we, Alison?' Beaming down at her. 'Now we've got another Tory government, the age of the entrepreneur has arrived with a bang. There won't be anything to stop me. All Maggie Thatcher's got to do for me is to keep her promises – and I don't think anybody can doubt she'll do that – and I'm a made man. By the time I'm forty, I plan to own a string of outlets and to have made my first million.' He spoke lightly and with humour but his audience did not doubt him. 'Only my *first* mind. Others will follow because nothing is too good for Alison.' He turned to his bride and raised her hand to his lips with a flourish. 'My wife, Mrs Alison Toan, is going to be a very rich woman. I give you my word.'

He also gave a signal to one of the waiters and, after a short pause the young man stepped forward with a large bunch of red roses. Rigg took them, like a king accepting tribute, and held them out towards his audience so that everyone could see that the flowers were bound together with red ribbon and that entwined through the bow at the centre was a string of freshwater pearls.

'For you, my darling,' he said to Alison. 'My first pearls for my first lady. For you to wear in our little love nest. Long may you be happy there.' And to appreciative applause, he fastened them round her neck.

But he hadn't finished yet. When the applause died down, he took a long envelope from his pocket, laid it in front of his bride, and waited while she opened it.

It contained two air tickets to Venice and reservations for a fortnight at the Cipriani Hotel.

'Oh Rigg!' Alison said, overwhelmed by his generosity. 'What a wonderful honeymoon!' And she threw her arms round his neck and kissed him with sheer delight while the wedding guests cheered and stamped their feet on the floor.

Down at the far end of the long table Alison's old school friends were misty-eyed at the romance of it.

'Wasn't that lovely,' they sighed to one another. The youngest of them, a girl called Sue, was so moved she was actually in tears.

'Not particularly,' Brad said in her brusque way. She held up her empty glass to a passing waiter. 'Fill that up for me sunshine.'

'Oh go on Brad!' Sue protested. 'It was a lovely speech. Like something on the telly. I wish they'd stayed to film it.'

'Hm,' Brad said, watching as the glass was filled.

'You're an old sour-puss,' Sue said, gazing at the bridegroom with open admiration. 'I think he's a dream. He's good-looking, he's rich, he's going to inherit a fortune when he's thirty-five, he's madly in love with Ali. I can't see anything wrong with him.'

'Well I can,' Brad said, helping herself to her neighbour's unwanted mints.

'What?'

'He's got a cruel nose.'

Chapter One

March 1990

When Alison Toan pushed her double buggy round the corner into Shore Street that March afternoon, there was a strange man standing on the edge of the kerb, gazing up at her house.

Strangers were a rarity in Shore Street which, despite its name, was actually a quarter of a mile from the beach and not much of a street either, just a short, litter-strewn alley, hidden behind the prestigious Edwardian shops in the Selsey Road. Most people in Hampton weren't aware of its existence. Why should they be? It was too inaccessible and too insignificant, nothing but one short terrace of fisherman's cottages. But it was where Alison had lived for the six years since her marriage.

Built at the turn of the century, the cottages were small and plain with slate roofs and no decoration. Each had a front door and two sash windows giving out on to the street, and, occupying half of a very small backyard, a narrow kitchen with a bathroom above it which had been added at a later date as an hygienic afterthought. The south side of the street was a muddle of garages and dustbins belonging to the Selsey Road shops and usually lined with parked cars. The far end was blocked off by the walled garden of an old people's home. Consequently, the nine families who lived on the north side of the street were thrown in upon themselves as though they inhabited an isolated village. They knew one another's business, recognised one another's visitors, and treated strangers with suspicion. It didn't surprise Alison at all to see curious faces peering from several of the windows at the one now outside her front door.

He was a non-descript man, small, neat and buttoned-down, wearing a dark suit and carrying a brief case, and he'd obviously arrived in the blue Sierra which was parked further up the alley in front of the butcher's garage.

Not one of Rigg's friends, Alison thought, as she walked towards him. Not that she knew many of her husband's friends, but those who did appear in Shore Street were expensively dressed and drove flashy cars like Volvos and Mercedes and BMWs. And he's not trying to sell double glazing either. He's too well dressed – and too sure of his authority. An office worker, she decided. Probably from the council, checking up on whether she'd paid the poll tax or something equally horrid. Well tough, she thought. You won't catch *me* out. She always paid her bills and taxes on the nose, *and* her share of the mortgage too, no matter how hard it was to earn the money. It had been very hard sometimes, particularly in the four years since Jonathan had been born. But she'd done it. Always. It was a point of honour with her. So you're wasting your time, Mr Council Official, if that's who you are. She was none too pleased to see him, whoever he was. After a long day's work at the holiday camp, all she wanted was a cup of tea and a chance to cheer the kids up.

It had been a bad day. Baby Emma had been so upset in the crèche that afternoon that they'd phoned through to reception with a request for Alison to remove her. Consequently Alison had spent the rest of the afternoon trying to attend to the campers with the baby climbing all over her lap and grizzling. Then Jon had been miserable when she picked him up from play school. Now all three of them were tired and grubby and needed their tea.

The stranger turned and smiled at Alison, as she trundled the pushchair towards him. He was assessing his subject, the way he always did on a visit like this one.

'Mrs Toan?' he said. He had a quiet, polite voice, a necessity in his line of work.

'Yes,' Alison replied and undid Emma's harness to ease her out of the buggy.

'Is your husband at home?'

What a silly question, Alison thought, settling the baby on her hip. As if he'd be at home at this hour of the day. She waited for Jon to climb out of his seat and then collapsed the buggy with a neat nudge of her knee. But she answered the man politely. 'He's at work in Chichester. He runs two jeweller's shops, *Rings and Things* in East Street or . . .'

'Yes. Thank you,' the man said. 'We know where he works.'

'Well that's where you'll find him.'

'We haven't been able to contact him at either of his shops, Mrs Toan. That's why I'm here. What time do you expect him home?'

'It all depends,' Alison said, opening the door and shepherding Jon into the house. 'He could be back for dinner or he could be late. He works long hours.'

'Ah,' the man said, hesitating on the doorstep. 'I see. Well then . . . I wonder if I could beg a few moments of your time.'

What a nuisance, Alison thought. But it might be business and she couldn't turn business away, no matter how tired she was. 'You'd better come in,' she said.

He followed her through the front door into the living room, wincing noticeably at the wreckage of breakfast things and discarded nightclothes they'd left behind when they rushed off that morning. Not for the first time since her marriage, Alison yearned for Rigg to be successful enough for them to buy a nice modern house with a hall, where casual visitors could be asked to wait. This house had no hall and no front garden and no privacy of any kind. You just stepped off the pavement straight into the one and only living room with all your debris exposed for any visitor to see.

'Sorry about the mess,' she said, picking up dressing gowns and pyjamas and hanging them over the banisters. 'We were late this morning and I've been at work all day. You won't mind if I get their tea while we talk, will you. It's been a long day for them.'

'No, no,' her visitor said. 'You go ahead.'

'I gather you want to see my husband about something particular,' Alison said as she hung up their coats. 'Is it jewellery?'

'No,' the man said, bluntly. 'It's about his VAT. I'm from Customs and Excise. I've got a letter which I am instructed to hand over to him.' He opened his brief case and took out a long buff envelope.

It was such a shock that for a few seconds Alison was speechless. To be visited by a VAT man was bad enough, but to be told he'd brought a letter that had to be delivered in person was worse. She lifted Emma into the high-chair and washed the child's dirty hands with a damp flannel, letting chores occupy her until she could think of an answer. Finally she decided to make light of it. 'Wouldn't it go in the post?' she asked.

'Not this time,' the man said sombrely. 'He's six months behind in his payments, Mrs Toan. We've sent him several reminders. We have to be sure *this* letter reaches him.' He held it out to her.

Alison's heart contracted with alarm. She took the letter and put it on the mantelpiece. Six months behind, she thought. It couldn't be true. Rigg wouldn't do such a thing. He was too good a business man. 'There must be some mistake,' she said.

'Not on our side, Mrs Toan,' the VAT man replied. 'We don't make mistakes.'

Despite his bland face and his quiet tone there was an air of confident menace about this man. It made Alison feel as if she'd committed a crime. She turned away from him and walked into the kitchen, to busy herself getting orange juice and biscuits for the children. To her dismay, he followed her.

'You will be sure he gets the letter, won't you, Mrs Toan,' he insisted. 'It's a final demand. You understand that, don't you?'

'A *final* demand?'

'I'm afraid so. The next stage in the procedure would be a summons, you see. I'm sure none of us would want things to go that far. Much better to get it all settled now, don't you agree?'

This was getting more serious by the second. 'Yes,' Alison said, and, because she wanted to end the interview and get rid of him so that she could think what she ought to do next, added firmly, 'I'll see he gets it. Was that all you wanted?'

'Nothing further,' he said. 'I mustn't keep you. I can see you're busy.' And he allowed her to escort him to the door.

'Who was that man?' Jon asked, peering at his mother solemnly over the rim of his mug.

'No one important,' Alison told him in as light a tone as she could manage.

'I don't like him,' the little boy said, frowning. 'He's nasty.' Under his mop of thick fair hair his brown eyes were earnest with feeling.

'Well he's gone now,' Alison said. 'D'you want a wafer? There's two each. Emma d'*you* want a wafer?'

Emma nodded her fair head and held out a chubby hand.

Alison's heart was thumping despite her outward calm. She folded back the wrapping and put the biscuit into the baby's fist. 'Be a good girl while I get the tea,' she said. She was aching for a cup.

But tea was only a limited comfort that afternoon. She sat at the pine table at the dining end of their one long living room, between Jon's chocolate-smeared pine chair and Emma's rickety high-chair, and drank two cups. Neither clarified her thoughts.

Despite his ease in company, his generosity, charm and good looks, Alison knew that Rigg often felt insecure. He never admitted it, but she could tell. He hated being wrong, especially if his mistakes were commented on. It made him touchy and bad-tempered. Part of her job as his wife was to smooth things for him, to protect him and put him at his ease. She was quite proud of her ability to handle him, even though she had to admit it wasn't always successful. But successful or not, it made her feel good, aware of being a supportive, loving wife. Like her Mum had always been. Although, naturally, she never told anyone what she was doing, not even Brad. The whole point of the exercise was that it had to be private.

During the six years that she and Rigg had been married, she had gradually worked out a set of ground rules that made their life together if not exactly easy – it was too stormy for that – then at least as comfortable as their passionate natures would allow. One of the most important was never to worry him when he was at work. He was furiously private about his work, almost – if it wasn't an unkind thing to think – secretive. Now and then, he came home in high good humour to tell her that he'd had a 'fabulous day' and that the takings had been 'phenomenal' but, apart from that, they never talked about business and he never explained where he'd been when he came in late. It was her fault really. Since the children had been born she hadn't had the time to show enough interest in what he was doing.

Now she would have to break her own rule and contact him at work. He ought to be warned about this letter, just in case it *was* important. She picked up the phone, rather nervously, and dialled the number of his shop in East Street.

It was quite a relief when his assistant took the call, that funny blonde girl, Norrie, speaking in her false sing-song.

'Rings and Thi-ings. How may I *help* you?'

'Hello Norrie. Can I have a word with Rigg?'

'Oh it's you Mrs Toan,' Norrie resuming her usual

voice. 'He's not here, I'm afraid. He's not been in all afternoon. He came in this morning, about tennish, but he didn't stay long. Just a few minutes, that's all. I haven't seen him since. Sorry. Have you tried *Baubles*?'

Baubles was the kiosk in one of Chichester's miniature shopping arcades where Rigg had started his entrepreneurial career. His assistant there was a skinny young man called Kevin, who sounded fed up when he answered the phone.

'Haven't seen him for four days,' he said. 'Came in Friday and emptied the till. I've no idea where he is. I never know where he is. I told that feller from the tax office. No good asking me.'

'Is he on a demo somewhere?'

'No idea. Didn't take any stock. Try *Rings and Things*.'

'I have. He's not there.'

'Surprise, surprise.'

Alison thanked him and put the phone down quickly before she could be led into saying something that might be construed as disloyal. The bitterness in the young man's voice had been too marked to be misinterpreted. The VAT man had been right. Rigg wasn't at either of his shops, and, what was worse, neither of his assistants seemed to expect him to be there.

Oh well, she thought, there's nothing I can do about it now. I shall have to wait until he gets home. Meantime there were the kids to feed, bath and put to bed, a meal to cook and the room to tidy, just in case he was early. Nothing infuriated him more quickly than an untidy room.

The letter stood on the mantelpiece like an unexploded bomb, while Alison did the chores. At midnight, when she finally went wearily up to bed on her own, its pale oblong was the last thing she saw as she climbed the stairs. It looked even more threatening by moonlight.

It must have been around three o'clock when she heard Rigg's key in the lock but, by then, she was too tired and he was too drunk for conversation. He scattered his clothes on the carpet, fell into bed, grunted that he was 'knackered', gave her a moist kiss and fell asleep in the middle of it. Three hours later, when the kids came chattering into the bedroom to start their day, she knew better than to wake him.

It wasn't until ten o'clock that he finally came scowling down the stairs, dishevelled and unshaven, scratching his head and grumbling for tea. Glancing at him, Alison felt a moment's pure admiration for him, despite her anxiety. Even in his early morning state he was handsome, with those broad shoulders and that narrow waist and those long, long legs. His face was striking – broad and bold, with a bushy moustache, thick sideburns, streaky fair hair, and eyes that were disarmingly mottled brown under dark brows. How could she do anything but admire him?

But there wasn't time for that now. She and the children had eaten their breakfast such a long time ago they'd forgotten it, the washing was done and hanging in the yard, they'd been down the road to get some shopping and there was only half an hour left before she had to set out on their long walk, via Jon's playschool, to the holiday camp and the afternoon's work. It was the worst possible moment to tackle Rigg about anything, let alone a visit from the VAT man.

I'll leave it till I've given him some breakfast, Alison decided.

But the letter was in his hand and he was already shouting, 'Whass this? Ali! Whass this?'

'A man brought it for you yesterday,' she said. 'Don't bother with it now. Have a cup of tea first.'

'Don't bother with it now,' he said, his voice rising. 'It's from the VAT office. It's a final demand.'

'I told him it was a mistake.' Alison said, glancing anxiously at the kids. But they were playing with their toys on the hearthrug and didn't seem to have noticed that anything was wrong.

'Mistake!' Rigg said crossly. 'That's putting it *mildly*. It's a disaster. Now I shall have to pay the bloody thing. Why didn't you refuse it? It wasn't addressed to you. You should have told him to take it away again. You'd have been within your rights.'

'Oh come on Rigg, be reasonable. How could I? He was on the doorstep. He knew I was your wife.'

'A bit of loyalty,' Rigg growled, 'that's all I ask.' He aimed a kick at Jon's painstaken tower of bricks so that they scattered in all directions. 'What are all these damn bricks doing all over the place?' Jon's lip trembled and Rigg glared at his son. 'Now he's going to yell. That's all I need! Well stop him, can't you.'

Alison picked Emma up and put out a guiding hand to lead Jon away from the line of fire. 'Don't take it out on the kids,' she said. 'It's not their fault you're behind with your payments.'

'I'm not behind with my payments.'

That was a relief to hear. 'Oh well, that's all right then.'

'No it's not "all right then". I've got all this money to pay.'

'But you said . . .'

'It's an outstanding account. That's all it is. I could have held it off if it hadn't been for you. Now you've landed me right in it.'

'So you *do* owe them the money.'

His voice was dark with disdain. 'Well of course I owe them money. Everybody owes everybody money. That's the way the business world works.' He crammed the demand back in its envelope. 'Nobody pays bills on time. You ought to know that. I've told you enough times. Especially to the tax man. Not before you actually have to. Or do you want me to hand over all my hard-earned cash to make interest for the state?'

Alison decided to stop the argument. She couldn't win it and it would only get worse. Emma was wriggling off her lap and poor Jon was frightened. He was all eyes and his little heart was beating like a hammer under her fingers. 'What do you want for breakfast?' she said because she couldn't think of anything else to say.

'I haven't got time for *breakfast*,' he said. 'I've got to find three grand by the end of the week. Where am I supposed to find three grand? Eh? You tell me, you're so clever.'

She had to answer that. It sounded too much like a cry for help. 'Perhaps you could ask your mother,' she said, annoyed that her voice was shaky. 'Perhaps she'd let you have something on account.'

'No I couldn't. You know that.'

'The bank then?'

'Don't talk to me about banks.'

'Then it'll have to come out of the takings, won't it.

You're doing well enough for that, aren't you? You were telling me only the other day . . .'

That suggestion infuriated him. 'Don't tell me what I'm doing,' he shouted at her. 'I can't just lay my hand on three grand whenever I feel like it. Money doesn't grow on trees.'

'Time we were off,' Alison told the children, keeping her voice bright and normal. 'Where are our coats?' All she could think about was getting out of the house, into the open air, away from his rage before it got any worse. She tumbled the children through the front door, dragging the folded buggy after her.

And there was her friend Brad, leaning up against the wall beside the window, gazing at the sky and smoking. She was wearing her old leather jacket with a new pair of skin-tight jeans and cowboy boots, and her hair was dyed scarlet and lacquered into a stiff plume above her forehead. At the sight of her Alison relaxed a little.

'Boo-ba-do, kids,' Brad said. 'D'you wanna McDonald's?'

Jon's eyes lit up. 'Yeah! An' chips.'

'Hop in then,' Brad said, striding off towards her battered Mini. She'd parked it right in front of Rigg's BMW. The contrast between the two cars couldn't have been more marked – his brand-new, bright red and gleaming with polish, hers ancient, dull brown and eaten with rust.

Alison's emotions were so muddled that she was hardly conscious of what she was doing: fear of Rigg's anger and annoyance at her own inadequacy; relief at seeing Brad and her car; embarrassment because the row must have been overhead. She shoved the buggy into the back of the car without speaking and she and the children climbed in and made spaces for themselves on the back seat among the usual debris – sagging cushions, empty cigarette packets, old newspapers, ancient chewing gum, broken-down shoes.

'All set?' Brad asked. And off they went.

'I thought you were on early turn,' Alison said, when she'd recovered enough to speak. Brad worked in the holiday camp too, as a waitress.

'Changed shifts,' Brad explained, 'so's I could get me barnet done. D'you like it?'

'It's wicked,' Alison approved, glad of a chance to talk about something other than her present problems. 'You look like a pop star. What does Tiny think about it?'

'Oh him!' Brad said disparagingly. 'He's yesterday's news. I've given him the elbow.'

Alison wasn't surprised. None of Brad's lovers lasted long. 'Hence the new hair style,' she said, shrewdly.

'Something like that,' Brad agreed as they turned out of the Selsey Road and began to drive alongside the promenade. 'What's up with the Great-I-Am this morning?'

The question stirred Alison's emotions all over again. 'Oh, nothing much,' she said, wanting to make light of the quarrel. 'You know what he's like first thing in the morning.'

'No. I don't, as it happens,' Brad contradicted sweetly. 'An' just as well fer him, if you ask me. If he shouted at *me* like that I'd have his guts fer garters.'

'What's guts?' Jon wanted to know.

'It means she'd be cross with him,' Alison explained quickly.

'He kicked my bricks all up in the air,' Jon said.

'I'd kick him in the . . .'

'Look at that boat Jon,' Alison side-tracked. 'See it. Right out there. See?'

There was a stiff breeze blowing and one of the fishing boats was having a hard time struggling back to the beach. White foam curved from its bows and it was rolling dramatically.

Brad looked at it too. 'Wouldn't hurt the Great-I-Am to do a bit a' work now an' then,' she said, 'stead a' sitting on his bum all day in that precious BMW.'

'He does work hard,' Alison said, springing to his defence. 'He was home really late last night.'

Brad made a grimace. 'I'll bet he was! An' where'd he been? Did you ask him that?'

'You know I didn't. I don't pry into his affairs. We trust one another.'

Brad looked at her friend through the driving mirror. 'You're a fool,' she said. 'You let him get away with murder.'

'He's not as bad as he sounds,' Alison said, hating the criticism, especially as there was more than a grain of truth in it. She *ought* to know where he was and what he was doing. 'I can handle him.'

'Yeah!' Brad grinned. 'Sounds like it.'

'It's just our way. That's all,' Alison tried to explain. 'All couples have their own life styles. We've been through all this hundreds of times, Brad. You won't change us.'

Somebody ought to, Brad thought. But she didn't argue any more because poor old Ali was still looking pale from all that roaring, and there wasn't any point in making her feel worse than she already did. 'I'm having a Big Mac,' she announced. 'What you having, kids?'

'It's all hot air,' Alison struggled to explain as they walked into McDonald's. 'He's got a short fuse, that's all. He'll have forgotten all about it by this evening.'

But although she was putting on a bright, brave face, she wasn't as sure as she sounded. The fact was she felt guilty about the letter and guilty about the row. Guilty – and a failure. With hindsight, she could see that she ought to have told Rigg about it the minute he got home. He would have taken it better then. Not well exactly, but better. He was always in a bad mood when he woke up and she couldn't pretend she didn't know that. She'd handled the whole thing very badly and now the kids had been upset and Brad had overheard the row. It was a disaster and it ought not to have been.

The afternoon brought an endless queue of problems to solve so that she was late finishing work, very late collecting Jon from his play-group and even later getting home. Lights were already on in most of the living rooms in Shore Street and the windows disclosed framed tableaux of her neighbours sitting at tea, some round the table, others squashed side by side on sofas, watching the telly as they ate. Entire families, children, mothers *and* fathers.

Pushing the buggy along the pitted pavement, past the first four lighted windows, Alison felt jealous and bleak. She couldn't help it, even if it was disloyal. If only Rigg wasn't always at work, if only he could spend more time with the kids. It would make such a difference – to all of them. He might even be better tempered in the morning if he could get a good night's sleep once in a while.

But once she was inside her own home, her good sense returned. It was no use thinking like that. All his time and every penny of their money *had* to go into the business. She'd accepted that right from the start. They'd both known it wouldn't be easy.

'Tea,' she said, lighting the gas fire. 'Get your coats off.' The warm glow lit the room and she sat back on her heels and let it play on her face for a second. Then the BMW drew up outside the door.

The sound threw her into a panic. Jon's bricks were still all over the floor; they were still in their outdoor things; Rigg's dinner wasn't even prepared, let alone cooked. His shadow filled the glass of the front door. His key was in the lock.

His arms were full of parcels, presents for Jon and Emma, a bunch of red roses for her, and he was smiling at Alison, the way he did just before he kissed her.

'Kitten!' he said lovingly. 'How could I have been so foul to my Kitty? Forgiven?'

She forgave him at once, almost unreservedly. And the presents were thrown on to the sofa so that she could be kissed – in his most practised and arousing way.

'Love you,' he murmured into her hair, running his fingers up and down the nape of her neck.

'I want a *drink*,' Jon said, tugging at her jersey. 'I'm thirsty.'

'Presents,' Rigg said, releasing her. 'Come and see what I've got for my Prince and Princess. The most expensive presents in the world. How about that?'

There was a Tiny Tears for Emma and a barrel full of Duplo for Jon. The first games began in front of the fire, Alison arranged her roses in the blue vase, and Rigg spread himself out on the sofa with the wrapping paper scrunched at his feet. Together they made a tableau every bit as heart warming as any of the others in the road – the happy family, gathered together after a hard day's work.

'What's for dinner?' Rigg said.

Dinner was cooked, eaten and appreciated, the kids were bathed and put to bed while Rigg had a short nap on the sofa, and the late evening settled to the softness of music and love-making.

'I'm a pig to my poor kitten,' Rigg said, when they'd both come and were lying side by side, relaxed with satisfaction.

'Never mind,' Alison said sleepily. 'Blame it on the VAT man.'

'That reminds me.'

'Um?'

'I found the money.'

Hadn't she known he would? He was too good a business man to be beaten by a mere three thousand pounds. 'Good,' she murmured. She was more than half asleep now and the word was slurred.

'Yes,' he said, 'Got it from the bank. We've got to go and see the manager tomorrow morning. You won't mind that, will you Kitten?'

'I've got to go too?'

'That's what the man said.'

She was too drowsed by love to ask why or even to wonder. 'All right,' she said. And was asleep.

Chapter Two

As Manager of the Chichester branch of the Camelot and Wessex Bank, Mr Arthur Drury took himself with total seriousness. He was a gentleman of the old school, more at home with ledgers and typewriters than computers and multiple loans, and as such, he had an instinctive distrust of Yuppies.

Nevertheless, he liked Rigby Toan. An enterprising young man, privately educated, of course, and doing well with his two jewellery stores. Over the last eight years Mr Drury had personally seen to it that the Camelot and Wessex had given Mr Toan all the backing he needed. Even now, when the young man was behaving like a Yuppie and offering his equity in the matrimonial home as surety for a loan, Mr Drury was predisposed to let him have what he wanted. Especially now that he'd met Mrs Toan. She was such a nice quiet young woman, the dependable sort, the kind of wife who would be supportive but not foolish.

'Will three thousand be sufficient for this expansion you have in mind?' he asked Mr Toan.

'Oh yes,' Rigg said, assuming his responsible expression. 'I'm sure it will. We mustn't overstretch ourselves. Not in a recession.'

'Quite,' Mr Drury agreed and the two men nodded at one another.

'There *are* risks to a transaction like this,' Mr Drury warned, smiling across his desk at Mrs Toan, 'and I would – um – be doing rather less than my duty if I did not make them known to you. Um – you and Mr Toan will both have to sign these application forms in the presence of a solicitor, that being the legal requirement with second charges.'

The warning puzzled Alison. She opened her mouth to ask what the risks were, but Rigg was speaking before her.

'That's perfectly understood,' he said smoothly. 'We've got an appointment at Spatchcock and Hornchurch in . . .' He looked at his watch (a Gucci bought to inspire confidence, like the BMW) ' . . . sixteen minutes.'

'Then I mustn't keep you,' Mr Drury said, impressed by the organisation. He rose out of his chair to signal that the meeting was over. 'I wish you success. And you too, Mrs Toan.'

They were out of the bank and into the pale sunshine in the street before Alison had a chance to ask any questions.

'What's all this about seeing a solicitor?' she asked as Rigg rushed her towards the centre of the town. 'You never said anything about seeing a solicitor. Is it going to take long? I promised Sally I'd be back in an hour.'

'Won't take a minute,' Rigg assured her. 'It's only a formality.'

'Why did he say . . .'

'Oh you don't want to take any notice of anything Mr Drury says,' Rigg told her firmly. He took her arm as they walked so that she had to lengthen her stride to keep up with him. 'He's just being an old woman. Here we are.'

The solicitor's office overlooked the old market cross that stands where it has stood for centuries, right in the centre of Chichester where the town's four roads converge, its eight stone arches providing a thoroughfare in rainy weather and the stone seat surrounding its central column making it an all-season meeting place. Originally designed as a butter market, it is a curiously romantic little building, like a Gothic crown set about with carved stone pinnacles and bejewelled by four shining clocks and as unexpected in a Georgian market town as an Arab in a crinoline.

Alison could see the eastern clock-face from where she sat waiting while the solicitor read through the papers they were going to sign. The sight of it increased her anxiety and her annoyance. She felt cross with Rigg for not telling her there were two interviews to attend. It had been very kind of Sally to agree to look after the kids, especially at a moment's notice, and she didn't want to impose on her by being late back.

'Yes,' the solicitor said, tidying the papers. 'This is all in order. However, there is one thing that has to be made clear before you sign. To take out a second charge on your home is not something to be undertaken lightly. You are signing over the equity to the bank. I want you to be quite clear about that. In the eventuality that you were to fall on hard times and be unable to repay the loan – which nobody would want, naturally, and which we all hope will not happen although we all have to face the fact that it could –

then the bank would be within its rights to repossess your house.'

'For three thousand pounds?' Alison said. 'They wouldn't do that, would they?'

'They'd be within their rights.'

'But that's preposterous.'

'That may well be the case, Mrs Toan, but these are the terms of a second charge. I have to point them out to you and to caution you as to the advisability of your actions.'

Rigg was shifting irritably in his seat, and Alison knew he didn't like the way the conversation was going but she pressed on. 'When you say you've got to caution us, it sounds as if you would be against it,' she prompted.

The solicitor's reply was sombre and serious. 'My advice to you, Mr and Mrs Toan, would be to find some other way of raising the capital you need which wouldn't put your home in jeopardy.'

'You think we'd be risking our home?'

'I think you should consider the whole matter very carefully before you put your signature to anything.'

Rigg was making a supreme effort to stay charming. 'We appreciate that,' he said to the solicitor. 'We've got to be careful.' He turned to smile a warning at Alison. 'We know all this, don't we darling. But it's only three grand. That's hardly going to break the bank, now is it? I can repay it in three months. Or less. Probably less.'

'But if the worst came to the worst,' the solicitor insisted.

'If the worst *did* come to the worst,' Rigg said grandly, 'and we *did* get into trouble, we could always sell the car.'

'Yes, of course we could,' Alison agreed, supporting him. What a sacrifice he was offering! That car was his most precious possession, the love of his life.

'It's a BMW.' Rigg ticked off the details. 'A 325i. Touring. Power steering. We're talking sixteen grand's worth of car here. So the bottom line is there really isn't any problem. That's the bottom line.'

Mention of such serious money did the trick. The solicitor was reassured, Rigg got his way, the forms were signed. After all, what was a mere three thousand pounds compared to sixteen grand's worth of car?

Surprisingly, when they were out on the pavement again, Rigg seemed distant and preoccupied. 'Sorry I can't give you a lift,' he said, 'but I've got an important meeting. You know what it's like. You can catch a bus, can't you?'

Alison was disappointed that he wasn't going to drive her home but she tried not to show it. 'Yes,' she said. 'All right.'

He was so eager to be off that he turned on his heel as she was speaking. He didn't kiss her goodbye and he didn't look back.

Still, she comforted herself, as she set off down South Street towards the bus station, at least the VAT man can be paid and that's what is important. She might not know much about business but she knew you didn't cross swords with VAT men. They had such power. They could walk in any time they liked and take your goods or your furniture or anything. She remembered hearing about one family where they took all the children's toys. She crossed the road and quickened her pace. There wasn't really any risk in signing this second charge. Not for three thousand. She'd been a bit surprised when Rigg hadn't told the bank manager what he really wanted the money for, but that only went to show how worrying pressure from the VAT man could be. It was a good job done. Really. A very good job done. The only snag was that she was going to be late back. If only the buses weren't so few and far between. And if only it wasn't such a long way home.

Rigg reached his destination long before she did and it wasn't either of his shops. After two sticky interviews, he needed a drink and the reassuring company of his friends, so he went straight to Ernie's Wine Bar.

Most of the crowd were already there and well away, flushed and cheerful with booze. 'Rigg!' one of them shouted. 'There you are. We thought you were dead. Where've you been, you old bugger?'

'Around,' Rigg said vaguely, heading for the bar. 'Here and there. What's your poison?'

Bragging voices swirled round him, cigar smoke spiralled into the rafters, the place smelt of beer, spirits and cheerful sweat.

'Now that's what I call a deal. Fifteen K and more to follow.'

'A stone bonker. Can't fail.'

'So what you been up to Rigg?'

'Nothing much,' Rigg said, getting ready to brag in his turn. 'Just secured a new loan, that's all.'

'Crafty sod! How much?'

'About eighteen K, twenty if I want it. Depends.'

'He's a lad our Rigg,' his admirers told one another. 'If anyone can beat inflation it's our Rigg. I dunno how you do it Rigg.'

Rigg stood at the bar, basking in the warmth of whisky and approbation. 'Flair,' he explained. 'I've got flair, in case you haven't noticed. First you've got to choose an advantageous position, then you've got to build up a good clientele. That's how it's done. Flair. That's all it takes.' Now the day could start again, and this time he could enjoy it. God knows he'd earned the respite. He'd had enough hassle in the last twenty four hours to last a lifetime. He drank his second whisky even more happily than he'd drunk the first, relaxing as it spread fire and confidence down his throat.

There was a stir of cold air at the door and, as if to set the seal on his recovery, there was his best friend Francis, tall, dark-skinned and formidable in his black biking leather, working his way towards him through the crush. His dark hair was still damp from his ride and he smelt of petrol and oil and hot metal.

'That girl of yours at the shop is a moron,' he said, flinging his gauntlets on the counter. 'Said you were out of town.'

'She knows nothing,' Rigg said. 'How long you down for?'

'Couple of hours,' Francis said. 'Got to be back by two. Partying tonight. Large scotch, since you're asking.'

'Partying?' Rigg asked, passing a fiver to the barman.

'Yep. You on?'

'Tonight?'

'Yep.'

'Why not?' Rigg said. It was just what he needed. Frankie's parties were always a riot. He'd never known one to fail. Endless booze, constant music, disco lights to dance to and darkness to cover everything else, lots of pretty girls to impress. There'd been a page three model there last time. 'I'll just have to grab some readies.'

It took Rigg less than five minutes to charge down the road to *Rings and Things*. Despite his boasts, it was actually a small unobtrusive shop in a narrow, two-storey Georgian terrace at the least prestigious end of East Street. Its clientele was nothing to brag about either. It consisted mainly of factory workers and shop assistants on the look-out for costume jewellery or a 'nice little ring', or local husbands after a cheap piece of jewellery for a birthday present or to salve a guilty conscience. Consequently, the stock was designed for impact rather than style and was made of silver, marcasite or very thin gold and set with cheap, pale stones. But he ran up huge electricity bills lighting his limited wares so as to produce as much dazzle in his window as he could, and, sometimes, he would allow one of his drinking cronies to haggle over the price of some 'choice piece' so that he could be persuaded that he'd struck an amazing bargain.

Not that there'd been many bargains struck in the last few months. In fact more often than not the shop was empty – as it was that morning.

Norrie was perched on a stool behind the counter, reading a magazine and twiddling her hair.

''Lo,' she said vaguely. But Rigg was already through the shop and half way up the stairs to the flat, leaving a waft of stale cigar smoke, burped brandy and excited sweat behind him.

'No time! No time!' he called back to her.

She listened as he trampled the floor boards above her head. He's packing, she thought. Had to be. There was nothing in the flat except a bed and the wardrobe where he kept his flash clothes – all those Gucci loafers and Armani suits and things like that. So where's he off to now? London again? Or will it be abroad? You never knew with Rigg. Sometimes he'd be away for absolutely yonks and come back with such a tan you knew he'd been somewhere glamorous.

'There's a lot of letters,' she said, when he reappeared with his hold-all.

Rigg snatched the pile from the shelf under the counter and flicked through them. All bills – surprise! surprise! – and one looked as though it was a final demand from Jaffa Jewels. Well they'd all have to wait. He hadn't the energy for any more hassle. Or the time. He opened the till and scooped out all the notes except two, scrabbled a handful of coins into his back pocket and strode through the shop towards the back entrance where his BMW was waiting.

Ten minutes later he was driving at speed along the dual carriageway towards the M23 and freedom.

After a cautious interval, Norrie nipped out to the back of the shop and opened the stable door to see if the BMW was gone.

Then she phoned *Baubles* to tell Kevin that Rigg had emptied the till and to ask him what they were going to do about wages. Kevin didn't have anything to offer on that except to suggest that they should ask Mrs Toan.

Norrie snorted. 'Mrs Whimpy Toan!' she said. 'She knows nothing.'

Which was true. At that precise moment Alison knew less about her husband's whereabouts than they did.

Her day had been so rushed she was quite relieved when he phoned her late that evening to say that he was in London and wouldn't be back 'for a day or two'. Well at least I can get cleared up, she thought, gazing round her untidy living room. It was littered with toys and dirty tea things again.

'You'll be all right won't you,' he said. His voice was distant and off-hand so she knew she wasn't to complain or ask for help.

'Yes, of course,' she said. 'I'm a bit short of cash, that's all. You haven't given me any housekeeping for quite a long time.'

'Well you won't need housekeeping now, will you. Not while I'm away.'

'Well . . .' she pondered. She was always chronically short of money what with feeding the kids and buying their clothes and paying half the bills and that awful mortgage. 'I suppose I'll manage.'

'That's my girl,' he said cheerfully. 'I might have to pop over to Spain for a few days to see about the flat.'

She only just stopped herself saying, 'That damn flat'. It had been nothing but trouble ever since Rigg bought it and he was always having to pop over 'to sort something out'. 'Oh dear,' she said instead. 'What's up?'

'Nothing much,' he said airily. 'I'll sort it out. Leave it to me. It's a nuisance but I'll do it. I've got to, haven't I? Part of the business. You can see that, can't you?'

'Yes, I can see that,' she said, trying to sound

understanding and failing. She gazed round her child-wrecked living room. It's a man's world, she thought. He goes shooting off to Spain and all that lovely sunshine, and I'm stuck here with the dirty nappies, hours of washing up and chocolate stains all over the settee.

'I want to talk to Daddy,' Jon said pulling at her jersey when she put down the phone after Rigg's hasty goodbye.

'Daddy's at work,' Alison comforted because the little boy's mouth was going square with distress. 'You know he can't talk when he's working. Tell you what, let's have fish and chips for our supper. You'd like that wouldn't you.'

'Ships,' baby Emma said, smiling hugely. 'Ships.'

'Yes,' Alison laughed at her, as she pulled Jon on to her lap for a cuddle. 'We know you like them, don't we Jon. You'd eat chips till they came out of your ears.'

'Ears,' Emma said, putting up both hands to feel them.

'Have you got a nose Emma?' Alison said, leading them both into the familiar game.

The nose was touched and named.

'Have you got eyes?' Jon said.

'Eyes.'

Thank God for children's games, Alison thought as Jon's disappointment was played away. But, loyal though she was to her absent husband, she couldn't help feeling that it wouldn't have hurt him to spend a few seconds talking to his children, no matter where he was or what he was doing. If he'd wanted to, he could have taken them all with him to that flat in

Spain and given them a holiday in the sun while he sorted out the problem. If he wasn't so secretive and touchy about his work, she might have suggested it. But it was no use thinking that way either. Rigg was a free spirit. He always had been. An entrepreneur. Once he's made his first million, he'll calm down, but nobody will ever change him. It was part of his charm, something she had to accept along with everything else about him – early morning ill-temper, floral apologies, boundless dreams, unexpected presents and skill in bed. And he could be wonderful when he liked. Look how he'd offered to sell his car. Asking no questions was a small price to pay in return for love like that.

'I got my coat,' Jon said, tugging her elbow. 'Are we *going*?'

A hundred and fifty miles away in Birmingham, in the offices of Jaffa Jewels, Mr Jefferson Fehrenbach was beginning to think that there were several questions he ought to be asking Mr Rigby Toan – to say nothing of the twenty other customers who were equally tardy in settling their accounts. He and his accountant were working late that night, filling in the VAT returns for Jaffa Jewels and checking the books. As they worked, they'd made a list of defaulters.

'If you'll take my advice,' the accountant said, 'you'll send someone off to make a few discreet enquiries. A salesman perhaps.'

'I'll look into it,' Mr Fehrenbach decided. One or two of his better salesmen were capable of a bit of sleuthing but the feller in Sussex wasn't one of them. 'I'll put Alexander Jones on to the worst offenders.'

'Start with the six who owe you the most,' the accountant advised and he drew neat lines under six names and addresses.

Which was how Morgan Griffiths of the firm of Alexander Jones (Investigation and Security) found himself dispatched to Chichester and Hampton-on-Sea to investigate the trading prospects of Mr Rigby Toan.

Chapter Three

It was a beautiful day for a drive – an Easter-egg day, full of hope and innocence, the sky heaped with flamingo cloud, the trees and hedgerows laced with new leaf, the long smooth hills of the South Downs richly green on the horizon. Just the sort of day Morgan Griffiths enjoyed.

He'd just returned from a fortnight's holiday with his family in Port Talbot, where he'd been rather cast down by the things he'd heard while he was in Wales. More pits were due for closure, two more of his cousins were out of work and Granddad was very ill with 'the dust', too short of breath to get upstairs and coughing incessantly. It was a relief to be back in Guildford, with plenty of work to do.

It had taken him a long time to settle into a new occupation after the accident. A broken collar bone, three cracked ribs and a fractured arm left him in too fragile a state for any heavy work – not that there was much available. In fact, he spent the first twelve months taking anything he could get; stacking shelves in a supermarket, driving a taxi, night watchman at a local cardboard factory. Then, just when he'd resigned himself to a life of ill-paid manual labour, he saw an advertisement for a 'strong-arm man' in a London security firm, and as both his arms had returned to full strength he applied for it and got it. It was a wrench to leave the family, but it was the right move to make. That job led to another and better, which in its turn led to Mr Alexander Jones, where he'd been ever since.

The assignment he'd been given that morning was going to be a doddle. Making enquiries about the credit worthiness of a small town shopkeeper was something he could do in twenty minutes. He would have preferred a difficult case, like his last one which had been a large-scale fraud and had taken him to central London for more than three months among seedy streets and never-ending traffic jams – and some very sharp operators. But work was work and there were always compensations. When he had sorted this one out, he planned to spend the rest of the day by the sea. It was just the weather for it.

He'd been to Chichester once before, when he first started work with Alexander Jones. He had a vague memory of a neat market town with a theatre at one end, a station at the other and a cathedral somewhere in the middle, rather impressive, with a green roof and a very tall spire. And there it all was, almost exactly as he remembered it, except that there were rather more shops shut down and the four main streets had been pedestrianised.

Rings and Things was easy to find and that was pretty much as Morgan expected it too. He stood outside the shop front and made his first notes – 'well-stocked window, paint in good order, cheap jewellery, no customers.'

Then he went in to pretend to be looking for a bracelet and to talk to the assistant.

It took less than ten minutes to find out what he

needed to know. The assistant was affable, if a little vague. She informed him that trade was 'up and down', that she hardly ever saw the boss and that he was off in Spain at the moment, taking a holiday.

'All right for some,' Morgan said, in his laconic way.

''E's got a flat out there.'

'Time-share?'

'Don't think so. I think he owns it.'

Morgan put the bracelet back on the counter. 'Not quite what I was looking for,' he said. 'Thanks anyway.'

'You're welcome,' Norrie said. 'You could try our other shop if you like. You might find something there. *Baubles* in the Bellingham Arcade.'

A perfunctory glance was all that was needed in the arcade. Morgan made a few more notes. 'Similar stock, well-lit, three customers. All signs of a business ticking over.' Now he only had to take a quick look at Mr Toan's house and the job would be done.

But where Chichester had been predictable, Hampton was a surprise. For a holiday town in springtime it was very run-down. The main shopping street was virtually empty, and except for a large Boots next door to an equally sizeable W. H. Smith, the shops in it were mostly down-market. There were several that were struggling on with very limited stock and plainly wouldn't last much longer. The rest of the town wasn't much better. The pier ended in a row of broken spars, the railway station was falling to pieces, and there was litter everywhere; trodden underfoot at every kerb, spewing out of every litter bin, blowing and tumbling along the promenade. The recession was really biting here.

Rigby Toan's house was the biggest surprise of all. 'Turn-of-the-century fisherman's cottage, about 40K, possibly less, poorly furnished,' Morgan noted from the car. 'Kid's bike outside, secondhand. Not the home of a successful shopkeeper.' Perhaps there *was* a reason for this enquiry after all. Then he got out of the car to knock at the door.

An elderly woman in an apron threw open the upstairs window of the house next door and leaned out to see what he was doing.

'You looking for someone?' she said.

'Mr and Mrs Toan,' he told her politely. 'I *have* rung.'

'He's in Spain,' the woman said. 'She's on the beach if you want to find her. Went off about half an hour ago with the kids. They've all got their red bobble hats on. You can see 'em a mile off.'

The day was conspiring to take him to the sea. He backed his car out of the alley, crossed the Selsey Road and drove the few hundred yards down to the beach to see what Mrs Toan could tell him.

It was a lot colder on the promenade than it had been in the town and there was a brisk south-easterly blowing. The tide was a very long way out and, under the shifting cloud, the sea was streaked with springtime colour; glass-green and duck-egg blue ruffled with creamy foam. A joy to the eye. But the long expanse of dun-coloured sand looked wintry, damp and chill and corrugated with long dark ridges like skin contracted with cold. The promenade was unkempt, spattered with pebbles, blobbed by thick cow-pats of tar and littered with flotsam, rusty tins, frayed lengths of orange rope tangled in seaweed, plastic bottles, most of them with German labels, old shoes, rags and rotten wood, the remains of an antique orange box smeared with something dark and sticky.

There were very few people about. Two or three elderly couples, bundled shapeless by coats and scarves, attempted an afternoon totter along the promenade. A man wearing earmuffs and a vacant expression scanned the shingle with a metal detector. A pack of mongrels sniffed among the rubbish and jumped, barking, from pebble to pebble. But there was no sign of a woman and two children, and not a glimpse of a red bobble hat.

Nothing daunted, Morgan crunched down the mounded shingle and set off along the sand eastward towards the black silhouette of the pier. If he could find Mrs Toan, all well and good; if he couldn't, he would take a good long walk along the beach to clear his brains before the drive back to Guildford. Already the taste of salty air and the rhythmic tumbling of the distant waves were lifting his spirits.

There was a group of kids playing among the struts of the pier. He could see skinny legs darting about and a huddle of dark shapes bending over a pool, and there was an empty double buggy standing beside one of the groynes. That's a tatty old thing, he thought, as he passed it. Then he realised that the damp-looking object draped over one of the handles was a red bobble hat. So they must be somewhere near. Probably under the pier. Now that he was closer to it, he could make out a dash of red among the group round the pool and as he watched four of the figures detached themselves and went running off towards the sea.

The clearance allowed him to see that the three who were left behind were two small children with big eyes and red cheeks and a young woman in long brown boots, blue jeans and a multicoloured anorak.

He walked towards her, mentally taking notes, thinking what an unlikely partner she was for a rich entrepreneur, how young she looked, and how ordinary, with her long dark hair swinging in a pony tail behind her, and how suitably coloured she was in that odd patched coat, sea green, sky blue, sand, stone, rose pink, as if she was part of the scenery.

As he watched, she side-stepped round the edge of the rock pool, glancing from right to left at her children. Her movements were so soft and fluid she looked as though she was swimming. She reminded him, suddenly, of the little mermaid in the fairy story that had haunted him so powerfully (and secretly) when he was a little boy. The details of the story opened out in his mind, how she lived under a spell, shorn of her fish's tail, rejected by her callous lover, doomed to dance on feet that cut like knives. At that point Morgan's thoughts were so confused that he lost his usual professional confidence and couldn't think how to open the conversation. Should he admit to knowing her name and tell her that he'd come to meet her husband? Or pretend that this was just a chance encounter? Or should he smile at her and hope *she*'d talk to *him*?

But he didn't have to make a decision, for just at that moment the larger of the two children jumped on to the flat rock that edged the pool, slipped on the seaweed as he landed and toppled face downwards into the water.

'Jon! You idiot!' the woman yelled. But both she and Morgan were beside the pool in two strides. Four hands reached out, instinctively and in harmony, and the boy was lifted up between them.

'No harm done,' Morgan comforted in his Welsh sing-song, as the kid blinked water and sand out of his eyes.

Alison wasn't paying attention to anyone except her son. 'You're soaked!' she said, crouching so that she was on a level with the child's streaming face. 'Look at you.' She tried to brush the moisture away from the front of his coat, flicking at it with the tips of her fingers.

'I couldn't help it,' Jon said, as water dripped from his anorak and ran down his boots to puddle on the sand. 'It was the seaweed. I didn't *jump*. It's not my fault.' His face was quite cross.

'No. All right. I know it's not,' Alison soothed, producing a tissue from her pocket to wipe his wet face. 'We'll have to go straight home now and get you out of those wet clothes.'

'Not go home,' Emma complained. ''tay on a beach.' And she took off at once and began to run along the sand, following the other children in their gallop towards the sea.

Alison stood up, ready to give chase. 'Stay there,' she said to her son. 'I won't be a minute.'

'I'll look after him,' Morgan offered.

Caught between the demands of her two children, she was glad of the offer. 'Thanks!' she said. 'That's kind of you.'

'Have you got far to go?' Morgan asked, when she came running back with the little girl straddling her hip. 'I've got a car on the promenade. I could give you a lift, if you like.'

Alison had no intention of taking a lift from a stranger, however kind. 'No thank you,' she said, polite but firm. 'We can manage. It's not far.'

She was looking at him for the first time and her eyes were the colour of the spring sea. Fish-shaped eyes, lively and shining, beautifully curved, finned with black lashes. 'It's no trouble,' he repeated with a little shrug.

The baby wriggled on Alison's hip. 'Don' wanna go home. Mummy! Don' wanna go home.'

She'll never manage two kids and a buggy up all those pebbles, Morgan thought. 'I'll give you a hand up to the promenade then,' he said, picking up the buggy.

She could accept that. 'Thanks,' she said, reaching out for Jon's cold hand.

They crunched up the shingle together and, because he was being so kind, she decided to make conversation.

'Are you here on holiday?' she said.

'No,' he told her. And then after a pause, 'I'm working.'

'Really?' she said. 'No, don't tell me. Let me guess. Frost's or Butlin's.'

'Neither.'

'Then you're not local,' she laughed.

'Is that all the choice there is – if you're local?'

'More or less,' she said. 'There's nothing else much. If you live in Hampton, you either make fridges or clean chalets.'

'My Daddy works in a shop,' Jon said importantly.

'He's got a big shop. In Chichester. A great big shop. That big.' Spreading his arms as far as they would go.

Morgan smiled at the little boy.

'Mummy an' me,' Jon confided, 'we work in Butlin's.'

'Is that right?'

'You go to play-group,' Alison corrected, as they reached the promenade. 'Mummy works in Butlin's.' She took the buggy from Morgan and opened it with her free hand. 'Hop in.'

'Don't go falling in any more pools.' Morgan said to the little boy.

And they went their separate ways.

Afterwards, as he drove towards Guildford and the report he would have to write, Morgan realised that there were questions he ought to have asked Mrs Alison Toan, but he'd been enjoying himself so much by the sea and he'd been so easy in her company that he hadn't wanted to pry. Not that it mattered. He knew all he needed to know about Mr Rigby Toan.

Chapter Four

Margaret Toan paid the taxi driver with a five pound note and the airy instruction that he was to keep the change. After a day in London, she felt her shoes pinching and her back ached as if someone was kneeling on it, but she smiled brightly – just in case any of her neighbours were looking – and, ostentatiously clutching her Harrods carrier bags, she let herself into the house.

Silence washed heavily towards her from its emptiness. There wasn't a single sound of life; no kettle boiling, no radio, no TV, nothing. The love birds huddled together in their tall cage in the bay window, miserably mute. Even the clock had stopped and there were no cards on the mat.

'What *is* the point?' Margaret said to herself. 'What *is* the point? If your one and only son can't even send you a card on your birthday you might as well give up.' It was always the same when her birthday came round, always this dragging fear that she would be forgotten. Even an exhausting trip to London, an expensive lunch and an even more expensive shopping spree hadn't blotted it from her mind for an instant.

Frantic for a G and T, she let her prestigious shopping fall to the carpet and teetered towards the cocktail cabinet. Glass in hand, she set about filling the house with necessary sound, switching on the TV, clumsily winding the clock, shouting at the love birds. On her way back to replenish the glass she caught sight of her frowning reflection in the mirror over the fireplace. 'Life can be very cruel sometimes,' she told it. 'I'm sixty three, for God's sake, and my own son can't even be bothered to send me a card.'

But then the voice of her vanity rose through the gathering fumes of alcohol to comfort her. 'You might be sixty three, but you don't look it. You're a beautiful woman.'

She drank some more G and T, touched her careful blonde hair, adjusted her pearls and rearranged the silk scarf at her neck. 'Yes,' she said, gazing at the charming image that was beginning to assemble itself in the mirror. 'I am. I always have been and I still am.' Softened by admiration, her blue eyes gazed back at her face. Even after a long day in London her set was still holding. Skilful make-up disguised the sharpness of her nose and her teeth were very, very good. You would have to look closely to know that they were capped.

The gin was working. As she filled her glass for the third time, her movements grew languid. Gold charms dangled from her wrist, clinking musically. The clock ticked, the TV chattered and applauded. She threw her hat and coat into a chair and spread herself elegantly on the chaise longue, glass in hand. 'Madame Récamier,' she said, 'has nothing on me.'

But she wasn't Madame Récamier. She was Mrs Margaret Toan – widow of Henry, mother of Rigby – and in a small irritable corner of her mind she knew that these days she wasn't even allowed the glory of her full and proper name. Behind her back, most of her neighbours and acquaintances called her Maggie. Such a nasty, vulgar nickname. Totally inappropriate for someone like herself and downright insulting when it was applied to the Prime Minister. To see those awful demonstrators on the television waving their silly placards and shouting 'Maggie-Maggie-Maggie! Out-out-out!' was almost as bad as being burgled. It was so disrespectful. No way to treat a great lady.

Mrs Margaret Toan put her empty glass on the coffee table and began to cry. Tears oozed from under her closed eyelids and trickled down over her upturned cheeks. She was so absorbed in her self-pity that it was some time before she became aware that the door bell was ringing.

She eased herself out of the chair and crept over to the window. There was a dark shape on the doorstep. 'Rigby!' she cried. 'Oh Rigby, my dear boy!' He hadn't forgotten. The dear, dear boy. He'd come to see her after all.

He was bearing his customary bunch of red roses and looking so handsome she simply had to kiss him.

'Sweets to the sweet,' he said, thrusting the roses at her. 'Happy birthday Mater.'

'For me?' she said, feigning surprise, the way she always did. 'Oh you shouldn't have.'

'Can't have my lovely Mater sitting in a room without flowers on her birthday,' Rigg said. As he always did.

The ritual continued as they walked through her cluttered hall into the living room. 'Do you still love your old mother?'

He brushed her cheek with his moustache. 'Passionately,' he said. 'You know I do.'

'And you've come all this way to see me, just because it's my birthday. On your busiest day too. So tell me, how's trade?'

She poured him a nice large brandy and they sat opposite one another in the two armchairs so that he could tell her what she wanted to hear – that trade was booming, that he was doing well, that the recession was bouncing off him.

Margaret Toan was too good a business woman not to know that the possession of two lock-up shops and a fisherman's cottage was hardly a business empire, even in recession-hit times. But she pushed the knowledge to the back of her mind. It was important for her to view her son as a potential success. If he were to fail, it would be absolutely intolerable. Failure was so demeaning and she hadn't spent all that money on a private education to have her only son branded a failure.

'Flair, that's all it takes,' Rigg was saying, waving his glass, in the sort of expansive gesture that went down so well in Ernie's Wine Bar. 'You've either got it or you haven't.' The trouble was the words didn't sound right in his mother's over-furnished parlour. They required the sort of instant response he always elicited in the wine bar. He chewed the end of his moustache, waiting for his mother to pick up her cue.

She agreed with him, whole-heartedly. That damp moustache was too touching. 'You've got it, my darling,' she said over the clink of ice. 'You'll soon have your first million. I can see that. I'll bet you're not far off it now, are you?'

It was balm to be believed. Rigg smiled modestly. 'Well, let's say I'm on my way.'

'You're so like your father,' Margaret said, extending their fantasy. 'He was so handsome and he had such pazzaz. I can see you going just the same way. Just exactly the same way. Oh my dear, you're going to be so rich and so successful. They'll be beating a path to your door. And mine too I shouldn't wonder.'

Perhaps this was the right moment to throw out a hint. 'Actually Mater,' Rigg said casually. 'I'm thinking of opening another outlet.'

She looked away from him, her expression vague. Then she got up and walked over to the cocktail cabinet to fix them both another-teeny-drink. 'Good idea,' she said, with her back to him. 'Why don't you?'

'Slight cash-flow problem, just at the moment,' he admitted, hoping she would rise to the bait.

She didn't. Spine still straight, she busied herself with the ice bucket. 'You'll soon solve that,' she said.

'It would be easier if I were thirty five,' he hinted, needled by the unfairness of his father's will. Everybody else got the goodies when they were twenty one. 'If I were thirty five . . .'

She turned and laughed at him with a gently mocking sound. 'Don't wish your life away, my dear,' she warned, handing the glass over. 'You'll be old soon enough, heaven knows.' Unconsciously she adjusted her silk scarf, fitting it more tightly round her neck. 'You don't want wrinkles before your time.'

'But if . . .' Rigg began. He had to press on. If only she didn't block him so.

'Let me tell you about my birthday,' Margaret said brightly. 'I've been to London today. Birthday treat. They've got some lovely things in Harrods this year. I bought myself a trouser suit. Would you like to see it? I could model it for you.'

Rigg smoothed his moustache with his forefinger, masking the disappointed droop of his mouth. It was so difficult to find the right note when he was talking to his mother. Too serious and she scolded him, too light and he was ignored. This time, his hint had been too subtle for her to notice. That was the problem. But he *had* to be subtle. He couldn't ask her outright. That would be demeaning. He'd feel too much like a kept boy if he did that. A mother's boy.

Meantime there was a fantasy to play out, compliments to pay, images to project. Sometimes he wished they could drop their guard, just once in a while, and tell one another the truth.

'Yes,' he said, summoning the warmest smile he could manage. 'Go on then. Show me how beautiful you are.'

Acquiescence always roused Margaret's affection. She touched his cheek with her fingertips. 'You *are* my boy,' she said.

'That's me,' he agreed. 'That's who I am.'

In the kitchen in her semi-detached house in Apple Orchard Close, Alison's mother, Elsie Wareham – widow of Bob, mother of Mark, Greg, Alison and Andy – was wiping her hands on a damp J-cloth.

'Oh go on then, sweetheart,' she said to her eldest granddaughter who had been begging permission to lick the bowl. The trifle was made, the cream had been piled on top and there was only a scraping left. 'You can if you like. You've earned it. You've been a real help to me this afternoon. Only be sharp about it or the others'll come back and you won't get a look in.'

At thirteen years old, Katy Wareham was already showing the promise of the pretty young woman she would soon become but she was still shy and, as Elsie knew, she tended to get pushed to one side by her younger brother William.

Fortunately Mark and Jenny had taken that young gentleman with them when they went to collect Alison and the children, and the others hadn't arrived yet, so she and Katy had time, and the kitchen, to themselves.

Katy wriggled into a comfortable position on the kitchen stool and used her forefinger to scrape the whipped cream from the sides of the mixing bowl – scrape, lick, scrape, lick.

'Gran,' she said, thoughtfully. 'D'you think Uncle Rigg'll come to tea this time?'

Elsie was diplomatic. 'I think he's still in Spain,' she said. 'If he's back in time he will, I expect. Ali said he might come back today because it's his mother's birthday.'

'I don't think he will,' Katy said. 'And if he does he won't come to tea. He never comes to tea these days.'

'I'm sure he would if he could,' Elsie said. Whatever her private opinion of Rigg's absence from her family gatherings, she was loyal to him in front of the child. 'He works ever so hard.'

'I feel so sorry for Aunty Ali,' Katy went on. 'She's always on her own.'

'Oh I wouldn't say that,' Elsie said, looking rather embarrassed. It wasn't right for a thirteen-year-old to criticise her uncle like that.

Fortunately at that moment a car turned into the drive.

'Here's your Dad,' she said. 'Just in the nick of time. Let's get those potatoes mashed.'

Car doors slammed, there was a babble of voices and before Elsie could empty the potatoes out of the saucepan, the kitchen was full of people. Alison was wearing a new fuchsia-pink sweater for the occasion and her arms were full of daffodils. Emma clutched a chewed teddy bear and Jon ran at full pelt to be picked up and swung about by big cousin, Katy. Behind them, Mark looked enormous in the doorway with his pretty Jenny all smiles beside him, and young William used his dark head like a battering ram to push past them and get in with the others. Then it was all kisses and greetings and the sort of noisy chaos they enjoyed.

Elsie was arranging the daffodils in her best glass vases when Greg and Susie purred into the drive in their Rover, with their two little girls sitting in the back seats and looking very pretty in pale pink track suits. Ten minutes later, Andy and Clare came rattling up in that old banger of theirs – Andy clutching a cooked ham 'to add to the feast'. Now there were so many people in the house that the kitchen wouldn't hold them all and they had to move on to the living room.

This was the moment Alison enjoyed most: being back in the family bustle with her three brothers, laughing, teasing and full of life, and her sisters-in-law gossiping and setting the table – and children everywhere. Strictly speaking, she should have gone to Margaret Toan's house after work that day, because it was her birthday, but she couldn't have borne to miss a minute of the get-together. Every time she saw them she admired her brothers more. There was such a strong family resemblance between them, even if Greg was shorter than the other two. They had the same way of moving, the same laugh, the same shock of thick dark hair, although Greg's was cut shorter than his brothers' because he was an executive in the Rover plant at Southampton and had to look the part.

It never ceased to amaze Alison that this huge family could be squashed so amicably into her mother's limited house. There were fifteen at a full family gathering – fourteen if Rigg didn't come – and the dining room was 'technically' only big enough to accommodate half that number. But they always managed. Andy and Mark opened the dividing doors between the two living rooms and the diners settled wherever they could. The oldest and youngest sat at the table, the rest squashed on to the sofa or packed two to an armchair, or sat cross-legged on cushions with their plates between their knees. They balanced glasses and bottles on every available bit of furniture and they talked nineteen to the dozen. Afterwards, Greg and Susie usually took the kids out in the garden or down to the beach while the remaining adults cleared the rooms and washed the dishes, talking and joking all the time. It was busy, and happy, and crowded with incident, like a holiday.

But on that Saturday the holiday atmosphere was broken by the late afternoon news. Andy was sitting at the far end of the table, happily munching his way through a mound of cold meats and salad and pickle, when he looked up to catch sight of a riot on the television.

'Good God! Look at that!' he said. 'Turn the sound up someone.'

'What is it?' Susie said anxiously. There were always far too many things on the news that weren't suitable for her two little girls.

'It's the poll tax,' Greg explained, glancing at it. 'Some sort of demonstration, isn't it, Mark?'

'It's in London,' Clare said. 'There's the National Gallery. It's in Trafalgar Square.'

It looked more like a battle field. They watched as police horses galloped into the square, and police in riot gear charged at the crowds, riot shields held high. Running bodies blurred across the foreground of the picture, crash barriers toppled, the pavement was littered with the wreckage of broken poles and smashed placards. But there were still plenty of placards held aloft for the cameras to pick out, their bold stark print proclaiming, 'PAY NO POLL TAX'.

'It's disgraceful!' Susie said, putting down her fork. 'They don't think of those poor horses.'

'Horses!' Andy said, looking at his sister-in-law disparagingly. 'What are you talking about? It's people, Susie. They're the ones getting cracked over the head. Ouch. Look at that. He's going to end up in casualty.' He spoke from professional concern, being a charge nurse in a casualty ward.

'Look at *that*,' Clare cried, as another demonstrator was dragged along the road by two policemen. 'Now that's nasty.' She worked in the same hospital as Andy as a theatre sister, and she, too, could assess the seriousness of an injury.

Susie tossed her fair hair. 'Well if they don't want to get hurt,' she said, 'they shouldn't come out on the streets making a nuisance of themselves. That's all I can say. They should stay at home out of harm's way. Just look at that! He's *kicking* that poor horse!'

Her face was quite pink. This is getting out of hand, Alison thought. Clare and Andy were bristling, Greg was looking protective, poor old Mum was worried. I shall have to do something or they'll start squabbling and we can't have that. Clutching her plate, she stood up, hooked the big tray from its niche behind the settee and began to pick her way round the crowded room, gathering dirty plates and their attention as she went. 'Come on slowcoach,' she said to Andy. 'You're always the last to finish.'

'Some of us don't bolt our food,' he laughed at her.

'Please Miss, I've been a good boy Miss,' Mark clowned. 'I've got a nice clean plate. See?'

Alison handed the tray to him and stood with her back to the television, masking its controversial pictures with the bulk of her pink jersey. While he added plates to the pile, she managed to turn down the sound and to switch channels.

Watching her gratefully, Elsie thought – yet again – what a dear loving girl she was, always smoothing things over and making things easy. Bob always used to say she was the family peacemaker and that was nothing less than the truth. Dear Ali. She smiled at her daughter across the heads of her volatile sons and daughters-in-law, and they exchanged a glance which contained understanding, gratitude and affection.

'Time for trifle,' Alison said, heading for the kitchen.

'Yes *please*!' Jon shouted, running after her. 'Can I have a really big helping? I *am* four.'

Their laughter at his eagerness blew away the last awkwardness.

Chapter Five

It was very late when Alison and her children were finally driven home from her mother's party, this time by her big brother Greg. Emma was in her pyjamas and so deeply asleep that she didn't wake even when Alison lifted her out of the back seat and carried her into the house. Jon was asleep too, but he woke up sufficiently to stagger across the pavement of his own accord.

'Can you manage?' Greg asked, as his sister switched on the light with her elbow.

'Yes. I'm fine,' Alison said. She could hear a television playing and she wasn't quite sure whether it was next door or in her bedroom. The sound made her heart leap. It could just be Rigg come home from Spain.

It *was*. She could see the flicker of blue light under the bedroom door. Dear Rigg. What a lovely end to a lovely day. She settled both the children in their beds and then went in to welcome him, aware of how much she'd missed him and how glad she was to see him again.

He was spread out on the duvet, with all their pillows mounded behind his head, watching television.

'Hello,' she said. 'When did you get back?'

He smiled at her briefly. 'Bout an hour ago.'

'I didn't see the car.'

‘Had to park it round the corner. There wasn’t a space.’

‘D’you want anything to eat?’

‘No thanks.’

She sat on the edge of the bed and put her arms round his neck. ‘Oh Rigg!’ she said. ‘It *is* good to see you.’

He kissed her. A long, lingering, exciting kiss. ‘Hello Kitten.’

‘Why are you still fully dressed?’

‘I’m not fully dressed. I’ve taken my shoes off.’

‘Correction,’ she said, unbuttoning his shirt. ‘Why are you fully dressed except for your shoes?’

He lifted her pink jersey over her head and threw it across the room. ‘I was waiting for you to undress me,’ he said.

It was a rapturous homecoming, the best for a very long time.

‘Oh Rigg,’ she said, when they were both catching their breath afterwards. ‘I *have* missed you.’ Her eyes were closed with satisfied fatigue. ‘I do love you so much.’

He pulled his arm away from under her shoulders and sat up. The movement made her wonder a little, because he usually went straight to sleep afterwards. ‘What is it?’ she said, her eyes still shut.

The mattress tilted. He was getting out of bed. This time she opened her eyes. ‘What is it? Is there something wrong?’

He was putting on his clothes. Why was he putting on his clothes? But he stopped long enough to look at his wife. It was a disquieting look, distant and calculating.

'No,' he said, pulling on his trousers. 'Not wrong exactly. A bit difficult, that's all.'

She waited and watched his expression. She knew it was serious – he wouldn't be dressing otherwise – and she knew she mustn't put pressure on him – because of the look he'd given her. But the longer she waited the more anxious she became.

'The thing is,' he said eventually, 'the thing is, I'm moving out.'

Alison didn't understand him. Wouldn't understand him. He couldn't be moving out. Not when they'd just made love. Not when they were so happy. 'Moving out?'

'Yes, yes,' he said, and now he sounded irritable. 'I'm all packed. I could have gone an hour ago. I've been waiting to tell you.'

'Packed?' she echoed. 'Packed.' Now she noticed the travelling cases standing against the wall with his squash racket and a bundle of fishing rods tied to the handles. Despite a desperate effort to stay calm, she began to panic. What had she done wrong? He couldn't be doing this! He mustn't!

'You mean you're *leaving* me?' she asked, her voice suddenly husky.

He strode back to the bed and put his arms round her. 'No, no, course not. We'll still be married. It's nothing like that. You mustn't think that. It's just . . . well I've got to live over the shop, that's all. I can't go on living here. Oh hell! It's because of the poll tax. If I live here and run the two shops I shall have to pay three lots of tax again.'

Distress made her blunt. 'Can't you afford it then?'

He answered bluntness with bluntness. 'Not this year. No. I can't. I've got to make economies.'

Alison was so upset she couldn't think what to say.

'It won't be for long,' Rigg said, breaking the silence. 'I'll soon be back.'

'How long?' she asked bleakly.

'Three months. Six. A year at the outside.'

'A year!' It felt like a lifetime.

He back-tracked at once. 'Well not a year. That's stretching it a bit. A matter of months, that's all.'

'But why now? You don't have to leave *now*, do you?'

'It's for a year's tax,' he explained. 'That's why. April is the end of the tax year. It's got to look as though I've left you by the time they send the next demand. Oh come on Kitten. Every couple has to make sacrifices.'

'Yes,' she said dully. But not this sort of sacrifice. That wasn't part of the plan.

'I'm doing this for you,' he said, taking her by the shoulders and gazing earnestly into her eyes. 'It's all for you. I know it's tough but if we can stick it out we shall soon turn the corner. You'll see. This is just a blip, that's all. Look at it that way. A blip. It'll soon be over and then we can start expanding again. By this time next year we could be on our way to our first million. Living in clover. Eh?'

It was what he'd said to her a thousand times but in her present state of shock it made no sense. How could he be doing it for her when he was leaving her? How *could* he be leaving her? How would she manage without him? What about the bills? When she'd recovered enough to look at him, he was pulling on his jersey and checking the straps on the two cases.

'Are you going to pay me any housekeeping while

you're away?' she asked, forcing the question out. And when he scowled she added, 'I'm sorry but I've got to know where I stand.'

'Well obviously not,' he said, reasonably. 'If I'm not living here you won't need money for my keep.'

She frowned with worry. 'Who'll pay the mortgage?' she asked.

'I will,' he said, smiling at her. 'Leave that to me.'

'All of it? Every month?' She had to be sure because it was a terrifying bill and she would never manage to meet her half of it without his housekeeping money. 'We won't go halves any more? You'll pay it all?'

'Yes, yes,' he said, rather tetchily. 'If you'll pay all the other bills. You can manage that, can't you?'

She didn't know whether she could or not. Things were happening too quickly for her to digest and she felt too bewildered and too frightened. But she nodded anyway.

'Right,' he said briskly, taking the nod for assent. 'I'm off then. I'll give you a ring. We'll get through it, you'll see. We never pretended it would be easy. Remember our pact, eh.'

'Our pact?' she said, feeling and sounding foolish.

'Our pact,' he said. 'Two individuals. Personal freedom. Give and take. That's what it's all about. I let you have the children. You got what you wanted.'

And with that he was out of the door.

She listened as he carried the cases downstairs, bumping them against the walls. She heard the front door open and shut, his feet walking away along the cracked pavement, the sound of his BMW starting up, purring off, diminishing into the silence. She felt more alone than she'd ever done in the whole of her life.

Turning on her side, she tried to be sensible and settle to sleep. But sleep was impossible. How could she sleep when her husband had just walked out on her? If he *had* walked out on her. Just for a few months, he'd said, hadn't he? But what did he mean by a few months? What did he mean by any of it?

'Remember our pact,' he'd said. Was that a clue? And if it was, what did he mean by it? She'd always remembered the pact. She'd lived by it. They both had. Because it was their invention, their freedom pact. She remembered how thrilled she'd been with it, when they first discussed it. Then it had seemed a wonderful idea, clean and daring, breaking all the fuddy-duddy rules of the older generation that Rigg despised so much. They were both going to be perfectly free – to live their own lives, go their own way, each spending their own money, each doing their own thing. Neither of them would suffer the ignominy of being a dependant. Even if they got married they would still be two individuals, two – what was it Rigg always said? – two free spirits. And that's what they had been. Hadn't they? Even when it was really difficult.

The more she thought about it now, the more difficulties she remembered. Sometimes, even in those early years, she'd found it hard to rustle up enough cash to pay her share of the bills and her half of the mortgage, even though she was working full time then and knew exactly how much money she had to budget with. When Jon was born, life got really difficult because she could only work part time and she was always short of cash. But she'd never complained. No matter what.

'Remember our pact,' he'd said. *'I let you have the children. You got what you wanted.'* It was almost as if he saw it as some sort of bargain. Surely he wasn't equating her right to have children with his right to walk out on them. *That* wasn't what their pact had been about. No, he couldn't have meant that. It was too ugly.

But thinking back on it through the long night, Alison had to admit it had given her a nasty shock to realise that Rigg's ideas about freedom didn't include any consideration of the possibility of a baby. Miserably, she remembered the day she had told him she was pregnant – and how he'd rounded on her.

'I'm too young to be a father,' he'd said. 'I thought we'd agreed to wait until we could afford it.'

'Yes, well . . .' she said, because she hadn't done it deliberately. 'It *was* an accident.'

'Well then, I think you ought to get rid of it.'

She'd been horrified. 'I can't do that,' she'd said. 'It's your baby Rigg. I want it.'

'But not *now*,' he said. 'You can have one later, can't you? I'm no good with children. Anyway, we're too young to be parents.'

'I'm exactly the right age,' she told him. 'Twenty five. That's quite old enough.'

'Not for me it isn't. Anyway we can't afford it. Wait till we're ready.'

'I could be too old by the time you're ready,' she tried joking.

But he was hideously serious. 'Get rid of it.'

'No.'

'Then you'll have to look after it,' he told her. 'I'm not getting up in the night to attend to some howling brat.'

'I'll look after it,' Alison promised eagerly. 'Anyway, they don't always howl. Some of them are dear little things. Ever so quiet.'

'Ours'll howl,' Rigg said lugubriously.

'Well you won't have to get up to it,' Alison reassured him. 'I promise.'

But he was still adamant. It had taken three difficult hours to get him to the point where he would agree to let her go ahead and then it was only because she'd told him she would be responsible for the baby's keep.

'All right then,' he said at last. 'You can have it. But it's your responsibility, don't forget. Nothing to do with me.'

And so it turned out to be. The baby's arrival revolutionised her existence, but Rigg's life style didn't change in any way. He came and went as he pleased, ate the meals she cooked for him, complained if his clothes weren't ironed to perfection, gave her grudging housekeeping money for his keep and still expected her to pay half the mortgage. She'd had to take all sorts of odd jobs in order to earn the money to feed and clothe herself and the baby and manage that mortgage. It had been a nightmare. Two years later, when Emma was on the way, she worked until the day before the child was born. But even with two children and less money, all the housework, the childcare and half the mortgage were still considered by Rigg to be her responsibility. And she'd never complained. Not even then.

Not even when he took out a second mortgage on the house and doubled the monthly repayments when she was heavily pregnant with Jon. She'd accepted it all like a good wife. But when Emma was on the way and he decided to apply for a third, and even larger mortgage, she was forced to say something. If it had been another loan to improve his business, or to buy a bigger house, she would have kept quiet and accepted it – the same as always. But he'd raised that mortgage to buy that awful holiday flat in Spain.

Rigg couldn't understand why she was complaining. 'Think of it,' he urged. 'Our own holiday home. A place in the sun. It's just what we want.'

'Not me,' she said, made bold by desperation and pregnancy. 'I don't want it. Think of the fares. And the repayments. It'll mean paying more than £500 a month. Where am I supposed to get that sort of money with two children? £280 is bad enough.'

'Every other month,' he said. 'Don't forget that. I pay my whack.'

'Please don't do it, Rigg,' she begged.

But she couldn't persuade him. He'd made up his mind. 'After all,' he said, 'this is as much for you as it is for me. I'm buying this flat for you and the kids. That's all I'm doing it for.'

He was so eager and hopeful and put so much pressure on her that she said 'yes'. And was ashamed of herself for being browbeaten. Because it *was* a mistake and she knew it.

And so here they were, with a terrifying mortgage – which she still paid every other month – and a flat in Spain that she and the children had visited only once and hadn't enjoyed at all. They'd ended up with food poisoning. There were more expenses and difficulties attached to the wretched place than she could bear to think about – maids who didn't turn up, tenants who stole the spoons, sinks to unblock, furniture to mend and condominium charges to pay. And now this, on top of everything else.

There had to be more to it than mere money. Perhaps he'd found somebody else. People always said the wife was the last to know when that happened. But surely she'd have noticed *something*. She'd always paid such attention to him. Such attention. But not enough obviously.

It couldn't just be the poll tax. But if it wasn't, that meant he was lying to her and that was unthinkable. Rigby wouldn't do that. Not without a very good cause.

Her mind spun the facts round and round, making no sense of any of them. No matter what arguments she used to console herself, she still felt deserted, bewildered and terrified. She was desperately in need of sleep, but she couldn't sleep at all.

Chapter Six

Mark Wareham breezed into the house at ten o'clock that morning.

'Come on kids!' he said. 'Aren't you dressed yet? We've been up hours and here you are still gobbling toast and Marmite. Shame on you!'

'Toas' a' marmi'!' Emma agreed, waving her slice at him.

'Buck up and finish,' Mark ordered. Then he noticed the dark circles under Alison's eyes. 'You look a mess,' he told her cheerfully. 'What've you been doing to yourself?'

Alison ducked her head. 'I had a bad night, that's all.'

'So I see. Have you heard the weather forecast?'

'No.' It had been all she could do to get the breakfast.

'Showers and bright intervals,' Mark explained. 'You'll need wellies and anoraks, kids.'

'Perhaps we should put it off,' Alison hoped. In her present state, she didn't want to go anywhere. Left to her own devices she would have stayed at home and brooded all day. But a woman with two small children rarely has the luxury of choice.

'Put it off?' Mark said. 'The idea! We're not going to let a little bit of rain stop *us*, are we kids?'

So she had to follow the family.

As Mark had predicted, it was a day of strong sunshine and racing clouds, of warmth so pleasant that they were all tempted to discard their coats, and rain so precipitate and penetrating that they were soaked to the skin before they could get them on again. Nevertheless, with one exception, they were determined to enjoy themselves no matter what the weather.

They strolled along the avenue of limes beside the castle, fed the trout until the water boiled with flailing bodies, took three boats out on the lake and sang their way round the central island, explored the bird sanctuary, identified ducks and avoided the geese and swans which were in a particularly aggressive mood that afternoon. All six children were soon happily dishevelled, the picnic was a success despite the rain, and Mark and Greg and Andy talked and joked and played games all day long.

But to Alison, still tussling with a fact she couldn't accept, understand or talk about, it seemed faintly unreal. If she'd been able to confide in one of her brothers it might not have been so bad – but that would have been disloyal and, in any case, what could she tell them? That Rigg had left her? If he *had* left her. Or that he was trying to save money by living somewhere else. That sounded heartless without an explanation. No, there was nothing she *could* say. Not yet. She would just have to keep her worries to herself, get through the day and wait until she was home again on her own and had the chance to think.

That night, in a supreme effort to be sensible, she sat down and made a list of all the outstanding bills, estimated how much they were likely to be and set the total against her wages. At first the sum didn't tally, and because there were no luxuries to trim, she couldn't see any way to cut costs. She didn't smoke or drink – except on the occasional excursion to the pub – and she rarely went out for the evening – except for a family get-together. After a lot of thought, she decided that if she cut out any new clothes for herself and, apart from new shoes, clothed the kids mainly from car-boot sales, she could probably balance the books. She sat back and rubbed her eyes. At least planning made her feel that she was beginning to get on top of things. I'll take it one day at a time, she told herself, and we shall manage. That night she went to bed tired out but this time she slept well.

Gradually, her life alone with the children acquired an acceptable pattern. Living from day to day left all the important questions unanswered but at least it kept the children calm. She was surprised by how well they took Rigg's absence. It could have been because they were used to long spells without their father anyway, or because she had managed to keep their lives as normal as possible. They even went round to visit Granny Toan and to take her a belated birthday card and a little pot plant. Although the old lady was rather drunk, she seemed pleased to see them and gave them some after-dinner mints from Harrods and let the children feed the love birds.

Nobody mentioned Rigg at all during that visit and Alison didn't tell her own family what was going on either. They were so used to seeing her without Rigg that it would have been surprising if one of them remarked on his absence now. There was no point in upsetting them unnecessarily, especially as everything would be back to normal sooner or later.

Soon Alison had persuaded her daytime self that on one level there was nothing too difficult to face after all. Rigg's departure had certainly cut back the housework. Now there was only one meal to cook every evening and no heavy jeans and sweaters to wash and dry. But at night she lay awake and wondered how many weeks her twilight existence would have to continue, missing his warmth in the bed, the sound of his breathing, the pleasure of his lovemaking. It was then she realised how difficult this parting really was. But she got on with her life just the same. There was nothing else she could do.

After ten days, Rigg phoned briefly to say that everything was going well and that if any letters came for him she was to keep them until he could come round and collect them. After five weeks, he suddenly arrived late one evening after she'd gone to bed and, to her surprise and delight, stayed the night.

As she was bundling the buggy out of the door the next morning she plucked up the courage to ask him – as casually as she could – 'How long will you be staying?'

He had a mouth full of cornflakes, so he couldn't answer for a few seconds. He waved her question away while he chewed, which made her heart sink. She knew what he was going to say and was out of the door before he could reply, hearing his voice from a distance as she lifted Emma into the pushchair. 'Can't say. Can't say, for Chrissake.'

He'll be gone by ten o'clock, she thought. And, of course, he was. But not before he'd made half a dozen necessary phone calls.

Not long afterwards the bills arrived at Shore Street: gas, electricity and telephone.

The gas and electricity bills were more or less what Alison expected, but the phone bill was for £137.

There's some mistake, she thought, staring at the awful figures. It couldn't really be that much. With trembling hands, she crammed it into her shoulder bag and took it to work. It was too alarming to cope with on her own. She'd show it to Brad at lunch time and see what she thought.

Brad's response was trenchant. 'You've got some-one else's bill,' she said. 'Ring 'em up an' tell 'em. What was it last time?'

'Half that.'

'Well then.'

Alison wasn't sure. 'They'll think I'm com-plaining.'

Brad laughed and brushed her coxcomb of red hair with the palm of her hand. 'You *are* complaining, sunshine. An' quite right too. You can't pay a bill that size. Unless the Great-I-Am's going to cough up for it. Or ain't you told him?'

'It only came this morning,' Alison said lamely.

'Phone 'em,' Brad said.

So that afternoon, instead of taking the kids down to the beach, Alison settled them with wax crayons and colouring books and dialled the exchange. There was no mistake. It *was* her bill.

'You've had several intercontinental calls,' the supervisor told her. 'That accounts for a large part of the increase.'

The shock dried Alison's mouth. 'Intercontinental calls?'

'To Spain. Fuengirola. It's all itemized. Would you like us to send you an itemized bill?'

'No,' Alison said weakly. 'No thank you.'

'There are three long calls to Birmingham at peak time,' the supervisor added. 'That's another large item.'

Rigg! Alison thought. He must have used the phone for his business calls. No wonder it's such an awful bill. Why hadn't he told her? He couldn't have *meant* to do this to her, could he? He knew how little money she had and what a struggle it was to pay the bills at the best of times. He must have made the calls and forgotten to tell her. Once he knew what had happened he'd pay for his calls and everything would be all right. Without thinking she picked up the receiver, feeling its weight in her palm as she dialled the number of the shop. £137! It was terrifying.

Norrie was on the other end of the line. 'Rings and Thi-ings. How may I *help* you?'

'I want to speak to Rigg, please,' Alison said.

'Just a minute,' Norrie said. 'I don't know whether he's here.'

The subterfuge made Alison cross. 'I know he's there,' she said. 'I can hear him talking. Put him on.'

There was a muffled pause. Then Norrie's voice spoke at a distance. 'It's your wife, Mr Toan.' And after some indistinct mumbling. 'She's *heard* you.'

More mumbling. Footsteps. A shuffle of paper. Then Rigg's voice, 'What is it, Kitten? Be quick. I've got a customer waiting.'

'I've just had the phone bill.'

'So?'

'It's for £137.'

It sounded as if he was laughing. 'I've had mine too. That was even bigger. Think yourself lucky.'

'They said you'd been phoning Spain. Had you forgotten to tell me?'

There was a short pause before he spoke again, and when he did the laughter vanished. 'No, I didn't forget to tell you. There wasn't any need.'

'But you've been phoning Spain.'

'Well of course I have. What do you expect?'

'But from this phone, Rigg. From our home phone. Spain is business. So is Birmingham. You ought to have phoned from the shop.'

'Well I couldn't, could I? Be fair, Ali. It was important business. I could hardly miss out on something like that just because I wasn't in the shop. I'd soon go bust if that was the way I had to go on. Or perhaps you want me to go bust, is that it?'

The accusation hurt her. She felt ashamed and humbled. 'No. Of course I don't. You know that.'

'That's all right then. Look I've got work to do. OK? Bye for now.'

'No!' she called. 'Just a minute. Don't hang up.'

'Well what is it? Be quick. Oh damn it all, Ali. Now my customer's gone.'

She apologised quickly, aware that she was being a nuisance. 'I'm sorry, Rigg. I didn't mean to . . .'

In a voice weary with resignation, he said, 'Oh well, that's it. He's gone now. What do you want? Tell me quickly. This is costing me money.'

'What about the bill?' she asked him doggedly. 'You will pay for the long-distance calls, won't you?'

'I've got a cash-flow problem just at the moment. Don't worry. I'll sort it out.'

'Yes, but when? If we don't pay, they'll cut us off.'

'I tell you what,' he said. 'You settle it now and I'll pay you back later. How about that?'

'Well . . .'

'Right,' he said, as though it was all decided. 'Is there anything else? I'm in a bit of a rush.'

She was so stunned to think that she was going to have to pay this entire bill after all that she couldn't think of anything else. And while she was dithering, he rang off. £137. Where could she possibly find a sum like that?

In the end it had to come out of the housekeeping, which turned her weekly trip to Tesco's into a nightmare.

She always did her shopping on Thursday evening because Jenny gave her and the kids a lift to the store and drove them home again afterwards. It was a very large store, superbly stocked and convenient – but it was situated on the northern edge of the town opposite Frost's where Mark worked; without a car, shopping there was impossible.

Mark never approved of it. He called it a temple to Mammon and said it was designed to part people from their money.

Now Alison could see what he meant. The place *was* built to pressurise. She could feel the weight of it as soon as she walked through the revolving doors, and it increased as she pushed her trolley towards temptation, with Emma sitting at eye-level with the biscuits and Jon free to run from one enticement to the next. She grew tired of the sound of her own voice saying 'No. We can't afford it,' exhausted by the perpetual disappointment on his face and frantic at the impossibility of adding up the bill item by item as she pushed from one heaped stand to the next.

Jenny shopped in her useful cheerful rush, following her shopping list and not worrying about anything. These days she always reached the check-out long before Alison. And that made Alison feel both inadequate and jealous. And being jealous made her feel ashamed because jealously was so ugly. And that made her bad-tempered with her children. She shouted at Jon for running, at Emma for grizzling with boredom, at both of them for wanting treats she couldn't afford.

'It's not fair!' Jon said on the third dreadful Thursday when they were standing in the queue at the check-out. 'We always have sweets. You said . . .'

'Not today,' she said, strained with the effort to stay patient.

'Why not? You said . . .'

'I told you. Mummy hasn't got the money.'

'Yes you have,' the little boy argued, with a four-year-old's implacable logic. 'You've got lots of money. It's in your purse. I saw you put it there.'

'Not enough for chocolate,' Alison tried to explain.

'Wanta cock-let,' Emma said, bottom lip drooping, ready to wail when she was refused.

'Don't you start,' Alison warned. 'I can't afford chocolate. Just sit still and keep quiet, there's a good girl. It's our turn next. Here we go! Through that old gap. That's better, isn't it. Hold on to the handle Jon.'

The check-out girl was tired too. She worked like a robot, passing groceries across the check-out, bleep by bleep, her face vacant and her mind elsewhere. When she tore the final bill from her machine and read the total, her voice was as empty as her expression. 'Twenty three pounds eighteen p.'

The figure spun Alison into a panic. It couldn't be as much as that, she thought, searching through the loose change in her purse. It had to be below twenty pounds. That was what she'd budgeted for. She was sure she'd added it up correctly. Four fivers and here they were. The change in her purse came to fifty six pence and the check-out girl was waiting with her hand out. Oh God! Now what was she going to do?

'I'm sorry,' she said. 'I haven't got enough. Something'll have to go back.' The shame of it was making her blush. 'I'm ever so sorry.'

The check-out girl sighed with annoyance. 'What'll it be?' she said.

Panic made Alison slow. She couldn't think. What could she leave out? Washing-up liquid? But how would she clean the dishes? The mince? But then what would they eat? The apples? Oh God!

The next woman in the queue was getting restive. 'What's the hold-up?' she said, glaring at Alison.

'I'm sorry! I'm sorry!' Alison sounded as frantic as she felt. 'It's just . . . I'm just . . .'

'Wanta cock-let,' Emma piped up. 'Mummy! Wanta cock-let.'

Control snapped. Alison was drowning in a torrent of anger and fear. 'Shut up!' she yelled. 'Shut up! How many more times have I got to tell you? I can't afford bloody chocolate. I can't even afford the bloody mince.' Shocked faces loomed before her. The check-out girl was open-mouthed. Emma was screaming, her mouth a dark O. Jon was clinging to the handle of the trolley, white-faced. I must get a hold of myself, Alison thought desperately. But she couldn't. 'We shall have to live on air,' she shouted into the din.

Somebody was standing behind her, somebody

familiar, somebody saying, 'Steady on Ali. It's not as bad as that.' Mark! She was torn between relief and shame.

'What's the problem?'

'I haven't got enough to pay the bill,' she said, cheeks blazing. 'I only brought twenty pounds.'

He was looking at the till, already taking command. 'You take the kids and go to my car,' he said. 'In the middle, down at the end. I'll settle up here. Give me the notes.'

He was back at the car before Emma had stopped crying. 'I'll just go and tell Jenny what's going on,' he said, 'while you put this in the boot and then we'll all go home. Good job I came across, eh?'

Alison was so tired it was all she could do to lift her shopping bags out of the trolley. Jon looked awful, as if she'd beaten him up. And Emma's poor little face was smeared with snot. She took a tissue out of her pocket and tried to clean her.

'My poor Emma,' she said. 'I *am* sorry. All better now?' And was reduced to tears herself when the baby smiled at her. How forgiving they are at this age, she thought, torn with remorse. It's more than I deserve. She tried to smile an apology at Jon and was hurt when he turned his body away from her and wouldn't respond.

'Home,' Mark said, striding back to the car and opening doors to urge them all inside. When he'd driven out of the car park and was heading down the dual carriageway towards his house, he asked, 'Now what was all that really about?'

Alison was so down that she told him, briefly but more or less accurately. She explained that Rigg had left her – temporarily – because of the poll tax, described how they'd arranged to split the bills and what a mess the phone bill had made of her housekeeping. 'It's my fault really,' she said. 'I should have budgeted more carefully. I'll get it right next time.'

Mark looked at her shrewdly and for several seconds. 'Is he giving you any housekeeping?' he said.

'Well no. I couldn't ask for that. Not when he's in . . . when he . . .'

'So you're trying to keep yourself and two children on what you earn at Butlin's. Is that it?'

'Yes,' she admitted, adding to salvage her pride, 'I was managing very well until the phone bill.'

'You're not supposed to keep a family on that sort of pay,' he said. 'Nobody is. You ought to be on income support.'

'I can't do that,' she said. 'That's taking charity.'

'That's taking back some of the money you've been putting into the system for years,' he said. 'How long have you been at work?'

'Fourteen years coming up.'

'Well then.'

Could she do it? she wondered. Was she entitled? It would certainly make her life a lot easier if she had a bit more money coming in every week. But the thought of going on charity made her feel demoralised. I'll be like a pauper, she thought, a beggar. 'We're not separated, you see,' she said. 'It's nothing like that. It's just that he's in a bit of trouble at the moment.'

'Never mind Rigg,' Mark said, frowning at her. 'You spend too much time considering his feelings. You always have. He can look after himself. What you've got to think about now is how to feed yourself and those two kids. That's what's important.'

Alison knew she ought to stick up for Rigg, but she didn't have the energy. 'Yes,' she said meekly. 'I suppose so.'

'Look in your child-benefit book,' Mark advised. 'I'm pretty sure there's something about it in there.'

It surprised her to discover that there was. She sat in Jenny's bright kitchen and drank the tea her sister-in-law had made for her and read the instructions carefully.

The next morning, even though she felt ashamed, she rang the Social Security freeline. It was remarkably painless. A calm voice asked her how many hours she worked and how much she earned and she answered as well as she could, pointing out that her wages fluctuated according to the season.

'I work good hours from Easter to October,' she said, 'but in the winter it's largely weekends and the odd day here and there, so I don't do so well then.'

'Get a claim pack from the Post Office,' the voice advised. 'Read it carefully and fill it in. I should think your best bet would be to go on Family Credit, but they'll tell you.'

'Thank you.'

'When you've been on your own for thirteen weeks,' the voice said, 'you can claim One-Parent Benefit, you know. It's only a fiver a week but it all helps. They'll tack it on to your child benefit.'

'Thank you,' Alison said again. 'I feel so awful asking for charity.'

'You mustn't do that,' the voice said kindly. 'You're just the sort of person these benefits were designed for.'

That afternoon Alison filled in the necessary forms and sent them off to Blackpool as instructed. In the evening she phoned Mark to tell him what she'd done.

'They say I am entitled,' she said. 'If I get this money it'll make all the difference. You were right.'

'Aren't I always?'

'You won't tell Mum, will you? She doesn't know about any of this. I'd rather she didn't.'

'It's OK,' Mark reassured. 'I'm not a blabbermouth.'

'Nor any of the others.'

'Nor any of the others, if that's the way you want it.'

'You are good to me,' she said. 'I don't know what I'd have done without you in Tesco's. I'll pay you back, the first thing I do next pay day. I promise.'

'What are brothers for?' he said.

After she'd put the phone down Alison sat in her empty living room and thought harder than she'd ever done in her life. She was ashamed to be taking charity and cross with herself for handling her lack of money so badly. I've been feeble, she thought. I could have worked this all out for myself weeks ago. It was all in my child-benefit book, if I'd looked. If I'm going to be on my own for any length of time – and it looks as if I am – I shall have to face up to things a lot quicker. Take responsibility. Grow up. It's disgraceful for a grown woman to wait for her brother to show her what to do. Not that it wasn't very, very kind of him, but I should have worked it out for myself. Well from now on I shall be a lot tougher.

Still, at least Mum doesn't know, she comforted herself, as she made a cup of tea. That was one good thing.

Actually it was a bad mistake.

Left in happy ignorance of the true state of her daughter's affairs, Elsie had no hesitation in listening to Rigby Toan when he came calling on her, unexpectedly, two weeks later.

She was clearing up after a rather messy family tea when he rang at the door.

'Hello Rigg,' she said. 'I'm afraid you've missed them. They've all gone home. Mark took them.'

'Yes. I know,' he said, giving her the full benefit of his brown eyes. 'It wasn't them I wanted. I came to see you.'

'Really?' she said. 'Not trouble is it?'

'Well . . .' he hesitated.

'You'd better come in,' she said. 'I'm in a bit of a pickle. I was just drying the tea things. Ali usually helps me but we've been all behind this afternoon.' She had led him into the kitchen as she was speaking, picked up her tea-towel and set to work again. 'You won't mind if I get on, will you?'

'No, of course not,' Rigg said. He hesitated for a second, then he took a dry tea-towel from the rack above their heads and chose a plate to dry.

Elsie was rather surprised because she'd never known him help with the housework before. In the early days, on the rare occasions when he'd joined them for a family tea, he'd sat in an armchair and gone to sleep while the others worked round him.

'Well then,' she said, 'what have you come to see me about?'

He looked distressed. 'This is terribly difficult,' he said. 'I don't know where to begin.'

'Begin at the beginning,' Elsie advised. 'That's the best way.'

'I'm at the end of my tether,' he said, contriving to look it. 'I don't know what to do and that's the truth.'

That sounded alarming. 'It's not about Ali, is it?'

'Well I suppose it is, in a way. It's Ali I'm worried about. Ali and the children. Oh God, this is so embarrassing.'

Nervous with all this odd talk, Elsie put down her tea-towel and turned away from the sink to look at him. 'Spit it out Rigg,' she said. 'Don't beat about the bush.'

Rigg gave her a long, troubled look. 'I'm so worried Elsie,' he confided. 'I'm afraid we're going to lose the house.'

The shock made her throat constrict. 'What do you mean, lose the house?'

'This is so embarrassing,' he said again. 'Look I'm devastated about this. I don't know how to tell you. I can't afford to pay the mortgage.'

Elsie felt she understood. Mortgages were the devil to pay. She and Bob had spent hours worrying over theirs. 'You've got behind, is that it? Well, if you'll take my advice, you'll go and see them and explain it. They'll probably extend the time for you.'

'No,' he said, 'you don't understand. It's much worse than that.' He scrunched the tea-towel between his hands. 'You haven't got a drink anywhere have you? I feel awful.'

'Not that sort of drink, no. I'm sorry. I could make you a cup of tea.'

'No thanks.'

Elsie poured a glass of water. 'Take that,' she said, 'go and sit in the front room, drink some of it and tell me what's what.'

Rigg sipped the water pathetically. 'Don't tell Ali for God's sake but I'm months behind with my payments. I haven't let her know about it. She's got enough on her plate looking after the kids.'

Elsie assured him she would keep quiet and Rigg looked touchingly grateful.

'So you're badly behind,' Elsie prompted. 'Is that it?'

He gulped. 'Months and months,' he admitted. 'It's a nightmare.'

'How much do you owe them?'

'Five grand.'

'Five grand!'

'Yes. Awful isn't it. I've tried all sorts of ways to raise the money. All sorts of ways. And nothing. Everyone's short you see. They say it's the recession.'

'Wouldn't your mother . . .'

'I can't ask her,' he said firmly. 'That's out of the question.' An eyebrow flicked up which always gave the impression that he was mocking himself. 'I can't be a mummy's boy, Elsie. Anything rather than that. Anything.'

'Well I don't see how *I* can help you. I don't know any rich people.'

'They don't have to be rich,' he assured her. 'All I need is someone with a little capital in reserve – someone with a nest-egg – someone who wouldn't mind letting me borrow five grand for a couple of months. That's all it would take. Just a few weeks to tide me over and then I could pay it all back – with interest if that was what they wanted. Oh God, this is so embarrassing. I'm sorry to burden you with all this.'

Elsie was thinking hard but she left her thoughts for the second it took her to assure him that it was all right.

'You've always been so understanding,' Rigg went on. 'You always have the answer. You don't know how much I've envied Mark and Greg and young Andy, having you to turn to. I can't turn to my mother, you know. She isn't strong enough. It would upset her too much. You can't upset people when you love them, can you?'

Elsie hardly heard him for she was deep in thought, savouring an extraordinary ego-enhancing idea. For the first time in her life she was in a situation where she could make a difference to someone else's life. She, plain Elsie Wareham, who'd never amounted to a row of beans in the sixty years of her existence, actually had enough money to give this young man what he was asking for. He wasn't to know, of course, but she had quite a nice little nest-egg tucked away – thanks to Bob's foresight. It had been £10,000 when the insurance man handed it over but of course Ali's wedding had eaten into it a bit and now it was just over £7,000. (Not that she begrudged Ali her wedding. It had been a lovely day and worth every penny.)

She had a sudden and total recall of the ceremony, of Ali looking so beautiful at the altar in her fairy-tale dress. Her hair had been longer then, and curling over her shoulders. Dear Ali. She'd been so proud of her that day. And Rigg had been so handsome in his tuxedo, she remembered, with a red rose in his button hole. They *were* a handsome pair and no mistake.

Lots of sunshine, she remembered. And roses.

The scent of them had been all round her as she stood in the pew with her gloves in her hand, waiting for Ali to walk down the aisle. The scent of roses and thinking what a dear girl she was and how much she deserved to be happy. The family peace maker.

Oh no, Elsie decided, pulling herself back to the present with an effort, she *couldn't* stand by and let them lose the house.

'Now look here, Rigg,' she said. 'It's just possible I might be able to help you.'

'Elsie!' he said, endeavouring to look surprised, although he'd known about the nest-egg for years. Ali had told him. 'What do you mean?'

'I might be able to lend you this money.'

'Really!'

'Yes.'

'What can I say?'

'Nothing,' Elsie said firmly. 'And especially to Ali. You mustn't breathe a word to her. I can't do anything unless you promise me that.'

'No, no. Of course. I promise.'

He's a good boy, Elsie thought, moved by the earnest expression on his face. He's doing his best.

Ten minutes later Rigby Toan left the house. He kissed Elsie goodbye on the doorstep most lovingly, as well he might. For he had her promise that she would go to the building society first thing in the morning and draw out £6,000 to lend him.

Chapter Seven

Morgan Griffiths was back in South Wales, dressed in his best suit, attending the christening of Hywell's first baby, who was to be called Morgan in his honour. He had a silver christening spoon gift-wrapped in his pocket next to Hywell's scribbled invitation to be the child's godfather.

It was grand to be back in Port Talbot again, to see the harbour glistening in the June sun, the steelworks steaming and the great bulk of the Mynydd, rising protectively above the town, green with ferns and stolidly immense. The strength and permanence of the Welsh mountains had always given him a feeling of security. He saw them as a barbican to those who live among them, a bulwark to the rows of stone grey houses that cluster like roosting pigeons along their lower slopes. Governments had the power to close pits and factories and to put entire villages out of work, but they had no dominion over mountains.

As so many of his family earned their living in mines in the valleys, it had always seemed fitting to Morgan that his home should have been tucked against the side of a mountain. As a child, he'd spent many hours at the top of their steep back garden, looking down at the three terraces Dad had cut to make lawns and vegetable beds, and out over the roof of the house to the distant blue of the sea below.

There was magic in that view and he never failed to respond to it. Even now, it was the first place he went to every time he came home.

His younger brother, Trefor, was calling to him from the bottom of the steps. 'Come by 'yere, Mor. Granddad's come.'

'How is he?' Morgan asked, running down the steps. Their grandfather's emphysema had been much worse that winter and they'd all been very worried about him.

'Better than he was, like,' Trefor said as they walked into the house. 'Not too bad, all things considerin'.'

To Morgan's eyes the old man looked very ill indeed. He was coughing too much, his skin was yellowy grey and his eyes looked weary. But he was so pleased to see them all, and so delighted to have yet another great-grandson that he made them forget 'the dust' and its consequences.

'There's lovely, issen it,' he said. 'Another little Griffiths, Gwen.'

Grandma sat protectively beside him, watching him anxiously as he caught his breath.

'Time for a beer Dad?' Morgan's father suggested.

'Not if we're going to get to the church in time,' Grandma said.

'Get me to the church on time, eh?' Granddad laughed. And he started to sing the song in his cracked, wrecked voice.

Morgan's three sisters, who were all dolled up and giggly, were highly amused by that and, straightening their hats, they threw open the front door and set off at a trot down the steps towards the road, with their children gambolling round them, all of them singing at the tops of their voices. 'Get me to the church, get me to the church, be sure and get me to the church on time.'

'Not right in the attic!' Granddad said affectionately.

Family, Morgan thought, following them happily. He knew that this was what he wanted more than anything else, a wife and family of his own. He needed to be part of a family, all day and every day not just on occasions like christenings and Christmas. He'd done very well for himself in the six years since he'd left Port Talbot. He'd got a job he enjoyed, a comfortable flat, a quality car, but it wasn't enough. He hadn't made the most important part of his plan come true. He wasn't married and, as far as he could see, he wasn't likely to be. Not in the immediate future anyway.

Because he was watching over Granddad most of the time, he managed his role in the christening rather badly, muffing most of his responses and holding his candle so awkwardly that it dripped wax on his sleeve. But Hywell didn't mind.

He and Bronwen were flushed with success and talked about it all the way back to their house on the estate. Baby Morgan had been so good; the weather was lovely; what a day it was.

Tea was taken, the cake was cut and presently they all trooped out into the garden bearing chairs and stools for the family photograph. It was none too warm out in the open air because a wind had sprung up and a shower was threatening.

'This'll go on for ever,' Trefor warned the happy

parents. His father was the photographer and he always took ages to arrange a picture.

'We don' mind,' Bronwen said, gazing at the infant on her knee. 'He's all wrapped up lovely and warm. Snug as a bug in a rug, issen it, cariad.'

Morgan *did* mind, although he couldn't say so. He was still watching Granddad and it was clear that the old man was getting chilled.

'Hurry up Dad,' he called. 'We want to get down to the pub today not tomorrow. Right Trefor?'

Unfortunately Thomas Griffiths wasn't a man to be rushed. He continued to give instructions in his unhurried way. 'In a bit, Dai. Put your arm round the back of the chair, like. Bronwen, could you shift towards the middle. Just an inch. That's it. Now then, "Cheese" everybody. Marvellous! One more?'

They let him use all the film in his camera. But then they hustled him off to the local to wet the baby's head, and Morgan made sure that the first drink was a warming brandy for his grandfather. And not before time.

It was an uncomfortable pub but they were so happy in one another's company that comfort was immaterial. There was a lot to talk about. Trefor told them stories about his life on the liner during his latest cruise, Dai and Hywell kept them laughing about the impossible fares they'd had. Between coughing fits, Granddad entertained them with stories of the new doctor in his village. 'Hassen got a clue, boy. Not a clue.'

But after the third round, the talk grew serious.

'I see British Steel are shuttin' Ravenscraig,' Trefor said.

'Eleven thousand jobs gone,' his father said.

'Poor buggers. What's it like here?'

'Tickin' over,' Thomas said. 'Just about.'

'Aren't you glad you retired, Dad?'

'No. Not really,' Thomas said. 'Had no option, did I?' He'd worked in the steelworks all his life and taking early retirement had been quite a blow. For the first few months he'd felt idle and useless. 'I'm gettin' used to it now.'

'It's a national disgrace what that woman's doin' to this country,' Dai said, wiping his moustache with the back of his hand. 'The way she's goin' on, by the year two thousand there won't be a pit left open the length and breadth of the country, nor a factory still working neither. We shall all be servants or working for the bloody Nips.'

'Total madness I call it,' Hywell agreed.

Distress was making Granddad cough. 'Breaks my 'eart,' he spluttered. 'Good men goin' to waste. I thought we'd 'ad enough a' that in the thirties. There's machines rottin' underground for want a' use, and miners rottin' above ground for want a' work, and coal bein' imported from abroad. *Imported!* Where's the sense in it? That's what I should like to know.'

'It's not a matter a' sense,' Tom said. 'It's a matter a' prejudice. We're the enemy within, don't forget. We vote Labour. There's a crime! We belong to unions. There's a crime! Good God man, barely human we are. We brought down a government once. Remember that. We got to be cut down to size, thrown on the scrap heap, put in our place. Revenge, that's what this is about.'

Granddad was now red in the face from coughing.

'My round,' Morgan said, making a deliberate break in the conversation to give the old man a chance to recover. 'Same again?'

'I'll come with you, Mor,' Hywell said. And he got up to follow his cousin to the bar.

'We got to change the subject,' Morgan said, as they waited to be served. 'The ol' feller can't take all this serious stuff. It gets him worked up. Look at the state he's in.'

'You're right,' Hywell said. 'He don't look healthy. But you won't get 'em off politics. Not now.'

'Talk about the baby,' Morgan advised. 'Get him thinking about his great-grandchildren. That'll calm him. He's too ill for all this.'

'Right,' Hywell said, looking back at Granddad's discoloured face. 'I'll do what I can, Mor. We can't talk babies all evenin', though.'

'Grandchildren then,' Morgan said. 'Just to give him a breather. He's got enough of them.'

'No thanks to you,' Hywell teased.

'Slow but sure, me,' Morgan parried.

Which wasn't something that could be said about Rigby Toan. That night he'd rushed Alison off her feet. He'd arrived in Shore Street just as she was getting the fish fingers out of the fridge, ready for the children's supper. He was flushed and excited and full of snapping energy.

'Look sharp and get ready,' he instructed. 'We're going out to dinner. You've got ten minutes while I buy my cigars.'

He was right. Ten minutes was all she'd had. It

had been a real scramble. All her usual baby-sitters had already made other plans. But Brad had turned up trumps and not only offered to baby-sit but said the kids could stay the night at her flat.

'They can eat their fish fingers with me,' she said, when she came to collect them. 'Can't you kids. An' if you're very good I'll let you watch my telly.'

'Is it good?' Jon wanted to know.

'It's wicked,' Brad told him. 'Better'n yer mother's.'

'You are a dear,' Alison said gratefully, putting mascara on her eyelashes.

'You deserve a night on the tiles,' Brad said. 'Enjoy yourself. You don't have to rush back. Remember, you're only young once.'

So here Alison was in the best Chinese restaurant in Hampton, stunned by the speed with which the outing had been arranged.

'I feel like Cinderella,' she said. It was a pretty accurate description, for half an hour ago she'd been giving the toilet its weekly scrub while the kids watched some rubbish on the television. It was almost too good to be true, to be sitting here on a nice comfortable chair, with a clean table-cloth under her plate, and wine in her glass, and lashings of good food keeping warm over the night-lights.

'That was first rate,' Rigg said eventually, wiping his moustache with his table napkin.

He looked very handsome in the soft light from the candles. Handsome and prosperous, in a new jacket Alison hadn't seen before. Perhaps this would be a good moment to ask him how he's getting on, she thought, if I'm careful not to sound too pushy. 'I gather things aren't quite so bad these days,' she said.

He smiled. So that was all right. 'No,' he said. 'Actually they're rather on the up.'

'That's good.'

'Actually, I'm thinking of buying another shop.'

That was such a surprise she could help showing it. 'Really,' she said, trying to keep her voice non-committal. Was he serious? Or just testing the water?

'I'll give you a tip,' he said, 'for what it's worth. The best way of getting out of trouble is to spend your way out. I'm going into partnership with Harry Elton.'

Alison had never heard of Harry Elton but she didn't like to say so. 'Oh yes.' So he *was* serious.

'We're putting up the cash between us. It's a new venture, Kitten. A video shop. It can't fail.'

Now that she knew she could show an interest, she began to ask questions. 'Where's it going to be?'

'Here in Hampton. Up at the Selsey end. There isn't a video shop for miles around. We shall be raking it in.'

It *sounded* plausible.

'Well aren't you going to congratulate me?' he said.

'Yes. Of course. You know I am.'

He leaned across the table towards her and took her hand. 'I'm doing this for you Kitten,' he said, nipping her fingers softly with his teeth. 'All for you. You know that don't you.'

'Yes,' she said. 'I do.'

'It'll be the answer to all our problems. We shall be coining it, you'll see.'

'Does it mean you'll be home again?'

'Yes. Of course. In no time at all. Good eh?'

'Wonderful!' she said, and meant it.

For the rest of the evening Rigg talked about the new shop, telling her how it was going to be decorated, and what it was going to be called, and what a great chap Harry Elton was.

'We make a great team,' he said. 'You'll like him, Kitten. Tell you what, we've got a chap coming in on Tuesday to start putting up the shelves. You could come down and see it if you like.'

'I work all day Tuesday.'

'Well Wednesday then. We're going to have them painted red. Nice bright colour. Eye catching. That'll bring in the punters.'

He went on talking 'shop' all the way home. And he was still talking as they undressed ready for bed. 'Course the overheads are small, being a lock-up, that's the real beauty of it. Did I leave my other jeans here? I could do with them now.'

'They're in the wardrobe,' Alison said, getting into bed. She was disappointed that he was paying so little attention to her. On their first night together after such a long time, and with no children in the house to distract them, she had hoped he would be more loving.

'I'll take my old trainers too,' he said, opening the wardrobe door and seeing them on the floor.

Alison closed her eyes. And didn't open them again until the alarm went off at seven the next morning.

Rigg was fast asleep, lying on his back, one arm flung above his head, chin shadowed with stubble, hair ruffled into a peak against the pillow. He didn't stir when she left the bed and when she'd washed and dressed he was still lying in the same position, sleeping peacefully.

She tiptoed down the stairs so as not to wake him and made breakfast as quietly – and quickly – as she could. Time was shorter than usual because she had to walk to Brad's flat to pick up the kids before she went to work. I'll give her a ring to make sure the kids are ready, she thought, picking up the phone.

At that point an ugly idea sprang unbidden into her brain. Rigg would be alone in the house with the phone after she left. What if he started making long-distance calls again? There'd be nothing to stop him. She looked at the clock on the mantelpiece. Three minutes to go. If she was going to do anything she'd have to do it quickly. Her cheeks were red with shame at her disloyalty, but it had to be done.

She took the phone out of its socket, wrapped the lead neatly round it like a parcel and put it in her shoulder bag. Then she set off for work.

The phone weighed on her all day, in every sense of the word, plaguing her conscience and growing heavier and heavier to carry around. She was very relieved when she got back home that evening and returned it to its rightful place.

It rang almost as soon as she'd plugged it in.

'Do you know your phone's been out of order?' her mother's voice said. 'I've been trying to get you for nearly an hour.'

'Yes. I'm sorry. I was in such a rush this morning I left it off the hook.'

'I met Mrs Maynard in Bobby's this morning. She says your Rigg's opening a video shop in Hampton. Just off the beach she says. Is that right?'

'Yes.'

'My word! He *is* doing well. Can he afford it?'

'Oh yes. It's going to make a lot of money.'

That's a relief, Elsie thought. Now he'll be able to pay me back and get straight. 'When is he going to open?' she asked.

Alison didn't know how to answer. Anything she said could lead to more questions. If she admitted that she didn't know, her mother would wonder why. If she wasn't careful she'd end up having to admit that she and Rigg rarely saw one another. Fortunately she was saved by Jon, who pulled at her elbow demanding to speak to Gran, and by the time she got the phone back the subject had moved on.

On Wednesday, she went to Rigg's new premises. For a lock-up shop it was surprisingly big. Even though it was forested with lengths of wood and floored with shavings she was impressed. There were two men in checked shirts and jeans hard at work with saws and hammers. The shorter of the two pushed his way through the shavings to find out what she wanted.

'I'm looking for Rigg,' she explained. 'I'm his wife.'

'He's not here, I'm afraid,' the man said. 'We was expecting him this morning. I'm Harry.'

'Harry Elton?'

'That's me.'

They shook hands and took stock of one another. Although it was hard to assess his character from his appearance, Alison was reassured by what she saw, for Harry was an energetic-looking man and obviously a worker. She guessed he was about forty. He had a friendly smile and a round, ruddy face that she would have called trusting if it hadn't been for his eyes, which were small and shrewd and as brown as pennies. His hair was curly and very dark but it was cropped short like a lamb's fleece, which gave him an air at once purposeful and vulnerable. Rough hands, clothes that had seen good service, a shirt pocket full of small tools, pencils and screwdrivers, a steel rule, a pocket torch. A worker, whatever else. The kind of man who would make a good business partner.

'How long's it going to take to get fitted?' she asked.

'Two more days,' he told her. 'The stock's being delivered the beginning of next week. With any luck we shall open for business on Friday, just in time for the weekend.'

'It all looks very good,' she said, as she took hold of Jon's hand ready to lead him out.

'Wait till it's open,' he said. 'It's in a good position.'

That was certainly true. The parade of shops was right on the corner where the Selsey Road curved down to the sea. We shall do well, she thought. Oh Rigg, you'll be able to come home again.

But when Rigg phoned her later in the week, he said he couldn't make any plans yet and there was no point in coming home until September. Alison felt her heart sink. 'But if this shop does well . . .'

'As it will. It will. It's a stone bonker.'

'Well then.'

'I've got to give it six months,' he said, 'otherwise I shall lose all the advantage of staying away since April. You don't want me to pay extra tax, do you?'

'No.'

'There you are then. Have you seen the window display?'

'No.'

'Go down,' he instructed. 'You'll love it.'

I'd love it more if you were home again, Alison thought. But it was too late to tell him because he'd hung up.

The house always seemed so empty after a phone call. She'd switched the mute button on the television as soon as he rang, now, with a sigh, she brought back the sound. But she couldn't concentrate on the programme, bright and loud though it was.

It was another two months to September and two months is a very long time when you are on your own with two small children to look after. Never mind, she told herself, it'll pass. Once this video shop gets going, he'll make so much money we shall be in clover. If he works there I shall be able to call in and see him now and then. He might even come home for lunch. I'll cook him some really tasty meals. That'll tempt him back.

But Rigg didn't work in the video shop. As it was shift work, morning and evening, he hired students to do it. In fact, Alison saw less of him in the month after the shop was opened than she'd done in the months before. It was rather demoralising. But he'd always said it would be hard. She had to admit that. He'd always told her they would have to make sacrifices if they were going to make that first million.

If only making sacrifices wasn't so lonely.

Chapter Eight

The August began with an act of aggression in the Middle East and a heat wave in Europe. On the second Saddam Hussein of Iraq ordered his troops to invade Kuwait, and the next day was the hottest in August since records began. Apart from the politicians, nobody in England took much notice of what was happening in the desert. The heat wave was another matter because it affected everyone. Railway lines buckled, runways melted, cars and tempers overheated. Even Alison found it hard to stay calm but she didn't lose her temper until Rigg arrived outside the house with a brand new BMW – black this time and an even more expensive model than the previous year's.

With commendable self-control, she restricted herself to asking whether he could afford it.

'I can't not afford it,' he said, admiring it. 'It's an investment.'

'But you're short of money,' she said. The anger in her voice was unmistakable. 'You've got a cash-flow problem. You didn't even repay me for that phone bill. Remember?'

'Slipped my mind,' he said, recognising that he would have to pacify her. He took a fifty pound note from his wallet and slapped it into her hand. 'There you are. That's my share. Now you can stop fussing. I don't know what you're fussing about anyway. This car's not going to cost all that much more than the other one. Less, probably, in the long run. I got a good trade-in price and there'll be no repairs or anything like that. Anyway, that's not the point. The point is I've got to have it. Imagine if I turned up to a business meeting in last year's model. They *would* think I was on the way down. Isn't she a beauty?'

Alison put the note in her pocket but she was so angry that she couldn't see anything remotely beautiful in his new acquisition.

'If you've got money to spend on a car,' she said, 'you can afford to pay the poll tax and live at home.'

'Don't be like that, Kitten,' he wheedled. 'This is for business. You know that. If you don't have a new reg, every year, you lose trade. I can't run *that* sort of risk, now can I? I know it must look a bit flash to you, but it *is* necessary.'

'If you've got that sort of money,' Alison insisted, 'you could have lent some of it to me.'

That surprised him. 'What for?'

'In case you haven't noticed,' she said, looking up and down the street meaningfully, '*I* haven't got a car. I've had a driving licence since I was eighteen and no car.'

'What do you want a car for?' he said. 'We've always gone everywhere in my car.' He decided to tease her a bit. 'Or isn't a BMW good enough for you?'

She didn't respond to the teasing. 'So you'll be giving us a lift to work,' she said flatly.

'Not bloody likely,' he said quickly and he wasn't teasing. 'I'm not having your horrible sticky kids wiping their fingers all over my nice new upholstery. Let

’em walk. Do ’em good.’ And he adjusted the sunroof and backed out of the alley as quickly as he could.

There *are* times, Alison thought, when he can be really unbelievably selfish.

In the cramped offices of the Alexander Jones Agency in Guildford, the windows could be opened only four inadequate inches. Outside, in the cobbled street that led uphill to the centre of the town, drivers ground gears, swore and sweated, the stink from their exhausts fouling what fresh air there was. Inside, the air was so stale and hot that by ten o’clock in the morning it was impossible to hold a pen, a civilised conversation or even an opinion. To make matters worse Mr Jones was clearing his desk before cruising off on his second holiday of the year. ‘Clearing his desk’ meant interviewing each of his three employees in turn to check on the current state of the cases they were investigating.

Morgan Griffiths was the first to occupy the hot seat because he was the most senior member of the team.

‘What’s the latest from Jaffa Jewels?’ Mr Jones wanted to know.

‘The shop in Maidstone’s gone bankrupt.’

‘We expected that.’

‘Eastbourne seem to be holdin’ on. Just about. They’ve promised a payment in September. The Chichester shops have just paid £1,000.’

‘Did we have to use any pressure?’

‘No.’

‘How many visits did you make?’

‘One.’

'Well that's all very satisfactory,' Mr Jones said, wiping the sweat from his bald patch with a crumpled handkerchief. 'If we can't bill them for a large fee at least we can claim efficiency. Anything new in this morning? No. Send Barbara in then.'

Barbara Kirkby was a married woman in her late forties. She grimaced at Morgan as he passed on the message.

'Don't tell me,' she joked. 'He's going to offer to take us all with him to the Mediterranean.'

'I'd settle for a day in Brighton,' Roger said. As the third and most junior member of the team he got all the worst jobs. For the last five days he'd been stuck in the office, manning the phone.

A day at the sea, Morgan thought longingly, remembering the long sandy beaches at Hampton. The thought suddenly sprouted into an uncharacteristic plan.

'Well why not?' he said. 'There's no reason why we got to do our paperwork *here*. We'd have to put in the right number of hours, make sure there was always someone here to man the phone. But we could rearrange our hours, if you see what I mean. We could take it in turns to be off for a day, couldn't we. Working away, like.'

It was a wonderful idea.

'We could fill in files on a train,' Roger said.

'Or on a beach,' Barbara said. 'And I thought you were the original upright man.'

The plan was agreed, which was how Morgan Griffiths contrived to be driving into Hampton again on a glorious summer morning.

Heat shimmered phantom pools across the road

ahead, the weald was languid, foliage sticky, stubble burnt brown. He drove at speed, wearing dark glasses against the glare and enjoying the slip-stream of cooler air as it blew past his cheeks. Despite the languor of the day he felt charged with excitement. First stop the beach, he thought.

In Butlin's holiday camp they were better prepared for heat. The campers spent their days in shorts and T-shirts, or skimpy swimming costumes, the pools were crowded, there were iced drinks a-plenty and every window in the place was opened wide. In the four huge restaurants, all the doors were open too, to dispel the heat from the central kitchen.

Brad was on duty that morning, cool looking in her black and white uniform with her scarlet hair tied back with a wide black ribbon. She was in a determinedly cheerful mood, saucing the elderly campers, petting the kids, teasing the girls and giving the eye to all the men she passed.

'There y'are kid,' she said to Jon, when she reached Alison's table. 'The biggest chocolate sundae in the whole wide world.' Because it was school holiday time he'd spent the morning in the camp play-group while his mother was working and he deserved a reward.

The child was overawed. 'Ta!'

'Eat it nicely,' Alison warned. He was wearing a pale blue T-shirt that morning and she didn't want chocolate stains all down the front of it.

'So how's tricks?' Brad said, tucking her tray under her arm and leaning both hands on the table.

'Complicated,' Alison told her. 'We've had six double bookings and one treble.'

'Typical,' Brad said, grinning. But then her expression changed, suddenly and most dramatically, from lifted smile to down-turned fury.

'Je-sus!' she said. And with that she was across the room in four strides banging into tables as she went. 'You bloody little git!' Before anyone could stop her she had seized one of the campers by the throat. He jumped to his feet, struggling to get away from her, but she shook him so hard that his head jerked back and hit the wall behind him.

The hall erupted, campers on their feet, shrieking, waiters and waitresses scattering in all directions, the timid panicking back to the kitchen, the foolhardy and the rubber-necks stampeding towards the fracas. By the time the crowd had thinned enough for Alison to see what was happening, Brad was turning out the young man's pockets.

'Hand it all over,' she was bellowing. 'And yer wallet, you thieving git.'

Alison could see a heap of coins and assorted jewellery on the table. Recognisable jewellery, most of it gold and all of it Brad's. Brad's hand threw down a bundle of notes. The camper's face was as white as paper.

But then the supervisor was at Brad's elbow, leading her away, and the camper took off and ran through the hall, knocking cups and cutlery from the tables as he went. Alison didn't know which way to look – at Jon, who was stolidly eating his ice-cream, at Emma who was picking smarties out of their carton one by one, at Brad who was being marched into the kitchen or at the camper who was being detained by two security guards just outside the open doors.

'I'll see you in the car,' Brad called to her. 'Wait for me.'

In thirty impressive seconds the restaurant was set to rights. Waiters were dispatched to clear the broken crockery, meals re-served, cheerful muzak relayed on the tannoy, the families who'd been sitting in the vicinity of Brad's attack moved to another and better part of the hall. By the time Jon had finished his melting ice-cream, nobody could have guessed there had ever been anything wrong.

But Brad didn't come back.

Alison took her children off to the toilets to clean their sticky hands. Then they walked through the camp to the staff car park and Brad's battered Mini. But there was still no sign of her friend. They waited twenty minutes as the sun baked the tops of their heads and the tarmac bubbled in the heat. Emma fell asleep in the buggy in a most uncomfortable position and Jon ran round the cars until he was red in the face and out of breath and desperate for a drink.

'All right,' Alison said, when he'd asked her for a third time, 'I'll just leave a note for Brad and we'll go home.' Which she did, adding as a PS 'See you on the beach.'

As the tide was out they walked home along the sands, paddling in the shallow water and stopping from time to time to splash their arms and legs and faces. Emma woke to scrabble out of her harness and then fell straight into the sea water, where she rolled like a porpoise until her dress was soaked and her arms were covered in sand. It was one of the best walks they'd had in a long time.

'We'll nip back to the house and get some drinks

and your buckets and spades,' Alison said, 'and then we'll come straight back and make a castle with a moat. How about that?'

Rapturous agreement. So rapturous that Jon actually agreed to sit in the buggy and be pushed so as to get home and back as quickly as possible.

When they returned to the beach, laden with bags and buckets and straw mats, Brad was sitting against the breakwater sunning her legs and as cheerful as ever. She'd moussed her hair into its cockatoo quiff, put on her full make-up and changed out of her black and white uniform into a scarlet T-shirt and a pair of purple and black cycling shorts.

'What's this?' she said to the children. 'Sand pies?'

'We're going to make a castle,' Jon told her.

'Tastle!' Emma echoed.

'Come on then,' Brad said. 'Bags I first go with the bucket.'

'What *was* all that about?' Alison said as the castle began to take shape.

'Thieving little git,' Brad said, shovelling vigorously. 'I found him in the pub last night. Took him home, didden I? An' he only went through my jewel box an' nicked my purse.'

'Oh Brad!'

'D'you see his face when he saw me?'

Jon staggered up the beach with a bucket full of water and hurled it at the moat. Most of it landed on Brad's legs.

'Cor! Lovely!' she approved. 'You can do that again any time sunshine.'

'What happened next?' Alison said, as she and Brad toiled together on either side of the moat.

'They called the police, didden they.'

'And?'

'Did I want to press charges.'

'And did you?'

'Not 'alf. I don't work my guts out day after day so's some thieving little toe-rag can run off with the goodies.'

'But what about you?' Alison said. 'Weren't they cross?'

'Oh yes,' Brad said easily, standing up to stretch her spine and to see how much further they'd got to dig. 'I got me cards.'

'They sacked you?'

'Well no. They would ha' done though. I give 'em me notice before they had the chance.'

'Oh Brad! What'll you do now?'

'Get another job,' Brad said cheerfully.

'But what if you can't?'

'I'll find something,' Brad said. 'Old people's home. Lavatory attendant. They're advertising for wardmaids up St Mary's.'

'Oh Brad!' Alison said. 'That's awful.'

Brad shrugged. 'They're only jobs,' she said.

'I wanta n'orange,' Emma said.

'An' you shall have one, my sunshine,' Brad said. 'Where's the bottle Ali?' She looked up the beach to where they'd left their belongings and her tone changed. 'I say Ali, there's a feller lookin' at you.'

'No there isn't,' Alison said, with the perfect confidence of being right. 'If any fellers are looking our way they'll be looking at you.'

'He's coming over,' Brad said. 'So we shall see, shan't we.'

Vaguely curious, Alison stopped digging and stood up to see what her friend was talking about. There was a man walking down the shingle towards them, a big, solid-looking man in a short-sleeved shirt and faded jeans, a man with a chunky face, gingery hair on his head and a lot of darker hair on his forearms. At first she didn't recognise who he was, but as he got closer and smiled at her, she remembered.

'It's the Welshman,' she said. 'Look Jon. Here's the man who pulled you out of the pool.'

'Morgan Griffiths,' he said. 'I saw you from the promenade. I thought it was you.'

'Alison Toan,' Alison said, feeling she ought to tell him her name. She introduced him to Brad.

He shook hands with them both, formally.

'We're makin' a moat,' Jon told him importantly. 'Mum's diggin'.'

'So I see.'

'You can dig too if you like,' the little boy offered.

He hesitated. 'What does your mam say?'

'More hands make light work,' Alison told him.

So he joined them, helped to finish the channel and enlarge the moat and was fed biscuits and orange juice as a reward for his hard work. Then he sat on the pebbles and watched while Brad and Jon went for a swim to cool down and Alison and Emma decorated the sides of the castle with shells. After a few seconds she looked up at him and smiled.

'You're always doin' things with your kids,' he said, feeling he ought to speak. 'Playin' games and makin' things.'

She took that as the compliment he intended.

'That's family life for you. We like doing things together, don't we Emma? We're going to Brighton on Monday. Me an' Brad an' the kids.'

'Won't you be at work?'

'No,' she said, patting the side of the castle which was in danger of dissolving. 'I'm taking four days holiday. To give them a few treats.'

'Very nice. Is your husband on holiday too?'

'No. Only me. He's got to work.'

'Ah.'

'So we're off on the razzle, aren't we kids? Brighton Monday, Hotham Park Tuesday, Portsmouth Wednesday.'

'Very nice.'

'Are you on holiday too?' she asked. 'Or are you working?'

'No,' he said seriously. 'Neither really. Just a day off.'

'Ah. Come over here a minute Emma, there's a good little girl. You need some more sun cream.'

He watched as she rubbed cream on to the baby's shoulders, hugged her and tumbled her about, and played their old, well-tried game. 'Who loves yer?'

'You do,' the baby said chortling with pleasure.

'No,' feigning surprise. 'I don't, do I?'

'Yes. Yes. You *do*.'

'Oh well then, I shall have to kiss your tummy.'

Squeals of pleasure. Breathless hugs. Sand sprayed in every direction in a loving skirmish.

She's so feminine, Morgan thought, admiring her gentle hands and the curves of her cheeks and her arms and her breasts. Her dark hair was laced with sand and her bare skin tanned to the prettiest colour.

In fact she was turning him on so powerfully he had to shift into a different position to hide the state he was in.

She looked across at him, smiling lazily, her eyes very green in the sunlight.

If she wasn't a married woman, he thought, I could really fall for her. Out a' the question, of course, but I can enjoy her company. There's nothing wrong with that. If she doesn't want me to be with them she'll soon say so.

'Isn't it lovely not to have to work,' she said.

'You look like an advertisement for the sunny south coast,' he said.

'The water's wicked,' Brad said, charging up the sand with Jon in tow. 'Come on in you lot. You'll love it.'

'Later perhaps,' Morgan said. He could hardly strip to his trunks, the state he was in.

The afternoon spread before them, idle with heat and well-being. The sea was spangled with sunshine and so warm that they all went for a swim one after the other while the children paddled and sat in the water up to their chins. Pond-sized ripples edged the tide gradually up the beach, and soon – too soon – the sun was an orange disc half way towards the horizon.

'We should be getting home,' Alison said regretfully, 'or these two'll never go to bed tonight.'

'Would you like a lift?' Morgan offered.

'No thanks. It's only up the road.'

She was already shaking the sand from the towels, packing her bag and stacking the plastic buckets one inside the other. Suddenly he knew that he didn't want to part from her. He had to think of some other way to prolong the day. Or find some excuse to see her again. Her and the kids.

She and Brad worked together folding the towels.

'I've got to be in Brighton on Monday,' he lied, looking at them. 'Maybe we could meet somewhere.'

He was a bit disappointed when it was Brad who answered him. 'Have you?' she said, giving him her teasing look.

'Yes. We could go for a meal perhaps.'

'It would have to be McDonald's,' she grinned.

'That's fine by me.'

'You don't want the kids tagging along, do you?' Alison said.

'Yes, course. It's the kids I'm invitin' really. It's their holiday, issen it.'

Alison thought about it, her head tilted against the sunlight. 'Well all right then,' she said at last. 'We'd like that, wouldn't we kids?'

'West Pier at ten o'clock,' Brad said, brushing the sand from her legs.

'I'll be there.'

'Well, well, well,' Brad teased, as she and Alison and the kids walked back to Shore Street. 'You're a dark horse an' no mistake, Ali Toan.'

'It's not like that,' Alison said, annoyed with herself to be blushing. 'He's after you.'

'I don't particularly want him. You can 'ave him if you like.'

'*I* don't want him,' Alison protested.

'He's all right,' Brad said. 'Not my cup a' tea, but a bloody sight better than the Great-I-Am.'

'Oh don't start that, Brad,' Alison begged. 'You know we can't agree about him.'

'When was the last time he came down on the beach with you an' the kids?' Brad wanted to know. 'Never.'

'Oh come on, Brad. He's just opened a new shop.'

Brad snorted. 'New shop,' she scorned. 'If he'd got any sense he'd be paying a bit more attention to his old wife.'

They were waiting for a break in the home-going traffic in the Selsey Road. It was very hot and stuffy now they were away from the beach, and the pavements were smeared with spilt drinks and dropped ice-cream. Alison suddenly felt weary. It was going to be a long, hot evening, cooped up in the house with the children, all on her own. Brad was right. Rigg ought to spend more time with them.

'It'll be nice at Brighton, won't it kids,' she said, deliberately changing the subject. 'There's a railway there runs all along the beach. I'll take you for a ride on it.'

In the event, it was Morgan who treated them all to the ride on the railway, and two on the merry-go-round, and one on the dodgems. They ate Big Macs and drank milk shakes. And after that they trooped off to the pier for candy floss and slides and a ride on yet another roundabout. It was a lovely day.

And Brad capped it by telling them over tea and buns that she'd got a job in the kitchens in the local hospital, starting Wednesday. 'Quite nice, really, all things considered. Lovely an' clean. I shan't be able to come to Portsmouth with you an' the kids Ali, that's the only thing, but I can't turn up an offer like this, can I?'

'It's a new wing,' Alison explained to Morgan. 'They've just opened it.'

'Mostly geriatrics,' Brad said. 'Poor ol' things. They got dining rooms up on the wards. I shall be serving 'em dinner, that sort a' thing.'

Working on Wednesday, Morgan thought, pleased by Brad's news. It meant he could have Alison and the kids to himself.

That evening, when Brad had been dropped off at her flat and they were driving to Shore Street – extremely slowly – he told his third lie.

'I might have a job to do in Portsmouth – well, Portsmouth area – Wednesday,' he said. 'If I do, perhaps we could meet there?'

'I can't let you go on treating us,' Alison protested. 'It makes me feel guilty. It must be costing you a fortune.'

'I enjoy it,' he said. 'It's nice to be with you an' the kids, like.'

In the intimacy of the car it was possible to venture a personal question. 'You haven't got kids of your own, have you?' she said. And when he took a long time to answer, she added, in case she'd been indelicate, 'Not that it's any of my business.'

'That's all right,' he said, acknowledging her sensitivity before answering her question. 'I don't mind you knowin'. No. I haven't got kids. I wish I had.'

His answer reassured her. He's enjoying their company, she thought. It's the kids he's spoiling, not me. The kids he's interested in.

'Wednesday then?' he said.

He looked so hopeful she couldn't refuse him.

This time they visited the sealife centre and saw the rays with their wonderful spotted backs, and plaice swimming about and burrowing into the sand,

and sharks so big and fierce that Jon had to hold Morgan's hand for reassurance.

When they got home, Morgan didn't fake excuses to see them again. He simply asked if he could come down on Sunday for a day on the beach. This time he was accepted without hesitation. They had established a pattern.

Chapter Nine

The long days of the August school holiday passed with their usual combination of languor and rapidity.

Brad settled into her new job at the hospital and was soon talking about her 'old dears' as if they were family. Emma and Jon took to calling their new friend 'Morgan' and climbing on to his lap as if *he* were family. The video shop opened and seemed to be doing well – although Rigg never phoned or visited *his* family. When Emma celebrated her second birthday, he didn't send her a card. Not that Emma noticed. She was much too busy unwrapping Morgan's present, which was a cuddle-sized teddy bear.

The sun shone intermittently, the rain was warm, campers and day trippers came and went. Morgan taught Jon to swim, and September was upon them before they knew it.

'Jon's going to school next week,' Alison told Morgan on that last Sunday afternoon. It was one of the warmest days of the entire holiday and they were on the beach enjoying it.

'Good for you, boy,' Morgan said, ruffling the child's fair hair.

'I've got a *uniform*,' Jon said. (Alison had bought it for him at a car-boot sale and he was very proud of it.)

'There's grand.'

'I don't know how he'll get on,' Alison said, when the little boy had gone rushing back to his sandcastle.

'You're not worryin' are you?'

'Well yes. I am a bit. It's a long day and he's so little and you never know how they're going to take things, do you.'

She looked so anxious that Morgan had to stop himself putting his arms round her to console her. 'He'll be fine,' he said. 'He's a good kid. You won't have any problems there, I can tell you.'

He's such a comfort, Alison thought, looking at Morgan's craggy face and his tough, scarred hands. He wouldn't say anything he didn't mean. You can depend on him. It occurred to her that she'd come to depend on him quite a lot over the last few weeks.

'We're going to have a tea party when I go to school,' Jon said. He'd worked his way round the castle and was facing Alison and Morgan again.

'That'll be nice,' Morgan said.

'We havin' Smartie cakes,' Emma said, from her pit beside the castle.

'You could have some too, if you like,' Jon said, looking straight at Morgan.

It was such an easy invitation that Morgan was touched, but it put Alison in a quandary.

Throughout the holiday she'd been feeling guilty about the amount of money Morgan had been spending on their behalf. He was so kind and so generous to them and she'd never given him anything, except the kids' company. An invitation to tea would be a nice way to repay him but it would mean inviting him into her home, and she wasn't sure whether that would be sensible or proper. It might embarrass him and it would certainly upset Rigg if he heard about it. It made her feel uncomfortable that Rigg didn't know anything about this new friend of theirs.

'Are you coming to tea with us then, Morgan?' Jon asked. He stood with his legs astride and his head held high, his entire body demanding an answer.

'Well . . .' Morgan began, and his voice sounded full of laughter. 'That depends on your Mam.'

The decision had been made for her. 'Yes, of course,' she said. 'If you can get the time off, and you'd like to, you're more than welcome.'

It seemed odd to Morgan to be driving down Shore Street again. This was only the second time he'd been there and so much had happened in between that he'd almost forgotten why he'd been sent to Hampton in the first place. He considered telling Alison the truth about it, worried that it was dishonest not to, and made up his mind to broach the subject over tea.

But when she answered the door to him, there was such a tense atmosphere in the house that it put all thought of Rigby Toan out of his mind.

She was rushing about. Darting from dresser to table. Tweaking at the table-cloth. Constantly on the move.

In the kitchen the kettle was as frantic as she was. It whistled and puffed clouds of steam into the living room.

'Sit up to the table,' Alison told the kids, hoisting Emma into her high-chair. 'I've got to make the tea.'

'Is there anything I can do to help?' Morgan asked, following her into the kitchen.

It was a small cramped space, overlooking the backyard, and everything in it was cheap, well used and cheerful. The teapot was red and cracked, the biscuit tin faded and battered, the mugs an odd assortment.

'No thanks,' Alison said, refusing to look at him properly. As she put the lid on the teapot her hands were so shaky that the china clattered. 'I've put a seat for you at the end of the table. Away from sticky fingers.'

Morgan sat where he'd been bidden and watched her butter bread, fill beakers and set plates away from the edge of the table. She's quick about her work, he thought. Like Mam. The domestic details warmed him, taking him back to the richness and poverty of his own childhood in Port Talbot; to toast by the fire and errands in the rain; to his cold bedroom with its cracked lino and the warm welcome he got when he came home from school; to Mam's chipped teapot and the caddy with its picture of 'Nelson aboard the Victory'; to the graduated row of boots and shoes lined up for Dad to polish every evening.

'It's a nice place you got here,' he said.

He'd hoped to put her at her ease but she accepted the compliment stiffly. 'I try to keep it nice.'

Then there was a long pause because neither of them could think what to say next. On the beach they'd talked in an easy sort of way about all sorts of things – work, the kids, the state of the world. Now, thrown together in the enclosed intimacy of her small house, they were suddenly tongue-tied. He drank his tea and sampled one of the Smartie cakes. She attended to the children and replenished empty tea-cups.

Left without conversation, the private eye in Morgan took over. He noted the poverty of the furniture, the pictures of the two children blooming on the walls, the pot plants thriving on the windowsill. If

Rigby Toan *is* making money, he thought, he's not putting any of it into this house. Even more curious was the evidence – or lack of it – that suggested he wasn't living in it either. There was no jacket on the hooks beside the door, no spare shoes, no newspapers or magazines. Lack of such things alerted Morgan to an intriguing possibility. Could they be separated? Not that it was any of his business.

'Are we going on the beach Sunday?' Jon wanted to know.

'Depends on the weather,' Alison said, and kissed him on the nose. 'You'd live on the beach if I let you.'

'I like it on the beach,' Jon said. 'It's happy.'

'Right,' Morgan agreed. 'So it is.'

For the first time since he'd arrived Alison looked at him. 'It's odd that,' she said. 'It *is* a happy place. You sort of leave your troubles behind when you're by the sea. I don't know why it is.' Just thinking about it was making her relax.

'Holiday?' he suggested.

'No. More than that,' she said. 'For me, it's something to do with being near the sea, I think. I don't know. It's hard to explain. I have a sort of affinity with the sea.' She paused and grimaced. 'No, that's pretentious. You can't have an affinity with the sea, only with people. What I mean is I always feel happy by the sea. As if it's the right place to be. As if I belong there. No matter how I feel or what's been going on, it makes me feel better to be down on the beach. It's so dependable, isn't it, the sea? Always different, never the same two days running, but always *there*, if you see what I mean.' Then feeling she'd run on far too much, she added, 'I'm talking nonsense.'

'You make a lot a' sense to me,' he said, setting down his cup. 'That's how I feel about the sea. First place I go to when I got somethin' to think about. I don't know why either. Per'aps it's bein' brought up on the coast, like.'

'Were you? Where?' He'd never talked to her about his childhood.

'Port Talbot.'

'The steel town.'

He was encouraged by the warmer note in her voice. 'You been there?'

'No,' she grinned. 'We did it in Geography.'

'It's not really a steel town,' he said. 'Not now. It's all make-up factories an' things like that. There's only about a quarter of the steelworks left. Beach is still there though. They can't close that down. I spent a lot a' time on that beach when I was a littl'un. Me an' my brother an' my sisters. A lot a' time.'

She already knew that he was one of a large family. 'How many sisters have you got?' she asked. This was better. Now they were talking more easily.

'Three. There are five of us.'

'I was one of four,' she confided. 'I've got three brothers.'

'We got somethin' in common then.'

They were smiling at one another, *almost* at ease. But then Emma pulled at her mother's elbow and held up her mug. 'More juice, Mummy. P'ease.'

Alison refilled the mug with orange juice and Morgan noticed that Jon was blinking with fatigue.

'Your Jon's nearly asleep,' he said.

'It's been a long day,' Alison said. 'I shall have to get him to bed soon. He won't last out till six.'

Awkwardness had returned. She was fussing with the cups and plates.

'Time I was off anyway,' Morgan said. For a tea party, this had gone on quite long enough. He stood up and walked across the room to the door. 'Thanks for the tea!'

Preoccupied with Jon but feeling she ought to see him out, Alison followed him, and waited quietly while he took his jacket from the hook beside the door.

It was a well-worn jacket, made of brown leather that had creased and faded over the years into a pattern of tawny stripes and black scratches. She watched as he put it on. It lay across his shoulders like a mane and the colour and texture of it suddenly made her acutely aware of him; of his tanned skin, his thick tawny hair, the power and strength of his body, the power and strength of those big, scarred hands. He zipped the jacket, quickly, smiling at her. And to her horror she realised that the sight of those hands was turning her on. My God! Actually turning her on – and with increasing strength.

'See you Sunday,' he said, waved at the kids and walked out of the door.

For a few silly seconds she knew she wanted to reach out and pull him back. But then – and just as well – he was gone and all that remained was surprise and guilt.

What a thing to have happened! she thought, as she lifted Emma out of the high-chair. What a way for a married woman to behave. She felt overwhelmed with guilt. I should never have invited him to the house, she thought. I knew it wasn't wise. We should have had this tea party on our own. Then she thought: what if Rigg were to find out I'd invited another man to tea? He'd be furious.

I'll tell him about it, she decided, the very next time I see him. Not every single detail, naturally. I'll say Morgan befriended the kids and we invited him to tea because he'd been so kind to them. I'll tell him the next time he comes here. Whenever that is.

In fact it was Friday evening, which was sooner than she was expecting.

The evening began like any other. Jon and Emma were in bed and asleep, Alison was in the kitchen washing up the supper things and singing along to an old Beatles LP and the neighbour's television was loud enough to hear through the wall. Without any warning, Rigg let himself into the house.

His face was twisted in such terrible anger and distress that Alison left the sink at once and ran across the living room to put her arms round him and comfort him.

'What is it?' she soothed, searching for any sign of an injury. Blood? Bruises? 'Rigg darling! What's the matter?'

'I'm ruined,' he said, his voice muffled by her shoulder. 'Ruined. It's all gone down the pan.'

She rubbed his spine as though he was one of the children, kissed his hair and murmured comfort. 'Oh Rigg, my poor love.' He couldn't possibly be ruined, not with the video shop doing so well. He'd got himself in a state, that was all, made worse by drinking too much. His breath smelt of brandy and his jacket and moustache of cigar smoke, so she knew he'd been in a pub.

Being comforted irritated him. 'I'm not your poor love,' he said, pulling away from her. 'I'm ruined. Don't you understand? That bloody Harry's run off with all the money.'

'Harry?' For a second she couldn't think who he was talking about.

'Harry Elton,' he said irritably. 'Who'd you think? He's a bloody crook. God knows why I ever trusted him. I'm ruined, Kitten. Finished. Oh, for God's sake, turn that bloody row off.'

She dealt with the hi-fi, eased him to the sofa, sat him down, wished they'd turn the telly down next door, tried to think of something helpful to say. But before she could find the right words, he began to weep. Alison felt her heart squeeze with distress at the sight.

'Just when we were doing so well,' he said, his voice thick with tears. 'Up and running we were. People coming in all the time. We took well over a grand last week alone. And now the bills are coming in and he's buggered off with all the cash and left me holding the baby. Christ, Ali, what are we going to do?'

Next door, guns were pinging and the music was building up to a climax. 'Is it a lot of money?' she asked.

'I can't tell you how much.'

She was silent for a moment while horses whinnied and American voices screamed through the wall. She knew it was no good suggesting the bank.

'If only I was thirty five,' he said. 'There'd be no problem if I was thirty five. Oh God, Ali, it's all so unfair. Why can't she let me have the money now, when I need it? It should have come to me when I was twenty one. Everybody else inherits when they're twenty one. There was no need to tie me up for ever like this.'

'Perhaps if you went and asked her ... explain what's happened ... she might ...'

'I'm not grovelling to her for my own money,' he said. 'If she can't give it to me without being asked, she's no sort of mother.' He paused and wiped his wet cheek with the back of his hand. 'Shc's no sort of mother anyway. A decent mother would have given it to me years ago, when I was first setting up. But would she? Would she hell? She's just a bloody awful, selfish woman, got to have mink coats and luxury cruises and shop at Harrods. She doesn't care what happens to me.'

'She does,' Alison said, defending her mother-in-law. 'She's very proud of you. She's always talking about you. You and your shops and how you're going to be a millionaire before you're forty.'

'I shall be a bankrupt before I'm forty,' Rigg groaned, and fresh tears ran down his cheeks. 'The video shop'll go bust. God rot that bloody Harry Elton. I can't even *run* the bloody place without a partner.'

'Do you mean he was working in the shop?'

The question enraged him. 'No, I don't mean he was working in the shop,' he said angrily. 'We've got girls to do that. He was my partner, for God's sake. My partner. We're a limited liability company. Or don't you know what that means?'

She didn't, but she couldn't say so, because that would have provoked even more anger. So she waited. Now that he was crying he would go on talking – he always did once he started to cry. Tears loosened his tongue.

'Rotten bugger,' he wept. 'I trusted that man, Ali. I would have trusted him with my life – my life, do you realise that? – and he does this to me. Just walks out. Walks out. How am I supposed to manage without a partner? Tell me that. It's bloody illegal for a start. We're registered as a two-partner company. I'm not supposed to trade on my own. I shall end up in prison. Oh Christ, Ali, what am I going to do?'

'Could you find another partner?' she suggested tentatively, in case it was the wrong thing to say.

'And have *him* run out on me next? Oh yes, that'd be lovely. That's just the sort of thing I want.'

'Well it would have to be someone you could trust,' she agreed. 'Someone you've known a long time.'

'There's only one person I can really trust,' he said, looking straight at her, brown eyes bloodshot, 'and that's you.'

'I'd do anything for you,' she said passionately. 'You know that.'

Even through the fog of misery and alcohol, he recognised the truth of that. 'Yes,' he said. 'I do. I do know that. If only you'd been my partner none of this would have happened.'

'But I couldn't have been your partner, could I? I haven't got any money.'

He looked at her for a long time. 'You could now though,' he said at last.

'Could I?'

'Yes. If you could bear to.'

Touched by the compliment he was paying her and

glad that one of his problems had been sorted out so easily, she kissed him lovingly. 'Well that's settled then,' she said. 'What do we have to do about it? Do I have to sign something?'

'No,' Rigg said, cheering visibly. 'It's very simple really. All I have to do is to substitute your name for his, and give you one of the shares.'

The idea of being a shareholder pleased her. She'd been his business partner in everything but name ever since they married. Now she would be his partner legally.

Rigg got up and peered into the kitchen. 'I don't suppose you've got anything to eat have you? I'm starving.'

She cooked him her last two rashers of bacon and two eggs. And afterwards they went to bed and made love most tenderly, as though nothing had ever been the matter. In the morning he came down to breakfast with the kids and left the house at the same time as they did, like all the other fathers in the road.

Much encouraged, Alison ventured an invitation. 'Sunday dinner?' she asked, as he switched on the ignition in his shiny BMW. Cooking a special meal for him would make amends for that tea party.

'Great,' he said, giving her his most loving look.

It wasn't until she'd pushed the buggy half way to the holiday camp that she remembered that Morgan was coming down on Sunday. Oh well, she thought. It can't be helped. I'll just have to phone him up and arrange some other time for his visit. He won't mind.

He minded quite a lot, although he was careful not to tell her or to reveal how he was feeling by the tone of his voice. It was the first time this husband of hers had put in an appearance on a Sunday. Although he'd always known that he would have to step down if that happened, now that the moment had come it filled him with unaccountable jealousy. It was far too strong a feeling for such a gentle friendship but it was undeniably jealousy and most unpleasant. Feeling rather ashamed of himself, he agreed at once that some other time would do and returned to his work. It was better that way.

Partly to assuage her conscience and partly to spoil her husband, Alison made a special effort with that Sunday dinner, treating the family to roast chicken and all the trimmings and one of her lemon meringue pies. If Harry Elton really had run off with all the money, there could be other problems to solve as well as the partnership. So Rigg could do with petting. Good food always makes you feel better and the one thing she was sure about was her prowess as a cook.

The day wasn't a success, although it began well: Rigg arrived clutching Alison's company share and handed it to her with a kiss and a joky, 'Howdy pardner!' But after that nothing went right. Jon spilled orange juice all over the carpet and Emma did nothing but grizzle and pick at her food. To make matters worse, it started to rain and there was no hope of going out for a walk to put them in a better humour.

Finger paints are the only answer, Alison thought. That'll keep them occupied while I wash up. And she got them out of the cupboard. It was a bad mistake.

Rigg watched in horror as his children dipped their fingers in the pots and smeared colour all over two sheets of sugar paper. 'Ali!' he yelled. 'Have you seen the mess they're making?'

Alison didn't even look up. 'They're all right,' she said.

After a minute or so, Emma started to paint her face, circling her eyes with green and daubing her lips black. It was more than Rigg could bear. 'Don't do that, you naughty little thing!' he said. 'Use the paper.'

Emma was annoyed. 'No,' she said doggedly. 'I paint me face.'

'No, you don't,' he said, seizing her hands and grabbing a tissue from the table to clean them. 'You don't paint your face and you don't use your fingers. Haven't you got a brush?'

'We don't use brushes,' Jon said. 'They're finger paints.'

'Don't be stupid,' Rigg said crossly. 'All children use brushes. *I* always did. And I wasn't allowed to make a mess with them either.'

Now that Rigg's attention was on her brother, Emma returned to the paint pots, dipped all ten fingers in the red paint and began to print red spots on the paper.

Her father pounced on her. 'What did I tell you, Emma?'

'I do it,' the child said fiercely. But when he advanced on her with another handful of tissues she lost her nerve and began to scream. And at that, Alison left the dishes and came out of the kitchen to rescue her.

'What's the matter with them?' Rigg shouted into the din. 'Why can't they play properly?'

'They are playing properly,' Alison said, picking Emma up and cuddling her.

'They're not normal,' Rigg said. 'There's something the matter with them.' They'd made him feel an absolute wally. Children ought to obey their parents. He hurled the box of tissues into the corner and stormed out.

'I think Daddy's horrid,' Jon said, matter-of-factly, picking up a piece of meringue that had been left behind on the table and putting it into his mouth with his paint-daubed fingers.

'So do I,' Emma sniffed.

'We mustn't be nasty to Daddy,' Alison defended. 'He's worried.'

'Why?' Jon said.

'Because a nasty man's stolen all his money.'

'Let's go down on the beach and see Morgan,' Jon said.

'Morgan's not coming today,' Alison told him. 'And anyway, it's raining.'

'That's not fair,' the little boy said. 'He always comes on Sunday.' His mouth was drooping, ready for tears.

I must nip this in the bud before they're both crying, Alison thought. 'Get your hands washed,' she said, 'and put your anoraks on, and I'll take you to the swings. You'll get wet but you'll have to put up with it.' I'll make my peace with Rigg, she thought, the next time he rings.

There was no communication with Rigg for the next two days, which was disappointing. Wednesday was Alison's afternoon off and she took the kids down to the video shop to see what was going on there. Now that she was a partner it was the least she could do.

The shop looked exactly the same as it had been the last time she saw it. The same scruffy-looking blonde was sitting by the till, there were customers drifting in and out, the sweets stand was well stocked. A bit too well stocked. Emma and Jon saw something on it that they wanted at once.

'Not this week,' she said. 'I haven't got enough money for sweets this week.' Extra bacon and a larger chicken had played havoc with her housekeeping.

'That's not fair,' Jon said automatically, but having made his protest, he allowed himself to be led away and didn't argue.

The blonde girl was serving a customer. Alison waited until the deal was completed and then stepped forward.

'I've come in to say good morning,' she said. 'I thought you ought to know I'm the new partner. I'm Mrs Toan.'

The blonde wasn't interested. 'Oh yes,' she said.

'I've taken over from Mr Elton.'

The blonde's voice was even more vague. 'Oh yes.'

Alison felt a bit downcast that her presence in the shop meant so little. But she pressed on. 'What's your name?' she asked, feeling she ought to take an interest.

'Marlene.'

'I know Mr Toan has a lot of people working for him.'

'Yes. He does.'

'Perhaps I could have a list of your names and addresses and the hours you work. As I'm a partner.'

'I'll draw one up for you if you like,' Marlene offered. 'There's not much else to do here of a morning.'

As Alison left the shop, pushing the buggy before her, the sea breeze fluttered the tail of her blue shirt. I've made an effort, she thought. I've started being a partner. Now we'll sort out all these debts together. They can't be that bad.

Then – because the sun was shining, the sea was green, and the breeze was ruffling the in-coming tide into a flurry of white-crested waves – she put Rigg, Harry Elton and the shop right out of her mind and increased her speed towards the sands.

CHAPTER TEN

Back at *Rings and Things* Rigg wasn't thinking about his debts at all. His friend, Francis, had roared up in a wonderful new Porsche 911. He was full of himself, as quick talking as ever, with his wallet crammed with tens and twenties and news of a party in Dorking that evening.

'The Crayfords' place,' he said. 'I don't think you've met him, have you? Fantastic guy. Hop in. I'll give you a spin. See you got another BMW. You really ought to go for a Porsche next year, you know. They're fabulous cars.'

Bliss, Rigg thought, as the Porsche gathered speed and began to eat the miles. This is the life. Those bloody bills can wait. If I haven't got the money I can't pay them. That's all there is to that. Anyway, it'll sort itself out in the end. It always does.

'What d'you think of it, eh?' Francis said, nodding at the dashboard.

'Fabulous,' Rigg said. 'You're right. I shall have one next year. It's about time I moved up-market.'

This was where he belonged, out on the open road in a luxury car, turning the other drivers green with envy and heading for a party in a luxury house where the guests would be rich and successful. It was the style he deserved. The life he was born to.

'What are they like, your Crayfords?' he asked, taking a cigar from Francis' glove compartment.

'Actually it's only old Charlie Crayford,' Francis said. 'He ditched his wife about ten years ago. Got a bit of a bore by all accounts, so she had to go. You know how it is. You'll like him. He's a great guy.'

He also lived in the sort of house Rigg had yearned for all his life. Set on a slope of the north downs, hidden from the world by an enormous hedge of rhododendrons, and surrounded by acres of grounds, it was a Tudorbethan pile, built in the twenties, with the recent addition of a Victorian conservatory, a billiard room and a magnificent indoor swimming pool, with a jacuzzi and a sauna on one side of it and a full-length bar on the other. And Mr Crayford *was* exactly the sort of man Rigg admired, expensively dressed, shrewd, bluff, with the full-fleshed, well-oiled ease that only comes with years of rich feeding. The current girl-friend was pretty tasty too, beautifully rounded with a mass of thick, red-gold, frizzy hair. And wonderfully attentive to her Charlie, hanging on to his arm and his every word. Oh yes, Charlie Crayford was undoubtedly a great guy.

Rigg and Francis were welcomed with champagne and Rigg was introduced to so many guests he couldn't remember a third of them. There were plenty of pretty girls though, and a lot of them seemed available. But, as it turned out, what he picked up that evening was a great deal more useful to him than a one-night stand.

Like many self-made men, Charlie Crayford had an opinion on most things. That night he laid down the law about the Common Market – absolutely intolerable what those French johnnies get up to . . . Mrs Thatcher – what a magnificent women, the saviour of the nation . . . the poll tax – can't see what all the fuss is about; it's perfectly fair; we all pay the same . . . protesters – ought to be locked up, every man jack of 'em . . . and bankruptcy, which he pronounced to be 'totally unnecessary'.

Rigg edged into the circle to hear more. 'I don't quite see that,' he said, deferentially. 'I mean, if you've used up all your capital and you can't raise any more, then surely bankruptcy is the only way you can go.'

'Not no more,' Charlie said, beaming at him. 'Not now the law's been changed. And about bloody time too, eh Jock?'

The man called Jock agreed that it was and for a few minutes everybody in the group spoke out in favour of the change, which, as far as Rigg could make out, had been brought about by a new insolvency law.

'Sorry to be naive,' he said when he could get a word in, 'but I've never heard of this new law and there's a friend of mine . . .'

'Insolvency Act, 1986. Section 252.' Charlie Crayford boomed above the din. 'What's he done this friend of yours? Run foul of the law? Or is it just the creditors?'

'Creditors,' Rigg said, adding quickly, 'as far as I know.'

'Tell him to find himself an insolvency consultant. That's my advice. They're the fellers. Find an insolvency consultant and apply for a voluntary arrangement. That's what he wants to do.'

'What's that?'

'It's a licence to steal,' Charlie said, chuckling.

'That's what it is. A licence to bloody steal. Right fellers? Works this way – you ask your creditors to let you have a couple of years to pay them. Not all the debt mind, but a nice heavy dividend, fifty per cent, say, or sixty, even seventy five per cent. It doesn't matter much because you won't have to pay it. Or not all of it anyway. In two years most of the buggers'll be bust themselves. Or they'll have taken the insurance money. Just so long as they vote to keep you out of the bankruptcy courts. One meeting, good consultant and Bob's your uncle. Nothing to pay and they can't do anything about it.'

It sounded too good to be true. 'Do they really do it?' Rigg asked. 'Vote like that I mean.'

'If they think they're going to get a bigger cut,' Charlie said. 'Greed, boy. That's what makes the world go round. Am I right or am I right?'

'You wouldn't happen to know where I could find one of these insolvency consultants, would you?' Rigg persisted. 'For my friend I mean.'

'Got a card somewhere,' Charlie said. 'In my address book probably.' He turned to the butler who was circulating with the champagne. 'Bring me my address book from the study, will you Kenwood?'

Three minutes later the card – and salvation – was in Rigg's hand. After that, the rest of the party was an irrelevant noise.

Elsie Wareham was very surprised to find such a bulky envelope lying on her doormat. At first she thought it was junk mail of some kind and made a face because it was such a waste. Then she saw that it was addressed to her personally, so she carried it off to the kitchen to read it over her first cup of tea.

It was a dreadful shock. Six pages of closely typed print, entitled 'R.L. Toan in voluntary arrangement', full of incomprehensible legal jargon and detailing so many dreadful debts that it made her head spin. After a lifetime spent in the shelter of Bob's daily caution over money, it seemed quite incredible to her that any young married man could have run up so many terrible debts, leave alone their nice handsome Rigg. She glanced through the list of creditors, which ran to four pages. If you totted up all the figures it would be thousands and thousands of pounds. Even with her limited grasp of maths she could see that. Did Ali know? she wondered. She must be worried out of her wits.

She turned to the next page and read it carefully. It informed her that there was going to be a meeting of creditors in the Ship Inn in Brighton in three weeks' time and that she was invited to 'prove her claim' – whatever that meant – and attend the meeting. I can't do that, she thought. What if the boys were to find out? They'd be furious with me, giving away their dad's money like that. Except that I wasn't giving it away, was I? I was only loaning it. And now it says I'll only get sixty per cent of it back.

Her toast lay on her plate uneaten, she stirred her tea and discovered she could not drink it, the announcer was saying something on the wireless and she couldn't make sense of the words. There was only the enormity of those figures, making her throat prickle. What was she going to do?

A ring at the doorbell brought her to her senses. Milkman, was it? She found her purse, tidied her hair and went to attend to it. But it wasn't the milkman. It was Rigg, smiling at her in his most charming way.

'I had to come and see you,' he said, as he walked in. 'You're going to have a document sent to you . . .'

'It came this morning,' she said, leading him into the kitchen. 'I was just reading it.'

'Then I've come in the nick of time,' he said. 'I thought I ought to pop round and explain it to you, otherwise you might worry.'

'I am worrying,' she said. 'It's dreadful, Rigg.'

He sat down opposite her at the kitchen table, caught her hands and held them between his own. 'It's not as bad as it looks,' he said. 'Honestly.'

'But all those debts, Rigg. All that money.'

'I don't owe all *that*,' he said. 'How can I explain it to you? It's sort of like a photograph. I had to list all the people I hadn't actually paid at the moment the list was drawn up. Doesn't mean a thing really. All the little ones'll be paid as soon as I've sold enough.'

'When will that be?'

'A day. Two or three days. A week at the outside. I shall pay you back in full, naturally. Every penny. You don't have to take any notice of that sixty per cent. That's just for the others.'

Elsie relaxed and he let go of her hands. 'Oh well,' she said. 'That's different then.'

'It's just the big firms that are the trouble,' Rigg went on. 'People like Jaffa Jewels. They're the very devil. Won't give you time to pay. Want their money yesterday. That sort of thing. That's why I've asked for this arrangement, do you see? It's to give me a few months to sort things out for them.'

'Yes,' Elsie said. 'I see.' But then she thought of something else. 'But it says here I've got to prove my claim.'

'Nothing to it,' her son-in-law said, picking up the statement. 'All you have to do is fill in this claim form. See. You enter the amount I owe you there and sign at the bottom there. Simple.'

'And that's all I've got to do?'

He smiled at her lovingly. 'That's all.'

'I haven't got to go to court?'

'Good heavens no. Not if you don't want to. In fact it would be better for Ali and me if you didn't.'

'Would it?'

'That's the other thing I was going to ask you. My consultant's very good and he says it would be better all round if Ali could get to the court and appear with me. Supportive wife and all that sort of thing. Only we couldn't take the kids . . .'

'I'll look after them for you,' Elsie offered at once. 'Was that what you were going to ask me?'

'You're a darling,' Rigg said. 'An absolute darling.' He kissed her warmly. 'Just one other thing before I go. You won't say anything to Ali about all those stupid figures, will you? There's no need to worry her and I shall have it all sorted out in a week or two.'

'No, no,' Elsie assured him. 'Leave it to me. I won't say a word, not if you don't want me to. What time will you bring the kiddies?'

'About ten o'clock.'

In fact it was nearer half past nine because, for the first time since he left boarding school, Rigg was up early. He arrived at Shore Street, dapper in his grey suit, at ten past eight on the prescribed October morning. There was even time for a cooked breakfast before he and Ali set out for Brighton.

Alison was so nervous that she burnt the bacon, and spilt cornflakes all over the table. Even though Rigg had explained everything to her and planned it all down to the last button – arranging for Mum to look after the kids, which was kind of him, and issuing strict instructions as to what she was to wear – she couldn't help worrying about this meeting. It could so easily go wrong, particularly in a recession. It had come as a shock to know that he had got into real debt, but he had explained that it was all due to Harry Elton running off with the money and, in any case, they were all negligible amounts and he could pay them off in no time. Even so it was cold comfort. It was all very well saying the creditors would be bound to vote for him to go on trading. They might not. And what would happen to him if they didn't? Poor dear Rigg, it's so unfair, she thought, admiring him (that pale grey colour always had suited him). It was all this awful recession causing the trouble, of course. He couldn't help it.

'Ready for the off?' he said.

She finished putting on the last application of mascara, checked her handbag, straightened her skirt. The suit he'd chosen was her smart blue one (a real power-dressing affair) with a short straight skirt and a little boxy jacket with padded shoulders. She could appreciate what a good choice it was, but she hadn't worn it since she got pregnant with Emma and the skirt was a bit too tight. She pulled in her stomach and buttoned the jacket over the bulge, standing on tiptoe to check the result in the mirror over the mantelpiece.

'You look fine,' Rigg said, standing behind her to comb his hair. 'We're a handsome couple.'

She should have felt proud at the compliment but she didn't. In that moment and with a perversity that shamed her, she knew she didn't want to be part of a handsome couple, didn't want to go to court, didn't want to be involved in any of this awful business. She wanted to be in her comfortable jeans and an old jersey, striding along the beach with the kids.

Rigg smiled at his reflection in the mirror. 'Ready?' he asked.

It didn't seem to take any time at all to drive to the Ship Inn. Rigg kept to the fast lane all the way, overtaking everything else on the road, and Alison sat beside him and worried. Usually, she enjoyed a trip to Brighton but now she took no pleasure from the familiar landmarks. Under the elegant curves of the white bridge, over the Adur, buffeted by cross-winds, along the long Hove promenade where the hotels reared up like honey-coloured cliffs, past the wreckage of the West Pier and the new frontage of the Grand Hotel where Maggie Thatcher had nearly been blown up . . . it was all simply a journey. And a journey, what's more, with a trial at the end of it.

They parked the car and she followed Rigg into the hotel foyer, feeling bemused and trying to look as though she was a guest. It was a very grand foyer, all panelled walls and thick carpets and elaborate flower arrangements. There was a dark-haired man in a business suit waiting for them at the reception desk and Rigg introduced them, 'Harvey Shearing, my insolvency consultant – my wife.' Alison was too keyed up to notice what he was like.

Then they were walking along a carpeted corridor, up a short flight of steps, along another corridor, and being ushered into a plain, square, empty room. It made Alison feel demoralised because it looked exactly like a classroom, with the teacher's desk at the front – covered in green baize and immediately under the window – and chairs set out in long rows as though they were waiting for the class. If there'd been a cane on the green baize she wouldn't have been a bit surprised.

Handbag on her lap, she sat down at the far end of the front row while Rigg and the man called Harvey stood beside the teacher's table and talked in low tones like conspirators. People began to arrive, ordinary people, but all of them holding brief cases and official looking folders. The seats filled up. A waitress served coffee and biscuits. Rigg and Harvey continued to talk. Two important people made an entrance and took up their positions in the front row. One was a woman with red hair and a lot of dangly jewellery, the other a young man with glasses that he had to keep pushing up his nose. The man called Harvey went over to stand behind the table and gave a warning cough. Rigg took a seat beside his wife.

'Is it going to start?' Alison whispered. She was so nervous that her hands were sweating.

'They're the Inland Revenue,' Rigg whispered back, jerking his head towards the redhead and the man with glasses. 'They're the ones we've got to watch.'

'Ladies and gentlemen,' Harvey said, oiling a smile over everyone in the room. 'If you're ready, I suggest we proceed. I have a few opening remarks to make and then I shall ask Mr Rigby Toan to give you a resume of his proposal, if you're agreeable.'

Afterwards Alison couldn't remember anything that was said in those important opening speeches. Harvey's seemed to go on for hours, explaining procedure and talking about the Insolvency Act. Then Rigg stood up and told everyone what a marvellous money spinner the video shop was, how his difficulties were all due to the recession, how he could cover the sixty per cent payment easily by selling his flat in Spain and how he could continue trading profitably in two of his outlets if they would agree. She worried because he hadn't said anything about Harry Elton and the missing money (which meant that he hadn't told them the exact truth). And when the meeting was thrown open to questions, her heart was pounding with anxiety in case they asked him something that would catch him out.

But Rigg was smooth as velvet, answering every question with an expression of transparent honesty which could have charmed trust from a cynic.

He agreed with the redhead from the Inland Revenue that his income tax would be paid within a twelvemonth. 'No problem. Once the flat is sold.' He estimated that the flat would sell 'well within the allotted twelve months'. He explained that the new rent for his largest shop was more than he could afford and that consequently he would have to close it down, 'no matter what the outcome of this meeting'. He smiled when they asked him if he had any other problems with any of his businesses. 'None that you don't all know about,' he said. 'Trade is down, but then it's down everywhere. My video shop – which is a limited liability company and doesn't come into the terms of this proposed agreement as Mr Shearing explained to you – my video shop is doing excellent business.'

'What's your weekly turnover in this business?' the Inland Revenue man asked, pushing at his glasses again.

'Well I haven't got the exact figures with me,' Rigg said, 'but I should say we average out at about a thousand a week.'

There was a murmur of approval at that, and the two from the Inland Revenue whispered to one another.

'Any more questions?' Mr Shearing asked when the buzz had died down. 'No. Then I suggest Mr and Mrs Toan and I adjourn to another room while you consider what you've heard. Is that agreeable to you?'

They adjourned to a cloakroom a bit further along the corridor, a dark, chilly space like something long abandoned. There were no seats but by that time Rigg and Alison were so tense they couldn't have sat down even if there had been. Rigg prowled the length of the counter and back, up and down like a caged tiger. Alison fidgeted from foot to foot, as their new ally smoked one cigarette after another and told them he thought it had all gone extremely well.

'Having a flat in Spain as your major asset could well prove decisive,' he said. 'They were all impressed by that.'

'Do you think so?' Rigg said.

'It's a strong proposal,' Mr Shearing said. 'If the Inland Revenue will buy it, you'll be home and dry.'

Privately, Alison thought the Inland Revenue would be most unlikely to 'buy' anything. But her mouth was too dry to venture an opinion.

‘They liked the sound of my takings, didn’t you think so?’ Rigg was saying, when the man with the glasses appeared before them to say that they’d finished their discussions and were ready to proceed.

With her heart in her throat, Alison followed the three men back into the schoolroom. Papers were passed to the teacher’s table. Mr Shearing made two neat piles of them, took a pen and a notebook from his brief case and did a few sums. Then he stood up and announced, with a perfectly straight face, that the meeting had voted in favour of the agreement. Mr Toan was to be allowed to continue trading, on certain conditions laid down by the Inland Revenue, which he was sure would be entirely acceptable to Mr Toan. The debts were to be paid off within two years, at sixty per cent which would be raised by the sale of Mr Toan’s flat in Spain. And that was that.

Rigg maintained his self-control until the creditors had left the room and there was no one to see him but Mr Shearing, who was beaming, and Alison, who was too stunned to realise what had happened. He gave a roar of delight, seized his wife round the waist and lifted her off her feet to kiss her.

‘We’ve won!’ he crowed. ‘We’ve won, Kitten! I never thought we would, but we’ve won. It’s all right. We’re off the hook. This calls for champagne.’

There were all sorts of things that Alison wanted to ask but they were private and had to wait until she and Rigg were driving home. By then her head was so muzzy with the champagne that she found it hard to concentrate. Nevertheless she struggled to put the important questions together and to pronounce the words clearly.

'You'll have to pay all these debts eventually, won't you?' she asked.

'That's years off,' Rigg said. 'We don't have to worry about that for months and months.'

'Does this mean you'll be able to come home now, Rigg?'

'Not quite yet,' Rigg said expansively. 'Have to wait till the dust settles.'

'But . . . if you're going to sell the shop you won't have anywhere to live, will you.'

'I'm not selling the shop.'

'But you said . . .' Surely he'd said . . . something about the rent being . . .

'That was just for the punters,' Rigg said, 'No. I shall keep the shop and close *Baubles*. Don't *worry* Kitten. We've got it made.'

Alison closed her eyes and gave herself up to the rhythm of the car and the euphoria of champagne. Rigg was right. They'd won. There was nothing to worry about.

Chapter Eleven

'Mummy! Mummy! Come quickly!' Jon's voice shrilled from outside the front door. 'Something terrible's happened!'

Alison was icing cakes in the kitchen. Mark was waiting to take them to Mum's in his car for Friday tea, so she was working quickly. Which was why the door was opened and the kids were out in the street, even though it was none too warm and getting dark.

Jon rushed into the house, holding something round and dark in both cupped hands. He scampered towards her, with Emma toddling after him, yelling, 'Mummy! Mummy!' at the top of her excited voice.

'Steady on!' Mark said, putting out an arm to stop their onrush. 'What have you got there?'

It was a baby hedgehog.

'It can't walk,' Jon explained. 'It keeps rolling about. Look.'

'Put it down on the floor,' Alison said. 'It won't walk on your hand, now will it.'

The animal was lowered, very gently, on to the lino. It lay on its side for a few seconds while the children squatted beside it and they all watched it. Then it gave a shudder and tried to curl itself into a ball, tucking its sharp snout down between its front paws and hauling up its hind quarters, painfully and with obvious effort. As it rolled they saw what was the matter with it. One of its back legs was sticking out in a most awkward way and bent at an impossible angle.

'It's got a broken leg,' Alison said, 'poor little thing.'

'You get on with the cakes and I'll put it out of its misery,' Mark said, bending down to pick it up.

Young though they were, Jon and Emma knew by instinct what being put out of your misery meant. They folded themselves across the injured animal, furiously protective. 'No,' Jon said. 'You're not to.'

Bending towards her children to reassure them, Alison noticed something else about the hedgehog. 'It's crawling alive with fleas,' she said in horror. 'I don't care what you do with it, but it can't stay in my kitchen, Jon. We shall all be lousy.'

'It's got a broken leg so we've got to look after it, haven't we?' Jon pleaded, but with determination in his face.

'I'll take it,' Mark said, trying to be tactful. 'Put it back where it belongs.'

But Jon wasn't going to allow that either. 'No,' he yelled. 'You're not to.' At that Emma began to roar and she went on roaring even though Alison picked her up and tried to soothe her.

'It's a poor little baby hedgehog,' Jon yelled with tears in his eyes. 'It doesn't want to be moved. It wants to stay here. *I*'ll look after you, you poor hedgehog!'

'Oh for heaven's sake!' Mark said into the uproar.

There was so much noise that Alison couldn't think straight. The entire kitchen seemed to be screaming; the pots and pans black as open mouths, the kettle gathering itself to squeal, the cooker swollen with unnecessary heat. 'Calm down,' she begged. And Brad's ordinary voice spoke into the racket.

'Boo-ba-doo kids,' she called from the living room. 'What's the problem? Blimey, it's parky in here. D'you want me to shut the door, Ali?'

Both children stopped crying and Jon rushed towards her for support, explaining about the hedgehog as he dragged her into the kitchen.

'Poor thing!' Brad said. 'We'll have to take it to the vet.'

Jon was still suspicious. 'What's a vet?'

'A nice man who makes animals better when they're ill,' Brad explained. 'Got a shoe box have yer?'

'It's crawling alive with fleas,' Alison warned.

Brad wasn't deterred. 'What's a few fleas between friends?' she said. 'Come on then kids. Look lively.'

The atmosphere in the kitchen had changed completely. Alison found an old shoe box, Jon produced a felted jersey for bedding, the injured hedgehog was lifted up and put in its new nest.

'Now it'll be all nice and ready for you in the morning,' Alison said.

'Morning?' Brad grinned. 'We're not waiting till the morning, are we kids.'

'You're not going now, are you?'

'Evening surgery,' Brad told her. 'Accident and emergency.'

'But what about paying for it?' Alison said. 'It'll cost the earth.' She felt mean mentioning money, but she couldn't afford vet's fees.

'My treat,' Brad said. 'Come on gang.'

'She's a case, your friend Brad,' Mark admired, as

he and his sister watched Jon being strapped into the back seat of the Mini and the car seat being fixed for Emma.

'She's a dear,' Alison said. 'And generous.'

The word reminded Mark of his sister's predicament.

'How's it going?' he asked. 'Are you managing all right?'

'We're fine,' Alison said, very firmly.

Mark looked relieved. 'That's all right then. Are those cakes packed?'

On the passenger seat of Brad's Mini the hedgehog lay in the shoe box in an uncomfortable heap and looked at Jon with one small sloe-black eye.

'Do you think it knows?' the boy asked.

'Don't ask me, sunshine,' Brad said, smiling at him through the driving mirror. 'I don't speak hedgehog.'

'Does the man we're going to see?'

'Bound to. Vets speak all sorts of languages.'

He was very impressed. 'Does he speak English?'

'He speaks everything,' Brad said, turning in behind a large house. 'Horse. Cat. Dog. Colorado beetle. We're here. Sit tight till I come round an' let you out.'

The two children followed her through a glass door and into a tiled surgery. There was a counter at one end and opening off it an open corridor with doors down one side, three of which were labelled: Surgery 1, Surgery 2, Surgery 3.

'Now we sit here,' Brad said, when she'd explained their problem to the receptionist, 'and wait for the vet to call us.'

The children were so awestruck by the clinical order of the place that they sat and waited in almost total silence.

'Does he know our names?' Jon whispered after a long pause.

'No,' Brad whispered back. 'But he knows mine.'

And so he did. Two minutes later he put his head round the archway and asked for 'Miss Bradshawe' and Brad got up and led them both into the corridor and through one of the mysterious doors into the surgery.

The vet was a gentle-looking man with a soft beard, drooping eyes and sloping shoulders, and he moved delicately, inching his body through the door after them and placing his feet as though he'd been told to be mindful where he trod. Jon thought he looked very nice.

'Let's have a look at him, shall we,' he said to Jon. 'We'll just lift him out of his box.' Which he did, very slowly and gently, turning the little creature on to its back, so that all four leathery paws were sticking up in the air, three scrabbling furiously, the fourth rigid.

'I'm afraid that leg is broken,' the vet said.

Jon and Emma stood with their chins resting on the table and watched intently. Their new hero spread one large hand across the hedgehog's belly to prevent it from rolling itself up, and lifted the broken limb with the other hand, examining it very gently with the tips of his fingers. 'It's a clean fracture,' he said to Brad. 'He must have been hit before he could roll up into a ball.'

'Can you make him better?' Jon asked.

The vet knelt down so as to be on a level with the

child's earnest face. 'If you leave him with me for a day or two I'll do my best. He's in a poor state just now, because he's so frightened, but we'll look after him and keep him warm, and when he's well enough, I'll give him a little whiff of something so that he goes to sleep and doesn't feel any pain, and then I'll set his leg for him and it'll be as good as new.'

'Promise?'

'I promise. You leave him with me.'

'There you are,' Brad said. 'What did I tell you?'

'I'll deal with his livestock too,' the vet said, looking at Brad. 'He's rather badly infested. He'll probably take two or three days to stabilise, but it's important not to operate too soon. Wild animals are more likely to – um – be finished off by shock than from injury.'

Brad was touched by the careful way he avoided saying the word 'die' in front of the children. And impressed by his tenderness when he eased the little creature into one of the cages standing beside the wall. He might look like a wimp but he was certainly a kind one. 'What are his chances?' she asked.

'Pretty good, but you can never be entirely sure. Not with an animal from the wild. Shock can – um – at any time for a fortnight after the initial injury.'

'I see.'

'I'll pack the wound with intrasite,' he said, 'to be on the safe side.'

'What's that when it's at home?'

'It's a premixed wound dressing. Looks like wallpaper paste, actually. Very good stuff. It absorbs all the muck so that the wound doesn't get infected, and after that it provides the ideal conditions for granulation – um – the first stage of scar tissue formation.'

'Sounds gruesome,' Brad grinned.

'It isn't really. It's part of the healing process.'

'So that's it, is it?'

'Phone us in three days' time,' the vet said.

'Who shall I ask for?'

'Oh, yes. My name's Martin Smith. Not very original, I'm afraid, but my patients don't mind.'

'Say goodbye to Mr Smith, kids,' Brad instructed. 'Time we went home and told your mum.'

The children said goodbye to the hedgehog and blew it kisses through the bars of its cage. Then Emma walked up to the vet and held out her chubby hand. When he put his own hand down to hold it, she shook hands – solemnly.

He understood that she was thanking him and took her perfectly seriously, squatting on his haunches so that they were eye to eye. 'You're very welcome,' he said.

That night, supper in Shore Street was a celebration. After her gallant rescue, Brad was the guest of honour, and the talk was all of hedgehogs and vets.

'I hope he comes up trumps after all this,' Alison said, when the children had finally been persuaded to go to bed and stay there.

'If anyone can, he will,' Brad said. 'He looks a bit of a wally but he knows his job.'

'Well we shall know in three days,' Alison said.

Three days are a long time to wait when you are only five and an eternity when you are two. Emma asked about the hedgehog at regular intervals all through the day, and Jon drew a picture of it at school and was allowed to bring it home for Alison to pin on the wall. On Sunday, when Morgan came down to take them to the park, he was shown the picture and told the full story at least three times.

'It's made quite an impression,' he said, as he and Alison were walking back to Shore Street through the gathering twilight. Both the children were in the buggy and fast asleep.

'It's practically all they ever talk about,' Alison said.

The trouble was it became her sole topic of conversation too. When Morgan phoned her towards the end of the following week, he didn't have a chance to explain why he'd rung before she started telling him about the hedgehog.

'It's had its operation,' she said. 'Imagine that. Total success, so they say. They're going to collect it tomorrow afternoon after school. Jon's so excited. I couldn't get him to bed. It's taken me an hour to settle him. I've just come downstairs. All this over a hedgehog! They've made a cage for it out in the yard. They reckon they're going to nurse it until it has its plaster off and then Brad's going to keep it in her garden for them.'

'What I rang to tell you,' Morgan said, 'was that I can't come down on Sunday. I've got to go to Swansea for a few days.' He'd had a phone call that morning from Mr Fehrenbach of Jaffa Jewels with instructions to go to a jewellers there and 'make enquiries', and, among other things, news of Mr Toan's voluntary arrangement, which had been quite a surprise. 'I might be able to call in and see you on my way back. How would that be?'

'Fine,' she said.

But her voice was so non-committal that he

couldn't tell whether she meant it. Damn that hedgehog, he thought, as he put the receiver down. I don't want to talk about hedgehogs. He hadn't got any clear idea what he really wanted to talk to her about. He just knew he wanted to talk.

The expedition to pick up the wounded animal began as Alison expected, the moment Jon came home from school. Brad was sitting in her car waiting for them and listening to the radio, so Jon collected the shoe box from the windowsill and he and Emma tumbled in among the rubbish on the back seat and were driven off at once.

The hedgehog was in its cage and actually walking about and sniffing the air. It had a neat blue bandage on its injured leg, but it didn't seem worried by it at all. While they watched, it ate a mouthful of mince.

'Isn't he lovely?' Jon said, admiring him.

'He's a great success,' the vet agreed. 'I'll put him in the box for you, shall I?'

This time the shoe box was lined with newspaper – Alison had burnt the jersey for fear of fleas. Right in the middle of the nest was a picture of Margaret Thatcher arriving at the Lord Mayor's banquet in a regal creation of black velvet and white silk. There was a quotation from her speech in big type above it, '*I am still at the crease, though the bowling is hostile.*' The first thing the little animal did when they'd lowered him on to the paper was to crap on the Prime Minister's face.

Brad was delighted. 'Bull's eye!' she said. 'Bully for you, Mr Tiggywinkle!'

They all laughed and so did the vet. But when Brad grinned at him, he stood up and turned away, shifting his shoulders about as if he was embarrassed. Then he opened one of the wall cupboards and stuck his head inside. The backs of his ears were dark pink.

Brad and the children waited. He's sorting out some pills, Brad thought, watching the back of his shaggy head. He seemed to be muttering to himself. 'What I mean Miss Bradshawe . . .' he began, after clearing his throat several times. 'I suppose you wouldn't care to come with me to . . .' Another cough. 'No – clearly this is presumptuous of me.' More throat clearing. 'Um.'

'You trying to ask me out?' Brad said.

Blushing violently, he pulled his head out the cupboard. 'Well yes. Put like that, I suppose I am.' Now that he looked at Brad he knew how stupid the idea had been. She was such a bright, self-confident woman she wouldn't even consider such a thing.

'OK then,' Brad grinned. 'Why not?'

Being accepted was such a surprise that it threw him into confusion. 'You don't have to . . .' he said. 'I mean. I wouldn't want to pressurise you.'

'Ain't a man alive can pressurise me,' Brad said. 'Where you gonna take me?'

'Brighton?' he suggested hopefully.

'When?'

'Tomorrow.'

'You're on. My name's Brad, by the way, in case you're wondering.'

'I'll call for you at seven,' he said, blushing again. 'I've got your address.'

'Are we taking our hedgehog home or what?' Jon wanted to know.

So they took the hedgehog home.

*

Alison had laid the table for tea and was watching the news. 'Guess what,' she said. 'Geoffrey Howe's resigned. He's made a speech attacking Mrs Thatcher.'

'Our hedgehog did a poo on her face,' Jon said.

'Whose face?' Alison said.

'Mrs Thatcher's.'

'Listen a minute, sunshine,' Brad said, watching the picture on the screen. 'This could be good.'

Sir Geoffrey Howe was standing in the House of Commons, green leather seats behind him, looking mild and avuncular and saying that the Prime Minister's attitude was undermining the authority of her colleagues. 'It's rather like sending your opening batsmen to the crease only for them to find, the moment the first balls are bowled, that their bats have been broken before the game by the team captain.'

'Good God!' Brad said. 'Fancy Howe putting the boot in. Mild old Howe. Things must be bad.'

'It won't make any difference though, will it?' Alison said, heading off to the kitchen to make the tea.

'D'you wanna bet?' Brad said gleefully.

'Aunty Brad's going to Brighton with the vet,' Jon said.

Now it was Alison's turn to look gleeful. 'You're what?'

'He's asked me out.'

'I thought he was a wally.'

'Yeh! He is. But he's been so good with Mr Tiggywinkle I thought I'd give him a try.'

It turned out to be rather more than a try, because by the time they got to Brighton the following evening, the leadership of the Tory party was up for grabs and Michael Heseltine had thrown his cap into the ring. Instead of going to the cinema, they spent the evening in a restaurant talking politics and when they finally parted, Martin found the excuse to ring her up the next day 'to see how things are going'.

They went at an amazing speed. On Tuesday November 20th Mrs Thatcher lost the first ballot by four votes. On Wednesday she vowed to fight on. By Thursday she was admitting defeat.

Six days later it was all over. The Tory party had chosen a new leader and the television cameras were clustered outside Number 10 to watch the Iron Lady leaving the seat of power she'd occupied for the last eleven years.

It was a moment watched with mixed reactions.

In Port Talbot, where Morgan watched the news with his parents, two of his sisters and their husbands, Mrs Thatcher's tears were greeted with triumphant cheers.

'Serves 'er right,' Thomas Griffiths said. 'Now she knows what it's like to be driven out a' your job.'

'Won't open any a' the pits she's closed, though, will it?' his eldest son-in-law said bitterly. He'd been unemployed since his own pit was shut.

In Elsie Wareham's front room in Hampton, Alison and her mother were full of sympathy.

'Poor woman,' Elsie said. 'I don't wonder she's crying. Fancy turning on her like that, after all she's done. I don't understand it, and that's a fact. It's enough to make anyone cry.'

'That's politics, Mum,' Mark explained. 'They thought she'd cost them the next election, so she had to go.'

Elsie snorted. 'They're off their heads,' she said. 'She'd have won them the next election, the same as she won the last three.'

In Brad's cluttered room in her flat over the dress shop, she and Martin Smith watched the news as they ate a take-away.

'I never thought they'd actually give her the boot,' Brad said. 'Not when it come down to it. Look at her face, rotten old bat.'

'They've been very, very clever,' Martin said.

'How d'you make that out?'

'There's an election coming, this time next year, or the spring after, right?'

'Right.'

'And all the signs are pointing to the fact that people want a change. There's too much unemployment, there's beggars in the streets, there's people living in cardboard city, there's riots, the system isn't working.'

'So?'

'So they've given us a change. They've done it for us. We've got a new government now, a new Prime Minister, Mr Nice Guy, and they've given him a year or more to dig himself in and show how compassionate he is and make everyone like him. It's very clever. When the election comes they'll vote for the change they've already got instead of going for the change they really need.'

'That's not clever,' Brad said. 'That's Machiavellian.'

'Well, I could be wrong,' Martin said, shrugging his shoulders.

But it sounded much too plausible to Brad and just the sort of trick the Tories were capable of pulling. 'They're a crafty lot of buggers,' she said, opening another can of lager. 'Do you think people'll fall for it?'

'The selfish ones will,' Martin said, opening his second can as well. 'The cult of the individual is all very well but there's a danger in it. It glorifies selfishness, you see. Look after number one. Never mind other people. Me, me, me all the time. Anything's permissible providing the end result is a profit. You can lie, cheat, steal, bully, it's all permissible. Me, me, me, you see.'

'That's the Great-I-Am you're describing.'

'Who?'

'The Great-I-Am. He's always on the make. Me, me, me all the time. You've got him to a T.'

'Who is he?'

'He's married to my friend Alison, poor cow. He's the father of the hedgehog kids.'

'Right.'

'Not that he's ever paid any attention to 'em, poor little devils. I don't even think he pays their keep. Ali doesn't say, but it wouldn't surprise me. She's always strapped for cash. He spends money like water. Well he would, wouldn't he? Swans about in a brand-new BMW while she pushes a second-hand buggy round town, wears Armani suits while the kids get kitted out at car-boot sales, never comes home, holidays in Spain – on his own. He's a bloody monster.'

'I gather you don't like him.'

'No. I don't. I can't stand selfish men. An' that man is selfish to the core. There's a rumour going round he's in some sort of trouble. Money a' course. If I were Ali, I'd be worried sick.'

'If you were Ali you wouldn't have married him.'

'Bloody right I wouldn't. I knew he was a wrong-un from the word go.'

'You're very shrewd,' he said admiringly.

'You're pretty sharp yourself.'

He smiled at her, not sure whether he could kiss her yet or not. 'Is that an invitation?'

'What for?' she said, knowing perfectly well and teasing him with her eyes.

He threw another hopeful glance towards the bedroom.

If he could be as dominant in bed as he is about politics, he'd be a winner, Brad thought. But there you are, you can't have everything.

Chapter Twelve

'Gone?' Alison said. 'Gone where?'

'I don't know Mrs Toan,' Norrie said. 'I only work here.'

There was a truculent note in the girl's voice that alerted Alison to more trouble. 'Hasn't he paid you?' she asked. 'Is that it?'

'Not since Friday fortnight,' Norrie said. 'That's why I wrote to you.'

'You mean he's been gone a fortnight?'

'Three weeks more like,' Norrie said. 'Well, he hasn't been in the flat for three weeks. I thought you knew.'

The two women stood on either side of the counter in *Rings and Things* and regarded one another.

So he's not been living with her, Norrie thought. They *have* split up. Kevin was right. She hasn't got a clue what's going on. Shall I tell her about the bills now or leave it till later?

Thank goodness Emma's asleep, Alison thought. She glanced down at the little girl, lying peacefully in her buggy wrapped in a rug. Now that she was nearly two and a half, she rarely slept during the day, but the bus ride to Chichester and the warmth of her rug had lulled her into a snooze. She pulled her thoughts back to the problem. Poor Norrie does look miserable. And no wonder if she hasn't been paid. What can I say to put things right?

'I expect he's seeing to the property in Spain,' she said at last, and then, trying to make light of it, 'It's always the same. He goes out there in a rush and he never bothers to tell anyone. There's always something to see to, that's the trouble. That place would fall apart if he wasn't for ever out there trouble-shooting.'

Norrie examined her fingernails, making it clear that she wasn't amused.

'Did he take the car?' Alison asked. (If he's left the car behind, he'll have gone to Spain.)

'Don't ask me. Could ha' done. How would I know?'

'Is it in the yard?'

'He don't keep it in the *yard*,' Norrie said scathingly. 'Not since he took to living at the flat. You won't find it in the *yard*. If it's anywhere it'll be in the garage.'

Garage? Alison thought. I didn't know he'd got a garage. But she didn't let Norrie see her surprise. 'If you'll show me where this garage is,' she said, 'I'll have a look and see if it's there.'

'It's locked,' Norrie said. 'He keeps everything locked.'

For the second time Alison was deflated. 'Do you know who he hires it from?' she asked, doing her best to be patient.

'The farriers, I think. Mr Kauffman.'

'Well there you are then. He'll have a key.'

Norrie wasn't interested in the car or the key. 'What about my wages?' she said.

'They'll have to come out of the till, I expect. Is that how he usually does it?'

'If they could ha' come out the till,' Norrie said wearily, 'I'd ha' done it myself like I did last time when he went to London. There in't enough in the till to cover one week's wages, leave alone three. It might be Christmas, but trade's terrible.'

'Well it'll have to come out of the bank then.'

'I only got paying-in slips. I can't take money out. That's why I wrote to you.'

'Leave it to me,' Alison said. 'I'll sort it out for you.'

'I wouldn't mind,' Norrie said, 'only I got me rent to pay Friday. And with Christmas coming up an' everything. You need a lot a' money this time a' year.'

Don't I know it, Alison thought. She'd been struggling for weeks to put enough aside to buy presents for the kids, hoping against hope that Rigg would put in an appearance and offer to go halves, as he sometimes did.

'I'll see about the car first,' she said. 'And then I'll deal with the wages.' If the worst came to the worst, she reckoned she could raid the till in the video shop. Just this once. It would make a muddle, but she could hardly leave Rigg's employees unpaid. That wasn't proper or fair.

She retrieved the key from Mr Kauffman and unlocked the garage. And the car *was* there, just as she'd suspected, beautifully polished and covered with a sheet, like a boat laid up for the winter. So he *was* in Spain. But why hadn't he told her he was going?

'I'll post your wages to you this afternoon,' she

promised Norrie. 'It'll be the first thing I do when I get home. I'm sorry you've had all this trouble.'

She was being so kind that Norrie felt rotten about having to give her more bad news. But it had to be done. She couldn't just ignore all those bills. Sooner or later someone would want to know why she hadn't handed them on.

'These come for Mr Toan,' she said, fishing out the bundle from the shelf under the counter. 'I been hanging on to 'em till he come back. But if he's in Spain, you'd better have 'em, I suppose.'

Alison took the letters and stuffed them into her shopping bag. A quick glance revealed that the majority of them were bills and she knew she couldn't pay them – but she couldn't leave them with Norrie either.

'Time to go home,' she said to her sleepy daughter, and eased the buggy out of the shop.

For the last few days she'd been thinking hard about the voluntary arrangement, wondering whether it was going to work and how Rigg was getting on and if he'd earned enough money to pay the Inland Revenue. It was more than eight weeks since the meeting and she hadn't heard a word about it. Nothing from Rigg, nor from anybody else. Just Norrie's postcard that morning. And now he'd shot off to Spain without telling anybody.

Of course he'd obviously gone there to sell the flat, if he could. But, as she knew very well, pulling off a sale in the middle of a recession was terribly difficult, particularly if it was a house sale. Now, and a bit late, she wished she'd paid more attention to what had been said at that meeting. There'd been some talk about conditions being imposed by the Inland Revenue, and if he was going to be out of the country she really ought to know what they were. She ought to visit the bank too, if she was going to be responsible for paying Norrie and the stream of boys and girls who staffed the video shop. And that was another thing, if Rigg had been in Spain for the last three weeks who'd been paying *them*?

Ah well, she thought, as the Hampton bus turned into the bus station, with a flurry of rain patterning its green sides, first things first. As soon as I've given Emma some lunch I'll go down to the video shop and sort out Norrie's wages. Then I'll write to Rigg, and then I'll see what else I ought to do.

The video shop was being manned that morning by one of the young men she'd seen there before. He had lank hair and pimples, and was wearing two holey jerseys, one more or less on top of the other. He put down the book he was reading and opened the till.

'There's some letters come for Mr Toan,' he said, when she'd taken out the cash she needed and written an IOU to put into the till. 'Is he coming in?'

'I'll see to them,' she said, holding out her hand. When he hesitated, she added. 'It's all right, I'm his business partner.'

'I wish I'd known that yesterday,' the boy said. 'There was a bloke in here asking for Mr Toan, wanted to know if there was a partner.'

Alison felt her heart sink. 'What sort of bloke?' she asked.

'Official-looking. In a suit.'

'I see,' Alison said, picturing the man with foreboding. 'If he comes in again, send him on to Shore

Street, will you? Ask him to make it after five o'clock, if he wouldn't mind, and then I shall be back from work. Now tell me, who's been paying your wages?'

'We take it out the till,' the boy said. 'Mr Toan knows.'

That's not very satisfactory, Alison thought. All those hands in the till.

'Who banks the takings?' she asked.

'Whoever's here on Friday and Saturday.'

'Right,' she said. 'I'll come in and do it from now on. Then I can pay you all at the same time. Will you tell the others?'

Outside the shop, the sky was bruised with storm clouds and the sea was leaden grey, with a strong tide rolling west towards Selsey Bill. The beach was deserted and strewn with flotsam, long strands of black weed, plastic bottles, rusty cans. Gulls wheeled and screamed above the shingle, their plumage bedraggled by the rain. The beach huts had been taken down for the winter and the two remaining kiosks were dark with damp, their bright summer paintwork peeled to the boards and their shutters creaking in the wind. This seascape gave no comfort to her at all.

And there were still the letters to attend to. That evening when the kids were asleep she took them out of her bag and read them one after the other, with a steadily sinking heart. They were all bills and most of them were second demands. She couldn't understand why they'd been sent. Surely the whole point of the voluntary arrangement was that it was supposed to put a stop to bills being sent until Rigg could afford to pay them? There must be a mistake somewhere.

She rubbed her eyes and looked through the letters again. Then she noticed that there were two final demands from Customs and Excise for payment of VAT which did not make sense either because they were for different amounts. So there was a mistake there too. Had to be. But the next letter she looked at was the worst of the lot. It was a summons to attend court for non-payment of a VAT bill for £3,669. And the date of the hearing was long past.

She made a pile of the bills on the table in front of her, as if neatness would help her solve the problem. The shock of seeing so much money owing to so many people had blocked her ability to think. She wanted to phone Mum or Mark and ask them for advice. If it had been anything other than the shop she would have done. But she couldn't tell them about Rigg's business affairs. Those were *her* worry. Nobody else's. It would be disloyal to talk to anyone else about them. The only person she had the right to call was Rigg and since there wasn't a phone in the flat, she couldn't do that either. But she could write to him. In fact, she *had* to write to him to tell him about the VAT summons. She couldn't ignore *that*.

The next day was a working day, but she spent her coffee break writing the letter and mailed it on her way back to the office. Then it was simply a matter of waiting for Rigg's reply.

He didn't phone and there wasn't a letter. She gave him three days' grace, because the letter might have gone astray or he might have gone to Madrid or somewhere else and missed the post. Then she wrote again. And just to be on the safe side, she sent a third letter the following day, with a postscript begging him, *please* phone.

But the only phone calls she received were from her mother to say she'd got a lovely little coat for Emma's Christmas present and how about coming round and helping her put up the decorations that afternoon? And from Morgan asking her whether she'd like him to book seats for the kids to see a pantomime in the New Year.

Unable to concentrate on anything except those awful bills, she was distant with both of them. Worry filled her days with tension and kept her awake at night. Something had got to be done. But what? What?

Eventually, on her next day off, she phoned the Ship Hotel at Brighton and asked them if they knew where Harvey Shearing could be found. They gave her an address in Ashenridge and the fax and phone numbers to go with it.

Feeling guilty to be making a fuss, she dialled the number, and, rather to her surprise, got through to Mr Shearing at once. She explained the situation as calmly as she could.

'Yes,' he said, 'I should think you're right. He probably is in Spain, selling the flat. So what's the problem?'

'I've written to him three times, but he hasn't answered.'

'That *is* a little odd,' his voice soothed. 'However you don't need to worry about the bills. Either keep them until your husband comes home or post them to me.'

Alison swallowed with relief. 'All of them?' she asked.

'Well not the ones appertaining to the video shop, naturally. As I understand it, that's a limited liability company and outside the terms of the voluntary agreement.'

'Oh,' she said. I find a hope and it's dashed straight away.

'Mr Toan had a partner, I believe,' Mr Shearing went on.

'Yes.'

'Then that's the person who should deal with it, according to the law.'

The word 'law' was beginning to sound like a threat.

'I'm afraid *I'm* the partner,' she said weakly.

His answer was cool. 'Mr Toan did tell me something to that effect.'

'Look Mr Shearing,' she said. 'I don't know where to begin in all this. There's a terrible VAT bill outstanding and I haven't got any money to pay it. If Rigg made a profit on the sale of *Baubles*, couldn't I have a sort of loan on that for the video shop?'

'That's outside my brief I'm afraid. I couldn't authorise payment from profits on Mr Toan's jewellery store, even if there were any, which I'm sorry to say is not the case.'

'Not the case?'

'No. He's been running at a loss for several months. The kitty is empty.'

'You mean there's nothing in his bank account?'

'A few pounds. No more.'

'What about the money he got when he sold *Baubles*?'

'*Baubles* hasn't been sold, Mrs Toan, as far as I'm aware. The owners can't find any takers.'

That was a surprise. 'What owners?'

'Solicitors in Worthing, I believe.'

Alison had half expected to be told that the sale had made very little but not that the shop didn't belong to Rigg after all. He'd always spoken so grandly about 'my three outlets'. And she'd always believed he owned them.

'I thought Rigg was the owner,' she said. The trapped feeling was getting worse.

'Oh no, no, no. Rigg only leased the place and he was behind with the rent, as I understand it. Very few small businesses actually own their own premises, you know. All three of your husband's were leased.'

Disappointment turned into shock. 'Oh dear,' she whispered, as energy drained away from her.

'I'm sorry,' Mr Shearing said.

'Yes, well. I suppose *I* shall have to deal with the VAT bill then.'

'I'm afraid so, Mrs Toan.'

I shall have to sell the car, she thought. There's nothing else I *can* do. He'll be terribly angry, because he loves that car so much, but I've got no choice. There's nothing else I *can* do.

But, as it turned out, even that wasn't possible.

Alison waited until Monday in case there was a reply to her last letter, without much hope because if Rigg hadn't answered by now it had to be because he wasn't in the flat. It was cold and dark by day, the evenings were fraught with anxiety, and tension was making her careless. She burnt her fingers taking the supper out of the oven, forgot she'd left a sharp knife at the bottom of the washing-up bowl and gashed her thumb and, finally, as she carried the ironing upstairs late on Sunday evening, she knocked her most precious ornament off the shelf with the corner of the pile and smashed it beyond repair.

Tomorrow, she promised herself, tomorrow I'll ring the nearest BMW dealer and see what he'll offer me. I can't go on like this.

But the next morning there was a letter from a finance company which put paid to her hopes completely. It regretted to inform Mr Toan that, due to non-payment of more than £5,000, the hire agreement between themselves and Mr Toan was now no longer valid and that unless he sent any monies owing within the next three days, they would have no alternative but to repossess the BMW he'd rented from them.

Alison was forced to read the letter twice before she could take it in. She had just poured milk on to her cornflakes but her throat was so swollen with rage and disappointment that she couldn't eat. Fortunately Jon and Emma were busy demolishing their toast and marmite and paying very little attention to what she was doing.

The letter trembled in her hand. It can't be true, she thought. It just can't. All through this awful business she'd kept herself going with the knowledge that, if the worst came to the worst, Rigg would be able to raise money on the car. He'd said it himself, over and over again, to her, to the solicitor. *'I can always sell the car.'* And all the time he'd been deliberately lying to her. Deliberately lying. She was shaking with anger at his cruelty. Because it *was* cruel. He'd led her on, allowed her to think she had money to fall back on and then run off and left her to find out it was all lies. How could he have done such a thing? He'd cut the last piece of solid ground from under her feet. It was hideous. Despicable.

But she had to face facts. There was no money at all, not from the sale of the shop, not in the bank account, not from the car. Rigg didn't own *anything*. He'd *never* owned anything and he owed the VAT man all that money and there was no way he could raise it. No way *she* could raise it. What on earth was she going to do?

That afternoon, while Jon was at school and Emma was playing an involved game with her dolls, she phoned the number listed on the larger VAT demand and asked to speak to the officer who had signed it.

He was patient but adamant.

'No,' he said. 'There's no mistake. The first demand is covered by the voluntary arrangement and refers to your husband's jewellery shops. That will be paid in full from the sale of a property in Spain. The other is the VAT outstanding on Hampton Videos.'

Oh God, Alison thought. No wonder the figures didn't balance. They're two different bills. 'But we've only been opened for six months,' she said.

'Two quarters,' the man told her, 'and neither of them paid and, as I need hardly point out, with considerable debts outstanding on both Mr Toan's other businesses.'

There was no arguing with that. 'How much do we owe on the video shop?' she asked.

'£3,669.'

'My husband's in Spain,' she started to explain.

'So you tell me,' he said. 'However, that doesn't concern us unduly. His business partner is liable.'

'That's me,' she said, her heart sinking. 'In other words, *I've* got to pay this bill.'

'I'm afraid so, as your husband isn't here to pay it and you can't contact him. That is the law.'

'But I haven't got any money. I'm on family credit.'

'You've got stock,' he said implacably. 'If you can't pay the bill, we are entitled to constrain the stock.'

The severity in his voice was making her belly shake. 'What does that mean?' she asked, her voice husky with fear.

'It means we send a bailiff to your shop and take possession of everything in it which we then sell at whatever price we can command, and use the proceeds to pay off your debt and any interest you may have run up and the bailiff's fees and so forth.'

She was horrified at the brutality of the process. 'You *can't* do that,' she said.

'We not only can, Mrs Toan, we often do. We live in bad times. Your husband isn't the only one to refuse to pay his bills.'

She was too busy to argue about Rigg's intentions. 'How long have I got?' she asked.

'Hold the line just a minute and I'll check.'

She held the line, and her breath, for what seemed more like ten minutes than one.

Then he spoke again. 'It went to court six weeks ago, as I expect you know. Your husband didn't attend the court. We kept him notified. You have till Monday next week. That's Christmas Eve. If you can get the money to the office by first post Christmas Eve no further action will be taken.'

She thanked him, as the condemned man thanks the executioner, so stunned by the shocks she'd sustained in the last terrible days that she was beyond tears. She was almost beyond reaction. Only her mind was working, quietly and with surprising calm, almost as though it didn't belong to her.

If they can sell the stock, so can I, she thought. I'd get a better price for it and if it's going anyway what's to stop me? I'll hawk it round all the local video shops and see what I'm bid. It's the latest stuff. It ought to sell. Rigg would be furious but she couldn't stop to think about that.

There was nothing in her mind except a dreadful panic to pay the VAT man. Her Christmas preparations were forgotten, the kids' presents unwrapped, no cards sent, the cake bereft of icing. She was short-tempered and clumsy, doing everything too quickly, making mistakes, shouting at the kids and, all the time, thinking and scheming – her thoughts raced – I'll try the shop in the High Street tonight, and if that fails, the one in Derby Road, and if that's no good, the one at the other end of the prom. I've got five evenings and I've got to do it. It'll mean running up an awful phone bill, but I've just got to.

Even when Norrie phoned to say that there were some men from a finance company come to take the car, she simply told her to get the key from the farriers and let it go. It meant nothing to her now. It was only another debt. It wasn't worth money.

But it wasn't until Friday evening that she finally persuaded a local shopkeeper to take the videos, and then at such a reduced price that there was only just enough to cover the VAT bill and pay for all the phone calls she'd made. He and his partner came down with a van later that evening and cleared the shop, videos, posters, sweet-dispensing machine and all.

'I'll come back on Monday morning and pick up the returns,' he said, as he gave her his cheque. And that was that.

Now there was only the till left in the shop. Alison emptied it of the few notes and coins it contained, remembering Rigg's excitement when she'd first visited the place. It had been full of paint pots and lengths of wood then. And promise. Now she'd closed it down and put all those young assistants out of work and ended Rigg's dream. She felt racked by guilt, aching with it. But what else could she have done?

She looked round at the marked walls, the dusty corners, the pile of dog-ends in the corner, the evidence of failure. If there'd been a broom she would have set to and cleaned it up, but as there wasn't she walked home to Shore Street to relieve Brad who was baby-sitting for her. It had been a long, exhausting day.

Brad was sitting by the fire, smoking and reading a magazine.

'They been ever so good,' she said. 'How d'you get on?'

'I got the money,' Alison said wearily.

'Knew you would,' Brad said. 'So that's all right then. You can come to me party.'

Alison wasn't sure she'd have the energy for a party. 'When?'

'New Year's Eve. Me an' Martin at my place. I

didn't like to tell you before with all this goin' on. Your Mum'ud look after the kids, wouldn't she?'

'Well . . .'

'Go on,' Brad urged. 'Be a devil. Do you good.'

'What if Rigg comes home for Christmas?'

Brad had serious doubts as to the likelihood of that but she didn't voice them. 'Bring him along an' all,' she said.

But there was no sign of Rigg, apart from a card that arrived on Christmas Eve. It was posted in Madrid and the message on it was traditional, wishing his 'darling wife' a happy holiday and saying how much he loved her. He didn't tell her where he was, or whether he'd received her letters or when he was coming home.

Chapter Thirteen

It was late on New Year's morning, and Alison was gradually recovering from Brad's party. She was fragile with hangover and keeping as still and quiet as she could. She and the kids had just got home from her mother's house and were sitting on the floor in front of the gas fire, playing with one of Jon's Christmas presents, a game for two players called *Downfall*. The room was so peaceful that when the phone shrilled, it made them jump.

Rigg! Alison thought. It had to be Rigg. At last! He hasn't forgotten us. He's ringing to wish us happy New Year. Despite his lies and all the trouble he'd made for her, he was still her husband.

'That'll be your Daddy,' she said to the kids as she scrambled to her feet.

But it wasn't. It was Norrie.

'I'm ever so sorry to bother you Mrs Toan,' she said, 'but do you want me to open the shop today?

In the relief of getting that awful bill paid, Alison had forgotten about *Rings and Things*. Now she realised that with the video shop and its earnings gone, the jewellery store would have to pay its own way.

'Is there any point in opening?' she asked. And then, feeling she'd been rather blunt, 'What I mean to say is what are sales like in January?'

'Non-existent,' Norrie said. 'It's only birthdays an' things really from now till Easter. Mr Toan usually shuts down for a fortnight after Christmas.'

'We might have to shut down for good,' Alison warned. It was only fair to tell Norrie the truth as her job was at stake.

She was relieved when the girl took it calmly. 'Don't surprise me,' she said. 'The video shop's shut int it? Kevin came in yesterday. He told me.'

'I had to sell the stock to pay the VAT bill.'

Norrie took that calmly too. 'Thought it was somethin' like that,' she said. 'So now what?'

'Meet me at the shop tomorrow morning about eleven,' Alison told her. 'And we'll see. Bring the keys and your paying-in slips. I shall have to go and see the bank.'

This time it was easier to take command. It was simply a job that had to be done and she was the only one to do it. This time she was prepared for bad news – which, inevitably, came.

At the TSB the bank manager was polite and troubled. He was sorry to have to tell her that there was no spare capital in Mr Toan's account. The reverse in fact. Despite reminders, Mr Toan had been seriously overdrawn since the middle of November. The Christmas takings had hardly made a dent into what was owing. Was he to understand that Mr Toan was no longer in the country?

'He's in Spain,' Alison said.

'Could you contact him?'

'Not just at the moment,' she had to admit. 'But Mr Shearing – his insolvency consultant, you know – *he*'d be able to tell you what's happening. I expect you've got his address, haven't you?'

'We have,' the bank manager said, but his tone was lugubrious.

The more I delve into this, Alison reflected, the more of a muddle it is. But at least she wasn't being threatened. Mr Shearing could see to the overdraft at this bank and take over responsibility for the other VAT bill. That was what he'd been hired for. All she had to do was to give Norrie a week's wages – the spare cash left over at the video shop would cover that – and then simply close the shop down. It was upsetting to have to shut yet another shop, but also a relief to have it all over and done with.

'What shall we do with the stock?' Norrie asked when she'd been given her last week's wages. 'We can't leave it here, can we? Someone'ud nick it.'

'We'll pack it all up into boxes and I'll get my brother to come over in his car and ferry it back to my house.' It can go under the bed for the time being, she thought. Then it'll be there for Rigg when he comes home and I can tell him everything isn't lost. I owe him that at least, despite his lies.

Alison and Norrie worked together for the rest of the morning, while the two children played among the wrapping paper. They packed all the rings and bracelets into boxes, wrapped up the charms and necklaces, and stacked the display trays one on top of the other, until everything was piled neatly in the storeroom and the shop was cleared of all its merchandise. All that remained for Alison to do was to return the keys to the landlord when the goods had been taken away.

Now, she said to herself as she and the kids caught the bus back to Hampton, we can get back to normal and start living our lives again.

'Theatre tomorrow, kids,' she reminded them all.
'With Morgan?' Jon wanted to know.
'With Morgan.'
'Wicked!'
Something to look forward to, Alison thought. Something light-hearted and entertaining. It's just what we need. Thank God for Morgan. He's been a real friend to us.

But next afternoon when she came home from work, Alison found a letter from the building society waiting on the mat for her. It was so terrifying it put her into a state of shock for the next twenty four hours.

Addressed to Mr and Mrs Rigby Toan, it advised that their mortgage repayments were now six months overdue, the total debt on the three mortgages they had taken out on the property now amounted to over £3,000 and that, unless repayment was received within the next three weeks after receipt of the letter, legal action would be taken to repossess the house.

Dear God, she thought, as she began to shake. Repossessed. Her mind filled with visions of the homeless – out on the street, begging, huddled to sleep in doorways, shivering in cardboard city. Homeless.

She wanted to scream that they couldn't do it; they mustn't do it; it wasn't fair. But if she screamed, she would frighten the kids and that wouldn't be fair either. In any case, she could scream all she liked but it wouldn't stop them repossessing the house. They *could* do it and they would. If she'd learned nothing else in the last few weeks, she had learned that. They could and they would.

She put the letter down on the table because her hands were shaking so much they were making the paper rustle and she was afraid Jon would notice. She wanted to rush out of the house and find Rigg and make him come back and pay this awful debt and sort it all out. She was full of terrible fury that he'd let this go on and not told her. Why hadn't he paid the mortgage? He'd promised he would and he must have known he was putting the house at risk. This was even worse than all the lies he'd told.

'I washed my hands,' Jon announced at her elbow. 'I's ready.'

Ready for what? she thought stupidly. Then she remembered the theatre trip. Morgan would be here at any minute. Oh God! A theatre trip! At a time like this.

But she couldn't disappoint them, poor kids. She had to go – didn't she – no matter what she might be feeling.

'Come on, Emma,' she said, trying to be cheerful. 'Let's go and have our wash too. We've got to be ready when Morgan comes.'

Worry weighed her down and made her shoulders ache and tightened the skin on her skull. She wanted to run away and hide, not face the world and his wife in a crowded theatre. Make-up, she thought, as she and Emma went upstairs to the bathroom. That's what I need. If I can't hide at least I can wear a disguise. Make-up and perfume. Where was that bottle of French stuff Rigg had given her?

It was stronger than she expected but she used it lavishly. As she drifted down the stairs in a cloud of scented air to answer Morgan's knock at the door, she kept on thinking; Dear God, what am I going to do? What *am* I going to do?

Morgan had dressed with particular care that afternoon too and he'd made a point of driving to Hampton in his own car. It was a two-year-old Sierra and not as flashy as the company cars but it was clean and spruce for the occasion, and he wanted to be honest about everything that day, even the sort of car he drove. Not telling Alison that he knew about Rigg's business affairs was beginning to prey on his mind. This afternoon he would find a moment to tell her.

He'd come well prepared for this outing with dolly mixtures for Emma and Smarties for Jon, and enough cash to take them all out for supper afterwards. It was going to be an occasion.

He was so happy to see Alison again that, at first, he didn't notice any difference in her, but when they were on their way to the Worthing Road he became aware that she was wearing a lot of make-up which made her look hard, and perfume which was much too strong. It was rather off-putting to be sitting beside her and smelling someone else but he told himself that this was her way of marking a special occasion and that he ought to be glad of it.

They drove along the promenade at Worthing where Christmas lights swung in their multicoloured glory, and turned in among the shops where the windows were hung with tinsel. There was a Christmas tree ablaze with light on the steps of the town hall, and a tangible sense of bustle and pleasure at the theatre; parents beaming and pleased with themselves, grandmas bulky and benevolent, and hordes of children in their best clothes and a high state of excitement. Alison seemed preoccupied but the children were thrilled by everything they saw.

Morgan and the children enjoyed every moment of the pantomime and ate ice-creams in the interval and a hearty supper when the show was over. But Alison was so subdued there were moments when Morgan felt she wasn't with them at all – even though he could smell that damned perfume everywhere they went. She clapped in all the right places but he noticed that she didn't laugh. She praised the food but ate hardly any of it. She didn't mention her husband, in fact she didn't talk about anyone or anything, and, at the end of the evening, when they drew up in Shore Street, she didn't invite him in. It was all slightly unnatural.

'I got a job in Manchester tomorrow,' he said, as she was easing the key into her front door.

'Oh yes,' she said vaguely, busy with her thoughts.

'I shall be away for several days, like.'

'Oh.'

'I'll write to you when I get back, shall I?' Morgan said, feeling he was talking to a stranger. Why is she behaving like this? Is she cross with me for some reason? She didn't seem cross, just distant and preoccupied.

'What?' she said as the door opened. 'Oh yes. Yes. You write.'

She's not the slightest bit interested in me, he thought sadly, opening the car door. She's got her own life and there's something going on in it and I'm not part of it. Why should I be? She's a married woman. I got no business chasing after a married woman, even if she never says a single word about her husband. I simply got no business.

But then she looked across at him in the light of the single street lamp in the alley and smiled straight into his eyes.

'Thank you for a lovely evening,' she said with more warmth in her voice.

Hope and desire leapt up in him at once. 'Did you enjoy it?'

'Yes,' she said. 'Very much.' But she had looked away from him and the vague tone had returned.

Hope so quickly dashed made Morgan's disappointment more acute. I'm wasting my time, he thought, slipping the car into gear. The failure of the evening sat like a weight on his shoulders. She was odd at that tea party and I ignored it. Perhaps I shouldn't have. I can't ignore the way she's acting now. It's a bit too obvious. I got to face facts. She's not interested in me. She's got other things on her mind and I'm wasting my time.

'Take care of yourself,' he said, as he put in the clutch.

She switched on the living room light and prodded Jon and Emma into the house. 'I'll do my best,' she said sadly. But oh! how difficult it was going to be.

Later that night, when the children were settled, Alison sat down in her empty living room and wrote two careful letters. The first was to the building society explaining that Rigg was in Spain and promising to do what she could to pay off part of the debt, 'as soon as I can'. The second was to Rigg, telling him what had happened and imploring him to write or to phone.

'Have you put the money for the mortgage aside somewhere?' she asked. 'If you could tell me where it is, or send a cheque to the building society, I'm sure they would call off the court case. Please do something quickly. We've only got until the beginning of February and that isn't long.'

After she finally got to bed she lay awake for hours. Her mind went round and round like a mouse on a treadmill, covering the same useless ground over and over again. If Rigg didn't write and she couldn't find out where he was, she would have to find the money or be repossessed. Where could she find £3,000? The bank wouldn't give it to her because she'd got no collateral except the home.

She toyed with the idea of asking her mother to lend her the rest of her famous nest-egg and knew she couldn't do it. That money was her mother's insurance and she'd already spent far too much of it on their wedding. What Dad would have said about *that* if he'd known didn't bear thinking about. He'd scrimped and saved for years to leave her 'comfortable in her old age'. Ali could remember him saying: 'She's a good woman, your Mum, she deserves to be comfortable.' No, the nest-egg was inviolable. It belonged to Mum. Whatever happened she couldn't ask to borrow that.

But what else could she do? She'd got nothing to sell, no valuable paintings or furs or expensive jewellery. Rigg's jewellery was cheap and cheerful and wouldn't raise much money even if she could find someone willing to buy it, which was unlikely given the state of the recession. Now if she'd got a string of pearls like his mother, she could sell *them*. They'd raise a lot of money. But then Maggie Toan had always had plenty of money. She was rolling in it. Mink stole, real pearls, shopping at Harrods, taxis everywhere. It always exasperated Rigg to think how much money his mother had – he was always on about that will and how unfair it was.

But of course! The will. That was the answer.

Maggie Toan was none too pleased to see Alison and the children when they arrived on her doorstep. She had already drunk three gins and tonic that morning and was feeling decidedly woozy.

'Ah yes,' she said, when she'd allowed them into her elegant parlour. 'Happy New Year to you too, I suppose. If such a thing is possible. Which I very much doubt with all this dreadful business going on in the Gulf. You won't let the baby touch my china, will you?'

'No, no,' Alison said hastily. 'They won't touch anything, will you, kids?'

In fact, they were both too awed to do anything in such an overpowering place, except lean against their mother's knees and suck their thumbs.

Now that they were in her mother-in-law's house, Alison couldn't think how to start the conversation. 'You don't happen to know where Rigg is, do you?' she said at last.

'He sent me a lovely card,' Maggie said. 'From Madrid.'

'But nothing else?'

Margaret Toan parried that because it sounded like criticism. 'I expect he's busy, don't you?' she said.

'Yes. I'm sure he is,' Alison replied, wishing her mother-in-law wasn't always so distant with her.

'Well then. You won't lop against that coffee table, will you Emma?'

Alison took the little girl on to her lap. She looked at the love birds in their ornate cage, the Dalton china in its display cabinet, the crystal wine glass in her mother-in-law's hand. 'The thing is,' she began, 'he hasn't paid the mortgage for six months and if he doesn't pay it soon, the house will be repossessed.'

Margaret Toan gave her little tinkling laugh to show how absurd her daughter-in-law was being. 'How ridiculous!' she said. 'They wouldn't do a thing like that. Not to my Rigby.'

'They would,' Alison said. 'If the money isn't paid, they'll repossess the house and we shall be homeless – out on the streets.'

'Nonsense!' Margaret rebuked her. 'You mustn't say such things. It isn't nice to tell lies.'

'I'm not telling lies. It's true.'

'You're telling lies,' Margaret said, as firmly as her fourth G and T would allow. 'You're telling lies and you're being hysterical. Kindly stop.'

'Look, I know you don't want me to tell you this . . .'

'I don't. Quite right.'

'I know. But I've got to. If I don't, these children will be homeless. Your grandchildren.'

'Oh stop, stop, for heaven's sake,' Margaret implored. '*I* can't do anything about it.'

'You could,' Alison said, her voice all entreaty. 'That's why we've come here. You could.'

'My dear, the only way anyone could help you would be to pay your mortgage for you. I hope you're not suggesting that I should do that.'

'Well not you exactly,' Alison said. 'I thought perhaps you might let Rigg have part of his money, in advance.'

Her mother-in-law's painted eyebrows rose into her platinum hair. 'What money?' she asked.

'The money from his father's will.'

'That,' Margaret said as sternly as she could in her drunken state, 'is nothing to do with you. That is a private matter between Rigby's father and myself.'

'But it's Rigg's inheritance.'

How irritating she is, Margaret thought. Some people have no discretion. She tried to dismiss the subject with a flick of her ringed fingers. 'It's no good talking to me about it,' she said. 'It's all legally tied up. Nobody can touch it.'

Alison held her mother-in-law's gaze. 'But couldn't you . . .'

'No. I couldn't. It's not up to me. My husband saw to all that. Take my advice, Alison, don't even think about it. I never do.'

'If I can't pay this mortgage we shall be homeless,' Alison said, making one last despairing effort.

The bejewelled fingers flicked again. 'No, no. You won't,' Maggie said lightly. 'Stop worrying. You'll only give yourself a headache, you silly girl. It'll all work out, you'll see.'

'People are being repossessed all over the place,' Alison said.

'Yes, I know. But they're stupid people. They're not like you and Rigby. Don't worry. It won't happen.'

In the face of such unyielding complacency there was nothing Alison could do. Taut with anxiety and disappointment, she took her children by the hand and made as dignified an exit as she could. There was no one else she could turn to. Dear God, she thought, as she walked the children home, if Rigg doesn't answer my letter and come up with the money, what can I do?

In Fish Lane, crows were riding the tossing branches of the Scots pine trees. They rose into the dark air, serrated wings outspread, cawing incessantly in their harsh, cracked way, both menacing and mocking. 'Waah! Waah! You're no good! You can't! You can't!'

That night she lay awake until four in the morning. The waking nightmare wouldn't go away and there was no way out of it. Not even sleep. For when she slept she dreamed of being dragged out of the house by a gang of masked men with guns. And they were laughing at her. 'Waah! Waah! You can't. You can't.'

Even Morgan's friendly letter from Manchester, which arrived the next morning, failed to cheer her. During the last few weeks she felt as if she lost a skin. Now she was acutely aware of all the cruel things in life. The early morning news was full of pictures from the Gulf where the crisis appeared to be coming to a climax. There were now, so the newsreader claimed, 420,000 troops in the region – from thirty countries – 2,200 combat aircraft, 530 helicopters, 150 warships. The British ground forces numbered 25,000 men of the 1st armoured division, 7th and 4th armoured brigades. And there they were, churning up the desert sand in their Challenger tanks and waving at the cameras as they passed.

It's like a game, Alison thought, watching them as

she set out the breakfast things. They're playing soldiers. But if this war starts, there'll be hundreds of people killed and it won't just be soldiers, it'll be women and children. She poured milk on to Jon's cornflakes – nice, ordinary, peaceful milk – and stood holding the bottle in the room she would lose in another three weeks, in the home she couldn't even think of as hers.

The newsreader was speaking seriously. 'The United Nations deadline for Iraq to withdraw from Kuwait is on Tuesday. So Saddam Hussein has effectively four more days to make up his mind to meet the United Nations' demand.'

He's got four days and we've got three weeks, Alison thought, putting down the milk bottle. He's got four days and he can get out of it whenever he wants to, but he won't. We've got three weeks and I'd do anything to get out of it, but I can't.

Chapter Fourteen

Chichester's county court stands on an island surrounded by a three-lane traffic system at the southern end of the city. It is next door to all three stations – bus, rail and police – but isolated from the general public by the incessant traffic which roars round it. To make matters worse, there is no obvious entrance to the place, just a discreet side door which you discover only when you walk along the footpath between its two main buildings.

Alison was in such a state that it took her several minutes to find the entrance and, by that time, she was extremely worried that she was going to annoy the court officials by being late. Ever since she'd received the letter giving her the date and time of the hearing, she had been in a state of acute anxiety – about the jewellery hidden under her bed, about whether the children were getting enough to eat, about the clothes she ought to wear to the court, about leaving the children for Sally to look after. In short, about anything rather than face the enormity of being made homeless.

Once inside the court, an old-fashioned office with a long wooden counter and wooden partitions from floor to ceiling, she found that the court officials were kindly and unexpectedly sympathetic. But by then she was so tense that she couldn't respond to them.

She walked obediently up a carpeted stairway, along a glass-sided walkway between the two buildings where the sun warmed her face, and into a waiting room where there were rows of seats against all the walls and three windows giving out to the traffic and the workaday world. There were two men and four women waiting silently, their eyes averted from each other.

Presently a young man in a suit arrived and called 'Mrs Alison Toan'. He said he was from the building society and asked her if she wouldn't mind giving him a few moments before the hearing began. Alison was too numb to mind. What were a few moments here or there? They wouldn't make any difference to the outcome of the hearing.

They stood in the walkway and looked through the glass at the wintry trees swaying in the cottage gardens on the other side of the road. 'I don't suppose you've been able to get in touch with your husband, have you?' the young man asked, and his tone suggested how little hope he had of a positive reply.

'No. I'm sorry. I haven't.'

'No, well,' the young man said, 'once they've done a runner you never find them. At least that's our experience. The thing is, are you going to oppose our application?'

The question bemused her. 'What for?' she said. 'I can't pay the mortgage, so what's the use?'

'Quite right,' the young man said. 'That really is the best attitude to take in a case like this. You'll have to move out eventually. If you'll take my advice you'll agree to it now and let us have the property as soon as you can so that we can get on with the business of selling it. The longer you hold on to it, the bigger the debt will be. It's £3,500 now, you know, and we don't close the mortgage until it's sold.'

She could see the sense in what he was advising. 'It's all right,' she said. 'I'm not going to oppose it. Sell it as quickly as you can. I've faced the fact that I'm going to be homeless.'

'I wish we didn't have to do this,' the young man said. 'It's a hideous business. But the law's the law.'

That was the judge's opinion too when Alison sat meekly before him in his chambers, which turned out to be a sunny room containing two long tables, one for him and the other for her, the man from the building society and another man who was introduced to her as the court clerk. He smiled at her so sympathetically that she was afraid she was going to cry.

But it was handled so quietly and gently, it was over before she had a chance to succumb to any emotion at all. The judge explained that the building society had the right to repossess her house 'within the next fortnight, if possible, alternatively within the next three calendar months', and commended her good sense in agreeing to move out as soon as she could find other accommodation. She signed the necessary papers, shook hands with the young man from the building society, and ten minutes later was out in the February cold, facing the roar of the traffic and with no further rights to the house she'd lived in since she was married.

Lorries rumbled past. Rain clouds stained the sky over her head a darkly ominous blue-purple. I've lost everything, she thought. I put every penny I ever earned into that house. There were months when I went without to pay that awful mortgage, and what was the good of it? I decorated it and furnished it and kept it clean and what was the good of that? Damn you, Rigg. Why did you do this to us?

But there wasn't time for anger. Or tears. There was a job to do. Straightening her shoulders, she set off to catch the bus to Hampton and the Social Security Office.

The woman behind the counter there was younger than Alison, but she was quick, sympathetic and extremely practical.

It didn't take her long to work out how much the council would be prepared to pay towards rented accommodation. 'I presume you'll be putting your name down for council accommodation too?' she said.

'Am I entitled?'

'You're a deserted wife,' the woman said. 'So yes.'

And so I am, Alison thought, looking down at her hands. 'I suppose there's a long waiting list,' she said.

There was. 'About two and a half years,' the woman said. 'Are you likely to go back to full-time work when both your children are at school?'

The question restored a little of Alison's dignity and made her feel less of a dependant.

'Yes,' she said. 'With any luck.'

'That's what I thought. I'll give you some leaflets to take home and study at your leisure. And there's a list of the local letting agencies. If you'll get back to me as soon as you've found a suitable place, we can sort something out.'

Finding a suitable place was easier said than done. There were plenty of houses to let but most of them wouldn't accept children and those that would were mostly beyond her means. In the end, after a demoralising traipse round all the letting agencies in the town, her 'choice' was narrowed to three possibilities, none of them good.

She chose a semi-detached house on a bleak estate to the north of the town, one of a terrace on the south side of a patch of scrubby grass called Barnaby Green. It was more than a mile from Jon's school, nearly as far from any local shops, none too clean and decorated in such glaringly ugly colours that it made her feel nauseous to see them. But it was a house, and within her price range, and she could have it if she wanted. She signed the agreement, comforting herself that it would not be long until she could find something better. Then she went home to her own, clean, beautifully decorated, repossessed house.

There were so many things to do. She knew she ought to write to Rigg and tell him what had happened but she couldn't face it. She knew she ought to answer Morgan's letters because he kept writing to her, but she couldn't do that either. Instead she struggled through the day, dragging from chore to chore, sunk in a new, frightening fatigue that weighed her down from early, woken morning to late, lost night. Now she understood what it felt like to have a millstone round your neck.

But she did her best. She notified the gas board about the date of her move, and the electricity, the poll tax, the phone, the water board. She accepted Sally's offer of the loan of half a dozen tea chests and began the miserable business of packing up her home, folding their clothes into cardboard boxes and wrapping spare china and jugs and vases in wads of newspaper to keep them safe in the tea chests. But she was working automatically and without power, like a creature in a nightmare, as if none of it was real.

And she still had to break the news to her mother and Mark. She chose her moment as carefully as she could, waiting until the next family tea.

'I've got some news for you,' she said brightly, when the meal was over and the table cleared. 'Do you want the good news first or the bad?'

'Is it about Rigg?' her mother said, looking worried.

'In a way,' Alison said. She was brittle with false brightness. 'What do you want then, good or bad?'

'Bad first,' Elsie said, 'and get it over with.'

Alison took a breath and plunged into her prepared speech. 'Well, the bad news is we've been repossessed but the good news is that I've got another place.' She smiled at them, one after the other – Mum, Mark, Jenny, young Katy, William – knowing how false the smile was. And it didn't work. They were horrified, and their horror intensified when they heard that the mortgage hadn't been paid for six months and that Rigg hadn't told her.

'But what was he *thinking* of, Ali?' her mother asked. '*Why* didn't he pay it?'

'More to the point,' Jenny said, 'where is he now?'

'He's in Spain, trying to sell the flat.'

'You mean he's walked out on you.'

'No,' Alison said with an anguished face. 'You mustn't think that. It's not like that at all.'

'All right then,' Jenny said. 'He's done a runner and left you to pick up the pieces. I think it's disgraceful.'

'No. No. Really,' Alison implored. She was very near tears and, sensing her distress, so were Jon and Emma.

'When's your moving day, kid?' Mark asked, coming to her rescue.

'Thursday week.'

He whistled. 'They didn't give you much notice, did they!'

'I could have had longer,' she told him. 'I wanted to get it over quickly.'

He was instantly and reassuringly practical. 'Have you ordered a removal van?'

'No, not yet.'

'OK. Then you can leave all that to me. I'll get a small one from Bennett's and make several runs. That'll be cheaper. I can do the first one before I go off in the morning – we'll get it packed the night before – and we'll finish off in the evening. Do you need a hand with the packing? Katy'll help, won't you, Katy?'

'And me,' William offered.

'We'll all help,' Jenny said.

'I'll manage,' Alison said stiffly. 'I don't want to be a nuisance.'

'Don't talk cobblers,' her brother said, leaning across the arm of the chair to hug her. 'Moves are an abomination. I've not forgotten ours. You'll need all the help you can get, believe me. Now then, let's get down to brass tacks. Have you got any tea chests?'

Even though she was prepared for difficulties, moving day was one of the worst Alison could ever remember. For a start, it poured with rain, so that they trailed wetness in and out of both houses. The bed frames were so rusty it took ages to dismantle them, the living room carpet was too long to go in the van and had to be bent in half, and there were so many boxes and packing cases piled up in the living room at Shore

Street that nobody could move more than two feet without barking their shins. Then, because she'd forgotten to label any of them, nobody knew where to put the cases when they arrived at Barnaby Green, and they piled up in the living room where they were even more of a nuisance.

'See you at tea time,' Mark said when he'd helped her unpack all the bulky stuff from the first load. 'If I don't go now I shall be late. Mind how you go.'

Jenny was driving him home to collect his car. 'I'll come back and help you till twelve o'clock,' she said, 'but I'll have to get off to the office then. You do understand, don't you? I know it's only a part-time job but I don't want to lose it.'

'I'll stay with you,' Elsie said, anguished by the look on her daughter's face. 'Don't fret.'

'If we can get the kitchen sorted out,' Alison said, 'I shall be fine.' She was determined to stay cheerful, even though both the kids were grizzling and Emma would keep saying she wanted to go home.

But the kitchen was so filthy they were still scrubbing shelves when Jenny had to leave. And by then Jon had discovered the box she'd packed their playthings in and there were toys littered all over the living room.

It was a long, dirty day and at the end of it, when Jenny and Mark returned with Katy and William and the second load of furniture, the place was still a tip and Alison was grey with dirt and fatigue. True, there were curtains at the living room windows, but they didn't fit and hung very badly. True, the cooker was connected and the food was stowed away in the fridge and the newly cleaned kitchen cupboards, but none of the china was unpacked. To make matters worse it was growing dark, and when Alison tried to switch on the lights she discovered to her dismay that there were no light bulbs in any of the sockets.

'Not to worry,' Mark said. 'I'll nip down to Tesco's in a minute and get some for you. Your friend Brad's on her way over. I saw her in the chip shop. Where's your plates? She's bringing in fish an' chips.'

'An' pickled onions, an' Coke, an' death by chocolate cake,' Brad's voice said from the door. 'How's that fer service?'

She solved Alison's problems with a flick of her hands. No light bulbs? They'd plug in the table lamps. 'And what about the radio, Ali? You need a bit a' music.' No pyjamas for the kids? They'll sleep in their pants and T-shirts. 'That'll be fun!' No plates? OK. Then they'd eat their fish and chips from the paper.

'Tuck in,' she said. 'Last one to finish is a cissy.'

The meal made Alison feel better. Company and familiar food made her feel more at home. Afterwards, when the meal was eaten and the lorry unpacked, and when Mark had taken her mother, Jenny and the children home with the promise that they would all come back over the weekend, she heaped the dirty dishes in the sink. Then, leaving the kids playing in the bath, she and Brad assembled their beds and made them up.

'We'll do yours an' all, while we're at it,' Brad said, narrowing her eyes against the smoke from the cigarette stuck to her lip. 'You'll need a bed to fall into when this day's over.'

'I could fall into it now,' Alison admitted. 'I'm so tired my bones ache.'

‘Still,’ Brad comforted, shaking out Jon’s duvet, ‘you got through the worst, aintcher?’

‘Yes,’ Alison said. ‘I suppose I have. I don’t know when I’ve ever felt so down.’

‘I’ll tell you one good thing about being at the bottom,’ Brad said, grinning at her.

‘Yeh, yeh. I know. There’s only one way to go. And that’s up.’

‘Well it’s a cliché,’ Brad admitted. ‘But it’s still true.’ And she gave Alison a hug.

When Elsie Wareham got home, the phone was ringing. It was Andy wanting to know how his sister had got on.

‘She’s in,’ Elsie said. ‘It’s a terrible pickle but she’s in.’

‘Tell her I’ll be down next weekend to give her a hand. If she wants shelves putting up or anything like that, leave it for me.’

‘All right. Mark’s been helping. And Jenny. And the kids. They’ve been ever so good.’

‘So she’s all right?’

‘Oh yes. Quite cheerful really. You know our Ali. She takes things in her stride. Always did.’

Neither of them would ever know it, because they would never be told, but they were completely wrong. At that moment Alison was sitting in the litter-strewn muddle of the living room in Barnaby Green, weeping and in despair.

Chapter Fifteen

Morgan Griffiths was hiding in a wardrobe, feeling embarrassed and extremely uncomfortable. Ever since the accident in the mine, he'd suffered from mild claustrophobia, so a wardrobe was the worst place for him to be. It was nearly ten o'clock in the evening and he'd been sitting inside this one for nearly half an hour. Although the door was open, his palms were wet, his heart was pounding and it was all he could do to control the urge to escape. But he sat it out because, unpleasant though it was, it was part of his job and he had to get on with it.

He'd been hired by Mrs Percy Whitmore, the lady of the house, who was suing for divorce. She was afraid her husband was going to attack her. Morgan and the wife were both wired for sound. He also had a walkie-talkie in one pocket and a portable telephone in the other. Roger, sitting in the car outside with a spare key to the house in his pocket, was waiting for the signal to join in should the husband become too violent.

For the last twenty minutes, husband and wife had been charging about downstairs, shouting at one another. There was no doubt that the man was bad-tempered and abusive. He'd plunged into a quarrel as soon as he entered the house and his language was pretty choice, but he wasn't being physically violent. Yet.

Feet sounded on the stairs and the argument rose towards the bedroom. Angry words and accusations; she sarcastic and whining, he enraged and bellowing. Action at last. Morgan eased the wardrobe door shut and put on his headphones.

Then they were in the bedroom, crashing about within inches of the wardrobe door. Feeling easier now that he had work to do, Morgan waited.

There was the sound of a slap and the woman gave a little shriek and burst into a torrent of abuse. It went on and on, punctuated by slaps and growls and at one point blurred as though she was being shaken. Under cover of the noise, Morgan opened the door a crack to assess if it was time to intervene.

Mr Percy Whitmore was a small, swarthy man in an electric blue suit. At that moment he was chasing his wife round the bed, punching at her as he ran. She ducked out of the way as well as she could, defending her head with her arms, so that some blows went wide of the mark. But some connected. There was a bruise reddening the side of her forehead and a trickle of blood running out of her nose and her eyes were huge with fright.

'Time,' Morgan said quietly to Roger. Then he opened the wardrobe door and stepped out into the room, stretching himself to his full height and bulk as he went. 'I think that'll do, sir,' he said.

The husband was so surprised that for a few seconds he stood stock still and gaped, first at Morgan and then at his wife.

'Who the hell are you?' he said.

Morgan gave his usual answer with his usual calm. 'Alexander Jones, detective agency. Here at your wife's request, sir.'

'You little whore!' Percy Whitmore yelled. 'You've set me up! You bloody little whore! I don't *believe* this.' And with that he sprang at his wife's throat.

He was very quick, but Morgan was quicker and much more powerfully built. Within seconds he had the man spreadeagled across the bed with his arms pinned behind his back. By the time Roger made his entrance the whole thing was over.

'Let me go, for Christ's sake,' the man begged. 'I can't breathe.'

His wife had retreated to her frilly dressing table and was examining her face in the mirror. 'Now what?' she said. Her voice was surprisingly calm for someone who had so recently been battered.

'That's up to you, Ma'am,' Morgan said. 'You could call the police and have him charged with assault, if that's what you want.'

'What do you think, Percy?' she addressed her husband through the mirror. 'Should I charge you with assault? You can let him go, Mr Jones.'

'Do what you bloody want,' Percy said, when he'd been released. 'You always do. Why ask me?'

'Because you're the one who's going to be charged.'

'I shall deny it, whatever you say.'

'You can't deny bruises darling,' his wife said, touching hers with the tips of her fingers.

'I can deny how they were caused.'

'I feel I should warn you, sir,' Morgan intervened, 'we have a recording of what has happened this evening.'

'What?'

'You're on tape, darling,' his wife said sweetly. 'It's all on record. You can't deny anything.'

For a few seconds, the man's face was so suffused with rage that Morgan was afraid he would start punching his wife again. But he recovered himself, picked up two brushes from the dressing table and began to tidy his hair.

'So that's it, is it?' he said calmly. 'What do you want. A divorce?'

'I don't know yet,' she said, even more sweetly than before. 'I shall have to think about it, won't I? It depends how you behave.'

'Do we have to have these two . . . ?' Percy asked, grimacing towards Morgan and Roger, who were standing back against the wardrobe, keeping still and observing carefully.

'Not if you don't want them.'

'Well I don't.'

'In that case,' the wife said, turning towards Morgan, 'would you mind, Mr Jones . . .'

Roger's face was registering more amazement than was professional. 'Of course,' Morgan said. Propelling his colleague before him, he left the room and the house as quietly and quickly as he could.

'I shall never understand women if I live to be a hundred,' Roger said, as they drove away. 'All that screaming and shouting and she sits there as cool as cucumber saying it's up to him and will we leave. You'd have thought they were discussing the weather and here we've been waiting about in the cold for hours and hours like idiots. I don't think she'll divorce him, do you?'

'Couldn't say,' Morgan answered, concentrating on his driving.

'I think it was all an act,' Roger said. 'I think they like an audience. She was putting it on at that mirror. Her eyes were going from one to the other of us all the time.'

'Just so long as she pays the bill, boy. That's all we got to worry about.'

'It's being rich, if you ask me,' Roger said. 'They don't have anything to do all day, so they make dramas. I'll bet she's got a dishwasher an' a charlady an' a gardener an' all sorts. I'll bet she never has to do a hand's turn from one week to the next. You never really know them, do you though? Women. You think you do and then they go and do something so stupid you can't believe it. My Dad says they're a breed apart, an' if you ask me, he's right.'

Do I really know her? Morgan wondered, thinking about Alison. I feel I do when we're on the beach and the sun's shining, but she was different at that tea party and different again at the theatre. It still hurt him to remember how distant she'd been then. I really don't know her at all well, he thought. I've only ever seen her with the children. She could be a different person when she's with someone else. How would I know? I don't even know what sort of person she is when she's with that husband of hers. If she's ever with that husband of hers.

The dazzling lights of the oncoming traffic took his attention for the next few seconds. Perhaps I ought to leave well alone, he thought. Try to find someone else to get interested in. Someone less complicated. Someone who isn't married. Even if they're not so tender-hearted and they don't have such beautiful green eyes.

But Jaffa Jewels of Birmingham had other plans for him.

Early the next morning, after Morgan and Roger had come into the office, Mr Fehrenbach phoned to say that he wanted someone from Alexander Jones to fly to Spain on his behalf to find Mr Rigby Toan.

'I've been hearing some rather disquieting rumours from Chichester,' he said. 'Apparently Mr Toan has shut down all his shops and done a runner. Without paying any of his creditors, naturally. Now I've just been on the blower to that insolvency feller and he won't tell me his address. Says he thinks he's in Spain. Fuengirola. But that's all he'll give me.'

'You want us to find him,' Morgan said. 'Is that it?'

'Right,' Mr Fehrenbach said. 'There's something fishy going on. I'm sure of it. That insolvency feller says there's nothing he can do to get our money for us if Mr Toan stays out of the country. I don't believe it. I've been on to some of the other creditors and they think we ought to take action. We're prepared to club together to pay your fee and your air fares and accommodation and suchlike – nothing too costly mind. Can you do it?'

'When?'

'The sooner the better. I've made some preliminary enquiries. There are quite a few cheap flights from Gatwick these days. Because of what's going on in the Gulf, I expect.'

Morgan didn't hesitate for a second. It was just the sort of challenge he enjoyed and the irony of hunting down Alison's husband gave it an irresistible zest. 'Right,' he said, reaching for the Portsmouth Yellow Pages. 'Leave it to me.'

He spent the rest of the morning phoning estate agents in Chichester, at first with little success. Two had heard of his 'friend Rigby Toan' but neither had sold him a flat in Spain. The man who answered his eighth call, however, was more helpful.

'Yes,' he said. 'I know old Rigg. Great chap. Haven't seen him around for ages though.'

'You didn't sell him his flat in Fuengirola did you?'

'No, sorry. Wish I had. Why?'

'I'm looking for something similar.'

'In Fuengirola?'

'In the same block if poss.'

'We haven't got anything in Fuengirola at all, I'm afraid. Try "Apartments in the Sun". They specialise in Spanish properties. Ask for Nigel. He and Rigg were very thick one time. Used to go up to London together with that chap Francis.'

'Cheers.'

Nigel was out with a customer. His secretary thought he'd be back in an hour but it was mid-afternoon before he rang. He turned out to be a pushy salesman with a well-preened voice.

'I hear you want a flat like Rigg Toan's,' he said. 'A wise choice, if I may say so, sir.'

'Right.'

'That was a real snip. A beauty.'

'Yes I know. That's why I want one.'

'In the same block?'

'Right. Rigg's isn't for sale again by any chance, is it?'

'Not with this company, no sir. Did you think it might be?'

'I hoped.'

'A faint hope, if I may say so. He was well pleased with it.'

'I know. That's why I want one the same.'

'Well now, we've got a slight problem there. Only a slight problem. No hassle. Quite solvable. I've got two absolute beauties – just the sort of thing, two bedrooms, pool, maid service, sea views – only they're not exactly in the same block. Did it have to be in the same block?'

'Well as near as I can get.'

'"Arabesque" is virtually next door.'

'That might do. How far is virtually?'

'Two blocks down. In the right direction, naturally. Shall I send you the details?'

'Fax them to me.'

Mention of a fax impressed this young man. His voice changed from suave to fawning. 'A pleasure, sir. They'll be with you directly.'

Which they were. Complete with a picture of a hideous white concrete tower block set against a black sky. Now all Morgan had to do was to book the first available flight to Málaga and arrange to hire a car at the other end.

By eight o'clock the next morning he was driving along the highway to Fuengirola, under the bright winter sky of the Costa del Sol, with a local road map and Nigel's specifications in his pocket, determinedly on the trail of Mr Rigby Toan.

The promenade at Fuengirola is four miles long and lined with concrete apartment blocks from one end to the other, so it took a little while to discover the one called 'Arabesque'. But it was found at last and so were the apartments two blocks down on either side of it. Now it was simply a matter of prowling the bars and restaurants until he found the ones Rigg used. And that took less time than he expected.

The fourth bar he tried was run by a burly American who said his name was Fred and was happy to acknowledge that Rigg was 'a great buddy'.

'I'm a friend of a friend,' Morgan said. 'Francis.'

Fred appeared to know Francis too. 'A great guy!' he boomed. 'You just missed him. They were all down last week, did you know that? That was some party! Rip-roaring or do I mean rip-roaring. Great guys!'

Morgan was wondering how he could ask for Rigg's address without appearing crafty or stupid. 'I thought he'd be here by now,' he said.

'Rigg?' Fred said, as if the idea surprised him. 'Naw! Not till midday. Never gets up till midday.'

'It's midday now,' Morgan glanced at the wall clock.

'Try the pool, honey,' a woman's voice said from behind the counter. 'He takes a dip most mornings.'

She was middle-aged, fat and affable. 'The thing is,' Morgan admitted to her, 'I've left his address behind. I can't remember whether it's "High Towers" or "White Mill".'

'"White Mill", honey. You try the pool. That's where he'll be.'

Back into the car, back to the white tower block with its inappropriate name, turning into the car park, walking out into the grounds among the tropical trees . . . heading for the bright blue oval of the pool, finding it hard to believe that March was still more than a week away because it was so warm out there. Warm enough to be sunbathing if nothing else. Was there anyone sunbathing?

Yes, there was. A fair-haired young man, sprawled out in a deckchair, fast asleep – designer jeans, his arms crossed over a faded T-shirt, sandals on his feet and an expensive jersey flung on the tiles beside him.

'Mr Toan?' Morgan said.

Rigg opened his eyes and squinted up at his visitor. He was heavy with sleep and bad temper. 'Who the hell are you?' he said.

'Friend of a friend.'

'Francis, is it? You've missed him.'

'Yes, I know. He was here last week.'

'Take a pew,' Rigg said, waving one hand at an empty deckchair. 'D'you want something to drink? I could send out for a beer or something.'

'No thank you,' Morgan said, pulling the deckchair into position so that they were facing one another. 'I've just had breakfast.'

There was a pause while the two men took stock of one another and the midday sun warmed the tops of their heads.

'You been here long?' Morgan asked.

'Too long,' Rigg said, looking sorry for himself. 'Bloody awful hole this is. Full of bloody old women and retired colonels.'

'I thought it was where the criminals came.'

'Criminals! That's a laugh!' Rigg said sourly. 'You don't get criminals here. They're in Marbella. Different altogether, Marbella. There's some life there. Too bloody expensive though, that's the trouble. You need to be a millionaire to live in Marbella.'

'Or a criminal.'

'Right.'

'So what are you doing out here?'

Rigg screwed up his eyes and looked crafty. 'Come to that, what are *you* doing?'

'I was told to look you up. Always do as I'm told, me.'

'I can't put you up. The place is a tip.'

'That's all right. I got lodgings in town. I'm only here for a day or two.'

'Sales rep are you?'

'Something like that.'

'Then you're lucky. You'll get back home.'

The self-pity on Rigg's face was too obvious to be missed. Morgan decided to play to it. 'Won't you?'

'Can't. I'm stuck in this hole. Stuck for years and years.'

'Sounds terrible.'

'It *is* terrible. You don't know the half of it. Two years I've got to sit it out here, did Francis tell you? No. Two bloody years. And all for a book-keeping mistake. That's all. A book-keeping mistake.'

Morgan made a sympathetic face and waited. So he hasn't put the flat up for sale, he thought. That'll interest Mr Fehrenbach.

'It's bloody unfair,' Rigg complained. 'It's not my fault. There's a recession going on. A worldwide recession. They should wise up. There's companies going down the tubes all over the place. *I* can't help it. It's all the banks' fault. Bloody vultures. One minute they're all over you – have some more money Mr Toan, have another loan, take out second charges – and the next minute, what are they doing? They're hounding you down, calling for blood. That's what they're doing.'

'Still, you got your wife with you,' Morgan said, trailing the bait to see what would be said.

Rigg sniffed. 'Don't talk to me about *her*,' he said. 'She's bloody useless. Wouldn't come with me, would she? Had to stay with the bloody kids. She thinks more of those bloody kids than she does of me, I can tell you that for nothing. Wife? She doesn't know the meaning of the word. You'd expect a bit of loyalty from a wife now, wouldn't you? But not her. D'you know what she did?'

'No,' Morgan said, keeping his face expressionless.

'She let them repossess my car. My beautiful car. This year's BMW. Top of the range. She let them walk in and take it away. You'd have thought she'd have put up a fight for it. But no. Not her. She just let them walk in and take it away. Wrote me a letter. Your car's been repossessed.' He picked up the jersey and draped it across his shoulders. 'Don't talk to me about wives.'

So now I know what you think of her, Morgan thought angrily. What a shallow young man you are. She's worth ten of you. Time this conversation is brought to a halt, he decided. He never functioned well if he was angry and, in any case, he knew better than to push too hard at a first meeting.

'*Duw!* Is that the time?' he said, looking at his watch. 'I shall be late for my appointment.'

'That won't matter,' Rigg said lazily. 'They don't worry about punctuality here. Everybody's late for everything. Lazy slobs, the lot of 'em.'

Look who's talking! Morgan thought, standing up

and gazing down at the recumbent form of his quarry. 'Better go,' he said. 'I don't like bein' late.'

'See you around,' Rigg said, closing his eyes.

'If you're on your own tonight,' Morgan offered, 'How about dinner?'

'That's very kind of you,' Rigg said, opening his eyes at once. 'I 'preciate that.'

I didn't think he'd miss a trick like that, Morgan thought. 'Fred's at eight?'

'Right.'

As he left the compound, Morgan looked back. The swimming pool was bright blue and shone in the sunlight as if it had been polished, the tropical trees looked like a film set, and Rigg was lying in his deck-chair in the midst of it all, with his eyes closed, apparently fast asleep.

I'll play this fish very carefully, Morgan planned as he drove out of the compound. He might look idle, but the lazy ones are often the cutest. Slow but sure, I think. I'd better find somewhere to stay.

He found himself lodgings in a hostel called the Sedeno which was right in the centre of the old town. His room had a balcony overlooking the trees in the garden and in any other circumstances he could have enjoyed it very much. But his mind was so fully occupied with stratagems that the beauty of it was lost on him. He'd dealt with several self-pitying crooks in the course of his career as a private eye so he knew the form. What he had to do was let him talk, pretend to be sympathetic, and hope it wouldn't take too long before he'd brought him to the point where he could persuade him to come home.

It took twenty four hours and considerable

patience. They dined at Fred's that night and Morgan saw to it that Rigg's glass was always full so that he was soon muddled with drink and awash with self-pity. He talked about the Inland Revenue and how unfair they were, about the banks and the folly of credit cards, about creditors and how cruelly they were persecuting him. He ended up with the story of his perfidious friend, Harry Elton.

'Walked off and left me,' he said, staring into the wine glass. 'Took all my money and left me. What's the use of anything. Entrepreneur, tha's what I am. Backbone a' the nation. Prosperity a' the nation depen's on me. An' what do they do? Walk off an' leave me. Stuck out here. No frien's. All on m'own.'

'Perhaps you should go back and show 'em you mean business?'

That ploy failed.

'Can' do that,' Rigg said. 'Got to stay here. Gave me word. Good feller. Stay here. British. Honour a' the fag – the frag – the f-lag.'

'Time I was off,' Morgan said. 'See you at breakfast.'

The following morning they met at the pool and Rigg was in a philosophical mood.

'I been thinking about what we were saying last night,' he said, when he'd greeted his new friend.

Morgan was surprised he could remember a word.

'Greed,' Rigg said. 'That's what it comes down to. Sheer greed. All these bankers. They want their money and they can't wait for it. They want it now. Yesterday. If I went back to England they'd have me up before the courts before I could say knife. They're a vindictive lot of buggers.'

'You're right there,' Morgan said, seeing his opportunity. 'That's just what they are. If you stay out here, they're going to set Interpol on to you. They'll have you brought back in handcuffs.'

That was a shock. 'Bloody hell! You're joking!'

'No. It's no joke. That's what they do.'

'They don't! How do you know? Anyway they can't. They don't know where I am.'

Time for the crunch. 'I'm afraid they do Rigg.'

'How d'you make that out?'

'They sent me over here to find you. I'm a private investigator.'

The news pitched Rigby Toan into fear and fury. 'Christ Almighty!' he yelled, leaping to his feet. 'Who did? Who sent you? Good God, can't a man get any peace! Who sent you?' Face suffused with anger, he balled his fists, bent over Morgan and shouted. 'You've got no right to do this to me. You're invading my bloody privacy. Tell me who sent you or by God I'll . . .'

Morgan didn't move or look away. He simply sat where he was, perfectly calm and perfectly contained, allowing his superior size and muscle power to speak for him. The technique worked, as it usually did. Eventually Rigg stood upright, shrugged and moved off towards the swimming pool.

'So you're a bloody spy then?'

'That's my job,' Morgan said.

Rigg thought for a while. Then he changed tack and became reasonable. 'So who sent you?'

Morgan answered reason with reason. 'You know I can't tell you that,' he said. 'It's more than my job's worth. I can help you though.'

'Oh *can* you?' Rigg said, still growling. 'I don't see how.'

'I been helpin' you already, if you did but know it,' Morgan said easily. 'I been a good friend to you. I know where you are but I haven't told them yet. *And* I can tell you what to do to get out of it. There's nothin' to stop me doin' that.'

'What do you mean get out of it? How can I get out of it? I'm stuck.'

'No, no. You're not. You got a passport, right?'

'Right.'

'So you get on the first flight out of here and go back to face the music.'

'I can't do that. I told you.'

'It's the only thing you can do, believe me. The longer you stay here, the worse it'll be when they catch up with you. Go back, face 'em, you spike their guns.'

'You really think so?' Rigg seemed uncertain. He was thinking hard, trying to work out if it would really be to his advantage. Since Francis had gone home he'd been bored out of his skull. It's not in my nature to be idle, he thought to himself.

'It's the only thing,' Morgan said, encouraging him.

'Go back and face 'em?'

'Right.'

There was a long pause while Rigg went on thinking.

'You know I appreciate this, Morgan,' he said at last. 'You didn't have to tell me any of this, did you?'

'No. I didn't.' Morgan gave a wry smile. He's a devil, he thought, but a smart one.

'No,' Rigg agreed.

'I tell you what I'll do,' Morgan said, clinching the deal. 'I got to fly back tonight. Tomorrow's Monday. I'll write my report when I get back to the office but I won't post it till Wednesday. That'll give you time to get back, see your insolvency consultant, start getting things cleared up. How's that?'

It was agreed. 'I appreciate it, Morgan,' Rigg said again. 'I really do.'

Below them on the other side of the promenade, the Mediterranean winked with a thousand wicked eyes.

Chapter Sixteen

Harvey Shearing's office was a bow-fronted Georgian shop in the middle of Ashenridge High Street. It was a classy-looking place, with fresh white paint and brass fittings to impress you on the outside and a green carpet and leather armchairs to welcome you within – just the right setting for a man who owned two restaurants, a hi-fi shop, a cottage in Normandy and his own private plane.

The 1986 Insolvency Act had opened the door to a new life for Mr Harvey Shearing. There are good pickings to be taken from a recession if you understand the rules, and Harvey understood them very well. Everything conspired to help him. With a General Election looming, the government didn't want a crop of bankruptcies to ruin their chances of a fourth term, so it was a good climate in which to persuade the courts and the Inland Revenue to endorse arrangements. He had plenty of clients. There were thousands of misguided fools around, men who'd sunk their redundancy pay in small businesses, made a pig's ear of it, and were now queuing up to enter into a voluntary arrangement to avoid the shame of going bankrupt.

On Monday morning he came whistling to work, ready to advise the next batch of inadequates, and was annoyed to discover that the mail hadn't been opened and that both his secretaries were huddled over the newspapers, reading the news.

'What's this?' he asked. 'What's this?'

'The troops have gone in,' Sandra said, looking up from the paper. 'It's operation Desert Storm.'

'I know that,' Harvey said. 'They invaded yesterday morning. What of it? There's work to do.'

Both women stopped reading the paper but, to his annoyance, he realised that neither of them was looking at him. He swivelled round to see what had caught their attention and found himself staring at Rigby Toan, unshaven, crumpled by travel and gloweringly angry.

'Good Heavens!' Harvey said. 'What are you doing here? I thought you were in Spain.'

'Don't give me that,' Rigg said belligerently. It had been an uncomfortable flight and, now that his car was gone, he'd been forced to travel to Ashenridge by train. 'You know bloody well what I'm doing here.'

'Come into my office,' Harvey said quickly. There was no need for the girls to listen to this sort of stuff. When they were safely behind a closed door, 'Now tell me. What's all this about?'

Rigg prowled to the window. 'Giving my address to a private eye,' he said. 'That's what all this is about. I thought you were my friend. Fine sort of friend you've turned out to be.'

'Sit down,' Harvey commanded, 'and tell me what's happened. I haven't given your address to anybody. The whole purpose of a voluntary arrangement is to keep creditors and debtors apart. Think about it.'

Rigg had been in such a rage at having his cover

blown that he hadn't stopped to think at all. Now he sat down and told his story, biting his nails between sentences, his language becoming more and more lurid.

'Well, whoever it was, old son,' Harvey said, when he'd finished, 'it wasn't me. If you'll take my advice, you'll go straight back to Spain and concentrate on selling the flat, the way we agreed.'

'But that was my hidey-hole,' Rigg said through gritted teeth. 'There's no point in having a hidey-hole if everyone knows where it is. Somebody hired a private eye to come and find me.'

'Then you'll have to find somewhere else to hide.'

'Oh lovely! That's lovely!'

'Meantime, I've got work to do.'

In a second Rigg's expression altered. 'You couldn't lend me a tenner, could you?' he asked. 'I had to buy a train ticket, so I'm cleaned out.'

'You can have ten pounds from petty cash,' Harvey said, taking a note from his wallet. 'I'll accept your IOU.'

'It's bloody impossible without a car.'

'I'm sure it is.' Harvey did not sound sympathetic. 'Now, if you'll excuse me . . .'

Feeling more and more sorry for himself, Rigg fed his anger all the way to Hampton. If Harvey hadn't given the private eye his address, there was only one person who could have done – and she was going to pay for it.

The train ambled through water-logged meadows on its approach to Arundel. Everything in the landscape was exactly the same as ever, the same straw-coloured reeds fringed the same putty-coloured river, Arundel Castle rose stolidly from the same wooded slopes, the same cows browsed in the fields. I'm the only thing that's changed, Rigg thought, and I've been stripped of everything that makes life worth living, my shop, my car, my privacy, all my achievements. The image of his precious BMW being repossessed made him yearn with anguish. I can't function without a car. I've got to get another one.

At Hampton, he took a taxi to his mother's house. Funds were parlously low but it was a gamble he had to take. It's all up to the old dear now, he thought. Let's hope she'll put her rotten hands in her pocket.

Margaret Toan had only just got up when he arrived. She was drifting about the kitchen in her dressing gown, smoking a cigarette and trying to get her mind into focus. She was delighted to see her darling, naturally, but he was in such an excitable state, and told her so much and so quickly, that she became confused.

'I haven't had breakfast, Rigby,' she said feebly.

'Have some then,' he said. 'I'm not stopping you. Imagine them taking my car. The cheek of it! I've had the most terrible time, Mater. Stuck out there in that God-awful hole. It's a wonder I haven't been ill, what with the worry and being on my own.'

'Shall we make some coffee?' she suggested.

'Yes,' he said. But he didn't offer to help her. Instead he continued with his stream of complaints.

Maggie was feeling pretty dreadful. 'Look,' she said, when he stopped to draw breath. 'Tell me what you want, my darling, and I'll see what can be done.'

She couldn't listen to any more of this. Even if it meant paying him, she had to stop him.

'£5,000 would do,' he said, at once and happily. 'To buy a new car.'

Maggie got up and went over to the sink. 'I can't give you that sort of money,' she said, struggling to turn on the tap and fill the kettle.

'But it's coming to me anyway, when I'm thirty five.'

'We can't talk about that,' she said. 'You're not thirty five.'

'Lend me one thousand then. For the deposit.' With a grand he could pay two instalments on a new BMW. He'd have to go to a different agent of course . . .

Fragile though she felt, Maggie Toan could still bargain. 'Five hundred,' she said. 'And that's not a gift, mind you. It's a loan. You'll have to pay it back.'

Rigg was doing sums. It was a measly amount but it would have to suffice. 'You're a darling,' he said, deciding on the soft soap approach.

'So I am,' she agreed. 'Now make this coffee for me, there's a good boy, and I'll write you a cheque.'

He did as he was told, with as good a grace as he could pretend.

'Where are you going next?' she asked, when he put the coffee in front of her. 'Oh darling! Not in a mug. Couldn't you have found a cup?'

'I'm going to see my wife, if you must know,' he said, turning back to the kitchen with the offending mug. 'My wife and my children.'

'They've moved,' she called after him. 'You know that, do you?'

Rigg poured the coffee into a cup, slopping it into the saucer. 'What?'

'She sent me a card with her new address,' Maggie said, watching his face as he balanced the coffee cup in one hand. 'It's on the mantelpiece. Under the clock.'

'She can't have moved,' Rigg said crossly. 'What's she playing at? Has she sold the house? Is that it?'

'Don't ask me, darling,' his mother said, dropping her aching head into her hands. 'I don't know what she's doing. She was talking a lot of nonsense the last time she came round. I kept the card, that's all.'

Rigg frowned at it for a long time. Then he put it in his pocket. He was annoyed with both of them, Ali for springing this on him, his mother for telling him about it. Well, he thought, this is one more thing Ali will have to explain and it had better be good. First I've got to get me a car.

Two hours later he'd passed on the cheque to a car dealer and he was behind a wheel again, feeling a lot better. It wasn't much of a car – only a Ford and much too old – but it belonged to him and he could always trade it in for something more classy. I'll run it in for an hour or two, he thought, and then I'll go to this Barnaby Green place and see what's happening.

Alison was at home and had been hard at work all afternoon. By the time she had to set off on her long trudge down to the school to collect Jon, she was feeling quite pleased with herself. The living room was clear at last, tea chests removed, cardboard packing cases folded away into the attic, bookshelves on the wall, TV in the corner, toy chest doubling as a windowseat. Her two grey-blue sofas looked rather peculiar against the floral wallpaper and that awful loud carpet, but she was planning to make half a dozen new cushion covers in bronze and gold to link up with the better colours in the room so as to play the worst ones down. As she closed the front door that afternoon and sniffed the aroma of the cakes she'd left cooling in the kitchen, it almost felt like home.

It was a surprise – and a shock – to find Rigg lolling against the doorpost waiting for her when she got back. After so many months without a word, the unexpected sight of him tossed her emotions into turmoil – anger at being left to cope on her own, relief that he'd come home to help her at last, shame because she was on welfare. But the children were thrilled to see him.

'Daddy!' Jon cried, hurling himself at his father's knees. 'You've come home!'

'Daddy! Daddy!' Emma echoed, scampering after her brother.

Rigg put out a hand to protect his trousers but he didn't look at either of them.

'Where've you been?' he said. 'I've been waiting for you for ages.'

'Down at the school to get Jon,' Alison explained, keeping her voice calm.

'All this time? Don't pull at my clothes, Emma.'

'It's a long way,' Alison said, gathering her daughter by the hand.

'Well open the door then. I need some tea.'

Although she knew she didn't want to, she let him in. She switched on the light and the gas fire, pulled the curtains, settled the children. Then she gave him tea and one of her fresh cakes, after taking the precaution of hiding the rest away in a tin.

'These are good,' he said, cramming the second half of his cake into his mouth. 'Got any more?'

'No,' she said.

But Jon was talking at the same time. 'There's lots in the tin, Daddy.'

'Go and get them,' Rigg said, licking the crumbs from his lips. And when the child hesitated, 'You don't want your poor old Daddy to starve, do you?'

The tin was retrieved and Rigg helped himself to four more cakes as though he had the right to them. That's my hard-earned wages you're eating, Alison thought, begrudging him every mouthful. Four cakes your kids won't eat.

'You're all right then,' he said, when he'd finished off the last crumb.

'All right?' She looked down at her hands, still scratched and bruised from the move, and remembered the backache she'd suffered over the weekend after shifting all that furniture about. All right?

'You sold the house,' he said. 'Did it make a profit?'

'It was repossessed,' she informed him, cold with anger. 'I had to go to court and be repossessed. We could have been on the streets.'

That wasn't the answer he expected, or wanted, but he pushed it aside. 'You're *not* on the streets though, are you,' he said. 'You're all right. You like your new house, don't you, kids?'

'We got a gardin,' Emma told him solemnly.

'An' a swing,' Jon said. 'It goes ever so high.'

'There you are then. You're all right.'

'We're a welfare family,' Alison said. 'If you call that being all right. We live on state hand-outs.' It shamed her even to say the words.

He ignored them. 'Got any more tea?' he asked. 'My mouth's like a parrot's armpit.'

She poured another cup and plonked it down in front of him, too angry to trust herself to speak.

'How many bedrooms have you got?'

She could answer that. 'Two.'

'Just right for the four of us, eh kids?'

Alison's anger was growing so alarmingly she was afraid she wouldn't be able to control it. He surely doesn't imagine I'm going to let him live here, she thought. He *can't* be that insensitive.

But he was. 'I came home at the right time,' he said, still addressing his remarks to Jon. 'Didn't I?'

'You can't stay here,' she said. 'That's out of the question. I only got this place because I'm an abandoned wife. I'm not allowed to cohabit. I'd get flung out.'

He laughed. 'Cohabit?' he said. 'You don't cohabit with your husband. Anyway I've got rights.'

'We were repossessed because you didn't pay the mortgage,' she said. 'Or have you forgotten about the mortgage?'

'Don't be like that, Kitten,' Rigg said and sent her one of his looks. 'I couldn't pay it. I had a cash-flow problem.'

Once upon a time a look like that would have reduced her to jelly. Now it had no effect at all. 'You should have told me you weren't paying it,' she said coldly.

'It was only a couple of months. I don't see why

they made such a big deal about it. You were paying, weren't you?'

'What do you mean, I was paying?'

'Your half.'

'I wasn't supposed to be paying half. You agreed to pay it. You said you'd take care of it.'

'Half of it,' he insisted. 'If you didn't pay your half, no wonder you were evicted.'

'We were evicted because you didn't pay *anything*. Not one single penny. That's why we were evicted.'

'Well then *you* should have paid it.'

That was so unfair it took her breath away. 'How dare you!' she said. 'Where am I supposed to get that sort of money? On what I earn!'

'At least you've got a job. Which is more than I have. I've been unemployed all these months. Stuck out in that dreadful hole, all by myself.'

She looked him up and down. He looked reasonably rested and healthy. Then she looked down at her shoes which needed repairing. 'Do you mean you've been in Fuengirola?'

'Of course I've been in Fuengirola. Where else would I have been? You know very well where I've been.' There was a reason why he should feel particularly aggrieved by all this, but he was so angry he couldn't think what it was.

'Then you must have got my letters.'

'Yes. I got your letters.'

'Then why didn't you answer them?'

His answer was surly. 'I had other things to do.'

'What things?'

'I was looking for a job, wasn't I?'

She didn't believe him. 'You could have worked in

a bar,' she pointed out. 'There were plenty of vacancies for bar staff when we were there.'

'In a bar!' he said, his voice heavy with outrage. 'Me? In a bar!'

'Better than being unemployed. At least you'd have been earning.'

'It's all very well for you. You can get work. There's a recession on, in case you hadn't noticed. In a recession women can get work. Men can't. I can't.'

Anger drove Alison to speak louder than normal. 'I got a job, Rigg, because I made it my business to get one,' she said. 'I took anything on offer. Scrubbing toilets, cleaning out chalets, anything. While you were sitting on your backside in Fuengirola doing nothing.'

'Don't you talk to me like that,' he threatened. His voice was so harsh that Emma began to whimper. 'I worked my fingers to the bone. And that's another thing.' Now he remembered his grievance. 'You gave my bloody address to that bloody private eye.'

'What?' Alison went over to Emma and lifted her on to her hip.

'You heard. You gave my address to a private eye, you stupid bitch.'

She felt the child's rounded belly press against hers. 'No,' she said. 'That's not true. I haven't told *anybody* where you were. I wouldn't do that.'

'He came straight to the flat, hounding me. If you didn't tell him, who did? It was you. You haven't got a loyal bone in your body. You're just a bloody, stupid, little bitch.'

This has gone far enough, Alison thought. Both kids were round-eyed with anxiety, watching him, and Jon had edged across the room until he was standing right beside her. 'There's no point in going on with this,' she said, keeping her voice as calm as she could. 'I didn't tell him. I don't expect you to believe me, but I didn't. Drink up your tea. I think it would be better if you went.'

'I'm not going anywhere.'

'You can't stay here.'

'Don't you tell me what to do in my own house.'

It was what he'd always said in Shore Street and it had annoyed her there, when she'd paid half the mortgage. Now it made her hot with anger. She'd struggled and worried, been repossessed – all on her own – coped with the DSS, the move, his VAT bill, closing the shops, the never-ending nightmare of the last few months, and he dared to claim this house. 'It's not your house,' she told him furiously. 'It's mine. And you're not welcome in it.'

He stood stock still for a moment, absorbing the change in his wife, then he sprang at her, fists clenched. 'You bloody little cow,' he roared and punched at her. The blow caught her on the cheekbone and knocked her to the ground.

For a few seconds she lay where she was, too hurt and stunned to move. He was engorged with anger, out of control, hulking over her as he punched and shouted abuse. Both the children were screaming. She knew she ought to try to protect herself, and to protect them, but it was as if she was stuck to the ground. Then he seized her by the shoulders, hauled her to her feet and shook her.

'I'll teach you to talk to me like that, you bloody little cow. If I want to do a thing I'll do it, d'you understand? I'll do it and you'll keep your bloody mouth shut or get your bloody neck broken. You're just a whore. You're all whores, all the lot of you. I hate you. Hate you. Hate you.'

Alison was now very frightened and fought him as hard as she could. She struggled to free herself, panting with terror, her heart pounding and jumping. 'Stop it! Stop it!' Jon was clinging to her legs, screaming as though he was being beaten too. She couldn't see Emma, although she could hear her weeping. 'Stop it!'

Out of the corner of her eye she saw the phone hanging on the wall and she fell towards it, thinking 999. I'll ring for the police. But he was too quick for her.

'Oh no you don't,' he said, and he tore the phone from its socket and hurled it through the window, curtain and all, breaking the glass.

The crash was so loud it stopped both children in mid-scream. Rigg seemed stunned. He stood by the broken window looking out with a bemused expression, as if he couldn't understand how it had happened.

Alison gathered her children on to her lap and tried to soothe them. They were both sobbing with terror, great gulping sobs that tore her with pity. 'It's all right,' she said, cuddling their faces into her chest. 'Mummy's all right. Don't cry, my darlings. Please don't cry! Please don't cry!' She inched towards the sofa, and crouched beside it, enfolding them against her body, ready to use it as a barricade if he attacked again. 'Please don't cry.'

Rigg was moving about the room. Oh God! What

was he going to do now? She could see his feet walking towards the sofa. But then she realised that he was crying too and shaking his head from side to side.

'Oh God! Oh God!' he wept. 'I don't know how that happened, Ali. I'm so sorry! Oh God! I'm so sorry.'

Alison knew the weeping trick of old and his tears meant nothing to her any more. She went on cuddling the children, stroking their heads and holding them close.

'Ali!' he pleaded, and knelt down beside her. 'Look at me, please. I'm so sorry. I'd give anything for this not to have happened. Believe me. I'm so sorry.' He was right next to her. 'Look at me, please. I'm so sorry.'

She looked up at him, her face ablaze with anger. 'Go away!' she said. 'Get out! Haven't you done enough damage? Get out! I never want to see you again. Never!' Then she turned right away from him and crouched by the sofa with her weeping children in her lap and her hair hiding her face.

There was a long, terrible pause. Then she heard the door being opened and slammed shut. A few seconds later an engine started up and a car was driven away. The children stopped crying. The house was suddenly very quiet.

Even though she knew he'd gone, Alison remained where she was for a very long time, rocking the children and soothing them and stroking their hair. One side of her face throbbed violently and all her teeth ached.

The sound of a children's television programme boomed and quacked through the dividing wall, bringing her back to her responsibilities. 'We shall have to get our supper, won't we?' she said. 'It's getting late.'

'Is Daddy coming back?' Jon asked fearfully.

'No.'

'Are you sure?'

'Yes. I'm quite sure.' The phone was still hanging out of the window in its bulge of curtain and the room was several degrees colder. I shall have to clear that broken glass, she thought, and fix the window. I wonder whether the phone still works. 'Come into the kitchen,' she said, 'and I'll get you a drink.'

But they wouldn't leave her. They clung to her legs while she retrieved the phone and swept up the glass. They followed her upstairs and into the bathroom while she cleaned herself up and tried to examine her face and teeth. One felt loose and she was going to have a black eye by morning as well as several bruises. They stood on the landing while she found a piece of cardboard for repairs and watched as she plugged the phone back into the wall and dialled Brad's number to see if it was still working – which it wasn't. They stood beside her while she cooked the supper that none of them could eat. And that night they both had nightmares and they both wet their beds. Alison had to find clean pyjamas for them and take them into her own bed for comfort at three o'clock in the morning.

I'm due to go into work tomorrow, she thought, as she lay unsuccessfully trying to get back to sleep. Brad's coming to pick me up at half past eight. I shall have to go down the end of the road and phone her and put her off. I don't want anyone to see me like this.

Chapter Seventeen

'Good God!' Brad said. 'I should just think he *did* hit you. The rotten bugger!'

'Yes, well,' Alison said, throwing a warning glance at the children inside the house. 'Not in front of the kids.' She didn't want to talk about it.

Brad was too angry to take the hint. 'You should've called the police,' she said fiercely. 'You could have done him fer assault. Rotten bugger.'

'Well I didn't,' Alison responded wearily. 'Anyway, it's over now. I'd rather not talk about it. I didn't mean to drag you out here, you know. That's why I rang.'

'You didn't drag me,' Brad said. 'The old dears are all fed and watered. This is my break.'

Alison was aware of a neighbour peering from behind the curtains in the house opposite and a new unreasonable fear scratched in her chest. She could do without Brad's concern, but she certainly didn't want to provide her neighbours with ground for more gossip than they already had. 'Come in and have a cup of coffee,' she said. 'The kettle's boiling.'

'I reported your phone,' Brad told her, stepping through the door. 'They said they'd be along some time this afternoon with a bit a' luck. But that could mean anything. Blimey! It's parky in here. Where's the gale coming from? Oh, I see.'

'Daddy threw the phone out the window,' Jon told her.

'Your Daddy's a pig,' Brad said. ''Lo Emma. Whatcher got there?'

'Playdoh,' Emma said. 'Tha's a cat.'

'Do a hedgehog,' Brad advised. 'Your Mr Tiggy-winkle's still in my garden.'

'Is he?' Jon said, much impressed.

'You'll 'ave to come an' see him,' Brad said. 'Tell you what, if your Mum wants a couple a' days away from everything, you could come an' see the hedge-hog, couldn't yer?'

'We'll be all right,' Alison said, putting a cup of coffee in front of her friend. 'Once we've got the phone fixed.'

'What about the window?' Brad asked. 'D'you want me to tell your brother to come over?'

'No. I can do it. I've got to be independent.'

'Well you mind what you're up to,' Brad advised, drinking her coffee. 'Glass is nasty stuff. And if the Great-I-Am comes back, don't let him in.'

Alison's answer sounded listless. 'No. All right.' She knew Brad was trying to help but she wished she'd go away.

'I mean it,' Brad said. 'Put a chain on the door and if you hear a knock, look out of the window to see who it is, an' if it's him, don't answer the door.'

'We'll be all right, Brad. Really. It won't happen again.'

'It won't, if you fight back,' Brad said, looking at her friend's battered face. 'Trouble is you been a doormat fer too long. You aint got the gumption.'

'Don't start, Brad,' Alison begged, her voice weary. 'I can't take it. Not this morning.'

'OK, mate,' Brad said. 'Only look after yourself, that's all. You don't want another basinful, do you?' She was thinking: a pity that Welshman wasn't here. He'd have stood up for you.

The Welshman had been too hard at work that day to get out of the office. In fact it was Thursday before he had any spare time at all. Then, and at the end of another hard-pressed day, he drove down to Hampton to see how Alison was. Now that he'd met her husband he had to see her again – if only to explain how he'd been involved in her affairs.

The town was even more run down than he remembered it, the High Street full of tatty cars, shops making fewer goods spread as far as possible, 'For Sale' signs everywhere. There were three of them in Shore Street, hanging like wooden flags outside the tiny cottages. The third one gave him a jolt, because it was nailed above Alison's door.

He parked the car and ran back along the alley, too concerned to walk. Good job I got down here today, he thought. If they've put the house up for sale there has to be a reason, and in this climate, with him in voluntary arrangement, it's probably a bad one.

When he reached her window, he was shocked to see that the curtains were gone and that the room inside was completely empty. Moved? In this short time? She can't have. Why didn't she phone and tell me?

There was a young woman ambling up the road with a baby in a pushchair and a little girl dawdling behind her. He approached them cautiously so as not to alarm her, but, being a resident of Shore Street, she knew who he was.

'You're the chap who took them to the theatre, aren't you?' she said.

'That's me.'

'I've just seen her up the school,' she told him. 'I'm Sally. I used to baby-sit for her. She never said you were coming down.'

'She doesn't know. It's a surprise, like.'

'An' you're the one surprised.'

He grimaced.

'I'm not supposed to hand this on to anyone,' she said as she wrote Alison's new address on a slip of paper. 'I think she had a bit of bother with some of his creditors. They were repossessed, you see. Anyway she doesn't want people to know where she is. But seeing as it's you . . . Do you know how to get there?'

'I got a map.'

'You'll need it,' she warned. 'It's all little cul-de-sacs up there. Go straight along the Selsey Road until you get to the roundabout and then take the second turning out. It's called Bersted Road. That'll lead you to the estate.'

It led him to Alison. She was trudging along the Selsey Road, pushing her double buggy, wearing jeans and that familiar patched anorak, and a shawl of some sort wrapped round her head, a dark plodding figure in the gathering gloom of late afternoon.

He cruised to a halt beside her. 'Like a lift?' he said.

She turned as she walked, her spine taut with apprehension, her face half hidden by the folds of the shawl. Then she recognised him. 'Morgan!' she said. 'What are you doing here?'

'Taxi service,' he told her. 'Hop in and I'll take you home.'

She was embarrassed. 'I'm not living at Shore Street any more. I've . . .'

'Yes,' he said. 'Your friend Sally told me. Hop in.'

'No, it's all right,' she said. 'I can manage.'

There were two cars behind him waiting to pass on the narrow road.

'We're holdin' up the traffic,' he said. 'Hop in.'

She dithered, biting her lip and looking down at the buggy. 'I can manage. You go on.'

The car drivers began to hoot their impatience.

'I'm not movin' till you get in,' he said. 'They can hoot all they like.'

She was panicked into a decision. She didn't want him to see the state she was in, but she couldn't cause a traffic jam. She lifted the kids out of the buggy, folded it and bundled them all into the car. But she didn't look at him, or smile, or thank him.

'You'll have to navigate,' he said, being deliberately cheerful.

She sat at the back with the children and kept her head down all the time, giving directions but hiding her face. Morgan's concern for her grew by the minute but he didn't say anything. He didn't even comment on the distance they were travelling. What a long way they have to walk to school, he thought. She really ought to run a car if she's got to live out here. Could she drive? He didn't know and it wasn't the right time to ask. Not when she was behaving so oddly.

He wasn't impressed by the house, with its broken window and its garish décor, but he didn't say that either. While she ran on ahead to open the door, he carried the buggy into the porch and skinned the kids out of their anoraks. Then he stood in the porch and waited to be invited in. She was so obviously upset that he didn't want to do the wrong thing.

She was a long time fussing about inside the house, switching on lights and setting a match to a gas fire. But at last she came back to the door.

Now that she had taken off the shawl, he could see her black eye and the bruises all down the side of her face. He was so horrified that he said the first thing that came into his head, without stopping to think.

'Alison, *cariad*, what's happened to you?'

'It's nothing,' she said, ducking her head. 'I had a bit of an accident, that's all. It's worse than it looks. I'm all right.'

'What happened?'

She looked past him into the dusk of the front garden, not wanting to tell him, wishing he'd go away. But Jon was standing beside her and before she could stop him, he blurted everything out.

'Daddy hit her,' he said. 'He came in and he shouted and screamed and then he hit her and she fell down on the floor and we all screamed and then he threw the phone out of the window.'

'It's nothing,' Alison said, her face stubborn. 'He was upset, that's all. Someone sent a private eye out to Spain to find him. It upset him.'

Morgan could feel his heart sinking, as inescapable facts jostled into his mind. This is all my fault. I persuaded him back. *Duw! Duw! I* did this. And in that second he knew he had to look after her and protect her, no matter what.

'That's a terrible bruise,' he said, cupping her chin very gently in his hand and tilting her face to the light. 'You seen a doctor, have you?'

His concern irritated her. 'There's no need for that,' she said, shaking his hand away. 'I'm all right. I provoked him, that's all. I should have been more careful.'

'What rubbish!' he said. 'He's got no right to treat you like this, even if you did provoke him, which I don't believe.'

'It's my responsibility,' she said stubbornly. 'I should have been more careful.'

'That's what battered wives say.'

'I'm *not* a battered wife,' she said, her face suffused with anger and revulsion at the very idea. 'He lost his temper, that's all. It was a one-off. I shall get over it.'

'He could have injured you.'

'Well he didn't. Anyway it's no business of yours. Why don't you leave me alone?'

'Because I can't stand to see the state you're in.' And he thought: Because I love you and it tears me to shreds to see how much he's hurt you and to know it's my fault. And was surprised at what he was thinking.

'Then don't look.' Don't you understand? I don't want to be talked about. I want to pretend it hasn't happened.

The anger between them distressed him so much that he couldn't think what to say next, and while he hesitated, impetus and opportunity were lost.

She was sharp with unshed tears. 'I can do without this,' she said. 'Thanks for the lift.' And she shut the door on him.

Left in the porch, Morgan watched her drawing the curtains against him and realised that he was shaking with fury. That bloody creature! he thought. That bloody, idle, hideous creature. To come home and knock her about like that. She must have been in a bad enough state being repossessed, without being punched in the face. He's a bloody monster. He ought to be laid out cold. But over and above all that, he was feeling ridiculously happy. I'm in love, he thought. I love her. And he began to grin.

Meantime there was the problem about what to do next. She'd switched on the television. He could hear a children's programme playing loudly inside the house, and Emma squealing. There's no point hanging about here, he thought. If I knock, she'll ignore me. Those curtains are like a barricade. She's had enough. I ought to have seen that before I started arguing.

Still, at least after years working for Mr Alexander Jones, he knew one possible tactic. That gentleman's motto was explicit. *'Give 'em space and try again.'* I'll come back next week, he decided. I mustn't rush her. I'll give her time to recover and *then* I'll come back.

Rigg, who had no such scruples, came back on Friday morning. He arrived on the doorstep at Barnaby Green just as Alison and the children were setting out for school. He had an arm full of red roses and a mouth full of abject apologies and he actually offered to drive them all to the school gates.

The children clung to her legs in fear and had to be coaxed into the car but Alison was surprised to find that she didn't feel any emotion towards him at all. She wasn't afraid of him, or annoyed by his return, or angry with him, or even sorry for him. She simply felt cold, as if he was a total stranger to her.

'I's been a pig to my Kitten,' he said as he drove

back again. 'I didn't mean to hit her. Is I forgiven? My poor iddle-diddle Kitten.'

She cut through the baby-talk. 'Well it's done now,' she said. 'It's no good talking about it.'

He took that as forgiveness and turned to other things. 'I saw Norrie in Chichester yesterday,' he said. 'She says you've got all my stock.'

'It's hidden under the bed,' she said. 'It's quite safe.'

'That's good,' Rigg turned into Barnaby Green. 'I'll take it off your hands. You don't want to tempt the burglars.'

He went straight upstairs as soon as she opened the door and was down again almost at once with the first of the boxes.

'I don't suppose you had a stock list, did you?' he asked.

'Yes,' she said. 'I made a list. Do you want a copy?'

'If you've got one.'

She found the list while he was stacking the boxes in the boot of his car.

'Great!' he said, folding it and putting it in his pocket. He seemed in a hurry to be off. 'Well that's the lot. See ya!'

Alison took Emma's hand and walked down the path after him. There was something surreal about this visit and, although she didn't want to prolong it, she needed to make sense of it. She leaned down to the open car window.

'Now what?' he said and there was no mistaking his impatience.

'Aren't you going to give me an address or something?' she said.

'What for?'

'Don't you think I ought to know where you are?'

Rigg shrugged. 'No,' he said. 'I'll be around.'

She insisted. 'If people write to you, I need to know where to send the letters.' She'd had several unpleasant letters from his creditors at the video shop, and it was only right that he should deal with them.

'Let them wait,' he said. 'I don't particularly want them to know where I am. Anyway I don't have an address. I'm sort of on the move. See ya!' And he crashed the car into gear and roared off.

His departure left Alison with a nasty taste in her mouth. He wasn't sorry for what he'd done to her. He'd only really come back to collect his stock. Still she thought, the flowers are lovely. I'm damned if I'm going to waste them. So she put them in a vase and arranged them prettily. Then she settled Emma with some toys and sat down at the table to examine her face in her pocket mirror.

It was the family tea that night and Mum would be expecting them. But she knew she couldn't go. Not with one side of her face so swollen and discoloured. If only bruises didn't take such a long time to come out. Another week and she might get away with it, but not today. The injuries were too raw, and too recent, and too obvious.

Elsie was most upset when Alison rang to tell her she wouldn't be coming.

'That's two weeks in a row,' she said to Jenny and Katy, as the three of them were setting the table. 'It's not like her.'

'She *has* moved house,' Jenny said, arranging biscuits.

'Yes, I know that,' Elsie said, 'but all the more reason to come, to my way of looking at it. You'd have thought she'd have liked a meal in comfort. It isn't as if she's got to walk here. Mark said he'd drive them over.'

'She'll come next week,' Jenny said, comforted.

'I know it's silly,' Elsie went on. 'But I've got a sort of feeling. It worries me. It's not like her, is it Katy? And I made this jam sponge specially.'

'Tell you what,' Katy offered. 'You cut off a big slice and I'll cycle over and give it to her and then you'll know she's got it and we'll all know she's all right.'

'You're a good girl, Katy,' her grandmother said. 'Isn't she a good girl, Jenny?'

'No good asking me,' Jenny said, basking in her daughter's well-earned praise. 'I'm biased.'

So the cake was cut and wrapped and packed in a tupperware container, and Katy cycled to Barnaby Green to deliver it. Consequently, she was the first person in the family to see Alison's bruises.

She was awed and impressed but splendidly unemotional. 'Did he hit you?' she asked. There was no disapproval in her voice, and more curiosity than shock.

Alison found it was possible to talk to her.

'We had a tiff,' she said. 'People do when they're married. It's nothing really. It looks worse than it is. There's no need to tell your Mum and Dad. Or Gran. It would only upset them.'

'Was that why you didn't come to tea?'

'Got it in one. I didn't think they'd like the look of me. You won't tell them, will you? He'll never do it again.'

Katy was proud to be the receiver of such confidences. It was a step into the adult world. 'Course not,' she promised. 'I won't tell anyone.'

But she told her friend Meriel, at break on Monday, naturally. They told one another everything and considered themselves experts on wife-bashing.

'She says he'll never do it again,' she confided. 'I don't believe that, do you? Once they start wife-bashing, they don't stop.'

'Sandra's dad hit her mum for years and years,' Meriel said. 'He broke her leg, d'you remember? She was hobbling about for yonks.'

'Men are gross,' Katy said,

'Your dad's all right.'

'Oh *he*'s different,' Katy said. 'He makes jokes.'

Mark was also very concerned about his sister, when the news got back to him via Meriel's mother and Jenny.

'What are we going to do about it, Jen?' he asked, when Katy and William had gone chattering off with their friends and they had the house to themselves.

'Leave her alone to get over it,' Jenny advised wisely. 'And don't tell your mother. She'd have a blue fit if she knew our Ali was a battered wife.'

'That bloody Rigg,' Mark scowled. 'I'd like to break his stinking neck, vicious little git. First he leaves her without any money and she has to close down all his bloody shops and then he comes back and beats her up. Why didn't she phone us, Jen? I'd have gone over and seen him off for her. Perhaps I ought to go over now. What d'you think?'

'I wouldn't, if I were you,' Jenny said. 'If she'd wanted our help she'd have rung. You go charging in and you'll make matters worse. She'll ask when she's ready. You'll see. Let her do it in her own time.'

So Alison was left to cope on her own over the weekend and surprised herself by how well she managed.

The summer bookings were coming in so there was a lot of work at the holiday camp, and although she was feeling terribly tired, she was glad to be occupied. Some of the campers gave her curious glances, but the girls who worked with her had the good sense not to comment on the state of her face, but simply kept her cheerful with jokes and cups of coffee. Jon and Emma may have been wetting their beds every night but at least Jon seemed all right at school and Emma behaved herself in the nursery, and they were pathetically good at home, offering to help her make their beds with the newly dried sheets and following her like lambs wherever she went.

On Tuesday morning, she came home from her shopping to find that the glass she'd ordered had been delivered, with a wedge of putty attached. She gave Emma every toy she could find to keep her amused and a stern lecture that she wasn't to come anywhere near the glass while Mummy was working, then she set about mending the window.

It was horribly difficult because the old glass was a pig to remove and the new glass was heavy and unwieldy and almost impossible to hold in place. But after a two-hour struggle, the window was back. There were cuts and scratches on three of her fingers, two of them still bleeding despite elastoplast, the putty was pitted with finger marks, the glass was smudged and smeared – but she'd done it and she'd done it herself.

I might be a deserted wife, she thought, as she surveyed her handiwork, but I'm not defeated. I can cope. It was a comforting thought to take with her on her long trek to the holiday camp and her afternoon's work.

Morgan was also feeling pleased with himself that afternoon because he'd just used his detective skills to particularly good advantage. At odd moments during the morning, he'd phoned the holiday camp to find out when Alison would be finishing work, provided an alibi for his early departure from the office and persuaded Roger to hold the fort. Now he was on his way to the coast. Everything had been timed to the last minute. He'd even made allowances for heavy traffic. Whatever happened when he arrived, even if she refused to talk to him, he was as prepared as he could possibly be.

Because it was such a beautiful spring day, it was actually quite a pleasure to wait outside the holiday camp. He listened as the campers drove in and out under the garish welcome sign, car radios blared pop music, and unseen children splashed and yelled in the open-air paddling pool. The long flag-poles clinked tinnily in the March wind, the sky was a riot of tumbling cloud and he could smell the sea through his open window. Just let her talk to me, he thought. That's all I want.

And there she was, pushing Emma in the buggy, walking towards him from the administration building. As she got closer, he saw that her black eye had deepened, her bruises had extended and changed colour and that she'd cut two of her fingers – how had she done that? – but she was smiling at Emma and looked a lot more cheerful.

He got out of the car and stood beside it hopefully. Would she acknowledge him? Or just walk past?

She saw him when they were a mere hundred yards apart and she didn't hesitate for a second. Touched by his kindness, she turned the buggy and walked straight across to him in her old friendly way. But when they were standing face to face, she remembered how badly she'd behaved the last time she saw him and she couldn't think what to say.

He smiled at her and mimed a chauffeur touching his cap. 'Where to, ma'am?' he asked.

'You are kind,' she responded.

He agreed with her, grinning. 'That's me.'

'To the school first,' she said. 'To pick up Jon.'

'Right, Jon first and then home.'

She put the buggy in the boot and strapped Emma into the back seat as well as she could. 'I suppose . . .' she began.

'What?'

'We couldn't go down to the beach for a little while could we? I haven't seen the sea for ages.'

'Nor have I,' Morgan said, understanding her completely. 'Hop in. The sea it is.'

Chapter Eighteen

The sea was peacock green that afternoon and patterned with rolling white-horses, the horizon a thick line of indigo blue. Over to the west, the beaches of the Selsey peninsula were clearly visible, yellow under the sun and edged with white foam. Over by the sailing club, the wind surfers were out, their fluttering sails skimming the choppy surface like butterflies, red and orange, emerald green, fuchsia pink, butter yellow. Beyond the pier, a lone brown dinghy headed out to sea, its bow ploughing to a white furrow, its stern low with the weight of an outboard engine sputtering grey smoke.

Emma toddled off to find a patch of sand to dig and Jon ran to the water's edge and began to throw stones at the waves. The shingle at the shore line was washed clean and bubbled with retreating water. Even the gulls, perched in a chorus line along the breakwaters, looked as though they'd been newly groomed. It was a bright, brisk, beautiful afternoon.

Yet the magic was not working, as Morgan could see all too clearly. Alison was quiet but not comforted. She didn't smile and she didn't look at him. She stared out to sea, biting her bottom lip.

'Lovely, issen it,' he encouraged her.

But she sighed. 'Sometimes,' she said, watching the dinghy, 'I wish I had a boat. I'd like to get in and head straight out to sea and never come back.'

This will have to be handled with caution, Morgan thought. 'That's a bit drastic,' he said, keeping his tone light and slightly teasing.

She sat down on the pebbles. 'Well not never, perhaps, but not for a very long time,' she said. 'What I mean is, I can see why people run away.'

'You'd like to run away?' Morgan said, sitting down beside her and glancing at her averted profile. It was her undamaged side and her skin looked soft and vulnerable.

'Sometimes. Yes. I would.'

She'd given him the chance to say 'Run away with me' but he knew this wasn't the moment. 'I used to feel like that when I first when to Guildford,' he told her.

'Did you?'

'Often. Homesick, I was. Didn't know anyone. Missed the sea. I used to think if I had a boat, I'd sail downriver and head for the Channel and go straight back home to Port Talbot. Daft the ideas you get.'

'You're very fond of Wales,' she said, more as a statement than a question.

'Yes.'

'Why did you leave? If you don't mind me asking.'

'Lost my job. I was a miner.'

'Ah!' she said. 'That's where you got those scars.' She had often wondered and never liked to ask.

'Right.'

The fact that he'd been a miner impressed her. There was something admirable about miners, something heroic that set them apart from the general run of mankind, as they worked in the danger and darkness of the mines. 'How long were you . . . ?'

'Down the pit?' he finished for her. 'Six years.'

'A long time.'

'It was,' he said. 'It was a good life though. We worked together, always helpin' one another, a team, like.'

'Wasn't it dangerous?'

'Sometimes,' he said, remembering the roof fall.

'I think it's awful the way they closed all those pits.'

'There's more to go,' he said with some passion. 'It's not finished. Not by a long chalk. They got a hit list a' pits still to go. We're Thatcher's enemy, you see, miners. She got it in for us.'

'Rigg's one of Thatcher's boys,' Alison said. 'He thinks she's wonderful. When they had that deregulation – do you remember? – and you could borrow as much money as you wanted from banks and building societies, he was so happy. He said we were made. And now we've lost the house and all the shops and I don't know where he is.'

That was news. 'Don't you?'

'No. He came back to see us the other day – after – well you know – but he wouldn't give me an address or a telephone number or anything.'

'Why not?'

Out there in the freedom of open beach and wild sea air, it was possible to confide. 'He says he doesn't want his creditors to know where he is. I'm not surprised. They've sent me some horrible letters. Really heavy. Threatening.'

'Why did his creditors write to you?'

'I'm co-director of the video shop. At least I was. They were addressed to him actually but I thought I ought to open them. They say he owes them money for the stock.'

'Then you'd better give the stock back to them.'

'I can't. I sold it to pay the VAT bill.'

'What, all of it?'

'It was a big bill. I had to close the shop.'

'Does Rigg know all this?'

'He ought to. I wrote to tell him when he was in Spain.'

'What have you done with the creditors' letters?'

'I left them in the house.'

What a mess, Morgan thought, and how cunning the creature's been. If she's co-director of that shop she'll be liable for all his debts there, and I'll bet he's got plenty. I should have told her what I knew about him. I ought to tell her now. But she was plainly too unhappy to be burdened with an unwanted confession. It would have to wait.

'They're bound to find out where he is sooner or later, aren't they,' Alison said. 'His insolvency consultant's bound to know. He can't hide away for ever. I think he's making a bad mistake.' She paused, gazing out to sea. 'But there you are. It's his life. He'll have to lead it the way he wants. I used to think I could help him. In fact I used to think I *ought* to help him. But I know I can't – not now. Not after he . . .' She touched her bruises, bowing her head. The conversation was going too far. She'd have to find some way to change it.

The intimacy of the conversation was taking Morgan's breath away and making him feel unsteady. After a moment, while she found her balance and he gathered his nerve, he dared to ask, 'Do you mind about him not living with you?'

She answered honestly. 'It's hard work, being a

single parent,' she said. 'I can't deny that. But in many ways we're better off without him. He wasn't easy to live with. Anyway, I've got used to it. He's been gone a long time.'

'How long?'

'Nearly a year.'

Could I tell her what I know about him now? Morgan wondered. Is this the time?

But at that moment, Jon came crashing up the beach over the pebbles. 'I'm starving,' he said.

They had a McDonald's and a Coke, which was much enjoyed. Then both children had an ice-cream, which they smeared on their coats. It was dark by the time Morgan drove them home.

'It's been a lovely afternoon,' Alison said, when he pulled up beside her garden path. 'I've really enjoyed it.'

'Am I allowed in for five minutes?' he hoped.

She looked at him for a few seconds and then smiled. 'Yes. Of course.'

It was a happy homecoming. They tumbled into the house together, switching on the lights and the television, filling the room with cheerful sound.

'Give me those coats,' Alison said to her children, 'and I'll sponge them down.'

'If you're good kids an' get to bed in ten minutes,' Morgan said, 'I'll tell you a Welsh fairy story.'

They were almost exemplary.

The coats were sponged clean by the time Morgan came downstairs.

'I'll just hang them in the porch,' Alison said. 'On the airer. Then we'll have a cup of coffee.'

The coffee never got made. Two minutes later she

came back into the room with a letter in her hand. Her face was ashen, the bruises etched in dark colour against paper-white cheeks. She looked so dreadful that Morgan was on his feet at once.

'What is it?'

She held the letter out to him. It was a notice to quit. *'The owners have intimated to us that your tenancy does not conform to the rules laid down . . .'* he skimmed the rest of it, looking for a date. She had till the end of March to *'find other accommodation'*. 'Oh Alison, *cariad!*'

His sympathy broke her control. Her face crumpled into crying as hot tears spilled out of her eyes. It was all too much. 'Just as I thought the worst was over,' she wept. 'I've worked so hard on this place. And now this.'

He had his arms round her before he could stop to think whether he ought to be holding her or not. 'My poor dear darling love,' he said into her hair. 'My poor dear darling.'

'It's not fair,' she wept. 'We haven't done a thing wrong. Not a thing. I mended the window. It wasn't my fault he broke it. I've broken my back keeping everything clean in case they came out to inspect us. Nobody's been near. How do they know we've broken the agreement?'

He drew her head on to his shoulder, smoothing her wet hair out of her eyes. She was warm in his arms and her skin smelt of the sea. It was such a joy to be holding her at last that he could barely speak. 'Don't cry *cariad*,' he murmured. 'I'll look after you.'

But she was too distressed to understand what he'd said. 'Why now?' she wept. 'Why like this? Why didn't they come round and see the place, talk to me, tell me? Why a rotten letter? It's not fair to tell me like this. Why didn't they give me the chance to explain? Somebody must have been telling tales. One of those old cats on the green. They're always spying, looking out of their rotten windows, tittle-tattling. I've a good mind to heave a brick through one of their rotten windows, whoever it is. I should have sailed away this afternoon in that dinghy. That's what I should have done. Oh Morgan, what am I going to do? I can't face another move.'

Still holding her, he eased her to the sofa and sat her down sitting beside her with one arm round her shoulder and the other cuddling her into his side. 'I'll help you, *cariad*,' he said. 'Don't cry.'

But a dam had been breached. There were too many tears to shed for her to stop now. 'We've only just got over the first lot,' she wept. 'You don't know how awful it was . . . to sit in a court and hear them say you can't live in your own house. It's like the end of the world. And moving . . . There were packing cases all over the place . . . and it rained all day . . . and Emma kept grizzling . . . and the dirt! Oh God, the dirt! We were *scraping* grease off those cabinets and the loo was *brown*. And now just when I've got it all nice, they go and . . . It's not fair. We had such a lovely afternoon too . . . down on the beach. Poor kids! They've both been wetting their beds since he . . . I have sheets to wash every morning. And now we've got to go through it all again. I can't bear it.'

He let her cry it all out, smoothing her hair and kissing her forehead until her sobs finally subsided and she sat up and blew her nose.

'I'm so sorry,' she said. 'I shouldn't have gone on like that. It's just . . .'

'I know,' he said. 'It's all right. You can say what you like to me. I love you.'

That made her weep again, slow tears this time, rolling out of the corners of her eyes and falling on to her jersey. 'Oh Morgan. Do you?'

He looked at her lovely eyes, knowing he would kiss her. The whites were bloodshot from weeping but the pupils were as green and clear as the sea that afternoon and her lashes were thick as seaweed, clumped and spiked by tears.

'*Cariad*,' he said. Then he kissed her.

When the kiss began it was the gentlest touch, a softness, mouth to mouth, as he intended, but within seconds his emotion and the sensations he was rousing combined to break his control and, holding her face between his hands, he kissed her with increasing passion, long and hard. Dazed by a surfeit of emotions, she kissed him back, her heart thundering. When he stopped they were both shaken by the power they'd unleashed.

'Oh Morgan!' she said.

'I love you so much,' he told her. 'So much.' And kissed her again.

'We've got to be sensible,' she said after the third kiss.

His eyes were drowsy with love for her. 'Why?'

'If we go on like this, we shall end up in bed.'

The thought made him groan.

'I can't,' she said, setting a preventive palm against his chest. 'You know that, don't you. Not tonight. I'm in enough trouble as it is. If you stayed the night I should be cohabiting.'

The word brought him to his senses. She was right. He couldn't make her run that sort of risk.

'But we'll cohabit one day,' he said, 'won't we?'

She was too confused to be able to answer. 'Yes. No. Probably. I don't know.'

That made him laugh. 'I *do* love you,' he said. 'More than ever now. But I'll go. You're right.'

'You are a good man,' she said.

'Or a fool.' She was still in his arms and he hadn't kissed her for two whole minutes.

She kissed him. Briefly but with delicious tenderness. 'No. Never that,' she said. 'You're a very, very good man.'

'Which means I've got to go now.'

'Well not now perhaps. But soon.'

'You're not to worry about that letter,' he said, when they finally parted more than an hour later. 'If you've really got to find another place, we'll look for it together. Right?'

She was so lulled by kisses she agreed. 'Right.'

'And I'll help you with the move. Right?'

'Right.'

'I'll phone you in the morning. Sweet dreams.'

She stood in the porch beside the damp coats and watched him into his car, watched him reverse and drive away, watched until the last red gleam of his tail lights turned the corner. It was as if she was hanging on to the very last of the evening.

He loves me, she thought. She felt slightly delirious but she knew what a difference this evening had made. From now on, she had someone to trust, someone to advise her and comfort her, someone to turn to. I'm not alone any more. He loves me. The sheer amazement of it filled her mind to the exclusion of everything else. He loves me. Her own feelings towards him were in such turmoil she didn't know whether she loved him in return or not. It was enough that she was loved. Loved and protected and cared for. I'll go down and see the agency first thing tomorrow afternoon, she thought. She had the strength to fight back now. He loves me.

The next afternoon Alison dressed very carefully for her visit. She put on her suit and a freshly ironed blouse, polished her handbag as well as her shoes, even took time to make up her face. It was important to be seen as serious and well-groomed.

But it was all a waste of time. Although the young woman who interviewed her was patient and sympathetic, the position couldn't be changed. The owners wanted Alison out and, as she'd only been given the tenancy on a month's probation, that was all there was to it. There'd been a letter, the woman said. Something about a breach of the peace. 'There was a man in the house, apparently, lots of screaming and shouting – so the writer says – damage to property. A window was it?'

'It was my husband,' Alison admitted shamefacedly. 'I couldn't stop him. I did try.'

The woman looked at Alison's black eye. 'So I see.'

'It's not fair to drive me out because of him,' Alison pleaded.

'No. I know.'

'Well then.'

'It's the rules, I'm afraid,' the woman said. 'Not much I can do about it. If they say you've got to go, you'll have to go. We've got other properties on our books, if you'd like to look at them.'

'No thanks,' Alison said. She was suddenly weary, all the euphoria of the previous evening drained away. Less than a month, she was thinking, and then I've got to pack up all over again.

She stood up, squared her shoulders and prepared to get on with the rest of the day. If that's what I've got to do, she thought, that's what I've got to do.

On her way back through the town, she saw Brad standing outside Quality Seconds contemplating a pair of floral leggings. Glad of the chance of a bit of friendly conversation, she crossed the road to greet her.

'Whatcher!' Brad said. 'What d'you think a' them?'

Alison tried to drum up some enthusiasm for the leggings but made a poor job of it. 'Pretty lurid,' she said.

Brad gave her a searching look. 'What's up now?' she said.

'Nothing much.'

'Oh come on!' Brad rebuked. 'You've got a real gob on. Spit it out.'

So Alison told her. There was no point in trying to hide her problems any more. They had a habit of becoming all too public.

'Charming!' Brad said, when she heard about the neighbour's letter. 'You'd better come and live with me an' the hedgehog, that's all.'

'We couldn't do that,' Alison said at once, then paused. Could they? It was very tempting.

'Can't see any reason why not,' Brad said. 'It'ud only be for a couple a' weeks, wouldn't it. We could manage *that*. You'd have to put up with Martin being around now an' then, but you wouldn't mind him.'

It wasn't the sort of decision to be made in a hurry and, in the more sensible part of her mind, Alison knew that. But in her present state, doomed to be homeless in a month's time and buffeted between hope and disappointment, it was a lifeline.

Two days later, she took her first step away from the difficulties at Barnaby Green and went to stay with Brad.

The children were delighted with the move. They brought their favourite toys with them and all their bedtime stories, they didn't have that horrid long walk to school, and because they never knew when she was going to swear or say something awful, Brad was wonderfully outrageous company. They learned to eat kippers for breakfast and slept happily one at each end in a single bed.

'We can see our hedgehog every day,' Jon told his 'friend Morgan' when he came down to visit them. 'He lives in the garden.'

'We live up the stairs,' Emma said. 'With lots an' lots of things.' Brad's chaotic untidiness was an endless source of treasure and adventure.

Alison was surprised by how happy they all were. Brad was content to let her do the bulk of the cooking. The kids were being good. There was always someone to talk to and the view of the sea from the living room window was a daily pleasure. Morgan came down to see her two or three times a week, and each visit was better than the last. In short, life with Brad passed at quite breathtaking speed. Soon the mad March winds were blowing them towards the end of term and the Easter holiday. On the last day of the term Alison finally found a house that would suit.

It was in one of the older roads in the town, one of a long terrace with a small, tatty garden, a living room, kitchen and bathroom downstairs and two sizeable bedrooms on the first floor under the eaves. It had been let out to students for several years so the carpets were stained, the walls were covered in the remains of posters and bits of Blu-tack and the whole place was grubby.

'But I can soon see to all that,' Alison said, as she and Morgan took their second look round. 'I've still got the carpet from Shore Street. I could put that down in here. It's got possibilities.'

'We'll work on it together,' Morgan said. 'And don't say "I can manage" or you'll make me feel unwanted.'

So the agreement was signed and the moving day fixed for six weeks hence. And then, just as Morgan was beginning to feel that things were sorting themselves out at last, he had a phone call.

It was late at night and he'd just let himself into his flat after his long drive back from Hampton. He picked up the receiver happily, thinking it would be Ali, phoning to tell him something she'd forgotten when they said goodbye.

But it was his sister Sarah.

'Sorry to call you this time a' night Mor,' she said. 'I called earlier but you were out.'

The tenor of her voice alerted him to bad news. 'What is it?' he asked.

She told him with characteristic directness. 'Granddad's worse.'

'Much worse?'

'He's dyin', Mor. Can you get home?'

Chapter Nineteen

It was very quiet in the back parlour at Blaenhydyglyn. When Morgan and Sarah edged into the room, the only sounds they could hear were the wooden rhythm of the clock in the hall, the lick of flames from the coal fire and the terrible rasp and crackle of Granddad's struggle for breath.

The old man lay on a mattress on the floor where he'd been for the last three weeks, his long emaciated body spread out in front of the fire and his nose and mouth covered by an oxygen mask. Nan sat in the shadows in her old nursing chair, supporting his white head against her knees. The disease had gradually drained him of all his strength. He hadn't been able to climb the stairs for more than three months and for the last four weeks it had been all he could do to struggle out to the toilet. As the days passed, he'd grown more and more cold, even though Nan kept the fire going night and day. Now he was felled and every breath was an agonising effort.

For a few seconds, Morgan was afraid they'd come too late and that the old man was already dead, for his face was an alarming yellowy-grey and, despite the mask, they could see that his lips were purple with lack of oxygen. But his eyes flickered open when he heard them approach and he recognised them both, the old glint returning briefly.

Morgan knelt on the floor beside him. 'How are you, Granddad?' he said. And then felt stupid to be asking such a question.

The old man coughed for a long time before he could speak, and when his answer came it was faint and hoarse. But implacable. 'Goin' boy,' he said. 'On the way out.'

'Is there anything I can do?'

'Stay by here a bit.'

'Of course.'

'That's all any of us can do,' Nan said. 'Watch and wait. Be with him.' She stroked his white hair, very, very gently, and spoke to him in Welsh, her words soft as a caress.

'We take it turn and turn about durin' the day,' Sarah whispered. 'One hour on, four hours off. Mam and Dad stay overnight. Alice and Megan were here this morning. That way it's possible.'

But only just. The approaching death cast its pall over the entire house and filled the little back room to the exclusion of everything except thought.

Morgan felt as though he had travelled backwards in time, as though he was a child again. Standing powerless at the edge of the family in a house where the living room was like an oven and the rest of the house was cold, he once more glimpsed the subliminal strength of emotions he could neither understand nor control.

He and Sarah stayed for their allotted hour, saying little and doing less. Some of the time they sat in the back parlour waiting to answer if Granddad spoke or needed anything. Once they simply stood by the narrow window in the back parlour and looked out at the hillside like naughty children put in a corner and told to watch the wall. They were both relieved when Dai and Hywell arrived to take over the vigil.

'How long's he been like that?' Morgan asked as he drove his sister back down the mountainside to her home in Port Talbot.

'Three days,' Sarah said tearfully. 'Poor Granddad. He won't complain, Mor. That's the dreadful thing. He's in agony most of the time, an' he won't complain.'

'He never did.'

'No. But it makes it worse somehow.'

The mountainside was lush with spring, young leaf shimmering with recent rain, young ferns curled like green hair. In the distance, Blaenhydyglyn looked timeless, with its long terraces of stone houses cuffed and collared with white coigns and lintels and its vertical streets set into the mountainside as neat and secure as studs. The pit where they'd all worked was long since closed, but the village had survived, school, club, pubs, steep street full of shops, the friends and neighbours. A neat, clean, orderly, caring place. He remembered how Nan used to polish the furniture every day, and sweep the dust from her doorstep. But she couldn't sweep it out of her husband's lungs. And now he was dying of it. *Myn uffern!*

They were well away from the village now, so the important question could be asked. 'How long's he got?'

'Days, hours, a week maybe.'

'*Duw!*'

'It's not fair, is it, Mor. He's worked so hard all his life and been such a good man. He shouldn't have to die like this.'

'No,' Morgan agreed. 'He shouldn't.' And he had a sudden and vivid recall of Mam crying on the day he'd told her he was going to work in the pit, crying for fear of the dust and the terrible knowledge of what it could do. 'You'll end up like your Granddad,' she'd grieved. 'Gaspin' your life out. Never catchin' your breath.'

It was a time for remembrance. That night he and his sisters and their husbands and children gathered for an evening meal at their parents' house before Mam and Dad set off for their nightly vigil with Nan. Granddad was remembered with jokes and affection all through the meal.

'I got the pictures of young Morgan's christening somewhere,' Dad said, searching for them. 'Here they are. Remember that one?' And there was the old man, with the infant on his knee, beaming in the midst of his family, with Nan hovering protectively beside him and a row of children at his feet.

'He's always been such a one for the family,' Mam said.

'We're all here now, Mam,' Megan told her. 'Except for our Trefor. Any news of him yet?'

'We sent a fax,' Dad said. 'They're in the West Indies, that's the trouble. It's bound to take a bit a' time.'

'He'll be here as soon as he can,' Morgan said. They had to be together now. It was the only strength they had and they all knew it.

Trefor phoned late that night. He was at Heathrow. Just got in. He'd hired a car and was driving straight down. 'Don't wait up, Mor,' he said. 'I got a key.'

But Morgan waited for him just the same. What was the point of going to bed? He couldn't have slept. Not with Granddad dying by inches just up the valley.

Night and day became interchangeable. They slept when they could, cat-napping in armchairs when they came off watch. Those off duty cooked meals for those still on. Those who were in Nan's house at mealtimes cooked for her and coaxed her to eat what she could.

'You got to keep your strength up,' they urged. 'Wouldn't do for you to fall sick now, would it?'

And Granddad's struggle went on inexorably.

On the second evening Morgan phoned Alison to give her what news there was. 'It can't be very long now,' he said. 'He's very bad. Are *you* all right?'

'We're fine,' Alison told him. 'Don't worry about us. You've got enough to think about without that. Just do what you have to do.'

But there was nothing any of them could do. That was the difficulty. Nothing except wait and talk and remember.

'It's all wrong,' Trefor said, on their second evening, when Mam and Dad had left for Blaenhydyglyn, and the rest of the family were sitting round aimlessly. 'He's been such a good man, good worker, good parent, good grandparent.'

'He was a legend in the pit,' Morgan remembered. 'Ask old man Griffiths they'd say. And look at all the hard work he did durin' the strike. I can remember him handin' out food parcels all hours down at the club.'

They all remembered the strike.

'What a time that was!' Megan sighed. 'All that effort an' they still closed the pits. You'd ha' thought after all our men have *suffered* down the pits, they'd at least have listened to what they had to say.'

'Tories've got cloth ears,' Morgan said. 'They never listen to anyone.'

'We were the enemy within,' Megan said. 'Do you remember that? Maggie's enemy within.'

'D'you remember Tess Thomas down by the factory gates,' Alice said, 'an' how we all crowded into her living room to watch TV? I don' know how we all got in.'

'They had a three-piece suite,' Megan said, 'by the factory gates for the pickets to use. Do you remember that? Buff it was. The local police used to sit on it side by side with the colliers.'

'That was before the heavy mob arrived.'

'That's right. An' a caravan. Two berth with twenty men packed inside like sardines.'

'Someone set fire to it,' Alice said. 'Just before Christmas. Burnt out it was. Be about eleven o'clock at night. Just before Christmas. D'you remember that Megan?'

'I remember the pickets had a break Christmas,' Megan said. 'They didn't come picketing over the holiday. It was bitterly cold.'

'I tell you what I remember,' Trefor said. 'I remember when the mass picket started and the miners came down from Yorkshire and Kent. There were two thousand men standing outside the gates and nobody made a sound. Two thousand men in total silence. That really impressed me. To be that controlled. Two thousand men in total silence, no cars runnin', no sound at all. It was like Christmas Day. I'll never forget it.'

'I remember when the women's support group pelted the police with eggs,' Megan said. 'You were there, weren't you, Alice. The police were furious. An' when they baton-charged us we ran into the houses trying to hide the eggs before we were arrested. You never saw so many eggs. We put them under cushions and upstairs in the bedrooms.' The memory was making her laugh, for the first time since their vigil had begun.

'I put mine in a bookcase,' Alice said, laughing too. 'Daft thinking about it now. We should ha' put them in the kitchen. But you don't think, do you? Not when you're frightened. You just do the first thing that comes into your head.'

'What days they were!' Sarah said. She was laughing like her sisters, with tears in her eyes, glad of the relief of this swift, black humour.

They were making so much noise that they didn't hear the phone ring. It wasn't until Morgan held up a hand for quiet that the sound finally reached them.

It was Mam. 'He's goin',' she said. 'I think you ought to come. Just the cousins.'

Laughter was done with instantly. Talk was superfluous. There was a scramble for coats, a rapid departure, the five of them squashed into Morgan's car, a silent journey through the sleeping town, across the bright lights of the M1 and out on to the hushed enveloping darkness of the Mynydd. 'He's goin'.'

If any of them had any hope that Mam was wrong, it was dashed as soon as they entered the house. The death rattle was loud and unmistakable in that dark little room. Granddad was deeply unconscious and Nan was grey with misery. Racked with pity and totally powerless they waited with her, taking it in turns to hold her hands as the terrible snoring sounds went on and on and on.

The hours passed and still it went on. Morgan

found himself praying for it to stop and was shocked to realise that he was wishing his Granddad dead. His dear, dear Granddad, who'd carried him on his shoulders as a little boy and gone rabbiting with him and helped him with his homework and worked beside him in the pit. *Duwydd mawr!*

The first faint streaks of daylight coloured the edge of the curtains. Birdsong began with a single tentative chirrup rising against the darkness and grew until it was a full-throated chorus. In the silence of the hall the clock struck five, leaden and loud. The fire was almost out, a single, pale pink coal dying on a bed of grey ash. It was Easter Sunday and another day. And at long terrible last, the old man stopped breathing.

The silence that followed was more dreadful than his death rattle had been. Alice began to cry. 'My poor, poor old love,' she wept. 'What did he do to deserve a death like this?'

For the rest of the day they comforted one another and attended to the chores that had to be done. The undertaker came to the house within an hour, grieving with the family because he'd known old man Griffiths for the last thirty years and couldn't bear the thought that he'd died of the dust.

But whatever they said to one another was little comfort. Death had knocked a hole through the centre of their lives, leaving them stunned and crippled, clinging together. The date of the funeral was set. Morgan phoned Alison briefly, then he drove back to Guildford to do what work he could. But the days were meaningless with grief.

'It'll be better after the funeral,' Mam said when he phoned her. 'You know you've said goodbye after a funeral.'

But none of them knew how they would withstand the event. To watch him being put into the earth. It was too horrible.

They gathered mutely, marked out from the rest of the village by their black clothes. They huddled together in the chapel as the choir sang and the spring sunlight made dappled patterns on the coffin. They listened with aching hearts as Dad spoke of the good man his father had been.

'I got a bit of a poem here to end up,' he said. 'I thought it would be fittin' bein' he was a collier all his life.' He read it clearly, his voice throbbing with emotion:

I saw white bones in the cinder-shard.
Bones without number;
For many hearts with coal are charred
And few remember.

'Amen to that!' Morgan said. And his endorsement was echoed by others all round the chapel.

Then they were out on the cold hillside and the words of the burial service were being sung into the breeze.

'Forasmuch as it hath pleased Almighty God of his great mercy to receive unto himself the soul of our dear brother here departed, we therefore commit his body to the ground.'

And there wasn't one person by the grave who didn't see the awful irony of those final words. 'Earth to earth, ashes to ashes, dust to dust.'

Chapter Twenty

Despite her reassurance to Morgan, Alison wasn't having quite such an easy time in Brad's disorganised household. They were now into their third week together and there were many irritations – endless dirty coffee cups, the bathroom in constant use, Brad's perpetual smoking, the way she was teaching the kids to swear – but all too petty to complain about. Not that Alison would have dreamed of complaining when Brad was being so good to them. So her sense of grievance gathered like a boil.

To make matters worse, Brad was fighting an urge to let rip too. The more she heard about Rigg's behaviour – and she'd heard quite a lot from young Jon – the angrier she became. But *she* couldn't say what she felt either. Ali had enough on her plate without that. So they lived together in a state of brittle over-cheerfulness that didn't help either of them, until, inevitably, matters came to explosion point.

The trigger was a letter from Rigg. Alison found it at Barnaby Green when she went over to do some packing after family tea on Good Friday. Now I shall know where he is, she thought as she picked it up. But there was no address on the letter, no date, not even a salutation. The message was brief and to the point.

'It is the Mater's birthday on Sunday. I have ordered

flowers Interflora to be sent to you Saturday. No knowing when they would deliver as it is Easter. You can deliver them Sunday morning. Take a little present from the children, chocs would do. We have to keep in with the old bat because of my father's will. More necessary now than ever. R.'

Alison was furious at being given orders in such a peremptory way. He always presumes I'll do what he wants, she thought. But she also knew that she didn't have much option. Rigg was right about keeping in with his mother because she had ultimate control over the will on which so much depended. If he was going to pay off his debts when the two-year arrangement came to an end, he would need every penny of it. She drew the line at chocolates but the flowers were an investment. She would have to deliver them.

They arrived in an Interflora van the following morning, just as she and Brad were setting out to work. A dozen red roses addressed to Mrs Toan. Twelve beautiful blooms, all with stems of identical length and heads of perfect scarlet, like a line of chorus girls standing ready to perform.

'Blimey!' Brad said, joining her at the door. 'Easter presents now! Who're they from? Morgan?'

'Course not,' Alison said. 'He wouldn't be so extravagant. They're from Rigg, for his mother. It's her birthday tomorrow.'

'Oh lovely!' Brad said with heavy sarcasm. 'What are you supposed to do with them?'

'I shall put them in water for the moment,' Alison said, deliberately misunderstanding the question. 'I haven't got time for anything else. We're late as it is.'

'That wasn't what I meant,' Brad said, scowling. 'Why've they come here?'

'I'll tell you later,' Alison said, running the tap for the roses. 'Can't stop now. Come on, kids, look sharp.' She hid the flowers in her bedroom and steered the children out of Brad's narrow front door, down the stairs, and away from criticism.

Next morning it was pouring with rain and then the trouble really began.

'You're not going out in *this*,' Brad said, when Alison put Emma's anorak on, 'for heaven's sake. You'll be drowned.'

'I must deliver the flowers,' Alison said, helping Emma into her anorak. 'It's her birthday.'

'I knew it would be those bloody flowers,' Brad said. 'Let her wait. What's she ever done for you?'

Brad turned her attention to the children. 'You don't want to go out in all this rain, do you, kids?'

Jon and Emma were glad of an ally. 'No.'

'I must do it, Brad,' Alison insisted. 'It's important.'

Brad lit a cigarette and glared at her friend through the smoke. 'You'll get soaked,' she warned.

They did. As they walked up Fish Lane a sudden, stinging shower came slanting down upon them, driving in through the inadequate plastic cover of the buggy and soaking right through Alison's anorak. Within minutes they were all as wet as if they'd been swimming in their clothes and both children were complaining miserably.

'Never mind,' Alison said, fighting to stay cheerful. 'It'll soon stop. It's only a shower. The sun'll come out in a minute and we'll all get dry again.'

Sure enough, by the time they reached Maggie's house the worst of the shower was over; but the roses were so battered they looked as though they were at least a week old.

Maggie Toan came to the door in an expensive négligé and regarded both the soggy group and the flowers in a disparaging fashion.

'They're from Rigg,' Alison explained, holding them out towards her.

'He phoned me this morning,' Maggie said, shaking raindrops from the cellophane wrapper. 'Dear boy. He never forgets my birthday, even when he's busy.'

Alison dripped on the doorstep.

'I'd invite you in,' her mother-in-law said, looking down her powdered nose at Emma and Jon, who were steaming behind their plastic cover, 'but you're really too wet, aren't you. Better get home, my dear, and change those children into dry clothes.'

So there was nothing for it but to trudge back along the promenade to Brad's flat.

Brad was back from her breakfast duty, cooking bacon and eggs for Martin who was sitting at the kitchen table with a wodge of Sunday papers under his elbow, reading a *Times* supplement.

'Good heavens!' he said, when he saw the state they were in.

'We got caught in a shower,' Alison explained, skinning the wet anorak from her shivering daughter.

'I told you so,' Brad said, banging about in the kitchen. 'This is all the Great-I-Am's doing. I hope you realise. If they're ill it'll be all his fault.'

It was exactly what Alison was afraid of. 'They won't be ill,' she said, repressing any guilt. 'They're good strong kids. Bit of rain never hurt anybody.'

'That bloody Rigg!' Brad said. 'If he wants his mother to have a bunch a' bloody flowers on her birthday he should come down an' do it himself. She's *his* mother, not yours. You let him trample on you.'

Alison knew that only too well and she didn't want to be told it. 'Yes, well, it's done now,' she said, leading the children into the bedroom.

'More's the pity,' Brad said, returning to the bacon, which was beginning to burn. 'Now look at this bloody breakfast.' She took her anger out on a can of beans, opening them with such force that the juice spilled out all over the cooker. But her annoyance still rankled. Martin got snapped at when he asked if there was another cup of tea, the Sunday papers were swept off the table on to the floor as she dished up his breakfast, and she smoked two cigarettes as he ate, puffing angrily and saying nothing, her eyes screwed up against the excessive smoke.

By the time Alison and her reclothed children reappeared in the living room, the atmosphere was so heavy with smoke and bad temper that Martin was beginning to think he'd have to find some excuse to leave, Easter Sunday or no. He'd always been uncomfortable on the edge of someone else's quarrel and to be exposed to Brad's anger was more than he could bear.

But she didn't give him the chance to speak or move. She attacked Alison the minute she was in the room.

'Got any more errands to run for him?' she mocked. 'Or can we get on with the holiday now?'

'Leave it, Brad, please,' Alison begged, glancing

anxiously at the children. 'Shall we do one of your jigsaws, Emma? What about the animal one? Would you like that one?'

'No. Damn it all. I won't leave it,' Brad said. 'It's time you learned a thing or two about that bloody husband of yours. He's a bloody crook.'

Jon had taken a picture book from the toy box and was reading it, much too quietly, glancing up at them from time to time out of the corner of his eye in a way that made him look both vulnerable and sly. Alison was sitting on the floor next to Emma, spreading out the pieces of the puzzle. 'Please!' she begged.

Martin tried to intervene. 'Brad, don't you think . . .'

There was no stopping Brad now. 'No, I don't think,' she said, glaring at him. 'And never mind please. He's a bloody crook and it's high time she knew it. Swanning around in that bloody BMW when she's pushing the kids about in a second-hand buggy; wearing bloody Armani suits when the kids are in reach-me-downs from a car-boot sale; three bloody shops when she's living in a slum.'

'It wasn't a slum,' Alison said, stung by the criticism. 'I won't have that. I kept it lovely and clean.'

'It was a slum,' Brad said intractably. 'Shore Street is a slum. Nasty, cheap, little houses and he's swanning about giving himself airs. The Great-I-Am. Millionaire. I don't think.'

'Well we haven't got a house at all now, have we,' Alison said, fighting back. 'Cheap or nasty. So perhaps you're satisfied. We haven't got anything. We're just a welfare family. The lowest of the low. A nasty, slummy, welfare family.'

'And whose fault's that?' Brad stormed on. 'I'll tell you whose fault. The Great-greedy-I-Am. I knew it was a mistake when he started all that malarkey with the mortgage.'

'He wasn't the only one,' Alison said hotly. 'All sorts of people took out second mortgages. Re-mortgaging is a fact of life.'

'Fact of greed more like. He milked that place for every penny he could get out of it. And you know he did. Milked it dry and didn't pay the mortgage. Re-mortgaging my eye! Pure greed, that's what that was. What did you get out of it, except debt? Did he buy *you* an Armani suit? No he didn't. Did *you* get a BMW? No you didn't. You got repossessed. It's all me, me, me with Mr Rigby Selfish Toan. And you let him get away with it.'

Jon had retreated into the corner of the room behind Brad's huge moquette settee. He was sitting with his head bent over his book, his face horribly pale, and Emma was scowling, her plump little hands shuffling the wooden pieces of the jigsaw, turning them over and over. For their sakes, Alison knew she ought to stop this conversation, now, while she could, but a hideous curiosity drove her on. 'What do you mean an Armani suit?' she said. 'Why do you keep on about Armani suits?'

'Because that's what he wears.'

'No, I'm sorry,' Alison said, spilling into anger. 'I won't have that. He doesn't. You're lying.'

'No I ain't,' Brad said, furiously. 'It ain't my style.'

'I was the one who took his suits to the cleaners. I know you're wrong.'

'Now you listen here,' Brad said, stubbing out her

cigarette and leaning forwards out of her chair so that her face was inches away from Alison's. 'I kept my mouth shut for years. I could ha' told you plenty about that ratbag a' yours, but I never. You wanna watch what you're sayin'.'

'You've always hated him,' Alison said. She was very near tears but she couldn't stop. Not now. Not with so much said. 'You never had a good word to say for him. Admit it. And I thought you were my friend.'

'I'm the best friend you'll ever have,' Brad said. 'I tell you the truth. And the truth is that Rigby Toan's been a liar an' a fraud an' a con artist right from day one. You're worth ten of him. A bloody, rotten, little con artist. He's conned you good an' proper.'

They were still eye to wild eye. 'You can't say that!' Alison cried. 'You're saying my whole marriage has been a fraud.'

Brad leaned back in her chair. 'Right,' she said, lighting up another cigarette. 'He's never told you anything. You've always been the last to know. Did he tell you about not paying the mortgage? No. Did he tell you he'd gone to Spain? No. Well then.'

Alison was on her feet now, facing her opponent, but she couldn't answer. Because it was true. She bit her lip and looked down at Emma, who was banging one of the pieces on the floor. She corrected the child automatically, in a dull voice. 'Don't do that Emma. You'll break it.'

'All that bloody silly cloak an' dagger stuff,' Brad went on. 'Running away to Spain. Skulking out there for months and months. Never tellin' you. Do me a favour, Ali. He could've told you any time he wanted. But he didn't want, did he? You weren't supposed to know, mate. Face it!'

Emma suddenly threw the jigsaw pieces into the air and began to scream at the top of her voice. 'I hate it! I hate you! I hate everything! It's horrid. I kick 'em in the goolies.'

'Stop it!' Alison shouted at her. 'Stop it!' But the screaming child was already far gone in fear and anger. She lay on the floor, kicking out wildly in all directions.

'That's it!' Alison said. 'We're going to Gran's. Get your coat, Jon.'

The little boy crawled out from behind the settee. 'It's wet,' he said.

'Never mind. Get it! It can dry at Gran's. You can wear a jersey. Go on! Do as I say!'

It wasn't fair to be shouting at Jon, not when he'd been so good and it was Emma who was throwing a tantrum. But she was too distressed to be fair. Her one thought was to get out of the house and away from Brad's criticism. 'Get up, Emma. Stop that row!'

'You don't have to go rushing out,' Brad said, backing down. But Alison was already on her way to her bedroom to snatch up the first three jerseys she could find.

'I can't stay here,' she cried. 'Not now. Not now I know what you think of me. I've got *some* pride.'

'That's just bloody silly,' Brad shouted. 'That's cutting off your nose to spite your face.'

The noise in the room was deafening, with Brad shouting and Emma shrieking in a high-pitched incessant scream. Red in the face and sliding along the floor, she writhed away from all attempts to put on her jersey. In the end, Alison picked her up, stiff and screaming, hoisted her bodily across her hip and bumped her out of the flat and down the stairs. The wet buggy was still in the lobby and still spattered with rain. 'Get in!' she yelled. 'Stop that row and get in!'

Carrying their wet coats in his arms, Jon followed them downstairs. He stood quietly beside the buggy while the fight continued and winced as Alison pushed Emma's arms into her harness. The little girl arched her back and fought with all her might, and she was still screaming as they set out on their long walk to Gran's.

'Are you all right?' Alison asked him as they were walking through the Pier Gardens. At least it wasn't raining and Emma was reduced to simply sobbing now, slumped in the buggy with her eyes shut.

'I feel a bit sick,' Jon said. And was, suddenly and precipitately, all over his shoes.

There was nothing to clean him with but tufts of grass from the edge of the lawns. We're like gypsies, Alison thought. Tramping about in all weathers, pushed from pillar to post, cleaning ourselves with grass, being complained about. Worse really. At least gypsies have got caravans to go back to.

'Come on,' she encouraged, looking from Jon's white face to Emma's blotchy one. 'Soon be at Gran's. We'll be better then. And that nasty old rain's gone. That's good, isn't it.' And we're away from the row. Walking out had put paid to that.

But back in Brad's flat the row was still going on.

Martin put his foot in it as soon as the front door had closed. 'Poor Ali!' he said. 'You *were* hard on her, Brad.'

'Nobody asked you!'

'I'm sorry,' he said, retreating before the blaze of her anger, 'but you were.'

'I was only telling her the truth,' she said defiantly. 'Look at the state of this room. She walks out – toys all over the place and I'm supposed to clear them up.' That was unfair: Ali did twice as much housework as she ever did.

Martin knelt down on the floor and began to gather up the pieces of Emma's wooden jigsaw. 'Perhaps you shouldn't have,' he ventured.

Brad was lighting a very necessary cigarette. 'Course I should have. Somebody had to.'

'Perhaps it wasn't the right time,' he said mildly, fitting the pieces into their box.

Brad tossed the match into the waste-paper basket. 'Oh there's a right and a wrong time for telling the truth, is there?'

For the first time in their relationship, Martin argued against her. It alarmed him but he felt impelled to go on. 'Yes,' he said seriously. 'I think there is. Sometimes it's not possible to accept too much truth. Really Brad. How can I put this? It hurts too much.'

'Well tough,' Brad said, glaring at him.

'We all need a space to retreat to when we're feeling insecure,' he tried to explain. 'Somewhere quiet and private where we can lick our wounds – understand why we're being hurt – come to terms with pain. Honesty cuts off our escape.'

Brad wasn't impressed. 'If you're such a chicken you've got to run away all the time,' she said, 'then hard cheese.'

'How can I make you understand?' he asked, addressing the question more to himself than to her. 'Suppose, for example, you're in love with someone and you don't know how they feel about you. Or you know how they feel and it isn't what you really want them to feel. Say you're looking for commitment, marriage, children, all that sort of thing, and she's – well, not ready to commit herself. That makes you very insecure. To be told the truth when you're in that sort of state would push you down into despair. You couldn't take it.'

Brad was too angry to understand Martin's message. 'You're telling me I mustn't tell the truth, is that it?'

Her ferocity unnerved him. 'Sometimes,' he said. 'Not always. It can be very healing sometimes. I mean, it's just it isn't always appropriate.'

'Now you listen to me, buster,' she said. 'If I want to tell the truth, I shall tell it. No matter what.'

'But you frighten people with it, don't you see?'

'Well if you're so scared, you'd better push off. I'm sure nobody's keeping you.'

It was the moment he'd feared ever since their relationship began, but he faced up to it valiantly. 'Do you mean that?'

'Yes I do. Go away.'

It was spoken so coldly, and with an air of such finality that he took his coat and left the room and the flat, convinced that it was over, and the sooner they put a distance between themselves the better. He was in such a hurry that he didn't look back and he didn't say goodbye.

Left on her own, Brad smoked her cigarette and

scowled at the dirty breakfast plates. Now that the row was over and the room was peaceful, Martin's words echoed in her head. She began to understand that he'd been telling her something else. Something more important and nothing to do with Rigg. Something about them. *'Suppose you're in love with someone,'* he'd said. And *'say you're looking for commitment, marriage, children . . . and she's not ready to commit herself.'* Did he want to marry her? Was that it? Why didn't he tell her, stupid fool? Did she frighten him? No! She couldn't accept that, she'd never frightened anybody. Anyway, it was all too late now. He'd gone and that was that. He needn't think she'd go running after him. She'd never run after any man in the whole of her life, and she certainly wasn't going to start now.

To her surprise and horror, she realised that her eyes were filling with tears. 'Damn smoke,' she said, blinking the tell-tale moisture away.

Elsie Wareham was surprised too. She had not been expecting Ali and the children to Sunday dinner and she could see from the state they were in that something unpleasant must have happened.

'What a nice surprise,' she said, holding the door open. 'Are you staying to dinner?'

'If you'll have us,' Alison said.

It was a joint so it would probably stretch. 'I shall have to put on a few more potatoes,' Elsie said. 'Is everything all right?'

'He was sick on the way over,' Alison said, turning her mother's attention to Jon's pale face. 'He's all right now.'

'Poor old Jon,' Clare said, coming up behind her mother-in-law. 'Was it something he ate?'

'Either that or getting wet,' Alison said, helping Emma out of the buggy. 'We went out earlier. Got caught in that shower.'

'I should just think you did,' Elsie said. 'Just look at the state of those coats. They'll have to go in the airing cupboard straight away or they'll spoil.'

'Has he got a temperature?' Andy asked, putting a professional hand on his nephew's pale forehead. 'No. Quite normal.'

The bustling welcome restored Alison's spirits. Family, she thought, that's what I need. That's what I've needed all day. To be back in a family where people care for one another. Not bossed about, or told off, just looked after.

So Easter Sunday turned out to be a pleasant day after all. Greg and Susan and the girls arrived in the afternoon and Mark and Jenny and Katy and William turned up in time for tea as they'd planned. In the evening Mark drove his sister and her two sleeping infants back to Barnaby Green.

He asked no questions when she told him she wasn't staying with Brad any more. He simply carried Jon upstairs to his unmade bed and covered him with a blanket.

'When's the move?' he asked as Alison carried Emma into the room.

'Thursday fortnight,' Alison told him. 'And not a minute too soon.'

After he'd driven away and she was on her own, Alison plugged in the television and went off to the kitchen to make a cup of tea. Her mind was full of that awful quarrel and she needed something to occupy her.

It occurred to her that walking out on Brad like that had left everything in a muddle. The kids' pyjamas were still in the flat and so were their books and toys. The fridge here was empty. There wasn't even any milk for tea, and no fruit or vegetables either. No matter how bad you're feeling, she thought, there's always work to do. I'll get what shopping I can tomorrow and I'll do the rest on Tuesday. We can go to the bus station. That always bucks us up.

Chapter Twenty-One

The bus station at Hampton is a local landmark. Built in the twenties, in the Art Nouveau style, with a façade of striking green and cream tiles, it was once the hub of all the bus services from Selsey Bill to Worthing, a place where Southdown buses arrived one after the other to green the High Street. More than eight double deckers could stand waiting in its tall hangar and still leave room for arrivals and departures, while out at the rear was a vast space where the buses were cleaned and serviced and garaged for the night.

Now, in the nineties and after privatisation, it is just a grubby relic; all buses gone, its façade chipped, its yard a car park, its lofty hangar housing yet another flea market. They sell plastic shoes where the Mystery Tour once set off on its daily adventure – and shoddy clothes, and a variety of hideous nick-nacks and cheap toys from China and Hong Kong. The one good thing about the place is a stall that sells fruit and vegetables of excellent quality and at a reasonable price. Which was why Alison shopped there.

On that Tuesday afternoon, she bought as much fruit as she could afford. She and the children had been shopping for most of the day. Now they were all tired and it was very nearly closing time. So she wasn't pleased when, just as they were walking out of the garage, laden with shopping bags, she heard a man's voice calling her name.

'Mrs Toan! Mrs Toan! Just a minute. Hold on a minute, Mrs Toan.'

The voice was insistent. Turning her head, she saw that a man in a denim jacket was running across the road towards them. He was red in the face and waving his arms. At first glance she was sure she didn't know him, but when he reached the kerb a memory began to stir. Wasn't he Rigg's partner in the video shop? The awful man who'd run off with all Rigg's money.

'I'm so glad I saw you,' he said puffing up to her. 'I been tryin' to find you for weeks.'

'We're in a rush,' Alison said, trying to avoid him.

'Don't let me stop you,' he said. 'I don't suppose you remember me do you? Harry Elton.'

'Yes I do remember you,' she said coldly. 'You were Rigg's partner in Hampton Videos.'

'I still am, more's my bad luck. You don't happen to know where he is, do you?'

'No. I don't! And if I did I wouldn't tell you.'

Standing in front of her on the pavement, he gave her a long searching look, while the late afternoon shoppers jostled on either side of them and Jon and Emma, sensing trouble, clung to Alison's hands.

'Look,' he said. 'I know I got no right to ask you, but what's he been telling you about me?'

'This isn't the place to talk about it,' Alison said, feeling embarrassed. 'You know what you've done.'

'No,' he argued, his brown eyes dogged. 'You think *you* know what I've done. You believe what Rigg told you.'

'Not always.' Not since her quarrel with Brad.

Two elderly women gossiped past them into the garage. 'Look,' Harry said. 'Will you come back to my shop with me? Please. I got some papers to show you.'

What now? Alison wondered. 'Well all right,' she agreed, 'but you'll have to be quick.'

'Thanks,' he said. 'Let me take your bags for you.'

She handed them over and he carried them round the corner to his shop, which was a small lock-up crammed with wicker furniture, scatter cushions, pine bookshelves and plant stands full of artificial flowers. It was closed for the day but he took out a key and opened the door.

'I was just popping out for a bite to eat when I seen you,' he explained. 'Bit a' luck eh? If you'll just wait one minute, I'll get 'em.'

'Are we ever goin' home?' Emma said plaintively, slumping into one of the wicker chairs. 'I's hungry.'

'There they are,' Harry Elton said, rattling through the bead curtain that separated his office from the shop. He had a battered blue box file in his hand. 'Look at that one first,' he said, and pulled out an official letter.

It was a summons to Mr Henry Elton, co-director of Hampton Videos, to appear in Chichester County Court. The date of the hearing was in four days' time and the reason for the summons was non-payment of £1,254 to one of the companies which had supplied Rigg with videos.

'I don't understand,' Alison said. 'You're not the co-director. I am.'

'Only wish you *were*,' Harry said dolefully.

'You ran out with all the money,' Alison said, 'and

he made me the co-director. He gave me one of the shares.'

'Ah!' Harry said, his brown eyes alert. 'So that's what he told you. I thought it'ud be something like that. I ran off with all the money, did I?'

'Didn't you?'

'We bought the goodwill of that shop between us,' Harry explained. 'Six grand it cost. Three grand each. We was going to pay it back to the banks bit by bit out of the takings, only Rigg took all the takings and it never got done.'

'All the takings?'

'Most weeks, yes. He used to dip in the till whenever he felt like it. There wasn't cash for the wages some weeks. It was a shambles. We was always rowing about it. Come the finish I said I'd had enough an' he was to pay me back my three thousand an' we'd call it quits.'

Now that Alison knew so much more about Rigg, it sounded all too probable. 'Did he pay you back?' she asked.

'In the end. Yes. Took a solicitor's letter. But he did cough up in the end.'

'So why have they sent you this summons?'

'Because I'm still co-director. Legally liable. He never registered the change.'

The information crashed into Alison's brain. 'You mean I've never been a director.'

'See for yourself,' Harry Elton said, retrieving another paper from the file. 'I had a company search done to get to the bottom of it. See. There it is. Hampton Videos. Directors Rigby Toan and Henry James Elton. The lazy bugger never registered the change. Excuse my French! It's still me. He took me for a proper sucker, I'm telling you. Four summonses. An' all for bills he's run up since I left the company. Nothing to do with me, any a' this, but I'm the one that's got to pay. They don't know where he is, so they come down on me. Co-director. Legally liable, so they say. Is that fair?'

Wicker-shredded shadows dodged and flickered in the congealing light, mocking like goblins. I was never a director. I didn't have to pay that awful bill. It was nothing to do with me. I struggled and worried and it was nothing to do with me. Brad's voice jabbed into her memory. *'All that bloody silly cloak an' dagger stuff. . . . Do me a favour, Ali. . . . He could've told you any time he wanted. . . . You weren't supposed to know, mate. Face it!'* He'd known all along that she wasn't the director of the video shop and he'd deliberately kept her in the dark. She'd turned herself inside out, sold the goods, shut the shop, and she could have walked away from it. She was filled with anger against him. If he loved me, she thought, how could he have treated me so badly? And there's dear old Morgan phoning all the way from Wales, on the day his granddad dies, just to see how I am. The contrast between them couldn't have been more marked.

'Now I ask you,' Harry Elton was saying, 'is that fair?'

'No,' Alison said. 'It's not. I'm sorry, Harry. I've misjudged you. I shouldn't have said all those things about you back there.'

'It's not your fault,' Harry said generously. 'It's that bugger of a husband of yours. Excuse my French.'

'Swear all you like,' Alison told him. 'He didn't pay the mortgage either. We've been repossessed.'

'You're joking!'

'I wish I were.'

'How are you managing?'

'We're on the social.'

'That's wicked,' Harry said. 'I thought I was in a bad state but this is much worse. The rotten bugger! Stitching up your business associates – well that's bad but you got to expect it in this day an' age – it's dog eat dog in the business world. But to carve up yer own wife. An' yer kiddies. Well, words fail me.'

'Yes, well . . .' Alison turned her head away from his anger.

'So you really don't know where he is.'

'No. I'm afraid I don't.'

'Someone ought to catch him an' clap him in irons.'

'Emma's crashed out,' Jon said, from his seat on the wicker chair.

'Oh no!' Alison said, threading her way through the furniture to her sleeping daughter. 'She mustn't do that. She's got to walk. We've got to get home.' But the child was fast asleep.

'Where's your car?' Harry asked. 'I'll carry her round for you if you like.'

'I haven't got one.'

'No car?' Harry said. He found that hard to believe. Surely everyone had a car these days. 'What happened to the BMW?'

'That was repossessed too.'

'You're joking!'

'I'm not. He didn't own it. It was only leased, you see, and he didn't pay, so they took it back.'

'I'll give you a lift,' Harry volunteered. 'I got me van out the back. Where d'you live now?'

I owe Brad an apology, Alison thought. She was right about all this. I ought to tell her.

'Could you take me to my friend Brad's?' she asked. 'I'll show you the way.'

So he drove them to Brad's flat, Jon perched happily among the packing cases in the back of the van, Alison in the passenger seat with Emma sleepily on her lap.

'We're all in this together,' he said, when they arrived. 'That's about the size of it. You, me, the suppliers, the banks. All victims, all the lot of us. There's my card, look. I've put my home phone on as well. If you hear anything give me a ring.'

'I will,' Alison said. 'I promise. And thanks for the lift.'

There were lights on in Brad's living room and Alison could see a figure moving about between the table and the kitchen. She still had the key to the flat on her key ring but she didn't think it would be fitting just to walk in, so she rang the bell. They all listened as Brad's shoes clomped down the stairs.

'Oh, it's you,' Brad said as she opened the door. She was still wearing her uniform under her denim jacket and she had a scarf tied round her head like a mop cap. 'What d'you want?' Her voice was most unwelcoming.

'To say sorry,' Alison told her. 'Oh Brad. You were right about Rigg. He *is* a liar. I *am* sorry I argued with you.'

'Well, well,' Brad said. 'What's brought this about?'

'I've found something out. Something awful. You were absolutely right. He's a crook.'

'You'd better come in,' Brad said, her tone changing.

They followed her up the stairs. The living room was untidier than Alison had ever seen it. There were dirty paper plates and used cups and glasses all over the table, on the floor, the television, the windowsill, even on the hi-fi.

'Had a few friends in last night,' Brad explained. 'I've just this minute got in.'

Alison began to clear up. It was one way to show how sorry she was. 'Come on, kids,' she said. 'Pick up the plates for Mummy.'

Emma carried one of the plates across at once, but Jon seemed to be rooted to the spot. He was gazing up at Brad with his mouth open and his eyes as round as pennies.

Alison turned her head too. And gasped before she could stop herself. For Brad had flung off her denim jacket and whipped the scarf from her head. She was completely bald, her skull rising pale pink and naked above a face made suddenly unfamiliar by lack of hair.

'Neat, eh?' she said, as they all stared at her.

'Did it fall out?' Jon asked.

'No,' Brad told him cheerfully. 'I shaved it off. On Sunday after you left. An' if you don't tell me I look gorgeous, I'll shave yours off an' all.'

Jon's eyes bulged with horror at such a threat. He put up both hands to hold his thatch of thick fair hair firmly on to his head. 'She won't, will she Mum?' he asked.

'No. Course she won't,' Alison assured him. 'She's joking.' But cutting off her hair wasn't a joke. It was an immolation.

‘Off with the old,’ Brad said brightly.

With a vengeance, Alison thought. But why?

‘Thought I’d go the whole hog this time,’ Brad said, running her hand over her scalp. ‘Whatcher think?’

‘Well . . .’ Alison said, delaying for as long as she could while trying to think of something complimentary to say. ‘It’s stunning. I’ll say that. But why did you do it? Was it because . . . I mean have you and . . . ?’

‘Oh he went Sunday, just after you lot,’ Brad said, making a face to indicate how little she cared. ‘He’s *really* old news now.’

She loves him, Alison thought, understanding intuitively. This is a penance. She’s punishing herself. ‘Oh Brad! I *am* sorry.’

Brad dismissed her sympathy. ‘Plenty more fish in the sea,’ she said. But the strain in her eyes gave the lie to the jaunty tone of her voice. ‘Tell me about the Great-I-Am. You said you’d found something out.’

It was almost a relief to tell her about Rigg’s wrong-doing.

‘Don’t surprise me,’ Brad said when the tale was told and the plates had all been cleared and thrown in the bin. ‘Have you told your mum all this?’

‘No. Not yet. I’ve only just found out myself.’

‘Well you ought to,’ Brad said, carrying a tray full of glasses into the kitchen. ‘I was talking to her yesterday on my way to the old dears. She still thinks you’re gonna get back together again.’

‘Oh does she?’ Alison said, grimly. ‘I’d better disabuse her of that idea, PDQ.’

Brad gave her a long, searching look. ‘Divorce?’ she said.

'I think so,' Alison said. It was a terrible step to take but it was almost inevitable now. 'Don't you?'

Brad flung her arms round her old friend and gave her such a hard squeeze it was quite painful. 'That's my girl,' she approved. 'That's the best news I've heard in ages.'

After that they spent a cheerful evening together and cooked a huge meal, Brad providing the meat and drink, and Alison the fruit and vegetables. Then they put the kids to bed and allowed the television to entertain them, quite like old times. Except that Martin wasn't with them. And he'd gone on the Sunday of that awful row.

'Tomorrer,' Brad said when they finally went to bed, 'you can go an' see your Mum. Tell her the good news.'

'I'll wait till Friday,' Alison said. 'Greg an' Susan are coming down so I can tell them all at the same time.'

'You do that,' Brad said. 'Confession's good for the soul.'

But even with Greg's steadying presence, Alison found this confession extremely difficult. She waited until tea was over and Jenny had taken all six children down to the beach because she didn't want to talk about Rigg in front of Jon and Emma. She had hoped it might be easier when they were all busy washing up. But it wasn't. The minute she mentioned Rigg's name, they pounced on her with questions, all speaking at once.

'So you've heard from him.' 'What's he going to do about the house?' 'Is he back here?' 'I hope he's giving you some housekeeping after all this time.'

'No, no,' she said. 'I don't know where he is. I met his partner.' And she told them what had happened, getting it over with quickly before they could interrupt and take away her courage.

Susan was outraged. Mark and Greg said they weren't surprised. Elsie said how sorry she was.

'But he'll pay people back,' she added, with a slightly strange expression, 'won't he?'

'Well . . .' Alison said. 'I hope he will, but I'm beginning to wonder.'

'He *must*,' Elsie said, swilling out the teapot, her forehead creased with anxiety. 'He can't just take thousands of pounds from all those people and not pay them back. That would be awful.'

'All what people Mum?' Mark said, hanging up his tea-towel.

There was a pause as Elsie looked from one to another. 'Nothing,' she said, and now she looked shifty. What a mistake I've made, she thought. Oh dear. What can I say now? She propped the washing-up bowl on its edge and led them through into the living room, hoping the subject would exhaust itself on the way.

'*What* people Mum?' Mark insisted as they settled themselves into the armchairs.

'I think you'd better tell us,' Greg said, leaning across to touch her hand.

Elsie sighed. 'I promised him I wouldn't.'

'Promised who?' Alison asked. The conversation was alarming her but she hadn't dared to speak until now because the suspicion that was growing in her was so distressing.

'Rigg.'

I *knew* it, Alison thought. 'Oh my God!' she said and sat down heavily. 'He's borrowed money from you.'

'Well yes. I had to let him have it. He was in such a state.'

'How much?'

'Well rather a lot.'

'How much?'

'Six thousand pounds.'

They were all stunned. But Alison was sick with shame and anguish.

'Your nest-egg,' she grieved. 'Oh Mum! All your money! All the money Dad . . . This is *awful*. I'm *so* sorry.'

'It's not your fault,' Elsie said into the silence.

But it felt as though it was. 'I married him,' Alison said. 'I brought him into the family. If I hadn't none of this would have happened. I didn't marry him so that he could do that to you.' Her face was strained with the misery and guilt of it.

'Yes, well . . .' Elsie said, trying to pass it off. 'It's done now. I'm sure he'll pay it back. When he's sold the flat in Spain. That's right, isn't it?'

'Yes,' Alison said, rather surprised. 'It is. How did you know?'

'They sent me a paper,' Elsie admitted. As it was all coming out now she might as well be hung for a sheep as a lamb. 'Well, lots of papers actually. One of them was a list of all his creditors. I thought it was a bit much at the time.'

'Have you still got it?' Greg asked.

'It's in Dad's box.'

'Could we see it?'

The box was brought down from her bedroom and the papers were found and passed round for her sons and daughter to see. They made shattering reading.

Alison was so shocked by the list of creditors that she had to read it twice before she could take it in. How *could* he have run up such terrible debts? Five thousand owing to an insurance company, eighteen to the Camelot and Wessex Bank – that couldn't be right – and scores of names and addresses, a thousand owing here, five hundred there. Who were they all? The list was four pages long and the last page was entirely given over to credit card debts. He'd been running ten credit cards and he owed money on all of them. Thousands and thousands of pounds. It made her ache to think about it.

Greg was reading the report on the creditors' meeting.

'You didn't go to this meeting, Mum?' he asked.

'No. I didn't like to,' Elsie admitted. 'He said he'd pay me back. That was enough for me. I didn't think I needed.'

'It's all right, old love,' he said, smiling assurance at her. 'I'm not criticising you. There's just something here I want to check.'

'I went to it,' Alison said. 'If I can tell you . . .'

Greg turned towards his sister. 'It says here, Mr Toan explained that his limited liability company was doing good business. "*If he could continue to trade, profits from the limited liability company would ensure the payment of a dividend of 60 per cent to his creditors.*" That wouldn't be a video shop, by any chance, would it?'

'Yes,' Alison said. 'It was.' Now what?

'And he actually stood up at this meeting and said it was a going concern?'

'Well yes. He did.'

'No,' Greg said. 'I'm sorry, little sis. But it wasn't a going concern. It was in debt to the tune of ten thousand pounds, to my certain knowledge.'

Oh God! Alison thought. That's even more than Harry Elton knows about. She felt as though she was in a trap, condemned to hear bad news for ever. 'How do you know?' she asked in a voice husky with fear.

'He came to see me the night before this meeting,' Greg explained. 'I didn't know there was going to be a meeting. He never said anything about it. But I can remember the date very well. It was the day after Susie's birthday. We offered him a slice of cake, didn't we, Susan.'

'A big one,' Susan agreed wryly.

'Well anyway, we sat him down and talked pretty generally for half an hour or so and then he said he'd come to see if I would like to buy the video shop.'

'What!' Mark exclaimed. 'He didn't.'

'He said I could have it for ten thousand pounds as a going concern.'

'Oh God!' Alison said, realising how grasping Rigg had been. 'It wasn't worth *six*. That's what they paid for it.'

'Surprise me,' Greg said. 'Anyway he wanted ten.'

'What did you say?' Mark asked.

'At first I couldn't make out why he wanted to sell. I told him I'd need to see some documentation first, articles of association, his last audited account, details of subsequent trading, an assessment of the market value of the premises, that sort of thing.'

'And did he show them to you?'

'No. He said he hadn't brought them with him. So I asked him if there were any debts outstanding. And he said, yes, one or two. So I said I'd need to know what they were and I wrote them down as he remembered them. They came to over ten thousand pounds. At which point I said, what he was really asking me to do was to put my hand in my pocket to the tune of twenty thousand pounds for a business in financial difficulties that I didn't need and didn't want. And you'll never believe what he said then.'

Alison waited, feeling she'd reached the point when she would believe anything.

'He said, "*Ah yes. But when you've paid off the debts, the first £1.50 over the counter will be pure profit.*" Pure profit! I shall never forget it if I live to be a hundred.'

It's just what he would say, Alison thought. He was never interested in anything but profit. It's all he ever talked about.

'So I take it you refused his offer,' Mark said.

'Too right I refused it,' Greg said. 'I thought it was dicey at the time. And then when I heard he'd gone into voluntary arrangement I knew how wise I was.'

'He's a bloody crook,' Mark said. 'I'm sorry Ali but I can't say anything else. To take Mum's nest-egg and then to try and stitch Greg up for twenty thousand.'

The walls were falling in on Alison where she sat, the ground shifting underneath her feet. This was worse than anything she could ever have imagined. To take Mum's nest-egg. Dear old Mum, who'd never had a penny to her name except what little Dad had saved for her. It was robbery. Cruel, barefaced, selfish robbery. Dear old Mum, who'd never willingly hurt anybody in the whole of her life, who'd worked hard and scrimped and saved to get by. And in he comes and swans off with all her savings. All her savings. He never had the slightest intention of paying her back. He won't pay anybody back. He'd have taken Greg and Susan's money too if Greg hadn't been wise to him. Mark is right. And so is Brad. He's a crook. A con artist.

'I'm so sorry,' she sobbed. 'So very, very sorry. Oh Mum, you don't know how sorry I am.'

'It's not your fault,' Mark said, putting an arm round her shoulder. 'How were you to know? He's a professional charmer. It isn't just you and Mum. He took us in too. He's taken all sorts of people in. You've only got to look at that list to see that.'

But Alison wouldn't be comforted. It *is* my fault, she thought. It's all my fault they've been put in this position. He's my husband. I married him. I'm responsible for all of this. I should have stood up to him long ago. I should have made him tell me what he was doing. I've been a coward.

Guilt pressed down upon her. I shall have to divorce him, she thought. There was no doubt in her mind at all. Even if I loved him once – and she wasn't even sure about that now – I can't love him again, not after this. I can't love him and I can't stay married to him. I've got to tackle him, get a divorce and be rid of him for ever. I shall make an appointment with a solicitor first thing tomorrow morning.

Chapter Twenty-Two

It was early in the morning when Alison arrived in the town centre to keep her appointment with the solicitor. The main road was virtually deserted, its pedestrianised red cobbles stained with oil, its brick-walled flower beds sprouting empty crisp packets and crushed beer cans among the shrubs. She walked from the bus stop to the corner of the High Street, shivering despite the padding of her anorak. The tremor was more nervousness than cold, for now she was mere seconds away from the break-up of her marriage. She knew that what she was doing was right and inevitable, but as she walked through the door into the carpeted ease of the solicitor's office, she felt more vulnerable and alone than she'd ever been in her life. What would she have to confess in these quiet rooms? What would she have to say? Would they despise her for failing?

The young woman at the enquiry desk was pleasantness itself.

'If you'll just take a seat,' she smiled. 'I'll tell Mrs Cromall you've arrived.'

The waiting room was full of comfortable armchairs and there was a television chuckling to itself on a low display table, but Alison was too keyed up to sit down and relax. She prowled around the room, pretending to look at the pictures on the wall, automatically tidying the magazines. Mercifully it was a short wait. After ten minutes, a young woman in a blue suit appeared at the door to introduce herself as Mrs Cromall's secretary and to ask her if she would be 'so good as to follow me'.

They walked up a flight of stairs, along two anonymous corridors, past several anonymous doors. Alison felt like Alice in Wonderland falling effortlessly down her long tunnel, not knowing where she was going to land.

But there was no white rabbit, just a middle-aged woman with an urchin cut, a welcoming smile and a briskly efficient manner. It didn't take her long to establish the salient facts about her new case – that her client was on family credit and would need legal aid and that the husband in the case had walked out on his family in March 1990 – over a year ago.

'Right,' she said. 'First things first. I think we'd better establish what the grounds will be for this action. We've got plenty to choose from: adultery, unreasonable behaviour, two years' desertion, two years' separation by consent – which means you both want this divorce – or failing everything else, five years' separation.'

'Which would be the easiest?' Alison asked.

'Separation by consent,' the solicitor said, 'if he'll agree to it. You'd have a year to wait, of course, but it's usually relatively straightforward.'

That was a disappointment. 'Would other grounds be quicker?'

'Possibly but not necessarily,' Mrs Cromall said. 'Would a year's wait cause problems?'

'No. Not really. It's just I thought . . .'

'Even quick divorces take time,' the solicitor pointed out. 'Separation by consent is less messy. Has he visited you since he left?'

'Now and then,' Alison said, remembering the terror of that dreadful time. 'Not often.'

'But he didn't stay? You didn't cohabit?'

'No.'

'Then look at it this way, you've served out a year of the time already.'

'I suppose so.'

Mrs Cromall wrote on the form in front of her. 'Quite straightforward, so far,' she encouraged. 'Now, about children. Do you have any children?'

'Yes. Two.'

'Dates of birth?' Mrs Cromall asked. When they were given, she added 'They're quite young then. Does he pay maintenance for them?'

'No.'

'Do you wish to apply for maintenance?'

'Could I?'

'Of course.'

'Then I will,' Alison decided. And why not? It's about time he paid for the children. They're his as much as mine.

'There is one difficulty I ought to point out to you,' Mrs Cromall said.

Alison's heart sank again. 'Yes?'

'If he comes to court and promises to pay you maintenance, your family credit will stop or be reduced according to the amount agreed, and there are no real powers to make him pay if he doesn't want to. Lots of husbands pay for a few weeks and then stop. It can take months to get a court order to compel them to pay and even then they can play the same game again, pay for a few weeks and then stop. From what you say, it seems within the realms of possibility that your husband might not always pay up. If that were to happen you could find yourself seriously short of funds, because, as I expect you know, it could take several weeks to reinstate your family credit payments. It's something to consider. Did he pay you regular housekeeping when you were together?'

'Well, more or less,' Alison said, feeling she had to be fair. 'Not what you'd call regular.'

Mrs Cromall looked at her client shrewdly. 'Then he might not pay up, is that it?'

Alison couldn't defend him. She had to be honest or she wouldn't have any money to feed the kids with. 'Yes. I'm afraid it is. He's never paid maintenance for the children, you see. We had an arrangement. If I wanted children I could have them, but I had to look after them and pay for them.'

'What you're saying is he didn't want them.'

'No. He didn't.'

'Then he won't want custody. To look on the positive side.'

'No. I suppose not.'

'Visiting rights?'

'He might.' She hadn't thought about it.

'How would the children feel about that? I gather they haven't seen much of him during the last year.'

'I think they'd prefer not to see him.'

Again the shrewd look. 'Because?'

Alison bit her bottom lip, hesitating. It seemed so disloyal to be telling all their most intimate secrets to a stranger. But what else could she do? She wanted this divorce and she knew it was bound to involve telling tales.

Mrs Cromall tapped her chin with her pen. 'Am I right in assuming that your husband is – shall we say – a violent man?'

It was a relief to have it put into words. 'Yes. I'm afraid he is.'

'It's useful to know,' Mrs Cromall said calmly, 'in case he refuses to agree to this divorce as you propose it and we have to fall back on other grounds. Perhaps you could tell me the extent of his violence.'

It had to be said. 'He knocked me about.'

The shrewd face melted with sympathy. 'Often?'

'No. Only once.'

'We must make sure he doesn't do it again,' Mrs Cromall said. 'You can take out a restraining order, you know.' She looked at the form again, checking the entries. 'Right. Now all I need for the moment is your husband's current address.'

'I'm sorry,' Alison said. 'I don't know what it is.'

'His last known address then.'

'That was Shore Street.'

'Now that's a problem,' Mrs Cromall said. 'We must have an address for service of documents. Is there anyone else who might know where he is?'

'His insolvency consultant might. Or his mother. I'll ask them.'

'Splendid,' Mrs Cromall said. 'There's no rush. We can't do anything until your two years are up but it's as well to get everything clear, just in case we have to change tack. In view of what you've just told me, you understand.'

'I'll see what I can find out,' Alison promised.

'Keep me informed,' Mrs Cromall said. 'You can phone in the address when you've got it, can't you?'

As they shook hands at the end of the interview, Alison felt deflated. After the courage it had taken to make this decision, it was miserable to have achieved so little. Especially when there was another awful moving day to face and the bulk of the packing to do, all by herself. She couldn't ask her family to help her this time. Not after the way Rigg had treated them. That simply wasn't on. Sighing, she turned up the collar of her anorak and set off into the wind.

That afternoon, she plucked up what was left of her courage and made the two phone calls she'd promised.

Harvey Shearing was no help to her at all. He didn't know where Rigg was and, when she pressed him, told her, with some irritation, that he didn't need to know until the date the first dividend was due. He was so off-putting he made her feel she'd been presumptuous to contact him.

Maggie Toan had been having an afternoon nap when *her* phone rang.

'No, my dear,' she said. 'I've no idea where he is. Why do you want to know?'

'I've got some letters for him,' Alison explained – with relative truth.

'Oh, I shouldn't worry about *letters* if I were you,' Maggie advised. 'He'll pick them up in his own good time.' She had a sneaking suspicion that Rigg and Alison weren't living together any more now they'd allowed the house to be repossessed. If the silly girl was worrying for an address, it seemed more than likely. If that was the case, she didn't want to hear about it. 'I daresay he's busy at the moment,' she said, 'rushing about all over the place. You know Rigby. He's always got so many irons in the fire.'

It was Alison's turn to be irritated. I don't need irons in the fire, she thought, just an address in Mrs Cromall's file. 'You're sure you haven't had a letter from him?' she prompted. 'That might have an address on it.'

'I've told you,' Maggie said, and her voice sounded sharp. 'I don't know where he is. Why should I? I never know where he is. I'm only his mother.'

You should try being his wife, Alison thought. She was weary with frustration and failure. She'd made the most difficult decision in her life and nothing had come of it. Nothing could come of it because he was so well hidden.

'Well, thanks anyway,' she said. 'I'm sorry I disturbed you.' And she hung up quickly and went back to her packing.

Chapter Twenty-Three

It was Saturday evening and Morgan was on his way to Hampton, driving with care because grief had made him inaccurate and clumsy. There had been so much to attend to after the funeral that his few days' leave in Wales had extended into a week. Now and at last, he was on his way back to Alison. As the miles ticked by, he couldn't wait to get to Barnaby Green.

It upset him to see how derelict the house looked in the fading light of that cold April evening. The flower beds were full of dead daffodils, their crumpled heads as brown as paper on their long, dark stems. The front door was ajar and there was a long white scratch down the paintwork. There were tea chests and packing cases stacked on top of one another against the living room window, pushing the curtains askew. The topmost case was covered with a double-page spread from a recent newspaper. He could see the headline as he walked up the path. *'Nearly 3 million unemployed.'* There was a kid's bike lying on its side in the flower bed and several toys scattered in the porch but no sign of Alison or the children. Feeling suddenly rather unsure of himself, he pushed upon the door and went in. There was no one on the ground floor at all.

'Alison,' he called.

'Up here, Morgan!' Jon's voice called back.

She was on the landing, struggling to manhandle a chest of drawers down the stairs, and had obviously been working hard for some time. Her hair was stuck to her forehead with sweat, her jeans and jersey were smudged with dirt and grease and she frowned as she hauled at the chest of drawers.

'What are you *doin'*?' he said, bounding up the stairs to help her. 'You can't move a thing that size by yourself.'

Now that he was close to her he realised that she was furious and tearful. 'Yes I can,' she said, tugging at it. 'I've got to. There's no one else to do it. We've got to be out of here on Thursday.'

'Put it down a minute,' Morgan said, pulling at her arm, 'while I think of the best way.' Ever since the accident he'd had problems carrying heavy weights.

She fought him off. 'I've got to do it. Don't you see? I've got to.' Then she turned to shriek at Jon, who had put his head out of the bedroom door to see Morgan. 'You go straight back to bed! Do you hear me? And stay there. I don't want you two getting hurt on top of everything else. Read your book.'

Morgan recognised the edge in her voice as hysteria. There was only one thing to do, and that was to get the chest of drawers out of the way and *then* try to calm her. He dragged himself away from his grief to cope. 'Right!' he said. 'You take that end, I'll take this. Easy does it.'

It was heavy even for the two of them and by the time they'd carried it into the living room his shoulder was beginning to pain him. But she wouldn't rest. There was a toy chest to bring down and a bedside cabinet and two cardboard boxes full of games.

'We'll do those,' he said, 'and then we'll stop. It's not good for the kids to be up there in the bedroom all on their own. They need settlin'.'

'They're my kids,' she said wildly, heading upstairs again. 'I'll do what I like with them. You can't tell me how to treat my own kids.'

'Alison, *cariad*,' he pleaded, following her. 'Nobody's criticising you. I only said . . .'

'Yes, you were. I heard what you said. You think I'm a bad mother. Well you're right. I *am* a bad mother.' She knew she had been treating the kids appallingly these last few days, shouting at them for nothing and sending them up to bed long before they were tired, but she couldn't help herself. The more guilty she felt, the more badly she behaved; and the more badly she behaved, the more there was to feel guilty about. 'I'm a bad mother – and a bad daughter – and a bad sister – and a bad daughter-in-law. I can't pack. I burn the dinner. I can't even make a phone call without upsetting people. I can't do anything right. I've got all those debts to pay. Brad's still bald and it's all my fault. And there's Mum and all that money. I should have seen that coming but I didn't. I've been sick with worry ever since she told me. You're right. You're right. You don't have to tell me. I can't cope with anything.'

How did we get into this? Morgan wondered. He made a supreme effort to sympathise with her. 'What's the matter?'

She refused to look at him. 'Nothing,' she said sarcastically. 'What should be the matter? My life's perfect.'

Sarcasm was more than he could bear. 'Well at

least you're *alive*,' he said. His voice was so bitter it stopped her in her tracks.

The realisation that she'd forgotten all about his grandfather was like being doused with cold water. 'Oh my God!' she said. 'Oh Morgan, I'm so sorry.'

But he wasn't listening to her. He'd sunk down on to the stair below her and was sitting with his face hidden in his hands. And he was groaning.

The sound filled her with such pity it made her ache. She'd seen Rigg weep many, many times, and all three of her brothers had cried at Dad's funeral, but she'd never heard a man groan with grief. She crept shamefacedly down the stairs and sat down beside him, with one arm round his huddled shoulders. To carry on like that when he was grieving! To forget about his grandfather! How could she have been so callous? 'I'm so sorry,' she whispered.

'He was such a good man, Ali,' he said, his hands still over his eyes. 'It shouldn't have been like that. It wasn't fair. I can't bear it.'

'No,' she said. 'I know.'

'I loved him so much an' now I shall never see him again. Never. It's . . .' But he could find no words to express this misery. There was only the pain of it.

'It feels as if someone's punched a hole right through the middle of your body,' she said, remembering. 'I know.'

He looked up at her, his blue eyes strained with grief. 'Yes,' he said. 'That's how it is. That's exactly how it is. How do you know?'

'I've been there,' she said simply. 'When Dad died.'

'Yes,' he said, and dropped his head into his hands again.

Now that her self-pity was drowned and her sympathy aroused, Alison knew, instinctively, how to help him. He needed to talk, to weep – if he could – to be encouraged to remember. Above all, he needed to be comfortable and comforted. She left him quietly and tiptoed into the kids' bedroom to kiss them good night and settle them, promising them a story when she'd finished 'a bit more packing'. Then she went back to Morgan to do what she could.

'Come downstairs,' she said, leading him by the arm. 'It's too cramped here.'

He allowed himself to be led, walking heavily and with little sense of where he was going. They sat side by side on her untidy sofa.

'Could you tell me about him, Morgan?' she asked. 'Or would that be . . . ?' She spoke very gently and tentatively because the expression on his face was so awful, but he answered her at once and with evident relief.

'He was such a good man,' he mourned. 'I know he was old, but he shouldn't have died like that. He should have died peaceful, in his bed, not strugglin' for breath, on the floor.'

She waited, knowing there was more. And more came, slowly, haltingly, but with gradual and increasing relief: about the death and the funeral, about Nan and how brave she was, about Granddad and what a fine man he'd been. He was remembered at home, out fishing, down the pit, among his family.

'Head of the family, he was. The one we all looked up to. Old man Griffiths. No matter what your problem was, he had an answer for it. Wasn't always the answer you expected mind. I remember he used to say: "*Nothin' ever came of forcin' things. Easy does it. Go with it, wait for the moment, then turn against the grain, an' you can take it all your way, sweet an' easy.*"'

'Sounds like sense to me,' Alison said, thinking about it. 'I've been trying to force things these last few days.'

'Is that why you were in such a state?'

'Yes.'

'Your turn now,' he said, remembering some of the babble of nonsense she'd been yelling. 'What was the matter?'

'It's nothing really,' she said. 'Just something I found out about Rigg.'

'Ah! What's he done?'

He had recovered sufficiently for her to unburden herself. 'It's Mum's nest-egg,' she said, and told him the whole story briefly, from the meeting with Harry Elton to her visit to the solicitor. The telling upset her and reminded her of how wicked Rigg had been and how hopelessly guilty she felt, but she remained relatively calm. 'I don't know how he could have done such a thing,' she said. 'To Mum of all people. And to touch Greg for twenty thousand.'

'Was that why you said you'd got to do all the packing yourself?'

'I didn't think I could ask them for help. Not after that.'

'But you don't think that now?' It was only just a question.

She answered honestly. 'I don't know.'

'They'll be hurt if you don't.'

'Yes. I suppose so.' Confessing to him had made her see things differently. 'It was so evil. That's what I can't get over.'

'The evil flourish like the green bay tree,' Morgan said sadly, remembering his grandfather's funeral. 'The good die of the dust.'

'I used to think I loved him once,' she said. 'Now I think it was just pity. He's very good at making people feel sorry for him. He keeps on about it. All about how badly his mother treated him, and how he loved his father and wasn't allowed to go to his funeral, and how people let him down and ran off with his money. I used to think it was all true. I'm not so sure now.'

It was the moment to come clean. 'Look,' Morgan said, turning so that they were face to face. 'There's somethin' you ought to know. Somethin' I should have told you ages ago. When I came down to Hampton that first day and met you, I was lookin' for Rigg.'

'Were you?' she said, intrigued to hear it. 'What for?'

'I'd been paid to.'

He waited for her reaction. But it didn't come. She went on looking at him, her expression thoughtful. 'I'm a private investigator,' he explained. 'Right? I was hired to investigate *him*. By one of his creditors.' Then he was afraid that he'd upset her because she screwed up her face and shut her eyes. 'I should have told you at the start but there was always a reason not to, d'you see. It wasn't the right time. I thought I might upset you.'

She opened her eyes, blinked and looked at him. The expression on her face was so extraordinary he wasn't sure whether she was going to laugh or cry. 'What you're telling me is: you met *me* because you'd been sent to find Rigg.'

'Right.'

'But that's funny,' she said. She was grinning at him. 'That's really funny. That's poetic justice. Serves him right.' Then she began to laugh.

Relief that he hadn't upset her made Morgan laugh too. The irony of it *was* rather splendid when he came to think about it.

'So you know about the voluntary arrangement?' she said, when their laughter died down. 'And him doing a runner to Spain.'

He'd come to the painful part of this confession. 'Yes,' he said, his expression changing. 'As a matter a fact, it was me went out there and made him come back. I wish I hadn't.'

She understood what he was worried about. 'It wasn't your fault he hit me,' she said.

They were both very serious. 'It was my fault he came back,' he said.

'He'd have hit me sooner or later anyway. That's the sort of man he is.'

'I'm sorry I brought him back, *cariad*.'

'I know,' she said gently. 'But if it hadn't been for you knowing about him, we wouldn't have met in the first place, would we?'

That was true and comforting.

'I'm going to check that the kids are all right,' Alison said, kissing his cheek, 'and then I'm going to rustle up a supper. We can't go on for ever without food.'

They ate what they could, found two cans of beer in the fridge, and went on talking. They talked until three in the morning – she reliving the anger and revulsion she'd felt as she uncovered Rigg's dishonesty, he telling the awful story of that death over and over again – talking and talking, healing one another with words.

At four, Morgan woke up to find that they'd both fallen asleep on the sofa. At a little after six, he woke again to discover that he was lying at full length and that she'd put a pillow under his head and a blanket over his legs. She must have gone up to bed, he thought, as sleep overtook him again, and was touched that she'd looked after him so tenderly. He didn't wake again until it was full morning and the children were standing beside the sofa with their picture books ready for him to read to them.

Alison was in the kitchen, dressed in her clean jeans and a pretty pink jersey, busy making tea. 'It's a lovely morning,' she said.

He stood beside her and looked through the kitchen window at the pale spring sunshine dappling the grass. 'Yes,' he said. 'It is.'

The pain of that long night had brought them very close together. Now they were warm and easy with one another and full of affection. He kissed her briefly and gently, loving her very much.

'I'll have Sugar Puffs,' Jon said, from the kitchen door. So the family breakfast had to begin.

'What are you goin' to do today?' Morgan asked, when they were all settled round the table.

'I've got the key to the new house,' she said. 'I'm going to do a bit of cleaning up.'

'I could help you, if you like,' he offered. 'I haven't got to start work until tomorrow.'

She smiled at that. 'I'd be grateful.'

'Then that's what we'll do. Would your mum look after the kids?'

'I expect so.'

'I'll drive them round.'

For a few seconds, Alison wondered how she was going to explain the appearance of a strange man at her mother's house so early on a Sunday morning, but she had too many other things to think about, and the work had to be done, so she set her misgivings aside and phoned. Elsie said she'd love to look after the children. Toys were chosen to keep them entertained and they all drove over.

It was a significant meeting, even though Morgan and Elsie both handled it with casual caution.

'This is Morgan,' Alison said, when her mother opened the door.

Elsie looked her visitor up and down. He's a funny-looking bloke, she thought. Kind face though. Nice blue eyes. She could tell from Ali's voice that he was important.

'We're going to clean up the new house,' Alison explained.

So he *is* important, Elsie thought. 'All right then. When d'you want them back?'

'Could they stay all day?'

They could. 'I could give them supper if you like.'

'We'll collect them in time for bed,' Alison said. 'Thanks ever so.'

'He don't say much, this Morgan feller a' yours,' Elsie said to the children as she took them into the house.

'He's Welsh,' Jon told her, seriously. 'He reads stories ever so good.'

'He sleeps on the sofa,' Emma said. 'In his socks.'

'Does he though?' Elsie said. 'Fancy that.' Oh yes. He *is* important.

Chapter Twenty-Four

Alison's second moving day was remarkably straightforward.

Mark drove the removal van, Brad looked after the kids and kept them overnight, Elsie hung the curtains she had adapted to the right length two days previously, Alison and Morgan unpacked, and Jenny cooked a meal and brought it over for the workers that evening. By the time all the helpers had left, the worst of the move was over.

After the rush and effort of the day, the evening was as soft as a rose, languorous, sea-hushed and full of strange scents and colours. Sunset stained the western sky with streaks of pale green and smudged purple and the clouds that drifted across the face of the moon were spindrift veils of lilac and grey.

'What a night!' Morgan said, standing by the garden gate to admire it. 'I never seen a sky that colour.'

She looked at him for a long moment, her face serious in the half light. 'Can I ask you something?' she said.

'If you like,' he said, wondering what she was going to say.

But it wasn't the sort of question he hoped for. 'Does your back hurt you?'

He wasn't sure he wanted to answer. 'Why do you ask?'

'I've been watching you. You carry things – oh, I don't know – sort of carefully, as if it hurts you. Does it?'

'Sometimes.' And as she waited, expecting more, 'I had a bit of an accident, down the pit. Broke a few bones.'

'Oh Morgan!' she said, full of sympathy for him. 'Why didn't you tell me? If I'd known, I'd never have let you carry all that furniture about.'

'That's why I didn't tell you.'

'Would you tell me now?' she asked.

So he told her as much as he could remember. She listened with total concentration, sharing every moment and sympathising with every emotion. What a terrible thing it must have been, down in that awful darkness, not knowing whether he would live or die.

'I do love you,' she said. The words were spoken in a rush of admiration and pity before she had time to consider them. But once said, she knew how true they were. She *did* love him. She'd loved him for a long time. She just hadn't admitted it.

Morgan had hoped for this moment ever since he first declared his own love for her but now that it had come he could hardly believe it. 'Truly?' he asked.

'Oh yes,' she said, putting her arms around his neck. 'Truly.' She was quite sure now.

They stood eye to loving eye under their romantic sunset, alone together, loving one another and aware of how strong their emotions were.

'Am I to stay the night?' he hoped.

If he was, there were things that had to be talked about. 'I'm not on the pill or anything.'

He looked down at her. 'I'll take care of you,' he said.

'Can you? I mean . . .'

'Fully prepared,' he said and felt he had to explain further. 'Not that I was expectin' anythin'. Just bein' on the safe side.'

She wasn't quite sure how to take that.

'An' I haven't got AIDS or anythin' like that,' he said.

That surprised her. 'How do you know? Have you been tested?'

'I'm a blood donor,' he said. 'They have to test you.'

'Of course,' she said, admiring him again. 'I might have known that. You're just the sort of person. A giver.'

'So it's all right?'

'Yes. It's all right.'

He took her hand and laid it tenderly against his cheek. She watched him, feeling full of love for him – until she suddenly realised that her hand was so black with grime it was leaving smudge marks on his face.

'I need a bath,' she said, abruptly changing mood. 'I'm filthy.'

'So?' he said, still holding her hand and smiling into her eyes. 'We're both dirty, come to that. What d'you expect? We been workin'.'

'A bath each,' Alison said. 'That's what we need. I've got some Radox.'

'There's romantic you are,' he laughed. 'Lucky the immersion's on.'

'I've got a bathrobe in the bathroom box,' she said, walking into the house. 'I bought it for Rigg ages ago, but he never wore it. Wasn't flash enough. Shall I find it?'

She found soaps, Radox, a whole stack of towels, even bathsalts. The only problem was that once they got upstairs they discovered that there were no light bulbs in any of the sockets.

'I was caught out like this last time,' Alison said, as they stood in the darkness in the kids' bedroom. 'I should have been forewarned.'

'I'll get the table lamp,' he said. 'We can use it like a candle.'

Which they did. And, although the central heating in the house didn't seem to work at all, there was more than enough hot water for two baths, his first and then hers.

Morgan waited for her to finish her bath in a state of such heightened desire he could hardly breathe. He prowled the bedroom. He sat on her bed in the darkness with the bathrobe wrapped round him. He stood by the window and watched the rich blue of the night clouds rolling endlessly by. The scent of her bathsalts seeped under the bathroom door, filling his mind with imagined glimpses of her beautiful nakedness, rosy under the water.

She entered the bedroom, softly, on pale bare feet, while he was looking out of the window. She was wearing a blue and green towel like a sarong and another turbaned round her head and she carried the lamp before her in both hands. In the amber light, her wet hair shone dark and glossy on her temples and her bare arms glowed as though they were giving off a radiance of their own. He was bewitched by the sight of her.

'Mermaid,' he said, admiring and desiring.

'I can't find my hair dryer,' she said.

'Are you always so practical?' he asked.

'No,' she said, smiling at him shyly. It was a protective device and a very necessary one. She was acutely aware that they were on their own in a bedroom, and that she had virtually invited him there, with no kids as chaperons, and a whole night before them. And to make her dilemma more acute, she knew she wanted him very much.

'Come by here,' he said, patting the bed. 'I'll dry it for you if you like.'

She tucked her sarong firmly in place, set the table lamp on the bedside table, and sat on the bed beside him in the pool of soft light it cast. The room was full of packing cases and tea chests, bulky ugly things, lurking in the shadows like prehistoric beasts, nails glinting. The bed was the one civilised object in the room, its duvet tinted amber by the lamp light, the pine bedstead rich as honey. Morgan waited beside it, patient and amorous, his robe dark as red wine.

'How's your shoulder?' she said, as he rubbed her hair with the hand-towel.

It was difficult to find even one word to answer her with, his desire was so strong. 'Better.'

'Good,' she said. She was breathless too.

Words deserted them both. He rubbed her hair dry, kissing her face whenever she turned it towards him. And her mouth whenever she would allow it – which was more and more frequently. Soon they were caught in a timeless, magical trance of rising desire, as towels and robe were flung aside – love driven, flesh eager, sense hungry.

'Now?' he asked. 'Is it all right?'

Oh yes. More than all right. Much, much more than all right. Inevitable and gratifying and magical.

Afterwards, when they'd got their breath back, they talked, relaxed and easy with his arm still under her neck and her head on his shoulder.

'I want to marry you,' he said, 'when you've divorced him. You know that, don't you.'

'Yes. I know that.'

'You will marry me?'

The question confused her. *Did* she want to marry him? She really didn't know. Marriage was such a risk. In any case, it was an academic question when she was still technically married to Rigg. 'Probably,' she temporised, not wanting to upset him by a direct refusal at such a tender time. 'I don't know. Possibly not. It's too soon to say. I can't even think about it while I'm still married to Rigg. I've got to get divorced first.'

But that's eleven months off, Morgan thought, and that's a long time to have to wait. A long time to live this sort of half life. But what else could he do?

'Don't let's talk about it,' she said, kissing him. 'I know it's childish, but I'd rather not think about it, not for the moment, not till I have to. We've had so many awful things happen to us in the last year, me an' the kids, I'd like a summer off just to enjoy life again.'

It was the least he could give her when she was in his arms and so loving. 'Then that's what you shall have, *cariad*,' he promised.

The next morning they both overslept. Alison woke first to the realisation that it was past eight o'clock and someone was hammering on the door. She got up quickly, put on her dressing gown and ran down the stairs. It was Brad, her bald head gleaming, delivering the children and the hedgehog.

'They've had breakfast,' she said, walking through into the kitchen. 'Mr Tiggywinkle didn't like the journey. I'd get him out in the garden pretty quick, if I was you, and you'd better burn the shoe box. Morning Morgan.'

He was standing in the doorway, dressed in his shirt and trousers and scratching his head.

For a second Alison was embarrassed to see him there and wished he'd had the sense to stay upstairs, at least until Brad had gone. Then she worried in case his presence in the house upset the kids. But neither of them seemed at all phased by it.

'Come an' see our hedgehog,' Jon said. 'We're going to put him in the garden.'

'He's done a huge poo in his box,' Emma confided.

'What's his name?' Morgan asked. And when he was told, 'There's lovely. Mornin' Brad.' Now that the first embarrassed moments were over, he was as easy as if he'd been living in the house for years.

'I'm off to work,' Brad said, 'or I shall be late for the old dears. They're all yours, Ali. They been ever so good. You here for the day, Morgan?'

'*Duw* no,' Morgan said. 'I'm due in Guildford in fifteen minutes.'

'Oh well!' she laughed at him. 'You'll do that easy. I'll come round after work, Ali.'

'Do you want breakfast?' Alison asked when Brad had gone.

'Why not,' he said, smiling at her. 'I'm so late now, there's no point rushin'.'

So Alison settled the hedgehog in its new quarters and began to cook breakfast while Morgan went upstairs to wash and get properly dressed. Despite their breakfast with Brad, the children decided they'd like cocoa and biscuits, so the four of them sat down to enjoy their first morning meal together, in their strange clean kitchen, at their familiar scrubbed table. Their lives seemed to have shifted into a new and more comfortable gear. They talked about the hedgehog and the move and their plans for the weekend. As the meal proceeded, it occurred to Alison that she and Rigg had never sat round a table like that at breakfast time in all the years they'd been married.

Afterwards Morgan kissed them all goodbye and drove off to Guildford and excuses. And on an impulse, Alison took the children down on the beach. She'd already arranged for Jon to stay off school until Monday so they had Friday and the weekend ahead of them to settle in. What better way to start it than to walk beside the sea?

It was another lovely spring day and they had the shore to themselves. The tide was on its way out, so the beach was washed clean and fresh and ready for a new day, the pebbles polished and the long sands ridged by the retreating waves. Above their heads the arc of the sky was already richly blue and below it the sea shone in the sunshine, the curve of each tumbling wave polished smooth as green glass. It seemed entirely fitting to Alison that she should be out in the open air and in such a beautiful setting after such a night. There were still problems to be faced and difficulties to overcome but for the moment she was simply and entirely happy. A new day, a new home, a new life.

'Oh kids!' she said, 'isn't it great to be alive.'

Chapter Twenty-Five

Like all complicated changes, Alison's transformation from deserted wife to established lover was achieved by degrees – not all of them easy and some of them surprising.

Over the next few days, she gradually put the house to rights and got to know some of her new neighbours. One, an outspoken redhead called Lola, was particularly friendly and had some useful information.

She called in one Friday to ask if Alison would like her to get anything from the local shops.

'No,' Alison said. 'I don't think so. That's very kind of you.'

'We've got to stick together,' Lola said, explaining her kindness, 'all us one-parent families.'

'How did you know that?' Alison asked. Once it would have been a shock to be so easily recognised; now she felt relaxed about it.

'I've seen you up the school,' Lola said. 'Takes one to know one, I expect. You get to know the signs after a while. That Welshman's just your feller, isn't he.'

'Yes,' Alison admitted, surprised at how quickly *that* news had travelled. 'My husband walked out thirteen months ago.'

'Join the club,' Lola grinned. 'You're the eighth in this street alone.'

'Is that right?'

'Too bloody right. There are skunks running out on their wives and kids everywhere you look. It's an epidemic. Still, I can tell you one good thing about it. In this neck a' the woods, you don't need to worry about the cohabiting rule. We don't grass one another up.'

That was a very definite relief, especially to Morgan, because he wanted to visit whenever he could and he'd been worried in case his presence in the house got Alison into trouble with the DSS. Reassured, he came down at least once during the week – when he wasn't working away – and every weekend. He usually arrived on Saturday night and stayed until early Monday morning, so Sunday became their special day. He and Alison had their first argument over whether or not he should pay her housekeeping, which he won easily, claiming that paying for his food wasn't 'cohabiting' and that, in any case, if he wasn't allowed to pay for the food, he wouldn't eat it.

The days became weeks and the time they spent together grew more and more rewarding and easy – although Alison had to accept that Rigg was still a part of her life. It annoyed her that she didn't know where he was and angered her that he still owed her mother all that money. She didn't talk about him to the children and tried to put him out of her mind, but Jon remembered him.

She was stripping the beds early one Monday morning so as to get the sheets out on the line before they went to school and to work, when the little boy asked one of his sudden questions.

'When Daddy comes back,' he said, as she fitted the clean bottom sheet, 'where will he sleep?'

Alison went on smoothing the sheet to buy time. It was such an impossible question she didn't know how to answer it. 'He might not come back,' she said, cautiously. 'I don't know where he is.'

'But he's my daddy,' the child protested. 'He's got to come back, hasn't he. He could sleep in my bed when Morgan is here.'

'He owes a lot of money to a lot of people,' Alison said. 'He can't come back till he's paid them.'

That meant nothing to a five-year-old.

'He hasn't seen the hedgehog,' Emma said from her perch on her own bed. 'He'll like the hedgehog, won't he, Mummy.'

'He might,' Alison said guardedly. 'Hop off for a minute, there's a good girl. I've got to change your sheets now.'

'They're not wet,' Emma said, with some pride.

'No. I know they're not. You're a good little girl.' Wet beds were gradually becoming a rarity. Thank heavens. But she'd hoped it was because they'd forgotten about their father and the way he went on. The problem bothered her all day.

'I don't understand it,' she confided to Morgan that night. 'I thought they were glad to see the back of him after the awful way he behaved last time they saw him.'

'He's still their father, I suppose,' he said. 'They're bound to think about him.'

I shall never be really free of him, Alison thought. He'll always be their father no matter what I do. That's one part of my life I can't change. And the thought depressed her.

By now, Morgan had become part of her family.

He was included in all their outings and sneaked off to the pub of an evening with Mark and Greg – and Andy and Clare whenever they were down. So it was only natural that when June began and it was the school half-term, he should invite her to Port Talbot for a week's holiday to meet *his* family.

The visit was an exhilarating success for, as Alison discovered on her very first evening, the Griffiths and the Warehams were similar tribes, warm, noisy and friendly. She was welcomed into the family at once, even – as Morgan's father joked – 'though you're not Welsh, which is a definite blemish. Still, we got to make allowances!'

Morgan drove her from house to house and cousin to cousin, to see Nan in her hillside house in Blaenhydyglyn, and Hywell and Bronwen in the valley, and little Morgan, who was a fine fat child who instantly befriended Emma and had to be carried about by Jon. They visited each of Morgan's sisters in turn and were fed like royalty at every house. They went to Swansea and the Mumbles as though they were tourists. And on their last afternoon, as the sun was shining, they climbed the green side of the Mynydd to see the panoramic view of Port Talbot from the top.

Alison thought it was breathtaking. 'You can see everything,' she said. 'Look Jon, there's the harbour, and there's the beach. I didn't realise it was so long, Morgan.'

'It's a good beach,' Morgan said, enjoying the sight of its sandy length stretching to the west of the town. From their crows' nest on the Mynydd, the waves rolling in to shore looked like lace frills. 'There's the steelworks, look Jon, where my dad used to work.'

'It's the size of them I can't get over,' Alison said, squinting into the sun. 'They're enormous.'

'That's nothing to what they were before the closures,' Morgan told her. 'You could see the glow of the furnaces as far as Swansea in those days. At night the sky was orange for miles.'

On the mountainside opposite, windscreens flashed like diamonds.

'Look at those cars, Jon,' Alison said. 'Aren't they tiny?'

'Morgan's car is 'normous,' Emma said. 'Isn't it, Morgan?'

'You ought to drive you know, Ali,' Morgan said. 'I wonder you don't learn.'

'I have learned,' Alison said. 'I passed my test when I was eighteen. I just haven't got a car, that's all.'

'Then get one.'

She laughed at that. 'What with?'

'I'll lend you the money.'

She laughed at that suggestion too. 'How would I repay you?'

'All right then,' he said. 'I won't lend you any money if you don't like the idea. I won't give you so much housekeepin' an' you can pay me back that way. You could have one of our company cars at its trade-in price. We've got two replacements on order for August. How would that be?'

It was a four-year-old Metro and, on those terms, just about possible. But when Morgan drove her to Guildford to collect it, she felt very unsure of herself behind the wheel of a car.

'I haven't driven for years,' she said.

'Why not? You had a car, didn't you?'

'That was his,' she explained. 'He wouldn't let me drive his precious BMW. Oh Morgan, what if I do it wrong?'

'You won't,' he reassured her. 'It's like riding a bicycle. It'll come back to you. Come on, we'll go for a spin in the country and you'll see.'

It was a disaster. She crashed the gears, she oversteered, she made a mess of her first right turn and finally – to her horror – she ran out of road on an easy bend. She'd come into the bend too fast, and she knew it, but she'd forgotten how quickly everything happens in a car. For a few frantic seconds she stood on the brakes and pulled on the steering wheel, her heart pounding. But it was no good. There was a bump followed by a dreadful scraping noise and by the time the car came to a halt she realised she had scraped the near-side bumper along a rough stone wall.

Fortunately there was no other traffic about. She got out of the driving seat and walked shakily back along the road to inspect the damage, feeling hideously ashamed of herself. There didn't seem to be much wrong with the wall, which was covered in scratches old and new – but the bumper was mangled.

'Oh God!' she said, staring at it. 'This is awful.'

Morgan wasn't worried. 'Soon have that fixed,' he said cheerfully. 'We all make mistakes in a new car.'

'But I've wrecked it,' she said.

'That's what bumpers are for. Slower approach next time.'

'You can drive back,' she said. 'I'm not driving any more. I'm not cut out for it.'

His face was suddenly stern. 'Don't be ridiculous,' he said crossly. 'I told you. It's simply a matter of gettin' used to it. That's all. Get back in the car.'

She was shocked to be treated so harshly. 'I told *you*,' she said. 'I can't. Not after this. Rigg was right. He always said I'd be a danger on the roads. I can't drive.'

'You can,' he said, opening the driver's door. 'And he's not right. This is a minor accident. Could have happened to anybody. Get in.'

Because he was being so positive she did as she was told. But sitting in the driving seat, she knew she was still afraid. 'I can't do it Morgan,' she said.

'Switch on the ignition,' he told her firmly. 'You're a good driver and now you're goin' to prove it to yourself and damn Rigg's opinion. You're goin' to take us back to Guildford – slowly. I'm here beside you. You won't make another mistake.'

She wasn't reassured, but she switched on the ignition and began to drive – very, very carefully, and watching out for other traffic. By the time she got to Guildford again, a little confidence was beginning to return.

'There you are, see,' Morgan said as she parked – quite neatly – by the kerb outside the office. 'Perfect. Now you're gettin' the hang of it.'

She was more herself now that the drive was over. 'I'm sorry I made a fuss,' she said.

'Nothin' to be sorry about,' he said. 'You frightened yourself. That's all. An' that's no bad thing. Keeps you on your toes. You're a good driver, *cariad*. Just a bit rusty, that's all.'

It had been such a disquieting experience, she felt she had to ask, 'You do still love me?'

He kissed her to show her how much. 'That's one thing you never got to worry about,' he said. 'I shall love you for the rest of my life. You're stuck with me – no matter how you drive. And just think, you can take the kids to all sorts of places in the summer holidays.'

'If I ever get used to it.'

But like so many things in this new life of hers, it took surprisingly little time to get used to, despite such a bad start. By the time the schools broke up in July, she was driving as if she'd been at the wheel for years.

In August, because the recession had put Spain beyond most pockets for the time being, the holiday crowds returned to Hampton in larger numbers than usual.

Gangs of spotty young men, raucous with drink, strutted the promenade, wolfwhistling the girls in their brief bikinis and their new holiday make-up – or ambled around the town, in frayed shorts and T-shirts and flip-flops, arms and backs and shoulders patched flab white and sunburn red. Plump matrons in tight floral dresses ate ice-creams, cockles, chips, and sticks of rocks, while their husbands grew red-faced in the nearest pub. The beaches were full of holiday makers. The adults oiled one another with sun-tan lotion or spread out to bake on their skimpy towels, while their children scratched the sand and leapt into the waves, chirruping and quarrelling like sparrows.

Elsie said it was quite like old times. But Alison was glad of the car to take her children away from the crowds. Especially as Morgan had to spend a lot of his time working in the North. It was a disappointment to her that, just as the new term started in September, he had another long assignment in Birmingham. But there was plenty to do, she knew he wouldn't be away for long and she was well used to coping on her own.

But in the middle of that first school week she had to cope with something that she couldn't have foreseen.

On Wednesday morning, when she and Emma came home after taking Jon to school, she was greeted in the hall by a terrible smell. I must have forgotten to pull the chain before we went out, she thought, and went into the bathroom at once to put things right.

The bowl of the toilet was brimming with sewage. Gagging, she pulled the handle to flush it away. But instead of clearing, the filth spilled over the edge of the toilet and trickled on to the bathroom floor.

'Who's done a poo on the floor?' Emma said, following her mother into the room.

'Keep out, there's a good girl,' Alison said while thinking. There's a blockage somewhere. I'd better check the manhole.

But when she went out into the back garden there was no need to check. The smell was almost as bad out there as it was in the house and when she removed the manhole cover the drain was full to the brim. It was enough to make anyone panic but she kept calm. No matter how dreadful this was, she was going to cope with it.

She settled Emma in the living room with some

crayons and a drawing book, went into the kitchen to look for a suitable tool and found a broom handle. Then she tied a scarf over her nose and mouth and braved the garden, took a deep breath, lifted the cover and began to poke about in the filthy mess below her. Nothing happened except for some obscene bubbling, and even after struggling for nearly half an hour the mess had hardly drained away at all. By then, she was feeling so sick she had to stop.

It'll have to be dealt with properly, she thought. It's no good me poking around, even if I had the time for it – which I haven't. It needs proper tools and someone who knows what he's doing. I suppose I shall have to find the money to pay for it, if I'm responsible. But was she? She had a vague recollection of some division of responsibility being mentioned on the contract she'd signed. Interior and exterior or something like that. Why hadn't she thought of it before?

She went back into the house, washed her hands and face very thoroughly and then found the box file where she kept all her papers. The contract was three documents down. Blah, blah, blah . . . *'the landlord to be responsible for rendering exterior paintwork, keeping the roof, guttering and drains in good repair . . .'* It was like finding herself suddenly in possession of a suit of armour in the middle of a war.

It took a little while and several phone calls to arrange her day to make room for a visit to the agency. But it was done and she still got to work on time, driving through the gates of the holiday camp as her watch said ten thirty. Thank God for the car!

That afternoon, she and Emma kept their appointment at the agency. It was a sticky interview, just as she'd feared it would be. Welfare families get short shrift from most agencies. It took her twenty minutes to persuade this particular agent that the contract actually meant what it said, and then he claimed he couldn't contact the owner and couldn't proceed without his permission.

'This can't be left,' Alison said doggedly, holding Emma tightly on her lap. 'I know you think I'm being a nuisance but there's no choice. If something isn't done this afternoon there'll be shit all over the landlord's garden.'

The word made him wince. 'You see my position,' he said, shrugging his shoulders and grimacing.

This world, Alison thought, is full of men shrugging their shoulders and walking off to let the women clear up the mess they've made. 'I've tried to unblock it,' she said, 'when I didn't need to, and I'm not doing it again.'

'I don't know what I can do to help you,' the agent wriggled.

She was pushed to fury. How dare he just sit there and say such things. It's his job to help. He takes a big enough cut. 'Perhaps if I brought a bucket of the stuff into this office,' she said, 'it would give you an idea.'

'There's no need to take that tone,' the agent said, but he was clearly rattled.

'It's urgent,' she said. 'I can't have my children living in a house full of shit. They'll get ill. If you don't do something about it, here and now, I'll go to the council and tell the public health people, and see what they have to say.'

That threat worked. 'I'll tell you what I'll do,' he capitulated. 'I'll send someone round this afternoon and see if I can contact the landlord tomorrow. When will you be home?'

'In ten minutes,' she said. And was.

I never knew I could be so fierce, she thought to herself, as she looked out into her bubbling garden. For a peace maker, I've put up a bloody good fight this afternoon. Being on your own certainly shows you what you're made of.

Two men arrived with a van full of equipment just after she'd collected Jon from school. They were very cheerful and competent and knew exactly what the problem was.

'Old pipes,' the older man explained. 'Weren't built to withstand all this water, you see. Neither was the drains. When they went in, there was no baths or washin' machines. Just a toilet out the back an' a tap in the sink. This pipe's cracked in two places. We'll put a new piece in for you. By rights the whole lot should come out and be relaid proper. That drain's too shallow, you see. We get blockages up an' down this road all the time, don't we, Matt?'

'But you can fix it?' Alison asked.

'Take the kids out for a walk and we'll have it done for you by the time you get back.'

So they went out to enjoy a lungful of sea air.

When they got back the drain was cleared and cleaned and Brad was in the garden watching the new pipe being fitted.

'You've 'ad a fine ol' game here, aintcher,' she said.

'That's putting it mildly,' Alison said.

'I come over to ask you round to supper,' Brad said. 'That Cyril feller's give me three trout. Whatcher think? Will the kids eat trout?'

‘No, but I will. They’ll have fish fingers. I’ll bring some.’

‘Great,’ Brad said. ‘That’s settled then.’

‘You couldn’t have come at a better time,’ Alison told her.

‘Your phone’s ringing,’ the younger man said.

Alison took the kids and went into the house to answer it. For the first time that day she felt relaxed and happy. She half expected it to be Morgan ringing from Birmingham. Wouldn’t he be impressed to hear how she had handled everything? But it was Katy and her voice sounded odd.

‘Are you all right?’ Alison asked.

‘I’m at Meriel’s,’ Katy said, and now there was no doubt that she was crying. ‘Can you come over?’

‘Katy dear! What’s the matter?’

‘It’s Merry’s cat. She’s been run over.’

‘Oh Katy!’

‘She’s not dead,’ Katy sobbed. ‘But she must be horribly injured. It threw her in the air.’

‘Where is she now?’

‘She ran into the bush in the middle of the flats. She’s just lying there swearing and she won’t let us near and we don’t know what to do. She could be dying. I’ve rung home but there’s no answer. Merry’s mum and dad are in Chichester somewhere and her brother’s gone out on his bike. Oh Ali, we don’t know what to do.’

‘I’ll come straight over,’ Alison said. ‘Don’t worry. I’ll be there in five minutes.’

‘What’s up?’ Brad said, coming into the hall.

Alison explained, playing the incident down as much as she could for fear of alarming the kids.

'We'll have to take her to the vet, won't we kids?' Brad said.

'We?'

'I'll come with you. You'll never get four kids *and* an injured cat in your car.'

The cat was still under the bush when they arrived at the flats. Brad parked her car as near to it as she could, backing up very slowly and quietly. Then she and Alison knelt down beside the bush and tried to see what state the poor thing was in.

'She's just under there,' Meriel said, tearfully. 'She's a tabby cat. Do you see her?'

She was panting and dishevelled but there was no sign of blood.

'Get a cushion,' Brad instructed. 'I'll see if I can inch her on to it without hurting her too much. Then we can carry her without upsetting her.'

The cushion was brought and the cat was edged on to it, very delicately, and carried very, very gently to Brad's car.

'You get in the passenger seat, sunshine,' Brad said to Meriel, 'and I'll lower her on to your lap. Don't touch her. Just talk to her quietly.'

'Are we going to the vet's?' Jon asked, looking in at the car window.

'We are. You go back and get in the car with Mummy.'

'He'll mend her for you,' Jon said earnestly to Meriel. 'He's ever so nice. He did our hedgehog.'

'You're not going to Martin's, are you?' Alison asked in surprise.

'Why not?' Brad said easily. 'He's the best.'

'But not when . . . I mean, don't you think . . . ?'

'This is a life we're talking about here,' Brad said. 'Good God, if I had to avoid all my lovers I'd never get out of the house. I took the trout from old Cyril.'

'He was different.'

'Right. He's just a moron who works on a trout farm. Martin's the best vet in town, so that's where we're going.'

Chapter Twenty-Six

Since the end of his affair with Brad, Martin Smith had been struggling against depression. During the day his concern for the animals kept it more or less under control. But at night he sat cooped up in his flat – in rooms that seemed to have shrunk – too miserable to go out. His trouble was that he was impossibly shy. Always had been. At school, there'd been whole days when he hadn't dared to open his mouth. Even now, as a veterinary surgeon with an excellent reputation, he was gauche in company. With Brad he had begun to feel at ease for the first time in his life.

Scrubbing up in the surgery after his last patient, he remembered her miserably. Dear Brad, with her mad hair and her untidiness and her rough voice. He could hear it now, as if she were in the next room.

'Mr Smith. He's the feller we want to see. Mr Martin Smith.'

Good God! He *could* hear her. She *was* in the next room. He stuffed the towel down at once and went through to the waiting room.

The sight of Brad's bald head gave him such a shock he felt as though someone had punched him in the stomach. Oh Christ! he thought, she's got cancer and she hasn't told me.

She was smiling at him brightly – too brightly – and

urging him to look at a cat. The waiting room was crowded with people. He registered that Alison was one of them, that she'd got her kids with her, and that they were all looking anxious.

'Yes,' he said, becoming professional. 'Bring her into the surgery, please. Just you and the little girl, if you don't mind.' He turned to Meriel as he opened the surgery door. 'She's your cat, is she?'

'Yes.'

'Well, let's have a look at her.'

He examined the cat very carefully, asking Brad to hold her steady when she swore, and murmuring reassurance to the girl from time to time. It didn't take him long to discover that the poor thing was badly injured and required an immediate operation.

'No bones broken,' he said, 'and that's one good thing. But I'm afraid there are some internal injuries and she's in shock of course. We shall have to operate on her.'

'Will she be all right?' Meriel asked.

'I hope so,' he said, but added honestly, 'It all depends on how bad her injuries turn out to be.'

'When will you operate?' Brad asked.

'As soon as we've prepared her,' Martin said. 'I'll phone you, shall I? Let you know what's happened.'

Meriel was crying again.

'Try not to worry,' he said to her. 'I'll do the very best I can.'

Brad was already on her way out of the door. There wasn't time for him to ask her how she was or to suggest a meeting or anything. 'I'll phone you,' he said to her.

'Ta,' she said. And was gone.

Alison and the others were still in the waiting room.

'She's in good hands,' Alison tried to comfort.

'The best,' Brad said fiercely. 'He's going to ring us.'

They took the two girls home, staying at both houses to talk over what had happened, and they were late back to Brad's flat to cook their special meal. It was well past the kids' bedtime before they began to fry the almonds. And just as they were browning nicely, someone rang at the door.

'Oh bugger that!' Brad said. 'Tell 'em to go away.'

It was Martin. 'I'm ever so sorry,' he said. 'The cat didn't make it. I thought I ought to come and tell you myself, seeing as . . .'

'Oh dear,' Alison said, standing aside to let him in. 'Poor little thing.'

'I'm so sorry.'

'We didn't really have a lot of hope,' Alison said. 'We could see she was bad.'

'Her spleen was ruptured,' Martin explained. 'She – um – it happened on the operating table.'

'Oh Christ!' Brad said. 'I hate it when anything dies.' Her eyes were full of tears. 'Look after the almonds, Ali, while I phone that poor kid. Oh, that poor little cat. It's not fair. Bloody drivers! They want locking up.'

'We tried really hard,' Martin explained to Alison while Brad dialled. 'It was the shock as much as anything else. There wasn't anything we could do.'

'Is the cat dead?' Jon asked.

'I'm afraid so,' Martin said.

Jon gave it thought. To Alison's surprise he didn't

seem disturbed by the news. He was simply curious. 'What happens to cats when they're dead?' he asked. 'Do they go to heaven?'

Martin was nonplussed by the question but he answered it honestly. 'I don't know.'

'People go to heaven, don't they?'

'If they're good,' Alison said, giving the standard reply.

'Aunty Brad'll go to heaven,' Jon said. 'She's ever so good. When she dies, she'll go straight to heaven, won't she, Martin?'

When she dies, Martin thought, so it is . . .

'Well that's that,' Brad said, returning to the kitchen. 'She was ever so upset, poor kid. If I had a gun I'd see to that bloody driver myself. You had any supper, Martin?'

'Well no, as it happens.'

'You can share ours if you like,' Brad said. 'We got three trout, but these daft kids won't eat it. They're on fish fingers, aintcher kids.'

'Yeh!' Emma said happily.

Martin stayed to supper. How could he refuse her anything when she was so ill and she was being so brave about it?

It was an extraordinary meal after an extraordinary day. 'I feel as if I've been awake for a week,' Alison said, when she'd told them both about her visit to the letting agency and how she'd bullied the agent.

'Bullying, bad drains and then that poor cat,' she said. 'I don't want another day like this in a very long time. Let me cut that up for you, Emma.'

'No,' Emma said. 'Do it mesself.'

Alison slumped in her chair. 'I haven't got the energy to argue.'

'Then don't,' Brad advised. 'Waste a' time arguing with that kid. Never waste time, eh Martin.'

'No,' he agreed, yearning to ask about her illness.

'Too precious, time is,' Brad said. 'What I always say is you're a long time dead.'

He winced. But both women pretended not to have seen his expression, assuming that he was remembering the cat.

When the meal was finally over, the children were exhausted too. Brad and Alison had to carry them down to the car. By the time Brad came back into the flat, Martin was up to his wrists in soap bubbles, washing the supper things.

'Ain't that just typical,' she teased. 'Leave you alone for five minutes and you put on a pinny.'

He waved his bubbly hands before him as if he was warding off evil spirits. 'Don't joke!' he begged. 'Not now. Tell me quickly. Are you very ill?'

'Ill?' she said, grimacing at him. What was he talking about? Then she realised that he was looking at her naked scalp. 'Oh my God,' she said. 'You think I've got cancer. You think this is chemotherapy.'

His knees suddenly felt weak. 'Isn't it?'

'No. Course not. It's me new hair style. You went, I looked at me barnet and I thought, that's your lot, you're off an' all. An' that was it.'

He was choked with relief, rushing across the room to hold her in his arms. 'Oh thank God. Thank God,' he said into her neck. 'I've been worried sick ever since I saw you.'

'Hey!' she said, lifting his head so that he was forced to look at her. 'Martin, you dear old thing. Do I mean that much to you?'

'You know you do,' he said passionately.

She gave him a hard, quick kiss, holding his face between her hands, her fingers in his beard. 'I'm flattered,' she said. 'Really. Look, I'm sorry I flew off the handle that time.'

He kissed her back, feeling like a man who'd come home after a long journey. 'I deserved it,' he said. 'I spoke out of turn.'

'No you never,' she argued. 'You were right. I could see that after. I *am* a bully.'

'Well . . . maybe you need to be.'

'You said I scared you.'

He tried to deny it. 'No. I'm sure I didn't. I wouldn't have . . .'

'Yes, you did. You said you wanted to marry me and settle down and have kids but you was scared to ask me. Right?'

'Well, in a way.'

'Never mind in a way. Am I right?'

'Yes. You are.'

'You can see why I'm a bully,' she said in mock exasperation. 'I can't get any sense out a' you unless I bully.'

'I don't mind being bullied,' he said, kissing her again. 'You can bully me any time you like.'

'Right then. Into the bedroom, you!'

That made him groan. 'Do you mean it?'

'If I say it, I mean it. You know me.'

He was picking up the most delectable signals. 'Have you missed me?' he asked with hopeful curiosity.

'Catch me telling you that,' she teased. 'You *would* get big-headed.'

*

Alison couldn't wait for Morgan to get down to see them that Saturday evening. When she heard his car she ran to the door to greet him. Both children were in bed and asleep so she could take as long as she liked to tell him what had been happening.

He was carrying a bunch of freesias, their sweet scent preceding him into the house. It surprised her because he'd never brought her flowers before.

'Happy birthday, *cariad*,' he said, kissing her.

She held the flowers to her face, enjoying their perfume. She'd forgotten all about her birthday. 'How did you know?'

'I asked your mother. You can have your card on the proper day, on Tuesday, but I thought you'd like these now.'

They walked into the kitchen arm in arm. 'I've given up having birthdays,' she said, putting the flowers in a vase. 'You don't have time for birthdays when you've got kids.'

'You do now you've got me,' he said. 'Now you can start again. I got you a little present too.'

It was a gold bracelet with a single charm attached to it – a little Welsh harp, strings, pedals and all.

'Oh Morgan,' she said. 'You darling. I've always wanted one of these.'

He was beaming. 'So your Mum said. Come in the living room *cariad*. I got some news for you.'

'You wait till you hear what I've got to tell *you*,' she said. And the whole story of her day tumbled out: how well she'd managed the drains and the man at the agency; how awful it was that Meriel's cat had died; and how Brad and Martin had been brought back together.

He listened and praised and told her she'd 'done marvellous'. But when she finally paused for breath, he had the oddest expression on his face.

'What is it?' she said. 'Morgan darling?'

'I had some news for *you*,' he said. 'I thought it was good. I'm not so sure about it now.'

'Tell me,' she said.

He wasn't even sure he wanted to do that. But she insisted. 'You've got to now,' she said. 'You can't say you've got some news and then not tell me what it is.'

So he told her.

Mr Alexander Jones had announced that he was going to retire and had offered Morgan and Barbara Kirkby first refusal on the business. The two of them had been working out the possibilities at odd moments during his stint in Birmingham. Now that he was back it was time to make a decision.

'Go for it,' Alison said at once. 'I think it's a great idea. You ought to be your own boss.'

'No, hang on. There's more to it than that. I'd have to sink all my savings in it. I been savin' that money for a house.'

'For us?'

'Right. It's high time you had somewhere decent to live. I can't bear you bein' on the social. I want to look after you properly. Especially now, after those drains an' everythin'. I think I ought to use the money for a house – now.'

'Well, I don't. Look. I coped with the drains, didn't I. After that, I can cope with anything.'

'It would take too long to save up again,' he said. 'It would mean waiting.'

'How long?'

'Months probably. Depends on how big a salary I take and when I sell the flat.'

'I can handle months,' she said easily. 'I'm getting used to it.'

That made him fierce. 'You shouldn't be used to it,' he said. 'You deserve better than this. I want to marry you *cariad*, an' settle down in a house of our own.'

Talk of marriage was something she parried almost automatically these days. 'It's going to take a long time to get my divorce,' she pointed out. 'I don't even know where he is. Take the job. I'm sure it's the right thing to do.'

Chapter Twenty-Seven

Rigby Toan and his great friend, Francis, were at Charlie Crayford's house in Dorking at a black and white party.

It was nearly two in the morning and most of the guests had reached a state of maudlin exhaustion. Lust-sated couples drifted back downstairs to rejoin the groups still upright round the billiard table or still drinking by the pool. Some of the more dishevelled sprawled on chairs and sofas or lay on the floor, blear-eyed and incoherent. The catering staff had left at midnight but the wining and dining had continued unabated, so there were dirty glasses and plates of half-eaten food on every available surface, including the stairs and the grand piano. Someone had been sick in the jardinière and somebody else had painted 'LUV YER' in fuchsia lipstick across the Victorian looking glass in the drawing room.

'Decadence!' Charlie Crayford said, surveying the scene from his vantage point on the leather Chesterfield. 'I love it.' The bosomy blonde slumped against his shoulder opened her eyes and tickled him under the chin. 'You can't beat it.'

Rigg was propped up against the bar, talking to Francis.

'No, come on Francis. Be a pal,' he said thickly. 'Don't muck about. I can stay 'nother night, can't I?'

'Can't be done, old fruit,' Francis said. He was drunk and earnest in equal proportions. 'Mater won't have it. Can't stand your socks, she says.'

'No, come on. Don't muck about.'

Francis tried to focus his eyes, failed, snarled and suddenly changed moods, switching in one instant from giggling tolerance to spite.

'You're such a *fart*, Rigby,' he said. 'Why don't you piss off an' leave me alone. Go an' scrounge a bed with somebody else.'

'There isn't anybody else,' Rigg said with drunken candour. 'They've all dis – rerted me. De – reted me. Dis – erted me. All the lot. I've got no friends. Nowhere to go. Nobody loves me.' His face was creased with scotch and self-pity.

'Serve you right,' Francis said, picking up his drink and gathering his strength to walk across the room with it. 'Shouldn't be such a fart.'

Rigg made one last soulful appeal. 'Oh come on, Francis. Be a pal!'

'Why don't you go home and sort out that wife of yours?' Francis said, standing upright with an effort.

'What d'you mean? Sort out that wife a' yours?'

'Sort her out. That's what I mean. She's got herself another man.'

Rigg was enraged. 'She has,' Francis said, continuing his progress across the room. 'Saw her myself, ol' fruit. Got another man.'

Red discs danced before Rigg's eyes. 'She can't do this to me!' he roared. He felt violated by the news. 'The slag! I'll kill her. She can't do this.'

Guests gravitated towards the uproar, avid for a spectacle, and Rigg found himself surrounded by questioning faces. 'What's up?' 'What's he done?' 'Who is it?'

'I shall kill her,' he announced.

His audience were delighted with that and followed him into the great tiled entrance hall. Someone found his coat and he was pushed into it. Someone else dug his car keys out of his pocket. 'You tell her,' they encouraged. 'Don't you let her get away with it.' 'Who is it?' 'What's going on?'

They trooped out of the house to where the cars were parked in neat ranks against the orchard wall; they cheered as he fumbled into the driving seat; they applauded as he zig-zagged down the drive, scraped the ornamental gates and, still in second gear, roared slowly off towards the open road.

It was hideously dark. Rigg could barely see the road and the hedges on either side of it were black obstructions, looming towards him. He tried blinking, he rubbed his eyes first with one fist and then with the other, but the darkness remained impenetrable. It wasn't until a lorry passed him going the other way and flashed its headlamps at him that he realised he hadn't switched his lights on.

Not that it did any good. The road was illuminated now and the hedges were grey in the headlamps, but he didn't know where he was. Apparently, the road led to a dual carriageway ahead but, even when he managed to read the signposts, they made no sense. He knew he ought to be heading south, but which way was south. Why don't they bloody tell you on their stupid signposts? Eventually, hoping for better things, he turned left into a narrow country lane, and left again. And found himself in a field.

He was lost, befuddled and desperate for a pee. What the hell! he thought, as he turned off the ignition. I shall stay here. She can bloody well wait for me. He struggled out of the car and crunched through the stubble to the nearest tree to empty his bladder. She's nothing but a slut, he told himself, as he fell into the back seat. He was asleep before his head hit the rip in the plastic.

When he woke it was bold, bright daylight and two faces were peering through the rear window at him. He felt absolutely awful. Just sitting up made his skull sting.

'Party,' he explained, winding down the window.

'Told yer,' the older head said to the younger.

'I need some coffee,' he said thickly. His mouth tasted like a drain.

They gave him directions to the nearest transport café, where he had three cups of coffee, managed to clean himself up a bit in a cracked wash-basin in the gents, shaved and changed his crumpled evening dress for a jersey and jeans. His white tuxedo was in a disgusting state but at least he didn't have to go on wearing it. That was one good thing about living out of a suitcase: you always had a change of clothes handy.

Then he set off on his journey.

As he drove and his head began to clear he remembered why he'd been so upset the night before. That bloody Francis, not letting him stay the night. Bloody cruel, when you think of all the money he's got. Stinking rich. Absolutely loaded. And he can't spare a single stinking bed for one single stinking night. You soon find out who your friends are when you're down and out. No one'll offer me a bed now. They're all the same, fair-weather friends the lot of them. When I had the money to stand them all drinks and take them off for jaunts in the BMW it was 'Stay the night. Pleased to have you. No problem.' Now they won't give me the time of day. Or buy me a drink. Francis had *locked* the drinks cabinet the last time. Charming! Lack of cash is an absolute pig. Especially when you can't do anything about it. He'd sold off the last of the jewellery yonks ago. And now that whore's playing around with another man. Won't let me into the house. Oh no! But she'll make room for someone else. Well, I'll soon sort that out. I'll report her to the social for a start. He needn't think he's going to live off my wife, bloody parasite.

He was rattling down the approach road to the town.

And that's another thing, he thought. This bloody car's had it. The tax disc was long out of date and he couldn't get another one without an MOT certificate. And he couldn't get *that* because there was so much work that needed to be done on the damn thing and they'd taken all his cash cards when he went into voluntary arrangement. Life was bloody unfair. It really was. Now where was this house? Barnaby Green. That's the place.

There were several dirty toddlers playing on the green but none of them looked familiar. He sat in the car watching them and pondering what to do next. Of course she could be at work. He'd forgotten she worked.

While he watched, a strange woman came out of Alison's door and yelled at the kids. 'Melvin! Come on in will yer.'

The child began to amble towards the house, trailing a stick across the scrubby grass as he went. The woman had gone back into the house. Rigg got out of the car and stood on the front lawn, blocking the child's way.

'Do you live here, sonny?' he asked.

The urchin was instantly aggressive. 'What's it to you mister?'

Rigg seized the kid's ear and twisted it. 'I asked you a question.'

'Leggo my ear!' the boy said, trying to pull away from him.

'Answer my question. Do you live here?'

'All right. All right. Yes. Me and my Mum.'

Rigg let go of the ear and gave the child his most charming smile. 'That's all I wanted to know.'

Now what? He had to find her. But how? He certainly wasn't going to crawl cap in hand to any of the awful women who lived round this green. The sight of their ghastly children was quite enough to deter him from that. They ought to be at school. Why weren't they?

School! Of course. Brilliant. She'll have to go to school to meet Jonathan. I can wait for her there. If I can find out where it is. The nearest one to Shore Street probably. He'd have started school while she was still there. It'll be on the road map. Bound to be.

He found the school just in time to watch the kids come back after their lunch. But there was no sign of Ali.

'What time do they let them out in the afternoon?' he asked a returning mum and discovered that it was ten past three.

He was back at quarter past, having fallen asleep in the car while it was parked on the sea front. The side road leading to the school gate was seething with people. There were children everywhere, swarming all over the pavements, hopping across the road in front of the lollipop lady, hanging onto arms and pram handles and one another, all chit-chit-chattering and all in the same hideous uniform. Pillar-box red, for Chrissakes! It made his eyes hurt to look at them. How was he supposed to find his own sprog in a wriggling mass like that?

The question was no sooner in his head than there Jon was, solemnly holding Emma's hand and walking down the side road with Alison.

Despite his bad temper, Rigg couldn't help noticing what a good-looking little boy his son was, with all that fair hair and that handsome face and those broad shoulders. Good cheek bones, too. Like his father.

Then he remembered what he'd come to do and walked quickly back to where he'd parked the car. If she knew he was watching out for her, she might not go home. She was cunning enough to pull a trick like that. What's she doing now? He checked as he eased into the car. Standing on the corner talking to a girl in a pink jersey. She'd better put on a bit of speed if I'm going to follow or I shall be done for kerb-crawling. He was gob-smacked when she got into a four-year-old Metro and drove it away.

It was none too easy to follow because there were so many children in the road and the minute he got going the lollipop lady stepped out in front of him, waving her ridiculous stick. He was so cross that he ground his gears as well as his teeth. Hurry up! he muttered, drumming his fingers on the steering wheel. Damn silly woman. Hurry up or she'll get away.

He caught up with her in a road crammed with parked cars and watched as she edged the Metro into a very small space. There was nowhere for him to park. He had to back out of the road and find a space round the corner. By the time that was done, she and the kids were out of the Metro and walking up the path into one of the houses. Quick! For Chrissake! he thought. Do something or she'll shut the door.

'Jonathan!' he called. 'Daddy's here! Where's my iddle-diddle baby?'

For a few seconds Jon stood still, fair hair ruffling, thumb half way to his mouth. Then he recognised his father and streaked down the road towards him. 'Daddy! Daddy! Look Mummy, look! It's Daddy.'

Alison looked up, instantly alarmed, but Emma was already bouncing down the road after her brother, her plump legs working like a clockwork toy. It was too late to call them back so she left the key in the lock and followed them, protectively. Seeing him again was a most unpleasant surprise. How did he know how to find me? she puzzled. I thought I was well hidden this time. And yet there he is, bold as bloody brass, standing outside my house as though he's got a right to it. He's so bloody arrogant. It annoyed her that he was looking so well-fed and well-dressed and full of himself. That's a brand new pair of jeans, and designer jeans at that. He's not short of money to spend on himself. But then he never was. Rigby Toan, the Great-I-Am. What did I ever see in him?

And yet he *was* handsome. Even in her anger against him she could still see that.

'Where did you get the car?' he asked belligerently.

That wasn't a question she wanted to answer. 'It's mine,' she said, upset because she sounded so aggressive. That's what you've done to me, Rigby Toan. You've changed my nature.

'I didn't know you had a car.'

'Well there you are,' she said, trying to lighten her tone. 'There's a lot you don't know about me.'

The light tone annoyed him more than the aggression. In fact, everything about her annoyed him. She didn't look right. She was a deserted wife, for Chrissake. She ought to look the part, downcast, a bit depressed, unsure of herself. Not striding along towards him like that. She'd lost a bit of weight, but it improved her, made her look taller and her legs longer. And that walk was downright provocative. Damn it, she had no bloody business looking like that, when he was living out of a suitcase.

Jon was clinging to his knees. 'Daddy!'

He's a nice-looking kid, Rigg thought, and *he* loves me. 'How's my iddle-diddle Princey?' he said, lifting the little boy into the air.

'Me! Me!' Emma said, tugging at his trousers.

'Don't spoil my jeans,' he warned, but he stooped to pick her up too. 'How's my ickle-wickle Princess?' At least my kids love me, he thought. He stood with a child on each arm, defying his unloving wife. The trouble was they weighed a ton, and the strain of holding them rather spoilt the effect.

'We've got a hedgehog,' Emma told him. 'It does big, big poos.'

Rigg had no idea what to say in answer to that so he turned his attention to Alison again. 'Aren't you going to invite me in?' he asked.

'If I must,' she said grudgingly. She knew it wasn't wise, but they had to talk sooner or later. She ought to tell him about the divorce and get an address out of him so that the papers could be served.

Rigg carried the children into the house and was very glad to put them down once the door was shut.

'I've got a bone to pick with you,' he said, plunging in to the attack.

She parried attack with attack, standing in the narrow hall with the children between them. 'Tell me about Hampton Videos,' she said coolly.

That deflated him a bit. 'What about Hampton Videos? That's old news.'

'I was never a director, was I.'

'That's all water under the bridge,' he said grandly. 'Over and forgotten. We don't need to go into that.'

His dismissive nonchalance made her angry. 'I half killed myself paying that VAT bill,' she said. 'I lay awake nights worrying myself silly about it and there wasn't any need.'

'So you've learned something,' he said, shrugging his shoulders. 'Now you know you needn't have bothered.'

She was appalled at his callousness. 'Don't you care what a state I was in?'

'Why should I? If you got in a state that was up to you. It's not my problem.'

Alison couldn't believe what she was hearing. 'Not your problem!' she shouted at him. 'It was *your* bloody shop. Why didn't you tell me I wasn't a director?'

'Why didn't you tell me you'd got yourself a fancy man?'

The question was so unexpected it took her speech away – but she should have known it would come. If you live in a town like Hampton you can't expect to keep secrets. He was bound to find out sooner or later.

'That's not what we're talking about,' she said, and she shepherded the kids into the kitchen. 'Time for tea.'

'Is Daddy having tea with us?' Jon wanted to know, looking back at Rigg.

'Daddy's leaving,' Alison said firmly.

'No he's not,' Rigg said, following her into the kitchen. 'Daddy wants an answer to his question and Daddy's going to stay here until he gets it.'

The kitchen seemed smaller than usual now he was filling it with anger.

'There's nothing to answer,' she said, pouring orange juice.

'You've got a fancy man.'

The accusation made her feel guilty and guilt made her flippant. 'So?'

'You're my wife.'

'Wife!' she said, spreading Flora on two slices of bread. 'Wife! You don't know the meaning of the word. You walk out of my life whenever you feel like it. You don't tell me where you are. You leave me to go to court on my own, to have my house repossessed, to live on the social, to scrape shit out of the garden. We're a welfare family because of you. Don't talk to me about being a wife.'

'I won't have you carrying on with another man.'

'Why not? You don't want me.'

'Behind my back. Making me a laughing stock in front of all my friends.'

'What friends? I'm surprised you've got any.'

'You're to give him up, do you hear me?'

'I'm not your property, Rigg. I've got a life of my own.'

'You're my wife.'

'Not for very much longer. I'm suing you for divorce.'

He was enraged. 'Don't be so bloody silly.'

'Oh silly, is it?'

'Behind my bloody back, making me a laughing stock.'

'You know your trouble,' Alison said, realising it herself at that moment. 'You don't listen. You don't hear what people are saying to you. You're so busy thinking about yourself you don't pay any attention to anybody else. Watch my lips! *I'm divorcing you.*'

'I shan't let you.'

'You can't stop me.'

'That's all you know,' he said, his voice gloating. 'I shall refuse to sign the papers and that'll be the end of it. That's all I've got to do, refuse to sign. You can't just divorce people when you feel like it, so don't you think it.'

He was so assured he made her doubt. Could it be true? He seemed to have the law on his side in everything else, so why not this as well? 'Please go away,' she said wearily. 'I don't want to talk to you any more.'

Any sign of weakness increased his cruelty. He grabbed her by the shoulders and shook her. 'You're to give him up, do you hear? I won't have my wife running around with another man.'

'Let go! You're hurting me.'

'You deserve to be hurt,' he shouted, increasing his pressure. 'You're a bloody little slag.'

Emma began to scream. 'Don't! Daddy don't!'

He turned carelessly towards the child and slapped her across the face. The blow was so hard it knocked her to the ground. For a split second she was too shocked to move or cry. Then she began to scream in terror, on and on like an animal in a trap.

White with fury, Alison wrenched herself out of his grip. 'How *dare* you do that!' She shrieked at him, swooping down to gather the screaming child in her arms. 'It's all right, darling. Shush! It's all right. Mummy's here.'

Rigg was in full fury now and very strong. He lugged them both to their feet and this time he slapped Alison, first on one side of her face and then on the other, over and over again, rhythmically so that her head rocked like a pendulum. 'You're to – give him – up. D'you – hear me? – Give him – up.' Now it was the other bloody silly kid making a fuss, clinging to his knees, impeding him. He kicked him out of the way. 'And you can shut up too.'

Alison lay against the wall where she'd fallen and sucked in her breath ready to fight back. She was pulsing with anger. To hit her was bad enough, but to kick Jon and terrorise Emma was so appalling she had to stop him. Frantic with anger, she seized the bread knife from the board and ran towards him holding it aloft.

'Don't you dare hit my kids,' she yelled. 'I'll kill you!'

He was startled by the attack but only momentarily. Then he made a spring at her, grabbed her right arm and twisted it so cruelly that she let the knife fall. 'Oh yes!' he mocked, pushing his face right up close to hers. 'What with?'

All she could see was his eyes, bloodshot, glaring and full of hatred. She fought back, trying to grab his throat. 'My hands if I have to.'

This time he punched her under the chin and made her choke.

They were fighting in a flail of arms and fists and scratching fingers, screaming at one another through the blows.

'Give him up!'

'Go away!'

'Give him up!'

'No!'

'Right then,' he said, standing in front of her, panting. 'I'll take your precious children and see what you think about that.' He made a grab for Emma's arm and began to drag her towards the hall, punching at Jon with one knee so that the child was propelled ahead of him.

'Leave them alone!' Alison screamed, struggling after him, both arms outstretched. 'In the front room! Quick!' she yelled at Jon, and was relieved when he bolted past Rigg's legs, bent double but running at speed. She seized Emma's T-shirt in both hands and held on to it, pulling with all her might, scrambling to keep her balance, falling against the wall. Emma screamed and wriggled. They struggled together for endless seconds, screaming and punching. Then, suddenly, the child's warm body was between Alison's hands. She gave one last tug and pulled her free, tumbling with her into the front room, Rigg on her heels. He had his foot in the door, wedging it open, but she pushed against it with her entire body, kicking at his shoe so that he withdrew his foot for long enough for her to shove the edge of the sofa in front of the door. Inch by inch, the door closed. 'Quick! Quick!' she yelled as much to herself as the kids. 'Push the sofa!'

Despite its weight, she managed to wedge the bulk of the sofa against the door. All three of them sat on it, huddled together, panting and weeping, while Rigg pushed on the other side. Twice he managed to force the door ajar, and the sofa bumped along the carpet, while the children screamed and Alison flung herself against the door. Then everything went quiet.

'Has he gone?' Jon whispered.

'Hush!' Alison whispered back. 'I don't know. Listen.'

They heard him panting on the other side of the door.

'Don't think you've won,' he said. 'I'll be back. You needn't think you've got away with it, Alison Toan. They're my kids and if I want to take them away, I shall.'

Then, and at last, they heard his feet stamping out of the door and down the path.

Battered wife, Alison thought, as she cuddled her weeping children, and wept into their hair. That's what I am. I can't pretend any more. Not after this. I'm a battered wife and these are battered kids. Emma's cheek was imprinted with the red mark of his hand and streaked with dark tear stains. Jon's face was grey white.

'You're not going to be sick are you, Jon?' she asked, stroking his hair. 'You'll tell Mummy if you're going to be sick.'

He nodded meekly. 'Is he coming back?'

'No, of course not,' she lied. 'But we'll wait a few more minutes just to be sure.'

'He won't take us away, will he?'

'No,' she promised. 'He won't. I won't let him.'

They remained on the sofa until they'd all stopped crying. Darkness filled the corners with shadow. They heard the six o'clock news beginning on next door's television, but they were too exhausted to move. Finally, when another hour had passed, Alison stood up and went out into the hall to phone Morgan.

'Are you doing anything special this evening?' she asked.

Although she'd made an enormous effort to keep her voice calm, he recognised the distress in it at once.

'What's up? What is it, *cariad*?'

'Rigg's been here,' she said flatly.

'He's hit you,' he said.

'Yes,' she admitted. 'And the kids.'

'Stay where you are,' he said. 'Keep the door locked. I'll be with you in less than an hour.'

She was still sitting on the sofa when he let himself into the house. She had a child on each side of her and the television was flickering in the corner unheeded.

He was appalled by the state she was in – her hair tangled, bruises on both sides of her face, blood spattered all over her T-shirt.

'Alison, *cariad*!' he said.

She didn't appear to hear him, but sat staring at nothing, her face blank.

He tried again. 'Have you had anything to eat?'

She shook her head, her face still expressionless.

'I'll feed the kids, shall I?'

Still no answer and no expression.

He got to his feet and bent to pick Emma up, but she screamed and clung to her mother. 'I want my Mummy! I want my Mummy!'

'All right,' he said, releasing the child. 'You stay with Mummy and I'll go and get you something nice to eat. What would you like?'

He cooked poached eggs. But they left them on the plates. He tried to coax them. But they only wept more. Finally he lifted Alison to her feet and led them all into the bathroom where he bathed all three of them together, gently and tenderly, taking care not to knock their bruises. Then he eased them out of the bath, dried them, helped them into their nightclothes and put them all into Alison's double bed together. And none of them said a word the whole time.

It was only when her head was on the pillow and her eyes were closed that Alison began to speak. Then she talked until the whole terrible story was told in an anguished jumble of tears and terror.

'I'm here now,' he said, over and over again. 'I won't leave you. 'You're all right, *cariad*, I'm here.'

'But what if he comes back? He said he was going to take the kids.'

'He won't. I won't let him.'

It was impossible to console her. 'But what if he does?'

'We'll pack up and go to Guildford and you can live with me.'

The suggestion put her in a panic. 'No, no. I can't. There's the school. I've got to stay here.'

'All right. All right,' he said, afraid of upsetting her any further. 'You can stay here and I'll look after you. He won't come back if I'm here.'

'He'll come back,' she said dully and turned her head away. 'He can do whatever he likes. No one can stop him, don't you see? He's been hiding away for months, owing people all that money and nobody's done anything. He gets away with it. He can do what he likes.'

'Not with me around,' Morgan said grimly.

But she was sunk in despair and wouldn't believe him.

Morgan sat with them until they were all asleep. And his anger was like a stone in his chest.

Then he went downstairs, retrieved his camera from his travelling bag, and returned to the bedroom to take several professional shots, first of Emma's battered face and then of Alison's. If Rigg wouldn't agree to a divorce by consent and she needed evidence, he would provide it.

Then he rang all three of her brothers. The time for sympathy was over. What was needed now was action.

Chapter Twenty-Eight

The Trafalgar Arms in Hampton is a pub designed for conspiracy. Once renowned as a haunt of smugglers and as the setting for a brutal murder during the Napoleonic War, it was built at the turn of the eighteenth century to serve the thirst of a few dozen local fishermen. Now, it is a tourist pub, playing its reputation for all it's worth.

On the outside, it is white-washed and squat, having settled so far down on its haunches that the floor of the public bar is a foot lower than the pavement. Inside, the beams are ebony black, the original bread ovens are still set in the fireplace, and a trap door behind the bar leads to a cellar like a dungeon. It is poorly lit, because the locals like it that way, with candles on every table and a log fire to provide warmth in winter. A place of shadows and plots and dark secrets.

Morgan Griffiths and Alison's three brothers were squashed knee to knee as they gathered around one of its undersized oak tables. But they were so angry none of them noticed.

'This has gone far enough,' Mark Wareham said. 'We shall have to sort him out.'

'Dead right,' Andy agreed. 'We can't just sit back and let him go on treating her like this. She'll have a breakdown.' He and Clare had been appalled at the state his sister was in and Clare had stayed behind at Mum's house specially to care for her.

'He ought to have his bloody head bashed in,' Mark said. He was full of aggressive anger, his face dark with it.

'We got to find him first,' Morgan pointed out. 'We don't know where he is. He could be anywhere.'

'Somebody *must* know where he lives,' Greg said, peering out of the window at the passing traffic. 'His car registration number would give that away, surely.'

'She didn't see the car.'

'Crafty sod hid it, I'll bet,' Andy said.

'First things first,' Mark told them. 'We shall have to watch over her for the next week or two in case he comes back. Would she go to Guildford with you, for a few days?'

'Wouldn't hear of it,' Morgan said.

'That's shock,' Andy explained. 'Give her time to get over the worst of it and she might feel differently. I wish you could get her to go to a doctor.'

'She won't. I told you.'

'What if you called one in?'

Greg suddenly sat up and stared out of the window. 'Hold everything!' he said. 'Guess who's walking along the promenade.'

'Never!' Mark said. 'He's not.'

'I'd know that strut anywhere,' Greg said.

They crowded against the leaded window, a face to a pane. Sure enough it *was* Rigg, walking briskly towards the pier on the other side of the road.

For a second all three brothers were nonplussed. It's one thing to sound off against an enemy, quite another to see him before you, there, in the hated flesh.

But Morgan had no doubts. Hunting was his profession.

'Stay there!' he instructed, already on his feet. 'I'll follow the bugger. Give me twenty yards, then you can follow me. If we're goin' to sort him out, we got to get him where he can't run.'

'Somewhere quiet,' Mark called as Morgan left the pub, 'so's I can kick his head in.'

'Fetch the car, Greg,' Morgan said at the door. 'He could have his wheels.'

It was growing dark, but even in the half light Rigg was easy to track. He walked with a purpose as if he was going to meet someone, his head silhouetted against the rows of winking lights that beaded the pier.

Senses fully alert, Morgan followed at a discreet distance. There were several people at the pier entrance – mostly couples or groups going in to play the fruit machines. A gang of boys thumped one another and leapt about, all flailing limbs and barking voices. A gang of girls sauced the boys and giggled, all bright mouths and tossing hair. But waiting in the entrance there was a solitary man in a leather jacket, smoking a cigarette. That'll be the one, Morgan thought. And it was.

The two men met, shook hands, talked, and began to stroll back along the promenade. Morgan took a quick look behind him to where Greg's car was turning slowly into the promenade. Then he insinuated himself into a group of people browsing through the postcards on the carousel outside the tobacconist. The little revolving stand allowed him a kaleidoscopic view of his quarry. Rigg and his companion were heading west along the promenade, deep in conversation, and easy to follow. Then, to Morgan's annoyance, they climbed over the railings that edged the prom and crunched across the shingle and headed for the nearest breakwater.

Damn, Morgan thought. If they're down there, they'll see us up here on the prom. We'll have to go round them. Where's Greg?

He was waiting in a parking space opposite the pier with Mark standing by the car keeping watch. As soon as they saw Morgan beckoning, they drove to the tobacconist and picked him up.

'They're on the beach,' Morgan said. 'Down there, see? Is there somewhere you can park a bit further along? We need to get the other side a' that breakwater, so that they're below us and they can't see us.'

They parked; they walked back along the empty beach, not saying a word; they sat in silence on the higher western side of the breakwater with Rigg and his friend on the beach below them; and they listened.

'I thought you bought that flat for your wife,' the friend was saying. 'Your wife and kids, you always said.'

'Don't talk to me about *her*,' Rigg complained. 'You've no idea what she's done to me, Norman. My life's been absolute hell these last eight years. Nag, nag, nag. How could I keep my mind on business with that going on all the time? It's no wonder things got mislaid. And then of course you get creditors down on your neck, threatening legal action because some piffling bill hasn't been paid.'

Norman made a commiserating noise. The three brothers stiffened with anger.

'And then, the minute I turn my back, she's off with some toy boy. I ask you Norman, is that fair? A toy boy. I've had to leave my work and come down here to sort him out. And that's not all. Oh no! She sold my shop. Three shops I had and she actually sold my last remaining outlet while I was away in Spain and couldn't do anything about it. Cut the ground from under my feet. What do you think of that?'

'That's tough,' Norman's voice said. 'Women are all the same.'

'Course if it hadn't been for her, I'd have been a millionaire by now. I had it all lined up. Three outlets – two jewellers and a video store – good car – BMW actually – second home – nice little flat out in Marbella. And now it's all got to go.'

'I'm not sure I want a flat in Spain, you know Rigg.'

'It's a snip,' Rigg said. 'Just the thing. It's a smashing place. Very free and easy, the Spaniards. And the women! You'd never believe what the women get up to. They're all over you the minute you get off the plane. You'd love it. What do you say?'

'I'm not sure.'

'But you're interested.'

'Well . . . I might be. Let's put it that way, I might be.'

'The thing is, Norman, this is such a hot property, I've got one or two other people after it. That's why I thought we'd meet on the beach. I'm holding them off, naturally, seeing as it's you, but I can't hold them off for ever.'

'Perhaps they'd better have it then, because I'm really not sure. It's a lot of money.'

'No. I won't do that, Norman. I'm nothing if not fair. When I met up with you again, I thought there's old Norman. That flat is just right for old Norman. Old school pal and all that. I ought to give him first refusal. So I tell you what I'll do. If you'll pay me a deposit by the end of the month – say five grand – it's yours with no more to pay until the New Year. I can't say fairer than that, now can I?'

'Well . . .'

'It's a snip,' Rigg urged. 'And don't say you can't lay your hands on five grand. You must be coining it with that cattery of yours.'

'Let's go up the Trafalgar and have a few jars,' Norman said. 'I'm getting parky sitting here.'

The listeners above them heard the shingle being crunched underfoot. Then a head appeared over the top of the breakwater and their cover was blown.

'Right you bastard!' Mark said, springing off the top of the breakwater and landing at Rigg's feet. 'We've got you!'

'I'd hop it if I were you, mate,' Morgan said to Norman. 'The flat's not for sale, like. He's connin' you. Belongs to his creditors, see.'

The man was already moving away, half running, his fag stuck to his lower lip. 'Thanks mate. Cheers.'

Rigg was being crowded against the breakwater.

'So it's all her fault, is it?' Mark said, pushing his face right up against Rigg's. 'She sold your shop, did she? You bloody, sodding, lying hound!'

'It was a sales pitch,' Rigg said, trying to edge away. 'That's all fellers. You know how it is. I didn't mean it.'

'I suppose you didn't mean to knock her to a pulp

either,' Andy mocked, seizing Rigg by the front of his jersey and pushing him against the nearest upright.

'She took a knife to me,' Rigg struggled. 'It was self-defence. Honestly fellers, you don't know what she's like.'

'I've seen her,' Andy said, thumping him on the chest, 'I know exactly what she's like. A punch bag. That's what she's like. I've seen Emma too. Did *she* take a knife to you, poor little kid?'

Rigg looked to left and right, frantically searching for someone to help him, but the promenade was deserted and the beach was empty except for one other man – a vaguely familiar man – who was standing by the breakwater, watching them. Rigg narrowed his eyes in surprise and partial recognition. 'Hello!' he said. 'I know you, don't I. Come and tell these boys they're makin' a mistake.'

'Oh I don't think they're makin' a mistake,' Morgan said, bruising into the circle. 'But then I'm prejudiced, see. I'm the toy boy.'

'What?' Oh Christ, what's he talking about?

'Alison's toy boy. The one you were on about just now. The one you had to come home to sort out. Remember?'

'Oh Christ!' Rigg said, trying to edge away from them. 'Look. It was a joke.'

'Very funny!' Morgan growled, following him, fists clenched.

'Now what?' Greg asked.

'We beat *him* to a pulp,' Mark said, punching Rigg's chest. 'That's only fair, isn't it Rigg?'

Rigg made a stand in the only way he knew. 'OK then,' he said, lifting his head and sticking out his chin. 'Beat me up. See if I care.' It was the technique he'd used to outface the bullies when they descended on him at his prep school and his tone of careless bravado was the same as it had been then.

It took the brothers off guard.

'See how you like a taste of your own medicine,' Andy threatened, but he didn't start punching. And neither did the others. They circled their enemy, prowling and scowling, but they didn't attack.

'Grab his legs,' Morgan said to Greg. 'We won't hurt him. Don't want to make a martyr of him like. We'll just clean him up a bit.' And he looked at the sea.

Greg took his meaning at once and seized the leg nearest to him. Within seconds Rigg was being borne aloft, spreadeagled between the four of them, as they carried him bodily down the beach. 'Steady on fellers! I can't swim.'

'You should ha' thought a' that,' Mark said as they waded into the sea. It was battleship grey and icy cold. Just the right punishment for a wife beater. 'Heave!'

They threw him as far as they could, watching his body as it tumbled through the darkening air to splash down in a confusion of white foam and frantic limbs. They cheered and mocked as he struggled to get up again and was knocked sideways by the oncoming waves.

Finally he scrambled to his feet, coughing and protesting. 'For Chrissake!' But what with the pressure of the water against his legs and the weight of his wet clothes dragging him down, he couldn't escape them, try as he might. As soon as he waded out they caught him and threw him out to sea again, taunting and roaring abuse.

'How d'you like being on the receiving end, Rigg?'

'Not so good, is it, you bastard.'

'D'you want any more, wife beater?'

'Come on fellers!' he begged, still trying to turn their wrath. 'Play the game!'

'Serve you bloody well right,' Mark said as they splashed after him for the third time and pulled him down, like hounds, into the water.

Rigg's teeth were chattering with cold. 'What do you want me to do?' he pleaded. 'I'll do anything, honest – only let me out.'

'Keep away from Ali,' Mark yelled at him.

'Yes. Yes.'

'Tell us your address,' Morgan said.

'Haven't got one. Really. On my life.'

'Bloody liar!'

'I haven't!'

They splashed after him, caught him and threw him in for a fourth time. Now he was too weary to get up but sat where he fell, with the water up to his chest.

By this time, attracted by the sound of splashing and shouting, a crowd had gathered. They lined the railings on the promenade, to watch the theatre being played out at the edge of the sea, cheering when Rigg was thrown in, applauding when he staggered out again. It was better than a Punch and Judy show – and very similar.

'What's it about?' a newcomer asked.

'Yobs,' her neighbour told her. 'They keep chucking that one in the sea.'

'You won't come out till you tell us,' Mark shouted.

'Go on boy!' someone in the crowd yelled. 'Tell him! I should.'

Rigg rubbed the sea water out of his eyes. There's nothing for it, he thought, I'll have to find some address or they'll keep me here all night. 'All right! All right!' he called. 'I'll tell you. It's 10 Riverside, Allingham Avenue.'

'Where's that?' Morgan asked as he wrote it down.

'Littlehampton. Now can I come out?'

To the disappointment of the watching crowd, they let him run along the water's edge, scramble up the shingle and stagger on to the promenade. Once there, he ran as fast as he could, partly to put a distance between himself and their wrath, partly to avoid the crowd, some of whom came in happy pursuit.

Down on the shingle, Morgan and the three brothers were loud with triumph and residual anger.

'"Play the game", I ask you!' Mark mocked, watching until Rigg was out of sight. 'D'you ever hear such rubbish?'

'He won't forget this in a hurry,' Greg said. Always the least aggressive of the three brothers, he'd surprised himself by his capacity for violence.

'He thought we were gonna drown him,' Andy gloated.

'Serve him right,' Morgan growled. 'He had it comin' to him.'

'Wait till we tell the girls!' Mark said.

They congratulated one another all the way back to Elsie's house, where they told their tale to the five womenfolk and were applauded and congratulated all over again.

Only Alison took the story calmly. She didn't laugh, or praise, or question or comment. She just sat on the sofa, listening and saying nothing. Whatever they'd done down there on the beach, it wouldn't alter her life in the least. The debts still had to be paid, she and the kids were still bruised and aching . . . they were still a welfare family. Even when Morgan told her they'd bullied Rigg's address out of him, she didn't react.

'You'll be able to divorce him now,' Morgan said, trying to cheer her. 'You'll be able to serve the papers on him, won't you, *cariad*, now you know where he lives.'

'Yes,' she said. 'I suppose I will.'

But she couldn't respond to anything. Ever since her beating, she'd suffered from a terrible, unfeeling lethargy, cutting her off from the world. The kids wet their beds every night and had nightmares that needed a lot of comforting. She did what had to be done, cuddling away their fears, washing their wet sheets and pyjamas automatically and with a curious lack of attention, as though they were simply chores like washing up or cleaning her teeth. She went to work and did her job quietly, keeping her head down. It didn't matter what anybody said, she knew she was lost. She was a battered wife. He could come back and beat her any time he wanted and nobody would stop him because the law was on his side. He could run away and refuse to tell anyone where he was and she couldn't do anything. She had to stay where she was. She had kids to look after, to feed and clothe and take to school. It didn't matter where she went, Rigg would find her. There was nothing she could do to protect herself. She listened to the excited predictions going on all round her and she didn't believe a word.

'You won't see him again for a very long time,' Mark was saying to her. 'If ever. I think you could say we've seen him off, wouldn't you Greg?'

'If I'm any judge,' Greg said, beaming at their success, 'he'll be half way to London by now.'

Chapter Twenty-Nine

Margaret Toan was having an early night. She planned to go up to Harrods in the morning and she needed a nice long beauty sleep for a trip like that. She'd eaten what little supper she needed, taken a bath, put her hair in rollers and treated herself to a revitalising face-pack. Her cigarette case was full, there was plenty of gin in the cabinet and a good film on the box, so all her most pressing needs were taken care of. Now she was settled for the evening, with five pillows behind her head, a glass of G and T in one hand and the remote control in the other. And some fool rang the doorbell.

She ignored it – naturally – even though it rang three more times. It would only be some wretched door-to-door salesman or Jehovah's Witnesses or something like that. Well they could jolly well go away and leave her in peace.

She was very annoyed when whoever it was started throwing gravel at her bedroom window. She watched as the little stones scratched down the glass and pattered on to the tiles below.

'Really!' she said to herself. 'This is too bad.' She climbed out of bed and went over to the window. And it was Rigby, standing on the garden path, looking very handsome and rather wet.

Margaret opened the window and leaned out.

'Rigby darling!' she said. 'What *have* you been doing? You look as if you've been swimming in your clothes.'

'Something like that,' he said.

'What a boy you are!' she said admiringly. 'Always up to tricks.'

Rigg wasn't interested in her admiration. 'Are you going to let me in?' he said.

'I'll be right down,' his mother said. And when she'd opened the door and he'd squelched into the hall, 'My word, you *are* wet and no mistake. Have you got any dry clothes to change into? You're making a damp patch on my carpet.'

He took off his shoes and socks and put them out on the doorstep. 'I'll change,' he said. 'Were you in bed?'

'I thought I'd have an early night.'

'I'll come in and see you when I'm not so wet,' he said, heading for the bathroom.

She followed his dirty feet up the stairs. 'I suppose you want to stay the night, is that it?' she said. 'You'll have to make your own bed.'

'Yes, yes,' he said rather tetchily. 'That's all right. You go back to your telly. I can manage.'

But it wasn't the same now. She couldn't concentrate on the film with him crashing about in the bathroom next door (and running off all her nice hot water). She poured herself another G and T, but his arrival had even taken the flavour out of that.

Despite his bravado on the beach, being attacked had been a nasty shock to Rigby Toan. The shower gradually restored the feeling to his numbed fingers and toes but it would take more than warm water to repair his pride. One thing was certain. He couldn't stay in Hampton. Not with thugs like that around.

He wrapped himself in one of his mother's thick towels while he rummaged through his travelling case for some clean clothes. Most of his shirts were too dirty to contemplate and so was his underwear. Fortunately there was a clean red sweater at the bottom of the case and that looked all right, even if his jeans were crumpled.

I'll get the old dear to pop this lot in her washing machine tomorrow, he thought, dusting his least objectionable pair of socks with his mother's expensive talcum powder. But what he had to get out of her first was some of the money that was owing to him. It was wicked to make him wait all this time for his rightful inheritance. She *must* give it to me now. Or part of it, at the very least. I deserve it. I need it. Good God, she must see that. I've never needed it so much. I'm on my uppers.

Suitably psyched up, he marched across the landing to do battle with his mother for what was rightfully his.

Margaret was sitting up in her awful satin bed, wearing her awful satin négligé, drinking a G and T and watching some awful film. Better butter her up first.

'Washed and clean,' he said. 'Now I can give my lovely Mater a kiss.'

'You're a great nuisance, Rigby,' she said, half teasing and half scolding. 'I'd just got settled for the night and now you've put me out. I hope you realise that.'

'I's a pig to my sweetheart,' he said. 'A rotten-otten piggy.'

The baby-talk placated her – as he knew it would.

'Well just so long as you know it,' she said. The film was getting to the exciting bit. She could tell by the volume of the music. Her eyes swivelled to the screen.

Her inattention made Rigg feel irritable and hard-done-by. Damn it all, he thought, she might look at me. We haven't seen one another for months. If she's going to watch telly all the time, it'll make things very difficult for me. I *am* her son, for Chrissake. 'Aren't you going to ask me why I've come to see you?' he prompted.

She answered question with question, automatically, sipping her G and T, her eyes on the screen. 'Why've you come to see me?'

'I've got no money.'

That didn't bother her at all. 'So what's new?'

'Seriously, Mater.'

'You'll get some,' she said, following the film. Yes, she remembered this bit now.

'I'm in debt.'

'Um.'

He leaned across the bed and switched off the telly. 'Listen to me, Mater,' he said. 'I'm in trouble.'

'I was watching that,' she protested. 'You're very discourteous sometimes, Rigby.'

'I'm in trouble,' he repeated, looking at her with what he hoped was a suitable imploring expression. 'Mumsie dear, you've got to help me.'

'You do exaggerate, Rigby,' she said, searching for the remote control. Where *was* the stupid thing? 'I'm sure it's not as bad as all that.'

Rigg slipped the remote control in the back pocket of his jeans. 'It's as bad as it can possibly be,' he said. 'I'm in serious trouble. I need a lot of money'

Margaret sighed. This would go on until she gave him what he wanted. Or part of what he wanted. And he was wasting her viewing time. 'How much?' she asked.

'Sixty grand.'

'Oh Rigby!' Margaret said, but she wasn't scolding: she was laughing and sounded almost affectionate. 'You're so ridiculously ambitious. Just like your father.'

'So will you . . . ?'

'He never did anything by halves, your father. He always thought big. You're just like him. "Twenty thou," he'd say. "That's all. We can manage that." And we never could.'

Rigg began to relax. She was going to come across, thank God. 'You'll see me clear, then?'

She squinted at him. 'Do what?' she asked, as if she'd forgotten what they were talking about.

'Let me have the money?'

'What money?'

'Oh come on, Mumsie, the sixty grand.'

'I haven't got sixty grand.'

'No, all right. I know you haven't got sixty grand. That's chicken feed to what you've got. You're rolling in it. We all know that. That's why I've come to you.'

She looked at him quizzically. 'Rolling in it,' she said slowly. 'Is that what you think?'

'Dad's money,' he said crossly. This wasn't the time for pretence. 'He was a millionaire. He left you rolling.'

She finished the G and T and laughed, once, a short harsh yelping sound, like a vixen barking. 'Your father wasn't a millionaire,' she said. 'Far from it.'

'But he left me my inheritance,' Rigg said easily. She could talk as much nonsense as she liked, providing she came across with the money.

'Ah! The inheritance,' she said, waving it away with red-tipped fingers. 'That's nearly a year away, Rigby. We don't need to talk about that yet.'

'Yes we do,' he insisted. 'I need to know how much I'm going to get.'

'Why?'

How many more times? Rigg thought. 'Because I'm in debt. I owe a lot of money to a lot of people. It isn't just a cash-flow problem. This is serious. I owe the Inland Revenue nine grand for a start and three grand to the VAT and they've got to be paid by the middle of October – that's only three weeks away. Three weeks! Do you understand that? So you see . . .'

Margaret's eyes grew shrewd. 'How much do you owe altogether?' she asked.

'Sixty – seventy grand. I'm not sure exactly. There's interest charges. Anyway I've got to have that money. You can see that, can't you? Or at least some of it. You wouldn't like your baby to be sent to prison, now would you?'

Margaret had listened carefully to what he had to say. Now she shrugged. 'Well, really Rigby, that's your affair. There's nothing I can do to help you, darling. Not with a debt as big as that.'

'Now look,' he said, face darkening. 'You will have your little joke, but this has gone far enough. I'm desperate, don't you understand? I need that money now. I've got to pay my preferential creditors in three weeks or they'll make me bankrupt. I'm not leaving till I get it.'

She lit a cigarette and poured herself another G and T. He was pleased to note that her hands were shaking. Then she looked at him for an uncomfortably long time.

'I'm sorry to have to tell you this, my darling,' she said, 'but there isn't any money.'

He was enraged to hear her say such a thing. 'This is no time for stupid jokes!' he roared.

Margaret gulped her G and T. 'I knew you'd be cross,' she said. 'It was all very well for your father with his tricks and plots, *I* was always the one who had to face the music.'

She's gone gaga, Rigg thought, looking at his mother's flushed cheeks and bleary eyes. 'What are you talking about?'

'There isn't any money,' Margaret repeated. 'There never was. It was one of your father's tricks. He was going bankrupt, you see, so he put all the money he had into a fund for you.'

'I know. He told me. I remember.'

That surprised her. 'Do you?' she said. 'You were only a little thing.'

'I was eight. I remember. There *was* money.'

'It was so that his creditors couldn't get it,' Margaret explained. 'It was a trick. After he went bankrupt he made me take it all out, so that he could start again. By the time he died, it was all gone.'

The shock of what she was saying was making Rigg's blood run cold. 'But you let me go on thinking . . .'

'We had to darling, don't you see? If you'd known what was going on, you might have told somebody and that would have got us into trouble. You were only a little thing. And then later on, after he died, well . . . it was a such a comfort to you I didn't like to spoil things. I knew you'd be angry if I told you. You always had such a temper, even as a little boy. And there wasn't any need to upset you, was there? Not then. The truth is always so ugly, isn't it darling. So destructive. I used to think I'd find the right moment, but it never turned up, you see. And you were so happy thinking he'd left you an inheritance. I couldn't destroy that for you, could I? I always say it was knowing you had money that gave you the confidence to get started.'

Shock was turning into his familiar, terrible anger. 'You let me go on thinking there was money all this time and it was all a lie. You lied to me. How could you *do* such a thing? I've banked on this money. I've planned my whole life on it.'

'I knew you'd be angry,' Margaret said, wincing. The expression on his face was one she recognised only too well and had always shrunk from. 'I *am* sorry, Rigby. But what else could I do?'

'Sorry!' he yelled. 'Sorry! So you bloody well should be. How am I supposed to manage now?'

'Your father had it, you see,' Margaret tried to explain. 'That was the way he was. If there was any money going, anywhere, he had it.'

His anger rose, exploded, spilled over into violence. He sprang at his mother, slapping her stupid, flabby face from side to side as he shouted. 'You bloody, stupid, lying old bitch! I'm ruined, I hope you realise. I'm ruined and it's all your fault.'

She scrambled out of the bed and struggled to run away from him. But he had her by the arms, shaking her. Then he was slapping her, over and over. She was desperately afraid but she knew she had to fight back. She couldn't let this begin all over again. Not with her own son. It had been bad enough with his father. She summoned her strength to oppose him.

'Get out of my house!' she yelled at him, 'or I'll call the police.'

'No you bloody won't,' he said, looking round for the phone.

That precious second's inattention gave her the chance she needed. She made a grab for the phone, her finger on the button. 'I will Rigg,' she threatened. 'I'll call the police and I'll tell them what you've done and I'll have you arrested. Is that what you want?'

It stopped him. He stood before her, panting and scowling but not attacking. 'That's evil,' he said. 'You're a bloody evil woman. You wouldn't do that to your son.'

She was fighting back now – the way she ought to have fought his father all those years and tears ago. 'You lay one more finger on me and I will,' she said.

Anger was still bubbling in his chest, the old black anger that had to be released – but there was something about her expression that inhibited him. Something that reminded him . . . of a voice . . . long ago . . . shouting *'Don't you dare hit your mother!'* It was unfair because it was his father who was hitting his mother . . . over and over again.

'Oh God!' he said, putting his hands over his ears. 'Oh my God!' Then he ran, scooping up his case from the bathroom, leaving his wet clothes on the bathroom floor and his wet shoes and socks on the doorstep.

Standing in the bedroom, still clutching the phone, Margaret heard his car start up – on the third attempt – and rattle tinnily away.

Now that he'd gone, she was aware that she felt ill. Shock probably. There was a dreadful pulse beating in her neck and she was finding it hard to breathe, as if she was climbing a mountain and the air was thin. But he'd left the front door open and she had to shut it. There were things to do.

She went downstairs, very slowly, holding on to the banisters for support and feeling so very ill she was afraid she was going to faint. If I can just get that door shut, she thought . . .

But as she reached the last step, a wave of violent sickness swept up through her body, as though she was drowning. It filled her throat and blackened her vision. She fell, arms outstretched, unconscious before she could call for help.

Chapter Thirty

Rigg was in such a state as he left his mother's house that he didn't know where he was going. He drove without purpose, automatically, simply putting a distance between himself and what he'd done. He was approaching the Chichester bypass before he came to his senses. Then he pulled into the nearest lay-by, switched off the ignition, leaned his head on the steering wheel and wept for a very long time, paralysed with guilt, sunk deep in self-pity.

I've hit my mother, he grieved. No matter what she did to me, I had no right to do that. Not to my mother. Only criminals hit their mothers. Criminals and the lowest of the low. I've put myself in with all the worst trash in the world, hitting my mother. I can't go any lower. This is rock bottom. I've lost all my money, all my shops, I can't pay my debts, I can't go back to Spain, I'm driving a clapped-out Ford, I'm on the run – and now I've hit my mother. Dear God! How did I come to do such a thing? I must have been out of my mind. What can I do to put it right? There was nothing. He couldn't do anything, with no money, no home and nowhere to go.

As his tears dried up, he realised that he was desperate for a drink and yearning to be inside a pub in the good old-fashioned easy companionship of men and money. But he didn't even have enough cash for a small scotch, did he?

After drying his cheeks on his sleeve, he fished out his wallet and checked. Not a lot, but more than he'd imagined. Right then. Next pub along the road. A quick one – or two – something to eat, someone to talk to. Anywhere rather than in this car.

The next pub turned out to be rather a prestigious place, set in a garden full of trees. It was so crowded that he had to queue for nearly ten minutes at the bar before he was served. But, for once, he didn't mind waiting. It gave him a much-needed chance to recover. It was quite a while before he noticed what sort of people were standing round him. Mostly yuppie, loud, and not worth cultivating – but there was one man, bellowing for service at the far side of the bar, who looked drunk enough to be touched for a drink or two.

He was a rough-looking chap, in his mid-forties, with receding hair and a face and figure not only shaped but coloured by a life-long appetite for beer. His complexion was patched red and purple, he was barrel chested and had a ponderous belly. But the best thing about him was that he was waving a fistful of fivers and trying to bully the barman. He'd be good company, if nothing else.

Rigg insinuated himself to the front of the queue and as he gave his order, he managed to catch the man's eye. 'What would you like?' he called.

'Scotch,' the man said. 'Double.' And when Rigg carried his two glasses to the nearest empty table. 'That's very good of you. I 'ppreciate that.'

'Any time,' Rigg said, enjoying the warmth of the scotch on his parched throat.

'You're a pal,' the man said. 'You could die of

thirst before they serve you here. Bloody lot.' Now that they were sitting opposite one another, Rigg could see that his new friend was on the edge of drunkenness, his eyes bloodshot and his speech slurred.

'It's the first time I've been here,' Rigg confided. 'What's the food like?'

'No idea. Take my advice an' stick to scotch.'

Well that fell flat, Rigg thought. 'I will,' he said. 'You're a local then?'

The man confessed he was from Petersfield but said he had very serious doubts as to whether he would ever see the place again.

'Problems?' Rigg prompted.

'Bloody car's died on me, hasn't it.'

'You mean you haven't got any wheels.'

'Did have. Got it as far as this place and it went and died on me. Bloody battery's flat. No bloody garage for miles. I'm sick of the bloody thing.'

'You're in luck,' Rigg said, thinking quickly. 'It just so happens I've got a car I want to sell.'

'Not here?'

'Here as ever is. In the car park. It's only a little run-around. I bought it for my wife.'

'Don't she want it any more?'

'Surplus to requirements,' Rigg said. 'She's run off and left me. Would you like to see it?'

So they went out into the covering darkness of the park among the trees.

'What d'you think?' Rigg asked when his new friend had inspected the car.

'It's in pretty good nick,' the man said, kicking the nearest tyre. 'No rust. Not too much on the clock. How much d'you want for it?'

'Cost me six grand,' Rigg lied.

The man laughed. 'That was a few years back.'

'Yes. What d'you say to a grand then?'

'Too much.'

'Six hundred?'

'I'll give you four.'

'Five,' Rigg hoped.

To his surprise, five it was. The man took another wodge of used notes from his pocket and counted out ten fifties. Rigg handed over the log book and the deed was done. Three minutes later, the new owner was roaring off towards Petersfield with his bargain and Rigg was heading back to the pub with his case in his hand and his loot in his pocket.

Unlooked-for success is the best balm for wounded self-esteem. I might not know where I'm going, he thought, but haven't lost the old charm. I've still got flair. And now I've got a few readies as well.

As he reached the wicket-gate, a brand new Peugeot purred into the car park. It was driven by a self-assured woman with diamonds flashing on her fingers and dressed in a very smart trouser suit, an Armani if he was any judge. Well, well, well. This could be interesting. Sensing another catch, or at least a useful pick-up, he turned away from the gate and lurked under the nearest tree to observe her.

The car was locked, the streaked hair delicately touched into place. Then she strode into the pub.

Where's she from? Rigg wondered, checking that the park was empty as he walked over to her car. It was beautifully kept, clean and neat and highly polished. There was a brief case on the back seat with a glossy brochure beside it. By the light of his pocket torch and by dint of craning his neck into an impossible position, he managed to discover that there was a Manchester address on the brochure. So far so good, he thought. Now for the lady.

She'd found herself a seat by one of the windows and was drinking a St Clements. And it *was* an Armani suit. If he could strike up a conversation with her he might be able to cadge a lift to Manchester. Which ploy should he use? Spilling the drink was probably the best. He edged through the crowd until he was beside her chair, waited until she was raising the glass to her lips and nudged himself forward, knocking against her arm so that some of the drink was spilled.

'Oh I'm so sorry!' he said, turning on the charm at full strength. 'I do hope I haven't spoiled your suit.'

She was mopping the spill with a tissue. 'No,' she said, smiling at him. 'No harm done. It's the table that's suffered.'

On the strength of that smile, Rigg moved into action. He offered to buy her another drink, brushed aside her protest, returned to her table with a laden tray.

'That's very kind of you,' she said.

'It's the least I can do.'

They talked generally for a few minutes, establishing that she was a dress designer called Carmen and that he owned a chain of jewellery stores.

'Rather Ratty Ratner stuff,' he admitted deprecatingly. 'Not your style at all.' And was rewarded with another smile.

'I was thinking of having dinner here,' he said, 'I don't suppose you'd care to join me.'

It was almost too easy. 'Yes,' she said. 'It would be a pleasure, Rigby. I hate dining on my own.'

So they progressed to the restaurant, a candlelit table, an indifferent meal, plenty of wine – and a rather more intimate conversation. Soon Carmen was telling him that she'd had several love affairs – some of them rather good – but had decided never to marry – on principle. And he was confessing that he'd married young – we were both so in love, you see – and had been cut to the quick by his wife's desertion.

'I make mistakes for the best of reasons,' he confessed. 'Actually I've done a rather silly thing tonight.'

She was intrigued. 'Have you?'

'I've lent my car to a friend of mine. Did it without thinking of the consequences. Now I haven't got any wheels.'

'Why did you do it?'

'He was a very old friend,' he told her earnestly. 'He'd broken down, you see, and he had to get back to Petersfield in a hurry. Wife expecting a baby.'

'So how are you going to get home?' she asked, looking at him over the rim of her wine glass.

'Taxi, I expect,' he said. 'Not all the way, naturally, because I've got a long way to go. But to the nearest railway station.'

'Where are you going?'

'Manchester.'

'At this time of night?'

'Trains still run overnight, don't they?'

She laughed. 'I can see you haven't travelled by rail recently.'

'You don't think I'll make it tonight?'

'Not by rail, you won't. Not to worry. I'll give you a lift if you like.'

'To Chichester?'

'No. Better than that. To Manchester. You're in luck. That's where I'm going. And as you've been so kind to me . . .'

'I'm the luckiest man alive,' Rigg told her, giving her the full loving benefit of his fine brown eyes. And for the first time that evening he wasn't lying.

Back in Hampton, a blue ambulance light flashed round and round the close where Margaret Toan had lived with her love birds for the last twenty years.

Her neighbours were at their gates, discussing the shocking news.

'Me and Doris found her, you know. We were looking out the front room window and we saw the door open. And I said "That's odd. I've never known Maggie Toan leave her door open before." Didn't I, Doris?'

'And then we saw this pile of old clothes lying in the hall,' Doris said. 'And we went across and the poor thing had had a stroke. She's paralysed all down one side, you know. Can't speak.'

'Poor Maggie,' her neighbour sympathised. 'What brought that on, do you think?'

'I couldn't say,' Doris said, 'but there was a pair of men's shoes on the doorstep. So it might have been a cat burglar.'

'Someone ought to tell her son,' her neighbour said.

'They'll do that up the hospital,' Doris said, as the ambulance men lifted their buckled stretcher. 'Look. They're taking her off now. I'll just nip across and tell her I'll look after the birds. At least that'll be one less thing for her to worry about.'

*

'I feel ashamed of myself,' Rigg said, as the Peugeot touched ninety. The motorway was virtually empty. Eight distant tail lights shone before them like disciplined red stars, the road signs hung in the sky in well-ordered blocks of bright neon blue. There was nothing to do but hold the wheel, keep a foot on the gas and talk.

'Do you,' Carmen said, glancing sideways at him. 'Why?'

'Letting you do all the driving,' Rigg said. 'It doesn't seem fair. Me sitting here like a slob and you doing all the work.'

'I don't mind,' Carmen said. 'I'm used to it.'

'I could take over for you if you like,' Rigg offered. 'Give you a rest. We could stop for a coffee somewhere.'

'You're too kind for your own good,' Carmen said. 'Most other men would have fallen asleep and let me get on with it.'

'Then they'd have been fools,' Rigg said gallantly. 'And they'd have missed out.'

'You're flattering me.'

'No, I'm not. When you've got to know me a bit better, you'll know I never flatter anybody. I always tell people the simple truth.'

Carmen wasn't sure about all this. He could be shooting a line. She glanced at him again to check but he was looking at her with an expression of such transparent honesty she couldn't doubt him.

'Then you must end up in a lot of trouble,' she said. 'Most people can't stand the truth at any price.'

Rigg allowed himself a sigh. 'Too right,' he admitted, with a doleful expression. 'You're talking about my wife there. I gave her every mortal thing a woman would want but she couldn't take the truth.'

'Some women are like that.'

'She interfered with my business. Wanted to be my partner, you see. It didn't work. She sold off three of my shops while I was out of the country. And my BMW.'

'Whatever for?'

'Debts I think,' Rigg said, giving her the doleful expression again. 'I didn't like to ask. After all, she *was* my wife. You're supposed to trust your wife.'

'Not to that extent, you're not,' Carmen said briskly.

'Well I don't now. I've learned my lesson.'

'Is that why you're coming to Manchester? To start again.'

'Got it in one,' Rigg said. 'You're a very smart lady. In every sense of the word, if you don't mind me saying so.'

'I don't mind you saying so,' Carmen said. 'We could turn off here if you'd like.'

'I wish I'd met you ten years ago,' Rigg said as they turned off the motorway. 'When we were both in our early twenties and I hadn't made such a hash of my life.'

The thought that, in his eyes, she looked a mere thirty two or so – even though she was actually forty six – was the most delightful thing he'd pushed her way that evening. An intriguing young man, she thought, as she drove into the next service station. 'There's a café here,' she said. 'We'll have some coffee and then you can drive the rest of the way.'

He drove her to her door, put the car in the garage for her and escorted her to the doorstep.

'It's been a wonderful evening,' he said. 'And I really mean that.'

'Where are you going to stay?' she asked.

'Somewhere in Manchester,' he said, waving a vague hand, as if it didn't matter.

'We're miles from the centre of Manchester, you know. It's all residential round here. How will you get there?'

'I'll find a cab. Don't worry. I'll manage.'

She made her mind up, rapidly, the way she always did. It was a risk to let a virtual stranger into her house, but it was daring too and undeniably exciting. 'You can stay the night here,' she said. 'I can't let you loose on the streets – not when you've been so kind to me.'

'You're a woman in a million,' he said. The courtesy light was shining into his face, so he smiled at her most lovingly. 'You've turned my life round this evening, do you know that. I was at my lowest ebb when I met you and now . . .'

'Now?' she asked.

'You've restored my faith in women, my beautiful Kitty Cat. Well I tell you – if it wasn't for the fact that we've only just met, I could kiss you.'

'I don't think it's quite the time for that, do you?' she said, looking in her handbag for her front door key. That was moving just a bit too quickly.

'No,' he said, back-tracking at once so as not to alarm her. 'It isn't. I'm sorry. I shouldn't have said that. It was presumptuous.'

He kissed her four days later, after he'd made himself indispensable around the house and told her the full tragic tale of how much he'd suffered in his short life – of his father's death, his mother's cruelty, his wife's extravagance, his partner's treachery. During the next two evenings, having roused her sympathy, he elaborated on the way his creditors had sent a private eye to Spain to harass him and described the agony he'd suffered at not being able to meet his commitments. By the time he got around to the terrible story of how his wife's three brutal brothers had set upon him and beaten him up in full daylight on Hampton beach – because they blamed him for his wife's extravagance – he was in Carmen's comfortable double bed and had taken up permanent residence in her house.

Chapter Thirty-One

November came in gently, as if it was early autumn, with most of the leaves still colouring the trees and a September mildness in the midday air. To Brad's disappointment the date on which an autumn General Election could be declared came and went and it was plain that nothing would happen until the spring. Meantime there was plenty of work to do at the hospital.

St Mary's had originally been a small cottage hospital built beside the main road to Chichester to cater for the minor accidents and injuries common to all small rural communities and to patch up the cuts and bruises of the holiday makers. But the growth of rest homes and nursing homes in the town led to such an enormous increase in the elderly population that it had to be extended and converted to cope. Now the original white cottage is buried in a huge, new, red-brick building full of geriatric units and all the attendant services they require – rheumatology, neurology, physiotherapy, speech therapy, water therapy, a day care centre, a restaurant, even a chapel. It is well staffed – because care of the elderly is one of the few growth industries in the area – and it is always well supplied with flowers – because there are plenty of local funerals. To walk up its wheel-chair ramp and into its well-lit, flower-scented corridors is like stepping into another world.

Brad enjoyed working there, even when her old dears were fractious. It was rewarding to watch them as they gradually improved and there were always new people to meet and care for. In fact, several new patients had arrived that very morning.

'Who've we got on *our* ward?' she said, adjusting her cap as she looked round the day room. Now that she and Martin were back together, she was growing her hair. At the moment it was just a soft pale-yellow down, like a day-old chick, and because it was so short, her cap was constantly slipping off. But her bright blue uniform was as smart as ever and her smile was as red as her nails. She looked totally out of place in such a placidly elderly setting, like a neon sign on a church.

'Ethel's back,' Staff said. 'Arthritis. You remember her.'

Brad saw the old lady and waved at her.

'The other one's new to us. She's come here to be rehabilitated after a stroke.'

'Where is she?'

'Still on the ward. Room C. She's finding it a bit hard to settle.'

'I'll take her a cuppa, shall I? What's her name?'

'Margaret,' Staff said, glancing at the white board. She had all the patients' names written up afresh every day.

Brad looked at the white board too. *Room C – Mrs Margaret Toan*. 'There's a turn-up for the books!' she said. 'I know her.'

'Well perhaps you can cheer her up then,' Staff said, swishing off to attend to another patient. 'She's rather down.'

Maggie Toan, Brad thought. Fancy it being Maggie Toan! She remembered all that fuss over her stupid birthday – bloody red roses! – and had a sudden and vivid memory of the lady, swanning into Ali's wedding in a mink stole and a picture hat, flashing diamonds.

But when she took a cup of tea into Room C, the woman lying in the bed wasn't the rich bitch of her memory, but a shrivelled old lady, with a lopsided face and short, unkempt hair, dyed tatty blonde and growing out white at the roots. She looked up at her visitor anxiously and tried to smile with the side of her face that was working.

'There y'are, darlin',' Brad said. 'Nice cup a' tea for you.'

Margaret took the tea in her good hand and tried to hold it steady while she sipped. It was difficult because the cup felt so heavy.

'I'll hold it for you, shall I?' Brad offered.

'Tha' 'ould be k-k-kind,' Margaret struggled, ashamed of her slurred speech. 'I had a s-s-stroke, you see.'

'There y'are,' Brad said, supporting the cup and talking to her in exactly the same way as she talked to all her other old dears. 'Don't you worry. You're doin' lovely.'

That afternoon, when she got home after her morning shift, she phoned Ali to tell her the news.

'I didn't know she'd had a stroke,' she said. 'You could ha' knocked me down with a feather.'

'Neither did I,' Alison said. 'Is she bad?'

'I've seen worse. They got her on speech therapy an' things. She'll have to go in a home though. She'll never manage on her own. They got a social worker comin' to see her at the end a' the week.'

'I can't imagine Maggie Toan in a home,' Alison said. 'She'll hate it.'

'I feel a bit sorry for her,' Brad said. 'I know she's been foul to you an' the kids – an' she must've been pretty foul to the Great-I-Am or he wouldn't have turned out such a skunk – but you should see her, Ali. She's pathetic.'

'I suppose I ought to visit her,' Alison said. She didn't want to. The trouble was that ever since Rigg's attack she'd felt weary and dispirited. She had to get behind herself and push, even to do the simplest things. The thought of driving to the edge of town and sitting in a hospital ward trying to make conversation with a woman who didn't like her and probably wouldn't want to see her, was more than she could cope with.

'Can I have the last bis-tik?' Emma asked, pulling at her mother's skirt.

'Share it,' Alison said. 'Half each. I'll think about it, Brad. Shall I see you in Tesco's on Friday?'

There was a surprise at the new firm of Kirkby and Griffiths that afternoon too. The third client to ring after lunch was Mr Harvey Shearing.

'Mr Fehrenbach recommended you,' he said. 'He thought you might be able to trace the whereabouts of a client of mine, a man called Rigby Toan.'

Morgan grimaced at Barbara. 'I could give you an address,' he offered.

'That would be most helpful. He hasn't been in touch for rather a long time, you see, and there's a little matter of a flat in Spain that has to be sold.'

The address was given.

'If I needed service of documents,' Mr Shearing said, 'I assume you could arrange it?'

'We could.'

'Excellent. If I get no answer from my letter, I'll be in touch.'

'Accordin' to Mr Fehrenbach,' Morgan said, probing for information, 'the first dividend on Mr Toan's voluntary arrangement was due for payment last month. Is that right?'

'Precisely,' Mr Shearing said. 'And nothing's come of it. As far as I know the flat hasn't been sold and Mr Toan still has the deeds. That's what I'm after. The Inland Revenue are getting restive.'

'Right.'

'I'll give him three weeks,' Mr Shearing said, 'in case he's travelling. If I don't hear from him after that, I'll get back to you. I'm beginning to think he's rather a slippery character.'

'Well, well,' Morgan said as he put the phone down. 'That was Rigby Toan's insolvency consultant.'

'And?' Barbara asked.

'I think we're goin' to have an official request to serve papers on him.'

'He's yours,' Barbara said.

'I hope so,' Morgan said grimly. 'It's high time he paid his debts.'

It took Alison nearly a fortnight to summon up enough energy to visit her mother-in-law. And then it was only out of a dragging sense of duty and after she'd made arrangements to leave the children with her mother.

Brad was on duty in the day room and keeping all her old dears happy.

'Slow down, Stan!' she teased, as an old man inched his wheelchair towards her. 'I can't have you rushin' about like that. You'll do yerself a mischief. Can't you keep him under control Nell?'

One of the old ladies giggled. 'He's too fast fer me gel,' she said.

'You wanna watch 'im then,' Brad warned.

They all laughed and nodded, old eyes gleaming.

'She's a one!' another old lady said to Alison. 'Our ray a' sunshine she is. Keeps us all on the go.'

'I can believe that,' Alison said. 'Hello Brad.'

'She's in Room C,' Brad said.

Alison had hoped that Maggie would be in the day room, with plenty of company to distract her and Brad around to keep the peace. Hospital wards are awkward visiting places at the best of times, and a room is worse. This one was small and square, with white walls and white sheets, regulation blue blankets and a regulation plastic jug. There was nothing to look at or talk about except the patient in the bed who was lying flat on her back with her eyes closed and her mouth open.

Shall I go away again? Alison wondered. Or just sit here till she wakes up? She was shocked by how frail her mother-in-law looked.

'I'm not asleep,' Margaret said, and opened her eyes slowly, rubbing her eyelids with both hands. 'Who is it?'

'It's me. Alison.'

'Could you come a bit closer?' Margaret asked. 'I can't see so well now.'

Alison walked right up to the edge of the bed, surprised by how close she had to get before recognition flickered in Maggie Toan's blue eyes. She was even more surprised when the old lady struggled to sit up and grabbed at her hand.

'I am glad to see you, dear,' she said. 'I'm sorry to have to receive you in here looking like this. Get my lipstick for me, will you. It's over there on the cabinet.'

Alison retrieved the lipstick and watched while it was applied. 'I'm sorry you're not well,' she said.

Margaret waved the commiseration away. 'My son's coming to see me soon,' she said. 'He's a wonderful young man and so good to his mother.'

'That's not what you told *me*,' Brad said, putting her head round the door.

'Ah well, you're medical staff, aren't you my dear,' Margaret said. 'We don't have to tell everybody.'

'Tell everybody what?' Alison said.

'He was going to hit me, you know. That's why I had this little stroke.'

'Oh Margaret,' Alison said. 'I am so sorry.'

This time her sympathy had an immediate and unexpected effect. Margaret plunged into such a diatribe that it made Alison's head spin. It went on and on in an endless complaint – about Rigg – about his father – about what an awful life she'd had to lead – and finally about 'that ghastly woman from the social security'. By this time Brad had removed herself, with a grimace at her friend, so Alison had to cope with it all on her own.

'She's going to put me in a home,' Margaret said, scowling horribly. 'Don't you think that's wicked?'

'Oh, I'm sure she isn't,' Alison tried to be tactful. 'I think she's just trying to look after you.'

'Nobody looks after me,' Margaret complained. 'I've always looked after myself. Always. Well I won't go in a home and they needn't think it.'

'Some of these homes are lovely,' Alison tried again. 'They've got sun lounges and aviaries and all sorts of things. You might like it.'

'I shan't,' Margaret said. Then her expression changed and became so crafty she looked like a little old witch sitting up in her blue bed. 'Anyway,' she confided. 'They can't get me into anywhere until my house is sold, because I shan't have the money to pay for it. They haven't thought of that. If I can't sell the house I shall have to stay here, won't I? And we all know what the housing market's like with all those repossessions on the market. All those silly feckless people.'

Anger at the old lady's selfishness rose in Alison with surprising strength. 'One of those repossessions was mine,' she pointed out.

'They're a drag on the market, that's all I know,' Maggie pouted. 'People should be more careful with their repayments. They shouldn't be feckless.'

'And that's your son you're talking about,' Alison said.

'Oh that's right,' Maggie said, swinging from complaint to self-pity in an instant. 'Don't mind me. You say what you like about me. I'm only a poor old woman, that's all. I should have died when I had this stroke and then you'd all have been satisfied.'

'You say things like that,' Brad said, striding into the room again, 'you won't get your tea.' She had an empty cup in her hand and was smiling brightly.

Maggie changed expression yet again. 'I feel really bad,' she said, looking pathetic. 'These young people don't know what it is to be old and in pain.'

Brad winked at Alison.

'Where's the tea?' Alison asked.

'In me pocket,' Brad said, giving one of her devilish grins. 'Ready then darlin'?' And she took a miniature bottle of gin and a small bottle of tonic from her apron pocket and poured them into the cup.

'Is she supposed to have that?' Alison whispered.

'No. Course not,' Brad said, lowering the G and T into Maggie's eager hands. 'Staff 'ud have a fit if she knew. There y'are darlin'. You get that down you. Soon chase away the blues that will. Little a' what yer fancy.'

It was obviously true. Margaret was cheering by the mouthful. Alison was astonished by how rapidly she swung from mood to mood.

'I might have a little nap now,' the old lady said to Brad when the cup was empty. She dismissed Alison with a wave of imperious fingers. 'You can go.'

'What d'you think of her?' Brad said as the two of them walked back along the corridor towards the day room.

'I think she's a nasty crabby old woman,' Alison said. 'She hasn't got a good word to say about anybody. All she thinks about is getting her own way. She was gloating because there won't be enough money to pay for her to go into a home unless she can sell her house.'

'Then the sooner it goes on the market the better,' Brad said.

'Who's handling it?'

'The social services,' Brad said. 'They couldn't trace the Great-I-Am and there ain't any other relatives, by all account, except you an' the kids. I told 'em you wouldn't want to be bothered with it. Right?'

The visit had given Alison an unexpected surge of energy. 'I think I shall call in to see Mrs Cromall tomorrow,' she said, 'and see how she's getting on with my divorce.'

She came home from the solicitors dark with rage. When Morgan arrived at her house that evening she couldn't wait to tell him her news.

'They've written three letters to Rigg and he hasn't answered any of them,' she said furiously. 'Not so much as an acknowledgement. Mrs Cromall says she thinks he's given us a false address. Isn't that just typical?' She was more animated than Morgan had seen her for weeks.

'We'll go and have a look,' he decided. 'If he's livin' there we shall soon see. If he's not, we shall see that too. I should've checked it out at the start.'

They drove to Littlehampton the following morning, in a shower of bleak rain, past sodden fields and over a putty-coloured River Arun, into a town awash with water.

Allingham Avenue turned out to be a caravan site and number 10 was a modern four-berth trailer that had obviously been unused for a very long time. Mail lay on the dusty floor in dishevelled heaps, curling at the edges and long since airbrowned and faded.

'Ain't seen a soul since the September before last,' the caretaker told them. 'She come over then fer a day or two. Couple a' visitors. She bought it fer visitors. About five years ago. Had a lot in one time – come over from Canada. Nothink since September.'

'The owner's a woman?' Morgan asked.

'She pays the ground rent,' the caretaker went on. 'That comes from the bank, reg'lar as clockwork. Direct debit, I should say. But you don't see her.'

'What's her name?' Alison asked.

'Toan,' the caretaker said. 'Mrs Margaret Toan.'

'The artful bugger's tricked us again!' Alison said later that night when she and Morgan were entertaining Martin and Brad to dinner. 'We all thought that was his proper address. I've been worried sick in case he suddenly came over and started on me and the kids again. And he's never been there.' The meal was over and they were sitting at the table finishing the wine.

'Well now you don't have to worry no more,' Brad said, picking a chunk out of the remains of her bread roll and nibbling it. 'That's one good thing to come out of it. An' I can tell you another one. Maggie won't have to wait until she's sold her house. That'll disappoint her. She can put her caravan on the market and go straight into a home as soon as she likes.'

That made Martin laugh, but Alison was less interested in her mother-in-law than her divorce. 'I can't divorce Rigg unless I can serve the papers on him,' she said. 'And if I don't know where he is, how can I do that? It's going to take years at this rate.'

'No,' Morgan said very quietly. 'It's not.' There was a determination on his face that Alison hadn't seen before, an expression that was both powerful and threatening. 'It's my job to find runaways. Right? OK then, I shall find him. Barbara can cope on her own for a day or two. I'm goin' to Spain.'

Brad's face fell. 'Now?' she asked.

'Right away.'

'Oh!' Brad said, and grimaced at Martin.

Alison was alerted. 'What is it?' she said.

'We was hopin' you'd be around over Christmas,' Brad said.

'Why?'

'We was hopin' you'd come to a weddin'.'

'What?' 'Whose?' Alison and Morgan chorused together.

'Ours,' Brad grinned at them. 'Me an' Martin. We're goin' legit. Sat'day after Christmas.'

'But that's great!' Alison said, her face beaming with delight. 'Congratulations. Oh Brad, that's great.' And she flung her arms round her friend and kissed her happily.

'Don't I get a kiss too?' Martin asked. And was kissed in his turn.

'So you'll come?' Brad said.

'I wouldn't miss it for worlds,' Alison said. 'You can go to Spain afterwards, can't you Morgan.'

He could. There was no problem about that. 'Why did you choose Christmas?' he beamed at Martin.

'She wants to wear holly,' Martin said, beaming back.

Chapter Thirty-Two

Brad's wedding was such a riot it stopped the traffic and caused a stir from one end of Chichester to the other.

The bride wore cerise pink. Her dress was a Mae West confection, made of satin, cut to reveal a generous and well-powdered cleavage and so tightly fitting that her legs were pinioned together from squashed thigh to manacled ankle. At the ankles it erupted into a fishtail froth of net frills in black, chestnut and gold, and to complete the picture she wore chestnut coloured gloves to her armpits, gold high-heeled shoes on her feet and a coronet of artificial cerise flowers on her newly dyed chestnut hair. Her bridegroom, standing beside her in his neat grey suit and an advanced state of nerves, looked like a fisherman who'd set out to catch a mackerel and ended up with a manta ray.

As they posed for the photographer, Brad certainly made an impressive picture, but she'd forgotten that a bride has to walk about on her wedding day and walking in a dress like that was virtually impossible. The best she could manage was to shuffle one foot in front of the other and she had to lean heavily on her bridegroom's arm to accomplish that.

The procession from the car to the Registry Office was a grotesque and giggling struggle, and when they tottered back, arm in arm after the ceremony, there was another hurdle to contend with that was even more ridiculous. They were greeted by a wheelchair guard of honour which was holding aloft a ceremonial archway of crutches and walking sticks, and as the arch was barely four feet high, they would obviously have to crouch to run beneath it.

'Blin' ol' Reilly!' the bride said. 'I'll never do it!'

Her guard insisted, cheering and stretching their old arms as high as they could. 'Go on Brad!' 'Show a leg gel!' 'Let's be 'avin' yer!'

But it was impossible. She simply couldn't bend at all, not from the waist, not even at the knee, struggle and wriggle as she might. In the end Martin had to unzip the dress so that she could lift the whole thing up in both hands and totter through. Passers by were delighted by such an unexpected striptease in the middle of a chill Saturday afternoon shopping and gathered to cheer as bride and groom negotiated the archway, with yards of net billowing before them and the bride's black tights and chestnut underwear revealed behind for all the world to see.

'That's made my day,' one man said to Alison. 'Is she an actress?'

'Nah!' another one said. 'She's a stripper. You can see.'

As soon as the newly-weds had scrambled to their car, Alison left the children with Morgan and ran to zip up Brad's dress.

'Turn round quick,' she said to her old friend, 'and I'll make you respectable before you get arrested. Or freeze to death.' But Brad was glowing with warmth.

'Gawd that's tight!' she said as Alison pulled at the

zip. The photographer was happily taking unconventional pictures while the admiring crowd cheered and clapped. They were quite disappointed when the happy couple finally got into their car and were driven away to the reception. But as it took a long time and an assortment of vehicles to transport the extraordinary wedding party, they stayed on to enjoy that spectacle too.

The reception was held at the Royal Maritime Hotel, where Christmas carols were playing over the tannoy and the banqueting hall was hung with Christmas decorations. There were Christmas wreaths on every door and a Christmas tree standing in one corner in all its brightly lit, baubled glory. And the wedding cake was the most amazing thing any of the guests had ever seen. Instead of the customary white royal icing, it was decorated in cerise pink and hung about with golden bells and good luck charms, and instead of a model bride and groom to top off the third tier, there was a pink birdcage with two artificial love birds crammed inside it, plumed in chestnut and gold and looking like two turkeys in an inadequate oven.

And naturally turkey was on the menu.

By the end of the meal the groom was looking rather the worse for wear because Brad had been keeping him well supplied with wine all through the meal in an effort to calm his nerves. But when the time came for speeches he swayed to his feet.

'Ladies an' gennelmum,' he said and blinked as if he didn't know where he was.

The guests shushed one another. Chairs were scraped into position. All faces turned towards the bridal table.

'Jush like to shay. Thank you all for coming . . .' the groom managed. 'Fredery jicket splurm . . . fredery jicket kenge spludgely.' And he beamed with triumph at his guests, smiled at his bride and fell sideways back into his chair.

His audience cheered and clapped and stamped. The Royal Maritime had never known such a successful wedding speech.

'Oh poor Martin,' Alison laughed. 'He'll never live it down.'

'Don't you believe it,' Mark said. 'They'll be queuing up to bring their pets to him after this. Some notoriety's healthy.'

'There's dancing next,' Katy said. 'How will he ever dance?'

He didn't, of course. They laid him out on the stage behind the drawn curtains with two cushions under his head and left him to sleep it off. But everyone else danced, even Brad who contrived to perform a stationary wiggle like a pink-clad chrysalis, and Emma who insisted on dancing with 'My-friend-Morgan', and Jon who insisted on dancing with everybody he knew.

After the third dance, Alison sat by the wall and watched them. He's so good with those kids, she thought. It's no wonder they love him.

An elderly couple were sitting on the bench beside her and, as the music stopped, she turned to talk to them.

'Isn't this fun!' she said. 'I've never been to a wedding quite like this, have you?'

The woman sighed and looked meaningfully at her husband. 'No. I haven't,' she said. 'And to tell you the truth I wish we hadn't come.'

Oh dear, Alison thought. I've trodden on corns.

'We're his foster parents you know,' the woman continued. 'So it's a great disappointment to us – well, you can imagine it, can't you? – a great disappointment to see him married to a woman like that. He was always such a nice, quiet little boy, a little gentleman. And now this. Have you ever *seen* such a freak?'

Alison looked across to where Brad was dancing with a child in each hand and her temper suddenly boiled. How dare they say such things?

'Brad's my best friend,' she said, springing to her defence. 'I know she looks a bit over the top today but she's the kindest girl alive. I think they'll be very happy.'

Her vehemence silenced her new companions and, seeing their discomfited expression, she felt she ought to explain.

'I had my wedding reception here,' she said. 'Seven and a half years ago. It was a very grand occasion. Traditional. White dress, white cake, lots of speeches. Everybody said how handsome he was, and how wonderful it was. We were the perfect couple.'

'There you are, you see,' the woman said. 'You prove my point.'

'No,' Alison said. 'Actually I don't. Appearances were deceptive. He might have looked handsome. He *was* handsome but he had a terrible nature. He beat me. I'm a battered wife. You wouldn't think that to look at me, would you? And those two little children over there, dancing with the bride, they're battered children.'

'My dear!' the woman said, with instant sympathy. 'How dreadful! Are you still with him?'

'No,' Alison said. And was glad to be able to say it.

Morgan was walking across the dance floor to rescue her. 'What you doin' sittin' here all on your own?' he said, taking her hand. 'Come an' dance.'

'What was all that about?' he asked when they were safely on the dance floor and he had both arms comfortingly round her.

She told him, briefly.

'*Da iawn*,' he said. 'Quite right. You got to defend your friends.'

'I told them about Rigg,' Alison said. 'That's the amazing thing. I was so cross, I told them about Rigg.'

'Good,' he said.

'Is it?'

'Sign of health,' he said. 'You're acceptin' it, see?'

I suppose I am, Alison thought. Somehow or other this wedding had unlocked her emotions, giving her back the capacity to feel – not just anger but laughter, affection, and now, as they swayed to the music, a sudden, unbidden shiver of desire.

She moved against him, enjoying it. It was such pleasure to be in his arms, cheek to cheek, like this, knowing they would end the evening in bed. Such pleasure.

'*Cariad*,' he said, holding her closer, in the flickering darkness, under cover of all the other dancers.

She kissed his mouth, briefly but lovingly. 'I'm glad you're not going to Spain until the day after tomorrow,' she said.

Chapter Thirty-Three

A sharp rain was falling as Morgan drove into Fuengirola. The place was a monochrome version of its sunlit self, the white apartment blocks bleak against a sky heaped with dark evening clouds, the Mediterranean grey-green and sullen. But the Sedeno was open and welcoming. Morgan booked in, had a wash and a meal. Then he huddled into his winter jacket and set off to Fred's bar to make his first enquiries.

While he'd been dining, the rain had stopped and the street lights had been lit. Their sudden brightness blacked out the wintry evening and dropped patterns of colour to shine and shimmer on the wet pavements. There were very few people about and although Fred's bar was much the same as he remembered, it was completely without custom. Fred stood beside the bead curtain, polishing glasses so as to appear busy.

He hadn't seen Rigg Toan for about a year, he said, as he served Morgan his brandy. He didn't know whether there was anyone in his apartment.

'Kids come in and outa here all the time when the sun shines,' he said. 'We get to know the regulars – guys like Rigg – but most of my trade is kinda transient, I guess.'

'Well cheers,' Morgan said, enjoying the brandy as it spread warmth through his throat and chest. No luck here. Perhaps he'd find something out at the apartment block.

This time, thanks to Alison, he knew the number of the flat so it didn't take him long to find it. He half expected the place to be empty, but there were lights in the window and sounds of music. He rang the bell.

The door was opened by a middle-aged man with a Midlands accent. He was wearing brightly patterned shorts and a T-shirt as though it was the height of summer, and he looked puzzled to find a Welshman on his doorstep.

'I'm lookin' for a man called Rigby Toan,' Morgan explained.

'Never heard of 'im.'

'He used to own this apartment.'

'Can't help you,' the man said. 'Like I told you. I never heard of 'im.'

'I hope you won't mind me askin',' Morgan said. 'Do you own the apartment now, like?'

'Come in,' the man said. 'It's too bloody cold standin' out here. No I don't own it. We rented it, didn't we Mabel.'

Mabel was a plump lady in a crimplene dress and carpet slippers. 'For a fortnight,' she said. '£400. Christmas holiday. We thought it was a bargain but it was ever so dirty. Are you from the agency?'

'No,' Morgan said, producing one of his new cards. 'I'm a detective. I'm looking for the owner.'

'Oooh!' the woman said. 'How exciting. Isn't that exciting Ossie? What's he done? Do sit down.'

Morgan looked round the flat, mentally making notes. The chairs were made of pine and thickly upholstered, but the table had been scored with a knife and although the walls were draped with Christmas decorations he could see that they were marked and stained. This has been a holiday let for quite a long time, he thought. 'Could you tell me how you came to hear of this place?'

'Advertisement,' Ossie said. '*Windford Chronicle*, wasn't it Mabel.'

'You got a phone number then, or an address?' Morgan asked.

'Yes. We did.'

'You don't happen to remember them, do you?'

'No,' Ossie said, shaking his head. 'We paid by cheque, you see.'

'And they sent you a key?'

'Right.'

'By post?'

'Right again.'

'So you got to return it?' This is better. Now I'm on to somethin'.

'That's right,' Mabel said. 'We got to return it. They sent a stamped addressed envelope.'

'And you've got that at home somewhere,' Morgan said, preparing to accept a disappointment.

'No,' Mabel said, beaming at him. 'I got it here. In my vanity bag. Stay there an' I'll get it for you.'

It was addressed to a woman. *'Mrs Silvester, 87 Moor End, Cogglesford, Nr. Manchester.'*

So he's sold it, Morgan thought. That won't please Mr Shearing. Won't help the creditors either. Still at least I got an address. It might not amount to anything, but it's a start. Suddenly, he was full of energy, eager to get on with the hunt.

'Cheers!' he said.

Back at the Sedeno, he made two brief phone calls. The first was to Barbara's home number to report progress.

'Glad you rang,' she said. 'Your Mr Shearing's been on again this afternoon. He's going to bring an action to bankrupt Mr Toan. We're commissioned to find him and to serve documents.'

'Marvellous!' Morgan said. 'Just what I wanted to hear.' And he rang Alison to tell her the good news.

'So what next?' she asked.

'Next Cogglesford,' he said, 'as soon as I can get a flight back.'

As she put the phone down, Alison felt horribly lonely without him.

She drifted about the empty house, needlessly plumping up plump cushions and straightening straight curtains. The kids were in bed and asleep and she'd turned off the TV when the phone rang. She'd taken down the Christmas decorations that afternoon and the rooms looked empty and bereft. Even the kitchen felt unused. The washing up was done and put away, the oven was clean, the worksurfaces washed down. In fact if it hadn't been for a pile of papers on top of one of the units it would have looked clinical. She reached up idly to remove the papers and put the final tidy touch to the place. And saw that it was one of Morgan's files.

Whatever made him leave it up there? she wondered. That's not like him. Then she turned it over and saw that it was a file on R. Toan. Curiosity aroused, she took it through into the living room, made herself comfortable on the sofa and began to read it. It contained the list of creditors her mother had shown her, and alongside every section, there were notes and comments in Morgan's sprawling handwriting.

'Three mortgages,' he'd written. *'Is A liable? For all or any? Check with Abbey Nat.' 'Second charges. Has he hung this on A? Check.'* And at the foot of the page. *'Are there any other charges that could concern A?'* Are there? she wondered, feeling cold at the thought. Surely there aren't any more debts for me to face. But Morgan was worried about it and, what was worse, he'd hidden his concern. There's nothing for it, she thought. I must find out if I am liable. It was a joint mortgage, so it's possible. I'll phone the Abbey National tomorrow and make an appointment to see someone about it when I come home from work.

The Abbey National office was full of people that afternoon, bustling in and out of the automatic door, queuing beside the counters, sitting at various desks, bulky in their winter coats, talking to young women in slim blue uniforms.

But Alison's interview was in a quiet, uncluttered room and the manager was a woman – which she found encouraging.

'I have the details of your case here,' the manager said. 'How can I help you?'

Alison looked at the computer screen and there it all was – both of their names, the Shore Street address, the value of their mortgages, something headed 'Negative Equity'. 'It's been sold then?' she said.

It had and there was a considerable shortfall.

'Am I liable for it?'

'The mortgages were taken out in both your names, so yes. You are liable. *Jointly and severally.*'

'Could you tell me how much?'

It was £24,000. Dear God! Alison thought. It can't possibly be that much. It gave her such a shock she had to swallow hard before she could bring herself to speak. 'There's no way I could pay that,' she said. 'I haven't got twenty four pounds, leave alone twenty four thousand.'

'You'll forgive me for asking,' the manager said. 'I don't mean to pry into your affairs. But are you and your husband separated?'

'I'm filing for divorce,' Alison said, 'but we're still technically married at the moment.'

'He's in voluntary arrangement, is that right?'

'Yes, but there's a court case pending. His insolvency consultant's going to make him bankrupt. He's been on the run from his creditors for nearly two years.'

'Is he working?'

'I don't know what he's doing. He's a very secretive man.'

'Properties in possession will contact him,' the manager said. 'And then we shall see how to proceed.' She gave Alison a curiously searching look. 'You know there's a second charge on this property?'

'Yes. With the Wessex and Camelot. But it was only for three thousand pounds.'

'Um,' the manager said. 'I'd check that if I was you. Have you seen the bank manager recently?'

'No,' Alison said, her heart sinking like a stone.

'Take my advice. Make an appointment.'

The manager of the Camelot and Wessex told her he was pleased to see her. 'It's been quite a while,' he said, when she was ushered in. 'I hope you are well. Do please take a seat. How may I help you?'

Alison took Morgan's file from her shopping bag and opened it at the list of creditors. 'There's something here I don't understand,' she said. 'I thought you might be able to explain it.'

'If I can be of any service.'

'The last time we met was when Rigg and I came to see you about a loan of £3,000.'

'Correct,' Mr Drury said. 'I have the file.' And he patted it by way of confirmation.

'The thing is . . . on this list . . . Well it says Rigg owes you £18,000. Is it some mistake?'

'No, Mrs Toan,' Mr Drury said sadly. 'No mistake, I'm afraid. That is the sum that you and your husband owe to the bank. In fact, it's rather more than that. There are interest charges you see.'

Alison could feel her heart falling through her chest for the second time that day. So it *was* true. And he'd said '*you* and your husband'. Dear God. 'But how has it grown from £3,000 to £18,000?' she asked. Inside her head she was urging him, please, please, look again. Tell me it's some kind of mistake.

'Your husband increased the loan,' Mr Drury explained. 'Did he not tell you?'

'No.'

She looked so bleak, sitting before him in the pale sunshine filtering through his striped curtains, that Mr Drury was full of pity for her. But commerce was commerce. There was nothing he could do to help her, no matter how much he might pity her.

'Let me get this straight,' she said. 'In addition to the £3,000 we borrowed in the first place, he took another £15,000.'

'Correct.'

'So we owe £3,000 between us and he owes £15,000.'

'No,' Mr Drury corrected. 'The total debt now stands at £18,000 plus interest and you are both liable for it "*jointly and severally*". The bank accepted equity in the matrimonial home, as you remember, but now I'm afraid there is negative equity on the property, since its repossession. I'm afraid you and your husband are liable for the debt of £18,000 "*jointly and severally*".'

'But I didn't know he was increasing the loan,' Alison protested.

'I'm sorry to say that is immaterial,' Mr Drury told her. 'You are still liable.'

Jointly and severally, Alison thought. He milked that house for every penny he could get out of it and now I'm not just responsible for the shortfall on the mortgage, I've got this loan to pay on top of everything else. Dear God! How could he have been so cruel? I wouldn't have done that to my worst enemy, let alone to someone I was supposed to love. I can't go on pretending it was just bad luck. He knew what he was doing, so he must have done it deliberately. He went on borrowing and he didn't tell me, because he knew that in the end I would have to pay. He was free to spend the money – on that bloody BMW and clothes and God alone knows what else – because he knew that when things got rough he could run away and hide and I'd be left to face his creditors. He told me all those lies about it being the recession and about other people doing him down, and all the time he was taking money from anybody he could con out of it, and cheating me, setting me up to be his fall guy. In that moment, sitting in that peaceful office, with its cut flowers and its stripy curtains, she knew that she was capable of hatred and that she hated Rigby Toan.

Manchester was dark and damp that afternoon, and full of traffic. But Morgan set about his work there cheerfully and immediately, just as he'd done in Fuengirola, hiring a car and booking in at a cheap hotel. Then he bought a local road map and drove straight out to Cogglesford. He was tired and he was hungry but appetite would have to wait until he'd seen the lie of the land.

Moor End was hard to find in smoky darkness and unfamiliar streets, but when he finally drove up alongside the gate of number 87, it turned out to be an impressive house, red-brick, detached, and with a long front garden half hidden by a hedge of privet and laurel. Whoever she was, Mrs Silvester certainly had the money to buy that flat. The signs of wealth were all there, large garage, new double glazing, burglar alarms under the eaves.

There were no lights on in the house, except a courtesy lamp by the front door. And no sound from it either. Morgan consulted his watch. Past eight o'clock, so it looked as though she was out for the evening. He was just planning to go and get himself something to eat and come back at closing time, when a classy Peugeot purred up the road and pulled in through the gates.

Two occupants – one male, one female – male driving, Morgan observed. Stumpy legs in high-heeled shoes emerging from the passenger seat. The man leaping from the car, slamming the door, one arm full of parcels.

'Have you got everything?' the woman's voice called.

'I'll come back for the booze,' the man called back. The voice was familiar. Was it? Could it be? Then he turned to face the woman under the courtesy lamp and it was Rigby Toan. No doubt about it. Rigby Toan in a classy suit, looking fit and well-fed and full of himself. Gotcher!

The woman had to be Mrs Silvester. She certainly held the key – in every sense of the phrase. Rigg had to wait on the doorstep until she opened the door.

'Come on, Carmen!' he called. 'It's cold out here.'

Morgan watched as the couple walked into the house, switching on lights as they went. Does he live with her? he wondered. And if he does, is he trading? He could be using her name as a cover. That would be interesting. There was no question of going off for a meal now. The most he could manage would be a quick take-away. The vigil had to be kept.

And a very long vigil it turned out to be. The lights stayed on in the house until nearly two o'clock in the morning. Nobody came in or out. There were only the faintest sounds of pop music when a door was opened somewhere at the rear. Once he saw the woman, briefly, as she came to an upstairs window to draw the curtains. The downstairs lights went out, there was a glow at the landing window and lights were lit in a bedroom. One bedroom? There was no way of telling, as he couldn't see the back of the house. The glow disappeared, the lights went out and now the house seemed to be in darkness.

He waited another half an hour, chill and stiff-legged in the confines of his car. Then he eased himself out of the driving seat, stretched, closed the car door with the merest click and crossed the road to give the entire house the once-over.

It was easy enough to get in, just a simple catch on the wooden gate at the side of the house and he was in the back garden. No lights anywhere. No sign of life. They were both in bed. Now and at last he could drive back to the hotel and catch up on some sleep.

He was back on watch at eight o'clock the next morning, breakfasted and with a morning newspaper to keep him entertained, but unshaven and still tired. He was just in the nick of time. He'd hardly had a chance to read more than the headlines when the door opened and the woman came out. She looked brisk and businesslike in a tailored suit and a long swing coat. Off to the garage, checking things in her handbag, and then the car was out and she'd driven away, leaving Rigg still in the house.

The vigil continued. Nine o'clock, ten o'clock, half past. He likes his sleep. Finally, at a few minutes before eleven, the gentleman emerged from the house, yawning and blinking in the sunshine. He was wearing jeans and a blue sweater under a denim jacket. So he keeps a change of clothes here.

Morgan watched as he ambled out of the drive and headed off towards the centre of town. It would be hard to follow him in such a quiet road without other traffic to mask his presence, and another car didn't arrive to provide cover until his quarry was almost at the end of the road. But he need not have worried. Rigg was in no hurry and was easy to trail.

Morgan followed him all day, first to a café for breakfast, then to Lawton Street for a browse among the shops, then to a boutique called *Carmen* – what else? – where he waited for nearly an hour while Mrs Silvester talked to a customer. Then the two of them took a very long lunch, and after that Rigg walked slowly back to the house and let himself in. So he *has* got a key.

There was no need to watch any longer. Now it was simply a matter of sending a fax to Harvey Shearing. *'Toan found. He is living at 87 Moor End with Mrs Carmen Silvester. Please send documents to the above address. I will serve them a.s.a.p.'*

Then he phoned Alison.

'I've found the bugger,' he said.

'Brilliant!' she said. And told him what she'd found out at the bank and the building society.

She sounded so strong and so much in control that he decided to tell her the whole truth. 'He's living with the woman I came to look for.'

The emotions of Alison's lonely week gathered and grew and became a red-hot fury. 'He's a devil!' she exploded. 'I don't think he's got any shame or morals at all. He loads all his debts on to me, without telling me, he pretends to be living in that caravan when he isn't, he lies through his teeth, he skulks in Spain for months, he hides away, and now he's living with another woman. I suppose she's keeping him.'

'Yes. It looks like it.'

'Then she's rich.'

'Very.'

'I'm coming up to this Cogglesford place,' she decided. 'I shall catch the first train tomorrow morning. Meet me at the station.'

'Come to Manchester,' he said. 'I'll meet you with the car. I should have Mr Shearing's papers by then. You can see them served.'

'I shall do a lot more than that,' she promised. 'I don't know when I've ever been so angry.'

I ought to be ashamed of feeling so furious, she thought, as the blood burned in her cheeks. But she wasn't. She was glad of it, aware that it was necessary and cleansing, and that Rigg deserved everything that was coming to him.

Chapter Thirty-Four

Rigby Toan was in ebullient mood. He'd slept very late that morning and now, bathed and shaved, perfumed and pampered, he was dressing for a very special lunch date. He and Carmen were going to persuade a mutual friend of theirs to set him up in business – trading under her name of course, to be on the safe side. They'd found suitable premises in the High Street. Now all they needed was a sleeping partner and this man was more than likely.

Aware of the importance of first impressions, Rigg had decided to wear his eau-de-nil Armani suit and his Gucci shoes. Standing before the mirror, which covered the entire wall in Carmen's gold and chrome bathroom, he stroked the luxuriance of his moustache, admired the remains of his Spanish tan and congratulated himself on his good fortune. Flair, he told himself. That's what it takes. Flair. You've either got it or you haven't.

All in all, life was beginning to pan out quite well. Alison had held him back. There was no doubt about that. He could see it quite clearly now. Whereas with Carmen he had this wonderful feeling that things were going to take off. Carmen wasn't perfection, naturally. All women are tricky. It was in the nature of the breed and she could be bloody bossy. All that silly business with the front door key, insisting that *she* was the one to open the door when they were together, even though he had a key of his own. Making arrangements for dinner parties without telling him. Things like that. But she loved him and she was very generous.

He'd persuaded all sorts of presents out of her – usually by telling her how badly he'd been treated by that slag Alison. Last week she'd finally agreed to put down the deposit on a two-year-old BMW for him. He'd angled for a Porsche but she wasn't quite up to that yet. Not to worry. A BMW would do to be going on with. It would mean he could get around to a few government auctions and pick up some of the bankrupt stock that was going cheap. There were good pickings to be had at government auctions. He'd sent off for one of the catalogues more than a week ago. Cost a pretty penny – but Carmen had paid. Now he was waiting to see which would be delivered first, the catalogue or the car.

The doorbell was chiming. He took one last look at his image, smoothed his hair and went down the stairs to answer it.

It was Alison and that vile Welshman of hers, standing in the porch as though they had every right to be there. The sight of them was such a shock that he said the first thing that came into his head. 'How the hell did you know where I was?'

'No, we weren't supposed to, were we,' Alison said quietly.

Rigg was already thinking up excuses. 'You can't come in,' he said. 'I'm only visiting. The lady of the house is out.'

'The lady of the house is Mrs Carmen Silvester,'

Morgan said implacably. 'She's at work, at her boutique. You live here. I got photographs to prove it.'

Is there anything they don't know? Rigg thought. 'You can't come in,' he repeated and began to shut the door.

Morgan moved at once, using one large foot as a doorstop. 'Now you don't want a scene, do you?' he said reasonably. 'If we was to start bangin' on the door, your neighbours would want to know why.'

'And I suppose you'd tell them,' Rigg sneered.

'Right.'

This was hideous. If Carmen came back and found them, the fat would be in the fire. 'Can't we go somewhere else?' he asked. 'What do you want?'

'A divorce,' Alison said. 'But that's not what we've come for.'

That annoyed him. 'Don't be silly,' he said. 'You don't want a divorce. And anyway, I'm not going to give you one.'

'You don't have to give it, Rigg,' Alison said calmly. 'I take it.'

She can't be talking to me like this, Rigg thought. She loves me. But this wasn't the old Alison he remembered. She was standing so tall, with an expression on her face he hadn't seen before, and she'd had her hair cut, hadn't she? Whatever she'd done, she looked gorgeous and she was turning him on rotten. 'You're my wife,' he said. 'And that's how you're going to stay. I'm not letting you free to marry someone else.' With a meaning look at the Welshman. 'So don't think it.'

She didn't even look at him while he was talking.

Damned woman. 'Well I haven't got time for chit-chat,' he said and tried to shut the door.

But Morgan's foot was still in the way. 'I got a letter here,' he said. 'I think you'll want to see it.'

Annoyance struggled against curiosity and curiosity won. 'What letter?'

'From a firm you used to deal with. Somethin' to do with money. A refund of some sort. Too valuable to go in the post so they said. I got to deliver it to you in person.'

Is he telling the truth? Rigg wondered. He could be. It's possible. There could be some back cash owing from somewhere. He hadn't kept records, so it was difficult to be sure.

'Oh all right then,' he said, taking the gamble. 'You can come in. But only for a minute. I've got a lunch date.'

Hence the clothes, Alison thought as she and Morgan walked into the hall. That's an expensive pair of trousers he's got on.

He led them out of the hall into a room that ran the full length of the house. It was a curious room. Although it was comfortably furnished with a *chaise longue* under the window and armchairs by the fireplace, down at the garden end there was a workbench covered in paper patterns, a stand filled with cottons and books of samples, a tailor's dummy with a length of cloth draped over one shoulder and one wall full of deep shelves packed with rolls of cloth like a draper's shop.

'So,' Rigg said. 'Let's have a look at this letter.'

Now that the two men were standing face to face in the full light from the French windows, Alison couldn't help noticing how totally different they were. Morgan, in his rough jeans and his leather jacket – dear, solid, dependable, patient Morgan – held out the letter in his scarred right hand, his face guarded. And Rigg stretched out an unmarked, work-shy hand to receive it. He seemed smaller than she remembered, and slighter, a slick, devious-looking man, his face full of hopeful greed. Once upon a time, she thought to herself, I thought he was handsome and strong. I believed in him. Now I can see how weak he is. He looks like a spoilt child waiting to be pampered. She was surprised that she hadn't seen that aspect of his nature before.

There was a long pause while he read the summons, colour draining from his face.

'This isn't a refund,' he said, breathless with anger. 'It's a bloody summons. From that bloody Harvey Shearing. You tricked me.'

'That's right,' Morgan agreed. 'It's a summons. And I got a warnin' for you too. If you ignore it you can be sent to prison for contempt of court.'

Rigg had no answer to that at all.

'That's it then,' Morgan said turning to Alison. 'We can go now.'

But Alison had seen the label in Rigg's eau-de-nil jacket, which was lying over one of the chairs.

'That's a bloody Armani,' she said, striding across the room to pick it up in disgust. Brad was right. 'You stinking toe-rag. You buy Armani suits. Your children get their clothes from car-boot sales and you buy bloody Armani suits.'

Rigg tried to deflect her rage. 'What of it?' he said. 'It's my life. I can spend my money how I like.'

'I'll tell you what of it,' she yelled at him. 'It's disgusting, that's what it is. Your children eat beans on toast because I can't afford anything better and you spend thousands on your own stinking back. We live in squalor and you ponce about in a BMW with your Gucci shoes and your Armani suits. Well this is one suit you won't ever wear again.' She had spotted a large pair of pinking shears on the workbench and before Rigg could stop her she seized them and hacked at the sleeve until the cloth was in jagged lumps.

'You can't do this!' Rigg cried, aghast at such vandalism. He wanted to rush at her, to tear the suit from her rotten hands, to hit her until she stopped. But he couldn't do anything. Not with that bloody Welshman brooding beside him.

'I'm doing it!' Alison said, working on the second sleeve with immense satisfaction.

'I'll sue you for wilful damage.'

She flung the mangled jacket into the corner and turned to face him. 'You do that,' she said. 'And I'll tell them exactly how you treated me. See how you like that.'

'I'd deny it,' he tried to fight back.

'We got the photographs to prove it,' Morgan said laconically. 'Handy sort of article, a camera. Time we were off, Alison.'

They walked out of the room leaving Rigg too stunned to move. 'You've ruined my suit,' he said.

'Actually,' Alison said, 'you've got off very lightly. If you hadn't been wearing the trousers I'd have cut them up too. See you in court.'

After they were gone, Rigg retrieved the wreckage

of his jacket and began to weep. He'd been duped, attacked, cut to ribbons like this coat. And what had he ever done to deserve it? I've only been trying to make an honest penny, he thought, that's all, and she walks in and treats me like this. Life is bloody unfair.

Morgan and Alison laughed all the way back to Manchester. And even when they were on the train and heading back to London, they were still laughing.

'That did me such a lot of good,' Alison said. 'I feel wonderful.'

'You were wonderful,' Morgan told her. 'I could have cheered you.'

She gazed out of the window for a moment. 'You know,' she said, looking at him again, 'when I was little, I never lost my temper.'

'Never?'

'Well, very rarely. I thought it was the worst possible thing a girl could do.'

'And now you've changed your mind.'

'Now I've changed,' she said. 'I'm a different person.'

'Better?' he asked.

'I'm not sure about that. Stronger. If you'd told me two years ago that I've stood up to Rigg like that and cut up his coat, I'd never have believed you. I've always been – well, really rather frightened of him up till now.'

'If you'd told me eight years ago that I'd lie through my teeth to get the better of a criminal, I'd never have believed that either,' Morgan said. 'I never told lies when I was down the pit. None of us did.'

'It's a funny old world,' Alison said, reaching out to hold his hand.

'It's Maggie Thatcher's world,' Morgan said. 'That's what it is. We've all learned to think her way. There was a time when lyin' was wrong. No two ways about it, it was wrong. You even expected politicians to tell the truth. If they told lies, they had to resign. Now, God help us, we expect them to lie. They say they're massagin' the unemployment figures. They're not. They're lyin'. And we accept it. She's turned lyin' and cheatin' and grabbin' everything for yourself into a virtue. Even greed's a virtue now. They call it good business or bein' an entrepreneur.'

'Like Rigg,' Alison said, thinking how greedy he'd always been, taking money from anybody he could persuade to give it to him, with no intention of paying any of it back. *It's business,* he used to say. *You don't understand it.* Well. I understand it now, she thought.

'I tell you one thing,' Morgan said, breaking into her thoughts. 'Mr Shearing'll be pleased to hear what you done. He's been steamin' at not being able to find the Great-I-Am. I shall ring him first thing in the mornin' and tell him the good news.'

'Tell him I'd like to see him,' Alison said. 'I've got some information for him.'

Harvey Shearing came all the way to Hampton to see Mrs Toan and took her and the children out to tea and cream cakes. He seemed older than Alison remembered him and more worn.

'I shall be glad when this case is brought to court and he's made bankrupt,' he confided. 'The trouble your husband's caused me!'

'He won't be my husband for much longer,' Alison told him. 'I've filed for divorce.'

'I don't blame you. I thought he was such a nice young man when we first met, but now . . . Still, enough of that. What was the information you had for me?'

Alison had it all written out. 'This is the address of the Abbey National branch where we had our three mortgages,' she said briskly. 'And this is the address and phone number of Properties in Possession, who are dealing with the negative equity, which is nearly twenty four thousand pounds. It's Rigg's debt, not mine. I think he ought to acknowledge it.'

'Indubitably.'

'And then there's the debt to the Wessex and Camelot Bank. I signed second charges for that because he told me it was only for three thousand pounds and it's actually eighteen. I think he ought to acknowledge that too.'

'Oh he will,' Harvey Shearing said grimly. 'I can assure you of that. He's messed us all about quite long enough.'

Jon was kicking Emma underneath the table. They'd been in a quarrelsome mood all day.

'Time we were off,' Alison said, putting down a hand to restrain him. 'I'll see you in court.'

'First Thursday in March,' Harvey Shearing said, signalling for the bill. 'It's all fixed. Not long now.'

It was actually less than five weeks and it passed so quickly that it felt like a fortnight. At the end of February Alison had a letter from Mrs Cromall, asking her to call in at the office to discuss the divorce. In a curious way that speeded the time along too. *'The papers have been sent to your husband's address in Cogglesford,'* she wrote, *'but having had no reply, we feel other arrangements will have to be made.'*

'I'm afraid we have to accept that your husband is going to play hard to get,' she said, when Alison arrived to see her.

'It doesn't surprise me.'

'We shall have to serve these papers.'

'Yes.'

'Let me explain how this is done.'

'Actually,' Alison said, smiling at her, 'I know how it's done. The new man in my life is a private investigator.'

Mrs Cromall was genuinely pleased. 'I'm glad to hear there's a new man in your life,' she said. 'That is good news.'

'I can give you better,' Alison said. 'Rigg's got to appear in court in Brighton in a few weeks' time to be made bankrupt. I could serve them on him there.'

'How very appropriate,' Mrs Cromall said. 'I'll have them prepared.'

I can serve them on him, Alison thought, just like Morgan did. There in the court. I can serve them and get a divorce and break clean away from him. Then I shan't be in limbo any longer.

Chapter Thirty-Five

So the preparations were made and the day of the hearing arrived. Morgan promised to be in the office all afternoon so that Alison could phone and tell him how she'd got on. Brad and Martin sent a good luck card, and so did Greg and Andy. Elsie offered to collect the kids from school and look after them until she got back. Mark and Jenny phoned at breakfast time to wish her well. All she had to do was to drive the kids to school and then head off to Brighton. But she was nervous. It didn't seem possible that the Great-I-Am was finally going to be brought to book. He'd got away with so much and for so long, it was almost as if he was impervious to any attempt at justice.

It was a miserable day, overcast, showery and as dark as winter. Brighton was full of damp shoppers, every other store had a sale, the West Pier was closed and falling to pieces, even some of the prestigious jewellers in the Lanes had gone bust.

But the judge's chambers were quiet, discreet and as dry as their occupant. There were only three people in the meeting when Alison arrived: Harvey Shearing, wearing a dark suit and a determined expression; the judge's clerk, sitting at a side table piled with papers; and Rigg, in yet another Armani suit. The sight of it charged her with angry energy. How many more of them has he got? But there wasn't time to say anything, or to present her divorcee papers to him, because the judge was in the room and taking his seat at the head of the table.

It was all handled so smoothly that it seemed to be over before it had begun. Rigg sat at one side of the table and she and Harvey Shearing at the other. After establishing who they all were, the judge asked Mr Shearing to state his case.

It was a damning statement which detailed all Rigg's nefarious activities since the voluntary arrangement had been entered into. The judge listened attentively, while Rigg looked out of the window, a bored expression on his face – as if it was nothing to do with him. Finally the long indictment came to an end.

'I feel I should also point out,' Mr Shearing concluded, 'that there is a possibility of criminal charges being taken out against Mr Toan, *vis-à-vis* the manner in which his liabilities were declared to the creditors at the first creditors' meeting.'

Rigg and the judge looked at one another.

'Have you anything to say to this, Mr Toan?' the judge asked.

Rigg was so shocked by what he'd just heard that he had to swallow hard before he could speak. 'I haven't done anything of a criminal nature, Your Honour,' he said. 'I declared everything. I was quite open.'

'That isn't Mr Shearing's opinion,' the judge said drily.

'I've been badly advised,' Rigg pleaded. 'I was led to understand that I was to receive a large inheritance when I was thirty five, Your Honour.'

'Did you receive this inheritance?'

'No, Your Honour. Not a penny. I could have paid off all my debts if I had.'

'What means do you have to pay your debts now?'

'Well none, just at present, Your Honour. However there is my mother's capital and property to consider. I shall inherit everything when she dies, being the only son, as I'm sure you understand. The house alone must be worth in excess of eighty thousand. I don't know the value of the contents, exactly, but it will certainly be considerable.' He was recovering from his shock now – becoming himself again. 'I think it's safe to say there'll be no problem about paying off debts once I own the house. It's really only a matter of time.'

Alison caught the judge's eye.

'Mrs Toan?'

'Mr Toan's mother is in a nursing home,' she said. 'She suffered a stroke after Mr Toan's last visit. The house and its contents have been sold to cover the cost of the home.'

Rigg's mouth dropped open with renewed shock and stunned disbelief. She couldn't have had a stroke, he thought. She's as tough as old boots. She's putting it on.

The judge checked his facts. 'So what you are saying, Mrs Toan, is that there will be no inheritance whatsoever.'

'No. None.'

That's not possible either, Rigg thought. There *has* to be money. They're all talking rubbish. What a good job I've got Carmen.

'I see,' the judge said. He spent several minutes

writing notes. Then he looked up and spoke to Rigg, directly. 'It seems to me, Mr Toan,' he said heavily, 'that you have behaved shamefully throughout this affair.'

Rigg looked away and declined to say anything more. Once I get that shop on the High Street, I'll paint it blue, he planned. Blue and white with cane chairs. And an aspidistra in the window.

'There is also,' the judge went on, 'the matter of two outstanding debts which you share jointly and severally with your wife and which she has indicated she is unable to pay. Given that this case is an application for bankruptcy at which all your liabilities are to be taken into consideration, you might care to accept responsibility for these particular debts.'

Alison looked at her husband. Her heart was beating so strongly she could feel it shaking the cloth of her blouse. Agree to it, she willed him. Do one good thing at least this afternoon.

Rigg's face was devoid of expression. 'As you wish,' he said. This is all academic. When my new shop opens, I shall be coining it so fast that debts like that will be nothing.

Is that it? Alison wondered. Does this make it legal? But there wasn't time to ask because the judge was speaking to her again.

'Mrs Toan,' he said. 'I see here that in – um – October 1990, you supported your husband's application for a voluntary arrangement. Do you have anything to say on your husband's behalf?'

'No, Your Honour,' Alison said, 'except that I am doing what I can to obtain a divorce from him.'

The judge nodded his head as if that were eminently sensible behaviour.

'Your application is granted, Mr Shearing,' he said. 'Mr Rigby Toan is declared a bankrupt. Mr Toan, in due course, you will be informed of the date on which you are to present yourself for examination by the Official Receiver. Good morning, lady and gentlemen.' And he rose to leave the room.

Quick, Alison thought, pulling her document out of her bag. Quick, quick. If I don't do this now I shall lose my chance.

'This is for you, Rigg,' she said. 'It's a petition for divorce on the grounds of separation by consent.' And she held it out to him.

Harvey Shearing was on his feet and looking surprised. The judge had turned. He and the clerk were both looking at Rigg. It was all highly irregular, but for a few seconds they all waited. And Rigg, feeling the official pressure all round him and still in a trance of shock and disbelief that she could be doing such a thing, held out his hand and took the petition.

It's not over by a long chalk, Alison thought. He's got to sign to show he accepts it. But at least he's received it. He can't pretend he hasn't, not with a judge as a witness. And he can't ignore it any longer. I've taken the first step. At last.

Outside the building, gulls were wheeling and mewing. The sun had come out and beyond the promenade, the waves were tipped with white light, like cut glass.

'Now,' she said to herself, 'where's the nearest phone?'

It took an age to find one, but at last she was inside one of the new time-capsule containers and dialling Morgan's number.

His voice answered almost at once. 'Morgan Griffiths.'

'It's over,' she said. 'He's accepted the papers. Oh Morgan, darling! It's over! He's taken on all the debts. I'm in the clear. And they've bankrupted him.'

'Are you all right?'

'I'm triumphant,' she said. It was the exact word for how she felt – relieved, vindicated, victorious, cleansed of all the worries and horrors of her life with Rigg, emerging from the long battle with a new sense of worth and a new strength of purpose. Triumphant. The world was full of dreadful things – debts and dishonesty, lies and cruelty, battered wives and beaten children, wars and revolutions and terrorists – but there was still hope at the bottom of Pandora's box, even at the end of the twentieth century. Change was possible. People could change. Governments could change. Her children didn't have to grow up like their father. Her life with Morgan could be different.

'Time for celebration,' Morgan said.

'Time for a new charm for my bracelet,' she said, dangling it for him to hear.

'Right,' he agreed. 'What do you want? A scroll or somethin'?'

'No,' she said and paused, smiling to herself. 'I was thinking more along the lines of a wedding cake.'

There was another pause while Morgan digested what he'd heard. When he spoke again his voice was warm and full of love. 'That sounds like a proposal.'

'It is, my darling,' she said, aware of how very much she loved him. 'I've found something out this afternoon.'

'Have you *cariad*? What?'

'I've found out how old-fashioned I am. I want to get married and settle down and live with you for the rest of my life.'

It sounded as though he was chuckling. Or crowing. 'Morgan?' she asked.

'My dear Miss Alison,' he clowned, speaking in a high falsetto. 'This is so sudden.'

'My intentions are honourable, Mr Griffiths,' she answered. 'Will you marry me?'

'Try an' stop me, *cariad*,' he said. 'Just try an' stop me.'

Here follows Chapter One of
Beryl Kingston's new novel available in Century hardback

ALIVE AND KICKING

Chapter 1

The war against Germany was barely a month old and all over Great Britain patriotism burned like fever. London was crazed with it.

Newspaper headlines grew taller by the day, bragging of victory at the River Marne: citizens strutted and preened: shop windows erupted into an enthusiasm of ribbons and bunting and brand new Union Jacks. Some windows sported a picture of King George and Queen Mary, looking severe, and a hand-painted slogan, like '*Britons Never Shall Be Slaves*', or '*For King and Country*', or even more passionately '*God Bless Our Boys!*'. Others gave space to the new recruiting posters, with their demanding, professional type, '*Do Your Duty! Enlist Now! Join Today!*' and their huge, noble faces – white whiskers drooping like the bags under their eyes – each one confident in the expectation that the young men of the capital would spring to the defence of their country in her hour of need. It looked and felt like a carnival – and on the third Saturday in September 1914, it sounded like one too.

It was just after five o'clock and the market in Lambeth Walk was at its busiest, the street almost impassable for stalls and shoppers, when there was a sound like a sudden clap of thunder. It was so loud that it made Rose Boniface jump. She'd been picking over the second-hand blouses at Mrs Tuffin's tot stall, looking for something decent to cut down for her younger sisters to wear to school. She'd already found a blue cotton for Mabel. Now she stopped, one hand on the white lawn of a lady's blouse that she was considering for Netta, and looked up at the sky.

'What on earth was that?' she said.

'Drums, you ask me dear,' Mrs Tuffin said, her eyes firmly on the merchandise. As befitted a lady of her trade, she was a decidedly blowsy woman with a plump pink face, plump pink arms, fat fingers, a bosom that billowed over the tight leather constriction of her belt, and hips like cushions bulging under her long black skirt. She wore one of her own blouses, a confection in bottle-green taffeta threaded with tartan ribbon and decorated by rows of small jet beads and, squashed on top of her bun of black hair, a large straw hat of indeterminate colour.

Standing before such an abundance of flesh and finery, Rose Boniface looked like a waif. At seventeen, she was no taller than she'd been at fourteen when she took over the care of her brothers and sisters and became the mother of the family – a mere five foot and skinny with it. Her neck was too slender under the soft twist of nut-brown hair pinned at her nape, her hands too small with thin supple fingers, her wrists so fragile you felt you could snap them by looking at them. Yet, despite a childhood marred by too much hard work, too many worries and too little food, there was a gentleness about her face that was quite remarkable. It was already womanly, oval-shaped and set off by a natural fringe of wispy curls. True, her cheeks were too thin, her skin had the town dweller's unhealthy pallor and there were poverty shadows under her eyes, but her forehead was high and broad, her nose retroussé, chin prettily rounded, mouth a perfect Cupid's bow and her eyes themselves were widely spaced, dark grey and fringed with thick brown lashes. In short, Rose Boniface had the makings of a beauty.

The sudden thunder-crack had progressed into rhythm. 'It's a parade,' our beauty said, eyes gleaming at the thought.

Mrs Tuffin could see her sale slipping away. 'Would you like me to put that by for yer?' she asked, tucking a straying lock of hair under her hat. 'It's a good bit a' cloth. You could come back for it tomorrow.'

Rose pulled her mind back to the business in hand. 'It's gone under the arms,' she said, lifting up the sleeves. 'It'll need a lot a' working over. It ain't worth thruppence, Mrs Tuffin.' She wasn't bargaining – she was too open and honest to do that – she was simply pointing out the flaws in the purchase.

Normally, Mrs Tuffin would have argued until a better price had been agreed but she liked Rose and knew what an effort she made to keep her family well fed and respectable.

'Tell you what,' she suggested, picking up another white blouse. 'I'll throw this one in an' all, and you can use it for repairs. It's in pretty good nick at the back. See?'

'It's a bad colour,' Rose said. 'I'd rather have that old ecru one, Mrs Tuffin, if it's all the same to you. The one with the torn sleeves. That'ud make a nice contrast.'

Mrs Tuffin considered for a second, as the music drew near enough for them to discern a tune. 'All right,' she said, making her mind up. 'As it's you, Rose, you can have the three for a tanner. I can't say fairer than that, can I, gel?'

The sixpence was handed over and the blouses bundled into Rose's clean shopping-bag. Now there was no doubt that the rhythmic noise *was* a band and at the end of the Walk, what's more. People were heading towards it all along the street, agog for excitement. Rose trotted after them and arrived at the Black Prince Road just in time to see the tail-end passing under the railway bridge. It was a detachment of the Queen's, marching briskly and preceded by a drum and fife band, drums in pounding unison, pipes squealing like pigs. What a lark!

To her surprise she saw her big brother Bertie, standing outside the pub on the other side of the road. She hadn't expected him home from work so soon, but there he was, tall and dependable and cheerful, nodding his head in time to the music. He looks just like Dad she thought lovingly, taking him in – flat cap, old jacket, muffler flying in the breeze – you can see what a worker he is. Dear Bertie.

'Whatcher Rose,' he said, as she crossed the road to join him. 'What price this for a lark, eh? If we was to run, we could catch up with 'em and see the whole thing from start to finish.'

So they ran, shopping forgotten, two of a great crowd hurtling off to enjoy the display. And were not disappointed, for seen from the front, the soldiers looked as grand as they sounded, their kit immaculate and their expressions determined. They were led by a resplendent recruiting officer, a sergeant major with a brick-red face and a chest like a pouter pigeon, and by the time they reached Kennington Cross, they had drawn a long, straggling crowd behind and beside them, like a magnet trailing iron filings – factory workers like Bertie, women out shopping like Rose, clerks with self-important expressions, grimy boys in rags, elderly gentlemen stepping out boldly in time to the music, and, down beside the well-polished boots and carefully wound puttees of the contingent, a flea-bitten collection of Kennington mongrels yapping themselves silly with uncontrollable patriotism.

The procession continued into Kennington Road and came to a halt outside the Town Hall, where it was greeted by a councillor, sweating under his ceremonial topper. The sergeant major took up a stand in the middle of the small green called Kennington Park, while his detachment stood in bright ranks on either side of him and drummed for attention. Within two minutes all trade and traffic had come to a standstill, as cars and carriages were ordered to stop at once, errand boys forgot their errands, eager faces appeared in every window on all five storeys of the houses round the green and the Saturday shoppers told one another there had never been anything to equal *this*, never in a hundred years.

The sergeant major surveyed the scene with satisfaction, fondled his moustache and silenced the drummers with a glance.

'This 'ere band,' he bellowed at his fascinated audience, 'will be playin' for the next two minutes. No more nor less! Two minutes. Then Councillor Thomas has got sommink to say to you, and *I* got sommink to say to you, and you won't none of you want ter miss a word of it, believe *me*. If you got friends what ain't here, do 'em a favour. Nip orf an' get 'em. Sharpish! 'Cause I tell you, they'll kick theirselves if they ain't here to hear this.' He paused to let his words sink in. 'Two minutes,' he warned, and shot another steely glance at his instrumentalists who instantly began to play their tune again, very loudly.

Young men scuttled off in every direction to do his bidding, more faces appeared at the windows, the crowd grew by the second and the band completed its two-minute entertainment with a drum crescendo, white gloves flying like birds. Then the councillor began his speech, which was blown into inaudibility by the evening breeze. But because he smiled a great deal and waved his arms about, his audience gave him a happy cheer when he seemed to have finished. Then the sergeant major took over again.

'Hever since our glorious vic'try at the Battle of the River Marne,' he bellowed, 'we got the 'Un on the run. Thirty miles from Paris they was when our lads got stuck into 'em. And what did they do then, lads? I'll tell you what they done. Beggared off out of it as fast as their little yellow legs'ud carry 'em. That's what they done. And for why? I'll tell you for why. For two reasons. Because your 'Un is a coward. And because the British Hexpeditionary Force is a fine body a' men, highly trained, perfessional soldiers, British an' proud of it.' He paused to give his audience time to cheer, which they did, with fervour. 'Nah then,' he continued. 'I come down here this evening, to give you the chance to join our victorious Army. Chance of a lifetime. Come Christmas, the German war machine'll be finished for good an' all. We nearly knocked the stuffing out a' them all-a-ready. So whatcher say boys? All you got to do is take the shillin'. Just think a' the benefits. Free grub, free uniform, free lodgin', *an'* seven bob a week on top of all that. You'll have the world at your feet my lads. The world at your feet an' any girl you want jest for the asking. There ain't a girl alive what don't love a soldier.' Appealing to the women in his audience. 'Ain't that right my darlin's? An' if you're a married man, sir – since you're asking – even better. Wife's allowance nine bob, wife an' child fourteen shillings, two an' a kick for every child on top a' that. You could live like lords. Like lords me lads. An' all you've got to do is cross the road to the recruiting office over there, an' take the shillin'. What could be simpler?'

What indeed, put like that? The recruiting office at the Town Hall was clearly labelled. The flags were flying. There was even an army sergeant standing by the door ready to welcome them in.

The sergeant major looked at the ranks of ardent young faces turned towards him and his world – at dark cloth caps and work-grimed clothes, at collarless shirts and frayed mufflers, at the trusting innocence of young men lifted by his oratory and, in their unaccustomed stillness, touched with glory by the setting sun.

'Well?' he demanded.

'He's right,' Bertie Boniface said to his sister. 'I ought to do it, our Rose.'

Rose tucked her hand into the crook of his arm and gave it a squeeze. Ever since this war had been declared, she'd known he would volunteer for it, sooner or later. She was so proud of him. 'A' course,' she agreed, smiling at him. 'You go our Bertie.'

A queue was forming outside the recruiting office and young men were running towards it from every side.

'Three cheers for our brave lads,' the sergeant major cried. 'Hip-pip-pip-pip! Hooray!'

Bertie ran at the second cheer.

I shall never forget this moment, Rose thought, watching him as he stood in the line. Our Bertie going for a soldier. And all them young fellers running to take the shilling and defend the country and everything. She was proud of them all. But specially Bertie, dear loving Bertie, who'd fathered the family ever since mum died, and worked like a Trojan to look after them all. He's so good, she thought. Always has been. Wait till we tell them in Ritzy Street. Won't they be thrilled!

It took a long time to enlist. By the time Bertie came striding out of the recruiting office, it had grown quite dark. The band had long since marched away, the gas lights were being lit and the air was chill and smelt of soot and smoke.

'Come on,' he said, taking charge in his usual way. 'Pie and mash tonight. We've got somethink to celebrate.'

So they stopped off at the Cross for five portions and a large bottle of ginger beer. Then they took the short cut to Ritzy Street through Windmill Row, across the main road to Courtenay Street – where some lovely, new, yellow-brick houses were being built for the Duchy and there were gas lights to mark the way – left by the pub and north for home, Rose trotting to keep up with her brother's lengthy stride.

Unlike the roads in the Duchy estate, Ritzy Street was short, narrow and poorly lit. It had once led down to the Thames, to a landing-stage between the Doulton pottery works and the Gunhouse stairs, but now it was cut off from the riverside by the railway embankment and the wide sweep of the London and South Western railway line, which filled the area with the chuff and clutter of engines, day and night, and dropped sulphur stains and black smuts on to doorsteps and curtains and any washing the inhabitants were foolhardy enough to hang out. The houses were built in long, soot-blackened terraces and each house contained a basement kitchen and nine living-rooms, three on each floor. It wasn't the most comfortable place in which to live, but it had provided a home for the Bonifaces at a time when they stood in danger of the workhouse, and for that Rose was fond of it and felt at ease and happy there. When they first moved in to number 26, they'd occupied the second-floor back, which was the worst room in the house; now they had graduated to the two front rooms on the first floor and she and Netta and Mabel had a bedroom of their own, divided from Collum and Bertie by a wall instead of a curtain.

Netta was leaning out of their bedroom window with her hands on the sill, watching out for them. The light from the gas lamp outside the front door edged her sharp features with gold, and made the long straggle of her hair gleam like dark water as it hung over the sill on either side of her gilded hands. But her voice was far from romantic.

'Where've you *been*?' she wanted to know. 'I been waiting *hours*. I'm famished!'

'Set the table,' Bertie called up to her. 'We got pie and mash. Where's the others?'

'Playing out,' Netta said in a tone that implied he was foolish even to ask. 'Where d'you think?' And she left the window to prepare the table.

Bertie put two fingers in his mouth and gave a long shrill whistle – once, twice, three times. It was his usual signal to call the kids home and, sure enough, after a second there was a scramble at the blocked-off end of the alley and one of Mabel's boots appeared at the top of the wall, followed by a black-stockinged leg and a flash of white pinafore. Then the rest of her body appeared and she sat on top of the wall, swinging her legs, ready to jump down. She was ten years old but, because she was simple-minded, she looked younger, short, stout and moon-faced, her clothes patched and grubby and her hair in perpetual tangles. But she was a cheerful creature and full of affection. ' 'Lo, our Bertie,' she called.

'Look at the state of you,' Rose scolded as her sister ran towards them. 'You been playing up the embankment again ain'tcher. Where's your ribbon?'

Mabel thought for a long time and then produced the answer, speaking slowly but with triumph as she always did when she'd managed to get something right. 'In me pocket.'

'Don't tell her off,' Bertie said mildly as the three of them climbed the stairs. 'Not tonight.'

'Why not tonight?' Mabel wanted to know, stomping up the stairs behind them. 'Why not tonight, our Rose?'

'Tell you when Col gets home,' Rose promised. 'Get your hands washed, there's a good girl. It's pie and mash and you like that don't you. Look sharp and then you'll get the beauty of it while it's hot.'

The gas was lit, the fire made up and Rose dished out the supper, while the others took it in turns to wash in the basin in the bedroom, splashing out just enough clean water from the ewer to cover the backs of their hands and emptying the dirty water away in the pail afterwards. And five minutes after his brother's whistle, as Netta was folding the towel and hanging it back on the rail, Collum came charging up the stairs, just as they all knew he would. He was nearly fourteen and although he was small for his age and as skinny as the rest of the family, he considered himself far too grown-up to come at a call. Five minutes was enough to mark the distance between obedience and independence and to set him apart from his younger sisters.

The meal began at once because they were all much too hungry to wait. For quite a while they ate without speaking, their five tousled heads bent low over their five enamel plates. Then, when they'd taken the edge off their hunger, Rose told them the thrilling news.

'Passed me A, they did,' Bertie said with justifiable pride. 'Think a' that. A. Fit for military service in the front line, the surgeon said.'

'Well a' course,' Rose approved, mopping her plate with a chunk of bread. 'What d'you expect, the size of you?'

'Military service in the front line,' Netta echoed, food temporarily forgotten, she was so awed by the importance of it. 'It don't half sound grand, our Bertie.'

'D'you have to wear a uniform?' Mabel asked.

' 'Course.'

'Won't he look a swell, our Rose.'

'I wish I could go for a soldier,' Netta said, gazing earnestly at her brother across the rim of her beaker. Her pale face was peaked with yearning, the tangle of uncombed hair that framed it making it look thin and huge eyed.

'Well you couldn't, could you,' Col said disparagingly. Sometimes Netta said the silliest things.

Netta tossed her head at him, swinging her hair. 'I don't see why not,' she said, defiantly. 'I could fire a gun as well as anyone, and ride a horse – if someone'ud learn me – and carry the flag.' She waved her spoon like an imaginary flag, her dark eyes ardent. 'I'd make a jolly good soldier. I could cut my hair off, couldn't I, and wear trousers and boots and everything. Who'd know?'

'I would,' Col said flatly. 'Anyway, you can't because you're a girl.' The world of war and soldiery was entirely masculine. There was no place in it for women. It was a matter of pride and patriotism, strength, nobleness, valour, comradeship, courage under fire – all the things women couldn't understand. And all happening now, in his lifetime, that was the wonder of it. 'D'you think it'll go on long enough for me to join up an' all?' he asked Bertie.

'Shouldn't think so,' Bertie said. 'We got them on the run, the sergeant said. Be over by Christmas, he reckons.' Then, pitying Col's disappointed expression, 'Still you never know, do you.'

The plates and beakers were empty so Rose and Mabel began to clear the table. Then Netta lifted the kettle from its hob on the fire and poured hot water into the washing-up bowl on the living-room wash-stand so as to clean the dishes, while Col and Bertie pushed the table into its usual position under the window and set the chairs in a neat circle round the fender. There was a routine to everything they did and a place for everything too, for their rooms were small and cramped and contained too many people and too much furniture to allow for any untidiness. In this one, beside the wash-stand and the table and chairs, there was also Bertie's single bed, which had Col's truckle bed tucked underneath it and did duty as a settee during the day, and a dresser which held all their most prized possessions, jugs and dishes, cloths and crockery, a row of well-read books and Rose's precious Singer sewing-machine.

That machine had been the family's most expensive purchase. But they all agreed it had been well worth the money, for Rose's skill at making over old clothes and running up petticoats and pinafores from old sheets and pillow cases had saved them the price of it many times over.

Now she settled beside the table, spread out the three

blouses she'd just bought and began to ponder while Mabel reverently laid the pin cushion, the tailor's chalk and the tape measure beside the blouses and threaded up two needles with white tacking-cotton.

In the pause between the end of the meal and the resumption of conversation, it was quiet and peaceful in their little room: Netta dried the dishes and Mabel put them away, working slowly but taking great pains to have everything in its right place; Bertie and Col took the boot box from the dresser and set to work to patch Mabel's boots; Rose cut away the worn cloth from all three blouses and began to unpick the side seams. This was the time of day she enjoyed most, the time when they were all back together again after work and school, at ease and happy in one another's company. The room was full of familiar domestic sounds – the occasional tap-tap-tap of Bertie's hammer, the clink of dishes, the shuffle of shifting coals, the purr and pop of the gas light, the steady clonking of mum's old painted clock on the mantelpiece. There were so many things in the room to remind them of their mother. The dresser had been hers and so had most of the treasures that crowded its shelves; she had made the rag rug on the hearth, the patchwork cushions on Bertie's bed and the embroidered sampler hanging in pride of place on the wall beside the fireplace.

It was a very ordinary sampler, worked in cross-stitch on a piece of rough canvas and signed and dated – '*Emily Jones her work aged 11 years June 1887*'. It depicted a rose-spotted house with four windows, a central door and a thatched roof. There was blue smoke rising boskily above it from a decidedly crooked chimney. Three square rabbits sat on their haunches on either side of it, and beneath, in bold capital letters, was their mother's motto, the precept they all tried to follow – '*Live With Dignity*'. And isn't that just what our Bertie's done today, Rose thought, looking at it. If she can see him now, she'll be so proud of him.

The last plate was dried and put in its place on the dresser, the wiping-up cloth was hung on its string to dry, the last nail was knocked into Mabel's boot, the mending-box tidied and put away. Bertie balanced his feet on the fender and hooked his packet of Woodbines from his inside pocket, ready for his evening smoke. He looked across at Col who was sitting on the other side of the hearth watching him with admiration, and, on a sudden impulse, held out the little battered packet towards his brother. 'Time for a fag?' he said.

It was carried off with such splendid nonchalance that no outsider watching them would have realised what an important moment it was. But Rose and Netta knew and drew in their breath in surprise and pleasure ready to enjoy what would happen next.

'Ta,' Col said, with equal aplomb. 'I don't mind if I do.' He'd been smoking out on the street with his friends for nearly a year now but never in the house. As he drew in the first bitter breath, he narrowed his eyes and smiled at Bertie with open affection – the two men of the house sharing a gasper for the first time. This *was* a day, and no mistake.

'You'll have to mend all the boots on your own when I'm gone,' Bertie warned.

'I don't mind,' Col said. 'I'm getting to be a dab hand with that old leather, ain't I gels?'

'Cack hand, more like,' Netta teased.

'Come over here and let me try this pattern on you,' Rose said.

Netta stood to attention while Rose chose a brown paper pattern from her pattern box and fitted it against her sister's chest, folding the paper into neat tucks and pinning it together until she was satisfied with it.

'I'll take the sleeves up,' she decided. 'We can lose a good four inches an' that'll make a nice new armhole. Then if I cut out four new side panels from the ecru, and new cuffs, bit a' lace round the collar, you'll look a treat.'

'What about mine?' Mabel wanted to know, breathing heavily at her sister's elbow. 'What about mine, our Rose?'

'Yours'll have a new yoke and a nice front panel. I shall cut out all this bit where the stains are, see. An' I shall put this pinky lace round the neck and the cuffs. I might even have enough left over for a hair-ribbon. How's that?'

'You're ever so clever, our Rose,' Mabel said, watching with admiration as Rose pinned the pattern to the back panel of the ecru blouse.

It was true, and they all knew it so well that Rose didn't need to respond. It was part of the background knowledge to their lives that they all took for granted – like the fact that they worked well as a family and were fond of each other, that their lives would get easier in two months time when Col was fourteen and out at work, that Bertie was always dependable and Netta sometimes tricky and that Mabel would always be simple-minded and that they would always have to look after her. It was on a par with all the other accepted truths that they didn't have to think about either, that husbands worked and wives kept house, that, except for Mabel, they would all marry and settle down in their turn and be happy like their mother and father before them, that London was the greatest city in the world, that the sun never set on the British Empire, that they were bound to win this war.

Col tossed his fag-end into the fire. 'Well, that's it,' he said, smoothing his hair with both hands. 'Time I was off or old man Porky'll get the 'ump.' He worked every Saturday evening at one of the fruit and vegetable stalls in the market at Lambeth Walk and his employer was a stickler for punctuality.

'We'll be up presently,' Rose said. This family usually followed him to market at about ten o'clock of a Saturday evening, because that was when the remaining meat was sold off cheap – and the stale bread and buns and the 'specks' from the fruit and veg stalls. Sometimes they could get enough to keep them going till the middle of the week – especially if Netta was in one of her saucy moods.

'My brother the soldier,' Col said, standing in the doorway. 'I can't wait to tell Porky. When d'you reckon you'll have to go?'

'Not for ages yet, I don't expect,' Bertie said. 'There was hundreds joining.'

But he was wrong. The British war machine was geared for speed and his call-up papers arrived a mere seven weeks later – two weeks before Col was due to leave school and start work in the vinegar factory.

He came home from his last day at work, emptied his pay packet on the table and sorted the coins into five neat piles.

'Now there's two weeks' rent to tide you over,' he explained to Rose, putting the first pile into its jar on the mantelpiece. 'And there's the coal, and the boot club, and that's the housekeeping. You'll be all right till I get me pay.'

'What about you?' Rose said, touched by his care for them. 'You'll need a bit a' money.'

There was still fivepence left on the table. 'That'll do me,' he said cheerfully, putting it in his pocket. 'Now you *will* be all right wontcher. I done all the boots and the lavvy's all scrubbed. This'll keep you going won't it?'

'Who's going?' Mabel said, screwing up her face. All this talk of money bewildered her. 'Who's going?'

'You know who's going,' Netta said proudly. 'Our Bertie's going. For a soldier.'